THE BEAST UNBURIED

Jeremiah thought he was seeing some brown and muddy tree-part until it bent at the elbow and splayed the bony fingers of its hand. Shapes like a shoulder and chest followed, covered by dirt-brown skin the texture of cured leather. A second arm wrenched itself free, a thick rope dangling from the wrist. There followed a horribly oblong head.

Jeremiah fought to believe it was a sickly bear they'd woken, but the scene before him looked more as if Satan himself had dug his way up from Hell.

The thing turned toward Jeremiah's father. It opened its mouth. Jeremiah saw the yellow-white teeth glisten, like the fangs of a wolf.

Jeremiah ran toward his father, but the Devil was faster. With speed and grace as wolf-like as its fangs, it leapt . . .

Praise for Stefan Petrucha
and His Previous Novels

"Petrucha's got the goods!"
—**GREGORY MAGUIRE**, *New York Times* **bestselling author of** *Wicked* **and** *Son of a Witch*

"Petrucha offers a reality-bending take on the idea of split personalities. [His] story should leave readers considering the power of fate versus choice and the internal urges and desires that regularly jostle for control."
—*Publishers Weekly* on *Split*

BLOOD PROPHECY

Stefan Petrucha

GRAND CENTRAL
PUBLISHING

NEW YORK   BOSTON

Book design by Giorgetta Bell McRee

Grand Central Publishing
Hachette Book Group
237 Park Avenue
New York, NY 10017
Visit our website at www.HachetteBookGroup.com.

Grand Central Publishing is a division of Hachette Book Group, Inc. The Grand Central Publishing name and logo is a trademark of Hachette Book Group, Inc.

Printed in the United States of America

First Printing: November 2010

10 9 8 7 6 5 4 3 2 1

ATTENTION CORPORATIONS AND ORGANIZATIONS:
Most HACHETTE BOOK GROUP books are available at quantity discounts with bulk purchase for educational, business, or sales promotional use. For information, please call or write:

Special Markets Department, Hachette Book Group
237 Park Avenue, New York, NY 10017
Telephone: 1-800-222-6747 Fax: 1-800-477-5925

To the memory of Dan Curtis and all the actors, actresses, and writers of Dark Shadows, which filled the B&W afternoons of my youth with a dread and fascination that's lasted a lifetime.

"When you're walking through the graveyard at night
and you see a bogeyman, run *at* it,
and it will go away."

"But what," replies the child, "if the bogeyman's
Mother had told it to do the same thing?"

—JEALALUDDIN RUMI, thirteenth century

BLOOD
PROPHECY

Prologue

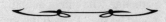

There was light.

Barely, in the dark.

Just enough to illuminate the dust floating in the prison cell air, just enough to make each speck shine against the stagnant black, just enough so that when Jeremiah Fall weakly waved his hand by its shackled wrist, innumerable motes of pale fire swirled between his fingers, as if they were all Creation.

Where was it coming from? The filthy straw covering the dirt floor held no surprises, nor did the dry rat corpses he'd kicked into a pile. The sandstone walls remained the same, and the ceiling was still twenty feet up, the same round stone sealing the exit. But the light had to be coming from somewhere.

He trained his eyes on the twirling motes. Each pinpoint shone with the same dull yellow. They pulsed, too, throbbing into and out of existence, unsteady as torchlight.

Torchlight. Of course. There must be some slight gap

between the stone and the ceiling, someone holding a torch in the room above. Who was up there? His guards? No. That motley trio was loud and drunk, always banging into walls as they cursed in French. The better soldiers were saved for more important tasks than watching a prisoner who couldn't possibly escape.

Who then? Someone who might actually listen to him? If it was, what would he say? Pardon me, monsieur, but if I don't find a way to stop it, the world will end six days after New Year's? Despite all he'd seen, Fall barely believed it himself. And he certainly didn't know what to do about it.

He didn't know. Not knowing had always bothered him, deep in his bones. Here, with nothing to feed his mind or senses, where every thought fell back on itself, not knowing nearly made him wish for madness.

His grandfather used to say that Jeremiah's insatiable thirst for knowledge would be his salvation. But here the constant grasping of his intellect was an agony that at times rivaled the black fire that roiled his belly. Aside from his churning mind, he'd been trapped here with a darker thing, a hunger that whispered to him so often and so well; Jeremiah Fall had long ago dubbed it *the beast*.

Beast and brain, with Jeremiah trapped between the two. And the lizard-thing didn't care about knowledge or salvation, only about itself. Even now, it told him that whoever was up there, despite whatever help they might offer, should be killed and fed upon. *After all*, it cooed, *even if you could explain, what would it matter to the coming darkness?*

It was not an entirely stupid beast and often quite convincing. Fortunately, the chains made its pleas moot. It was crucial Jeremiah stay in control. His visitors might at least tell him the date. Then, at last, he'd know how much time was left.

Ever since he had been captured, the possibility he could prevent the end of all things was the only reason he had to hold on to sanity, to existence. That was why he hadn't died with Amala, why his mind hadn't been reduced to nothing, why the beast had yet to conquer him completely. He told himself that, but he knew he was lying. He didn't know why he had survived.

It had been sometime in early October 1799 when the French soldiers found Jeremiah by the stone, deep in the territory of their enemy, the Ottoman Empire. He wished he'd put up a fight. But then, his soul crushed, he let himself be chained.

When they saw how sunlight burned him, they stuffed Jeremiah in the largest sack they could find and kept him there the entire journey. Somehow they'd made it past borderlands where eighty thousand Turkish troops had massed, preparing to reclaim what the French had taken from them. He couldn't see in the sack, but he could hear. Long before their words did, the relief in the soldiers' voices told him when they were back in Egypt. He figured the journey at roughly two weeks, but, unfed and drifting in and out of consciousness, he couldn't be sure. That would put him at the end of October.

Relief was brief for his captors. They soon learned that their beloved general, Napoleon, had returned to Paris, his Middle Eastern occupation cracking at the seams. Meanwhile, the native insurrectionists, their numbers bloated by Arab jihadists from across the Middle East, grew more daring every day.

As they brought Jeremiah into Cairo, a haphazard encounter with a narrow doorway tore the sack. The hole let him glimpse the moonlight bathing the orbed minarets, square fortresses, and princely palaces. Before the sack was patched, he had his wits about him enough to plead for the date, to ask how much time the world had left. He was refused.

His inner beast wanted to fight them, but he didn't. It was only after they dragged him down stone staircase after staircase and he saw the pit they planned to put him in that he finally struggled. But the chains were thick, and he had not fed in so long, that it was too late.

Whenever his guards lifted the stone cover to lower a bucket of food, he begged for the date again, but they remained mute. The only courtesy offered was the occasional bottle of wine, which he didn't drink.

At first, he pretended to eat what food they gave him, thinking he might count the days based on the number of times the bucket appeared, but he lost count. After that, he gave up, letting them marvel at how he stayed alive, hoping his survival, at least, might elicit a conversation.

It didn't, but once enough untouched buckets were recovered, a black-bearded guard held a torch down into the cell, illuminating the pile of desiccated rat carcasses. The three guards puzzled over it, debating the meaning as if they were part of the group of intellectuals Napoleon had taken with him on his invasion of this country. When the pile was bigger each time they checked, they reasoned, correctly, that Fall was somehow sucking the vermin dry, using their blood to stay alive. Then they talked, not to him, but among themselves.

"Chat noir avec des yeux rouges," they called him. *Black cat with red eyes. Mouser.*

After that, the bucket no longer appeared, leaving Jeremiah so alone he longed for the moments he could hear them stumble and curse in the room above.

Since then, how long had it been? Weeks? Months before this bit of light struck the dust? Could it be December already?

A clanking chain pulled against a groaning wooden wheel. The great circle lifted. Sand rained from its circumference. The invisible crack of torchlight swelled into a cone. He heard the rustling of clothes and the cautious river-murmur of whispered speech.

Freed of its mooring, the cover swayed slightly, affording a view of his visitors' legs. Instead of frayed, dirty cloths and worn sandals, the newcomers wore polished leather boots and clean blue pants. There were four soldiers, stiff, silent, and not alone.

A fifth set of legs held a belly so rounded that it strained against its fine frock coat, the typical dress of a French intellectual. It was an odd sight against the aged sandstone, but Jeremiah was well aware that Bonaparte had enlisted 150 scientists and artisans for his latest adventure. In Paris, they'd fallen over one another for the chance to be near their beloved general, not even knowing their destination until days before the massive fleet's arrival. If this was one of those intellectuals, a savant, that was a hopeful sign. At least he'd be sure to *know* the date.

A sixth and final figure, even more out of place, wore the dark robes of the Church. A priest? Fall almost laughed to think the proud, atheistic French needed a priest to deal with him. Good, then. If the savant proved difficult to convince, the priest might be more open to believing in the end of the world.

A rope ladder unfurled. The small log tied to its end for weight thudded into the straw. One by one, the soldiers climbed down. Their faces were masks, but their bodies provided some information. The dry heat rising from their uniforms told Jeremiah it must be daylight. He could smell it on them. That, and a bit of fear. Fear of him.

Two of the soldiers aimed their smoothbore muskets at his chest. The remaining pair set up a brazier, laying several iron tongs of different shapes and sizes at its side. Smoke soon curled from a small fire, adding a dimmer glow to the torchlight and a burnt odor to the rank dungeon air.

So they meant to torture him.

As the irons heated, the scholar climbed down, taking pains to make his descent look easy. He was young, midtwenties, roughly the same age as Napoleon, but of more average height. Extreme discomfort emanated from his body. The copious sweat on his brow further indicated his poor physical condition. He surveyed the soldiers and the brazier and then sighed with theatrical exasperation. When his gaze reached Fall, his full lips turned downward in a frown. Despite his airs, the doleful eyes peering from behind his thick spectacles shone with intelligence.

Still above, the priest croaked, "Geoffroy, will you steady the ladder?" The aged voice was so high-pitched it recalled one of the crones from Shakespeare's *Macbeth*. A witch in priest's clothing.

Reluctantly, the young man turned from Fall and held

the thick ropes. The priest inched down, shaking. Cotton hair and white, wrinkled skin jutted from the top of shadow-black robes. Even on the ground it appeared as if the tall man's legs would buckle. Geoffroy, seeing no option, steadied him.

"*Merci*. My muscles are stiff from the journey and do not recover as quickly as they once did."

"May I suggest a tincture prepared from the ground bones of a mummy, Father Sicard? It's quite a palliative. I can have one of our surgeons prepare a vial."

"No, please," Sicard said, fixing his mottled brown eyes on Jeremiah. Despite his frailty, he was the only one who didn't smell of fear. "I'll keep my faith in prayer and trust all bones to the Lord."

Jeremiah lowered his head in a bow. "Messieurs, I beg you, tell me, what is the date?"

Geoffroy turned toward Fall with an expression that made Jeremiah hope he would actually answer. Instead, he gestured as if presenting a rare animal. "Remarkable, no? So long in total darkness, no food, no water, no worse for wear. He even retains his manners."

"No one speaks more sweetly than Satan," Sicard said. "See how his eyes glow with hellfire."

Geoffroy shook his head. "I think not. They glow from the torchlight."

Sicard tsked. "How sad that in these otherwise enlightened times, the presence of the Devil is so often ignored. Try to remember I'm here because of my experience with the otherworldly."

Geoffroy clucked his tongue. "You're here because France holds Rome and your knowledge of Bible history is useful. That supposedly diabolical glow occurs only because the fellow's pupils are dilated to an abnormal extreme, the way a cat's eyes reflect in the night." He faced Fall. "Step forward."

Having no reason to refuse, Jeremiah obliged. As he entered the cone of brighter light cast from the ceiling's opening, the red sheen faded from his eyes, making them a more earthly blue. He walked as close to the two men as his chains permitted, then straightened in his torn desert robes, to better present himself.

"More human, now?" the savant asked. Sicard did not respond.

Geoffroy moved in a semicircle around Jeremiah. "The face is gaunt, but handsome, perhaps even friendly. Auburn hair is straggly. His body is lithe but not without muscle. Shocking health, given the lack of food."

"The Devil changes form at will."

Jeremiah spoke again. "If you won't tell me the day, at least tell me whose acquaintance I have the pleasure of making?"

The scholar raised an eyebrow. "Very well. I am Étienne Geoffroy Saint-Hilaire, representing the Institut de l'Égypte. My studies involve...unusual animals, so it was felt my skills might apply here. Father Sicard is, well, as is obvious, a member of the Church."

"Honored," Fall said. "I am..."

Saint-Hilaire waved his hand. "Jeremiah Fall, American. You fought against our troops as a mercenary alongside Murad Bey during the Battle of the Pyramids. You were captured and put in our work camps. In Rosetta, you discovered a stone of historic significance and were rewarded. Rather than show gratitude, you escaped and ambushed the caravan that was taking the stone here to Cairo. Had not our valiant soldiers tracked you into enemy territory, you would possess it still."

"The caravan was attacked," Jeremiah said. "I tried to protect it."

The savant ignored him. "Your earlier history is more difficult to ascertain with certainty. Likely you are the same Jeremiah Fall who battled alongside the colonists during the American Revolution. It is less likely, despite the father's beliefs, that you are the same Jeremiah Fall who fought *against* the colonists a hundred years earlier during King Phillip's War."

"Perhaps I just take good care of myself?"

Saint-Hilaire looked as if he were about to smile.

"He doesn't deny it," Sicard interjected. "He extends his existence by feeding on the blood of infants and virgins." He pointed a bony finger at the carcasses. "Rats, when he has no choice."

"Only animals," Fall said. "I only feed on animals. The same as the rest of us."

Saint-Hilaire peered over his glasses, first at Fall, then at Sicard. "There is a scientific explanation for his unique capacities, even perhaps for his long life."

"What?" Jeremiah and Sicard asked simultaneously. They exchanged an awkward glance.

Saint-Hilaire removed his spectacles and cleaned them with a handkerchief as he spoke. "Where the waters of the Nile meet the sea, I discovered an astounding fish, one with lungs that can breathe air. Now why would such a thing exist? Likewise, why are there creatures like the ostrich, which have the vestiges of wings when clearly they cannot fly? Instead of folktales, I resort to reason. I propose these are all indications of a unifying structure present in all species, an *ur*-form. Such a form would be capable of sometimes producing combined aspects, such as the lungs of an air-breather in a fish, the eyes of a predatory cat in a man, and so on. Why not also increased longevity?"

"Blasphemy," Sicard said. "You focus your mind on the Creation, but are blind to the Creator."

Saint-Hilaire sniffed. "The Church still says that the earth is the center of the universe despite the evidence. Why? So that God may reward the faithful for disbelieving the minds and eyes He supposedly gave them?"

"Please listen. The stone is *extremely* dangerous," Jeremiah said. "More than you can imagine."

Saint-Hilaire put his glasses back on and focused on Fall. "As I hope I've just shown, monsieur, the French can imagine a great deal. Our immediate interest *is* indeed the stone. Were you hoping to sell it to the British?"

"You have to keep it guarded..."

"The Mamluks? That would explain why you brought it into Ottoman territory."

Jeremiah sighed. "We had to take it to a holy place to try to destroy what was inside it. So we brought it to Al-Qurnah, where the Tigris and Euphrates meet. Eden. Where mankind was born."

Sicard sneered. "The garden was destroyed in the deluge that only Noah and his family survived. You went to that place to serve Lucifer. Admit it."

"No. Not serve. And not Lucifer, exactly." Fall lowered his head. He wished he could somehow simply *show* them what he knew about the world's fate, let them see what he'd seen. But all he had were the words he knew sounded absurd: "We were there to try to stop the end of the world."

The scholar threw his head back. "*Mon Dieu*!"

Using the savant's arm to steady himself, Sicard came forward. "His lies are intended to agitate you. See how it's working?"

Saint-Hilaire pulled away so quickly, the old man nearly fell. "I am surrounded by jihadists, insurrectionists, and plague! Our soldiers, my own countrymen, think my sample cases contain stolen treasure from the tombs and try to steal them! Must I deal with this superstitious stupidity as well?"

"Superstition? I think not." The old priest waddled over to the brazier and lifted one of the hot irons. Its tip, in the shape of a cross, was so heavy that he couldn't keep his wrist straight. "Tell me how your theory of... an *ur*-form was it? Tell me how it explains his reaction to sunlight or the need to keep him in not one, but four chains?"

Saint-Hilaire's eyes fluttered. "I don't have all the answers right now. Certain diseases make the skin sensitive to light. I've seen hysteria induce feats of strength."

Sicard turned toward Fall, holding the glowing red iron. Saint-Hilaire looked sideways at it and said, "What do you hope to prove with that?"

As the priest came forward, Jeremiah backed into the shadows. His unearthly state enabled him to vanish into the darkness, but he would still be chained. Best to keep that trick secret for now. It was hard, though, with the beast inside him growling. It didn't like pain.

"Watch," Sicard said.

The old man, suddenly possessed of both energy and strength, stabbed forward, pressing the cross into Fall's shoulder. The metal hissed as it seared through his skin and into the muscle. Jeremiah screamed and went to his knees.

To distract himself from the pain, Jeremiah struggled to stay focued on what was around him. He saw Saint-Hilaire wince and noticed that the soldiers were watching this show of weakness with contempt. The rough-and-tumble, battle-weary men barely tolerated the intellectuals. Now, trapped in Egypt, it seemed, they hated them.

Saint-Hilaire straightened. "You think that proves he fears your cross?"

Glancing at the soldiers, the scholar grabbed a second heated poker, flat-pointed. With forced detachment, he pressed it into Fall's leg.

Jeremiah screamed again, rolled to his side, and moaned.

"You see? Same reaction."

The priest shook his head. "You misunderstand. I wasn't trying to prove the power of the cross." He bent over, careful not to get too close, and pointed his gnarled finger at the pulpy shoulder wound. "I was attempting to show you...this."

The boiling flesh of the wound subsided, and the frayed skin began to knit back together. Saint-Hilaire's eyes went wide.

"Do you explain *that* by virtue of science or does the unholy magic of one of Satan's minions now seem more reasonable?"

"As I said...the fact that I've no natural explanation...at this moment does not mean one does not exist."

Fall struggled back to his knees. "Just tell me the day, and I'll tell you whatever you want to know."

"Give him nothing," Sicard said, "but another taste of the fire."

Saint-Hilaire narrowed his eyes. "Why is the date so important?"

"I want to know how much time is left."

"Before the end of the world?" Saint-Hilaire said. "Is it some sort of metaphor? Are the British planning a land invasion? The Ottoman?"

"No. Something worse."

The fire from the brazier glinted in the intellectual's eyes. It was clear he felt he was on to something. He took a step closer to Jeremiah.

Take him, the beast said.

"Careful, Geoffroy," the priest croaked.

Put your teeth to his throat. He's pale, but plump.

Saint-Hilaire held his ground. A desire to show manliness in front of the soldiers trumped his fear. "Tell me, what's worse than an invasion from the British?"

Feed.

Fall answered slowly. "Seventy French soldiers were sent into Ottoman territory to find us."

"Twenty," Saint-Hillaire said.

"There *were* seventy. Men who had wives, children..."

"The constant darkness has brought on dementia, Monsieur Fall. I've seen the reports. Twenty men."

"That's all that's left now," Fall said. "The other fifty weren't just murdered; they were eradicated, wiped from creation, from history, even from memory. The thing in the stone did that. And what it did to them, it will do to everything."

Feed.

"Geoffroy," Sicard said softly. "Step back."

But Saint-Hilaire stared a while longer, as if trying to evaluate Fall's honesty from the look in his eyes. Finally, a slight smile played on his lips. Would he believe? No.

"What non—" he began.

Before he could complete the word, Fall grabbed the Frenchman and brought his neck to his open mouth. Sicard and the soldiers saw the fangs and gasped. Though Saint-Hilaire could not, he felt their tips poised against his flesh.

Free the talking fool from his delusions. You need the strength.

Fall's voice, lower now, echoed in the small room. "Tell me the date...please."

He heard Sicard's quick breath, heard the soldiers shift, uncertain, heard Saint-Hilaire swallow, heard the life-giving liquid pumping through the savant's veins. The sound was so sweet, Jeremiah was so weak, and the beast knew it.

You know he's not going to tell you. Why not...

"It...it's Décade II, Quintidi de Brumaire de l'Année VIII de la Révolution," Saint-Hilaire blurted.

Fall closed his eyes and moved his lips, mumbling.

"He casts a spell! Shoot him!" Sicard cried.

Before the infantrymen could decide whether to obey, Fall hurled Saint-Hilaire at them. They were barely able to move their bayonets out of the way in time to keep from stabbing the scholar as he tumbled to their feet.

"It's no spell!" Jeremiah said. "I'm only trying to figure out..." He became aware of the results of his calculation just as he began the sentence. Since their bloody revolution, the French started their own calendar, with its own months and years. "November 5, 1799. It's November 5."

He fell back on his haunches and exhaled, leaving his captors utterly confused.

Without help, Saint-Hilaire rose. By the time he had adjusted his long coat, he managed to appear more insulted than terrified. He blinked, looked down, wiped his forehead with his handkerchief, and then met Fall's gaze. "You have your date. Will you tell us what we wish to know?"

"Everything," Fall said, "from the beginning. But trust me, it isn't the sort of thing anyone would ever wish to know. I'd have sooner died than live to tell it... if I hadn't died already."

1

April 14, 1644
Dedham, a township of the Massachusetts Bay Colony

Even with the sun tempered by the tall pines lining the field, Jeremiah Fall sweltered in the simple clothes of the godly. His broad-brimmed hat was stifling. His shirt clung to the sweat on his back. His legs baked inside the black pants. If only the plow weren't stuck again. Straining against it, he feared passing out, until a final, forceful push sent his hand skidding along the handle, where a wooden shard stabbed the meat below his thumb.

"Ah!" he said, clenching his teeth. He should've checked to see what blocked the plow. His impatience could've cost them the blade. Hurt, angry with himself, his father's favorite aphorism came to mind: *Arrogance is folly.*

His shame would be double if Nathan had seen. Fortunately, his father was too busy struggling with a second, ox-pulled, plow to notice.

The ox, though, turned its wide eyes toward Jeremiah in seeming judgment. Mary Vincent, his mother, had named it Patience. If merriment were not forbidden, he'd swear she'd done it as a joke.

Arrogance is folly. An important lesson. Pulling the sliver free from his hand recalled another; splinters hurt more coming out than going in.

As a thread of blood inched along his thumb, Jeremiah sighed and inspected the plow head. A rough sphere nested in the dirt. Another rock to be dug out by hand.

Meanwhile, Nathan and the ox began their fifth line for the day. They'd hoped for fifteen, but after the first hour, Grandfather Atticus was too tired to help. This next line would be the first to cross the mound that marred the terrain's flatness. What would his father do, Jeremiah wondered, when he reached this thing that looked like the dome of a buried giant's head? Suspicion of anything unknown might make him till around it. The Faithful, named Puritans by those who scorned them, were forever uncertain which parts of the New World offered Eden, which hell. But the Falls were also stubborn.

Atticus, Dedham's unofficial ambassador to the natives, said the mound was a mystery even to Kanti, the female leader, or *sachem*, of the small Algonquin village a few miles north. Hard to tell, though, how much his addled grandfather heard and how much he'd imagined hearing. One thing was certain: The Algonquin were convinced it was too early to break new soil. There'd likely be another snow.

Nathan, loath to heed native advice, refused to wait. Like the townsfolk, he felt the only purpose of contact was to draw the Algonquin closer to the Lord, not to be drawn into their savage ways. But wouldn't *some* advice be welcome? In Essex, the Falls had been carpenters, and in all their years here they had gained little expertise with the land. Could it still snow? To Jeremiah, the air smelled of spring. Even the forest didn't offer its usual foreboding sounds and shadows, only the playful breeze.

No, not only.

At the tree line, some low, wavering shadows coalesced into human form. Jeremiah tensed, wary of an Indian attack, until he recognized the figure. It was Chogan, the young Algonquin who enjoyed watching their labors. Speaking of arrogance, the boy's grin made it clear he'd been seen only because he'd allowed it. The Algonquin didn't consider pride a sin.

Still, the question behind the smile seemed reasonable to Jeremiah: "Why don't you take our advice? Snow is coming. Why work so hard for nothing?"

How often had Jeremiah explained that labor brought them closer to God? How all men were sinners since Adam was made from the dust, only the chosen fated to find heaven? A man made from dirt was the only part Chogan understood, and that only because it matched some heathen belief. If Jeremiah did return to school, maybe he'd find a better way to explain. Not today. The boy was already gone.

"Jeremiah, come quench your thirst!" Atticus called. The familial connection between the three men was written on them as clearly as the *begats* in the Bible. The only difference was the blue eyes Jeremiah shared with his mother. "It's a harmless hunger. Chogan would tell you the same."

Nathan halted Patience. "We do not follow the example of the godless."

Atticus cackled. "How can they be godless if God created them?"

Nathan gritted his teeth. Atticus's loose speech had caused them trouble for years. The voyage to the New World had turned to months. As they starved, a storm had hit. Jeremiah's infant brother was swept overboard. Ever since, the old man had given voice to the most questionable thoughts. More recently, the fever, which weakened him and brought Jeremiah back from school, left his tongue even less willing to censor them.

Nathan tried to be patient. "I beg you remember the second article of the covenant I put my name to so we might join this township: 'We shall by all means labor to keep off from us all such as are contrary minded...'"

Atticus's eyes lit up as if he were possessed by an impish squirrel. "Then all Dedham should be empty! I've yet to meet a man whose mind wasn't contrary to itself."

As Nathan's brow furrowed, the sweat that had accumulated in his thick eyebrows ran down the side of his face. "Don't play with the words as if this were a game, father!"

"Why not? The Lord plays with words!" He held aloft his prized Geneva Bible. "Thou shalt not eat of the tree of knowledge, for on that day, thou shalt die! Yet Adam lived 930 years! Matthew tells us the Lord said, 'He that is not with me is against me,' yet Luke tells us He said, 'he that is not against us is with us!' What is this if not play?"

For years, Dedham had tolerated Atticus. His exchanges with the Algonquin kept the community abreast of their plans. But since his fever, the old man went too far.

"Each time you speak, talk of our expulsion grows. Never mind how you destroy the chance of Jeremiah's return to the Harvard School. What becomes of us when homeless?"

"What do they say in town?" Jeremiah asked.

Nathan shook his head. "They recall we are the family who arrived on that cursed ship long ago, that we were shunned at Watertown even though they sorely needed carpenters." His hand shook as he wiped the sweat from his brow. "Make certain the work is its own reward. Do not think too much on school." He added, "But, take that drink. We've yet some time before darkness."

Obeying, Jeremiah walked to his grandfather and took the ladle.

"Dying doesn't frighten me, only the thought I might keep you from school," the old man said.

"Don't worry, grandfather. The extra yield from these acres will surely let father hire John Fisher to make up for..." His voice trailed off.

The old man nudged him. "For my becoming half a man. Half mad. I know. But I'm helpless against it. Though it's over a decade past, the tempest that struck our ship remains inside me like the whirlwind that appeared to Job."

"Go back to the house for a nap. You're tired."

Atticus crinkled the skin around his brown eyes. "I'm too awake."

Jeremiah patted his grandfather's shoulder, surprised how bony it was.

"Jeremiah, Jeremiah," Atticus went on. "The prophet Jeremiah went down to the potter's house and saw the potter break the vessel he was working on. So the potter abandoned it and made another. Then the Lord said to Jeremiah, 'Cannot I do with *you* as this potter does? As the clay is in the potter's hand, so are you in mine.'"

The sun sank lower, the air shifting from cool to cold, as if something thick and powerful had rolled into the field alongside them. A chill moved up along his back. Atticus's dismal tone haunted him, certainly, but was this sudden dread just despair or were his senses trying to warn him of something real?

There *was* something different. He turned, planning to tell his father, only to see that Nathan had led his ox to the edge of the rounded earth. He was at the moment of deciding, go around or through?

The word Kanti used to describe not the mound but its essence was *chepi*. Atticus likened it to the stories of the fairy folk he'd heard in Essex, demoted angels thrown from heaven. Not evil enough for hell, they roamed the earth kidnapping babes from their cradles. Kanti assured him it had more to do with a long-ago plague that nearly wiped out the Abenaki tribe. An Abenaki might know more, but their new settlements were far north, among the French.

Was it Abenaki ghosts Jeremiah felt watching from the woods?

Nathan ordered Patience forward. The ox dutifully put its cloven feet upon the rising earth, pulling the plow behind. As the metal blade edged forward, concern flickered across Nathan's face. Did he feel the dread, too? No, it was mere annoyance, the expectation of hitting another rock. As the plow slid deep into the mound, quickly and easily, Nathan Fall smiled.

Jeremiah hadn't seen his father smile since before the

loss of baby Jim at sea. His mother claimed he had smiled the day Jeremiah left home for Boston to exchange his skills as a carpenter for academic lessons. While he believed her, he'd not seen it with his own eyes. As the dirt yielded further, the satisfaction on his father's face was clear.

Perhaps he was thinking that now the field might be sown in time and Jeremiah could return to school. What he said was, "It's all right, Jeremiah. It's soft, like clay."

But arrogance is folly.

The plow suddenly rolled sideways. Patience lowed in distress and seemed to be sinking. Jeremiah thought the plow's weight must be dragging the ox down, but strangely, the creature's thin bovine legs, though scrambling, moved downward in the opposite direction.

Had they hit a deep hollow, a sinkhole?

With their sole ox in danger, Nathan didn't hesitate. He leaped atop the mound, drew the small scythe from his side and freed the animal from the harnass with two quick swipes. But Patience continued to sink, as if something beneath the dirt were drawing the creature down. Nathan grabbed the ox by the horns, stared into its panicked eyes, and shouted, "Harr!"

Patience obediently stiffened and attempted to stand.

It seemed the danger was over until the ox's large form jutted back toward the hole as if yanked. From what Jeremiah could see, the animal's back leg was caught on a thick root. Patience kicked free of it and stumbled down the mound, nearly knocking Nathan over in the process.

The thing that had held the ox, however, continued to rise. Jeremiah thought he was seeing some brown and muddy tree part until it bent at the elbow and splayed the bony fingers of its hand. Shapes like shoulder and chest followed, both covered by skin the texture of cured leather. A second arm wrenched itself into the air, a thick rope dangling from the wrist. There followed a horribly oblong head.

Jeremiah fought to convince himself it was a sickly bear they'd woken, but it looked more as if Satan himself had dug his way up from hell.

Patience limped across the field, blood flowing down its back leg, leaving the thing to turn toward Nathan. The shifting of its body revealed a visage that at first brought to mind a tangled mass of dried grass and peat. Then it opened its mouth. Even from this distance, Jeremiah saw the yellow-white teeth glisten against the dark earth of its form, like the fangs of a wolf bursting into moonlight while night rendered its body invisible.

Jeremiah ran toward his father, but the Devil was faster. Free of the mound, it snapped the remaining rope that bound its legs and pushed aside the fallen plow. The earthen-brown layer covering it, which Jeremiah had taken for its skin, fell off in wet clumps with each muscle it moved. What lay beneath, its true skin, was the same, but lighter in hue. With speed and grace as wolflike as its fangs, it leaped. In midair, it craned its neck forward, as if those bared teeth could pull it forward faster. As it flew, what looked like a long head fell away. The oblong thing slapped to the ground, stems of aged feathers rising. A headdress?

As Jeremiah prayed for more speed, the figure grabbed Nathan's neck and drew him to its teeth, sharp and distinct, and bit into his neck. Jeremiah shivered, a queasy nausea erupting in his stomach.

Nathan tried to hit the creature, to injure it or push it away, but the efforts of his strong arms looked like the thrashing of grass against boulder. His father's neck was split open like the spring lamb they'd killed last year, and the creature drank the spurting fluids. As it sucked in Nathan's blood, the skin around its neck thickened, its shoulders reddened, and its chest swelled.

Jeremiah knew it was too late. His father's body no longer fought, but twitched. Refusing to trust his intuition, he jumped onto the length of the sideways plow and hurled himself into the thing. He hit with his full weight, but the thing didn't fall, and instead moved only an inch along the mound's soft earth. Jeremiah's gaze met two lidless eyes. They looked more like stolen eggs embedded in a rat nest, their whites marred by the tiny branches of dead veins, the pupils sparking with an old, angry hunger.

Trying to grab hold, Jeremiah's hands scrambled against its rough form. Some of the ash-brown hide was vaguely supple, like half-dried beef, the rest hard as stone. When he pulled at it, his fingers slipped as they had on the plow, earning not splinters but drier clumps of dirt, revealing the pallid skin of a corpse beneath.

What was it? What was this world that it could have made such a thing?

The creature's back, no longer protected by dirt, was now struck by sunlight. The thing went rigid. Smoke snaked from its body. There was a loud hissing like water on hot coals. The light burned it.

Though Jeremiah's instinct wanted him only to join Patience and flee, the mind Atticus had praised mere moments ago forced him into attacking again. This time, he didn't try to move it or hurt it. Instead he focused on pulling away as much of the earth covering as he could, bringing to light more and more of its gray skin. As he did, he thought he saw the remains of a breechcloth and leggings on its unearthly body.

Recognizing Jeremiah as the cause of its increasing pain, the creature paused from feeding long enough to swat him away. Years ago, Jeremiah had been knocked down in a fistfight when an older youth called his grandfather insane, but this was different, more like swinging by rope into the face of a tree. Jeremiah's neck felt twisted. As he tried to stand, his legs did not wish to cooperate. He forced himself to his feet, but he was swaying, uncertain how long he'd stay conscious.

He thought he'd lost this fight and likely his life, until the grotesque odor of burning flesh assailed his nostrils. His mind had found the right thing—perhaps the only thing—to do.

Its skin reddened and curled in large round wounds, as if eaten like bark in a fire. Air rushed from its mouth as if it were trying to scream. At first, it didn't stop assaulting Nathan, but its agony soon surpassed its urge to feed. It picked its head up, chin and cheek glistening with blood. It hesitated as if weighing whether to drag Nathan off with it, then dropped him and raced for the shade.

Jeremiah staggered to his fallen father and cradled his bleeding form.

Eyes no longer focused, Nathan muttered, "Patience. Save Patience or Mary Vincent will be upset."

"The ox is safe," Jeremiah whispered, though he had no idea if that was true.

It had all happened so fast. Atticus neared them

only now, croaking as his lungs gasped for breath, "Nathan…Nathan…"

Jeremiah didn't look at his grandfather. His gaze was torn, head snapping back and forth, between his dying father and the thing racing for the woods, thicker and thicker tendrils of smoke curling from its form. As it disappeared among the trees, it found its voice, screaming long and loud, not just in anguish but in unmistakable fury.

As the screeching drenched him with fear, the words came to Jeremiah again: *Arrogance is folly.*

He wondered, did the aphorism apply to the Devil's world as well as God's?

2

Three days later, the snows came, thick and heavy. Day and night, a mad wind whipped the white air, covering hills and woods, river and sky. Cold whiteness veiled the farmhouses and filled the lanes. At first, the snow left the echoes of shapes, but in time, it covered those until nothing recognizable remained.

"Thou art all my good in times of peace, my only support in days of trouble..." Mary Vincent Fall said.

In the sudden, tumultuous privacy of their grief, only she spoke of salvation as she cooked and kept the fire burning in their stone and brick hearth. Atticus was left with moans and mumbles, half singing, half chanting whatever Bible passages came to mind. Jeremiah didn't speak at all.

"Thou art my one sufficiency when life shall end."

For now, she seemed content to keep them fed and warm, looking forward not only to the afterlife, but also to the day a headstone could be set on her husband's grave. It would have a winged skull carved on each side of the tympanum, signifying the journey from the physical to the spirit, and once it was complete, paying for it would cost them much of their savings.

Jeremiah knew he'd have to discuss their more mortal future with her soon, but was loath to add to her burden by telling her the Falls would soon be expelled. His own heart was torn between numbness at his father's horrid death and anger at all of Dedham for what seemed a betrayal, not only of his family but of common decency.

The morning following the attack, when Jeremiah asked for help in laying his father to rest, Goodman Broggin, the thick-limbed, slow-thinking patriarch of one of the few families who'd even bothered to visit, had said, "The ground, it's too frozen."

It was only when Jeremiah and Atticus took their shovels and left to dig the hole themselves that the other men were shamed into assisting. After the burial, they followed Jeremiah to the broken mound, shaking their heads at him and his story. There he found the rotting headdress, thinking it would be the proof of his word. It fell apart in his hands, looking like mere clumps of mud.

Jeremiah asked them, for their own good, to help track the thing, but Broggin, apparently now their spokesman, predicted it would be useless.

It was at the end of that conversation that Chogan, his father, and Kanti arrived. More of the tribe wished to come and show their respect, but Jeremiah refused them, fearing how the townsfolk would react. The Algonquin however were willing to track the beast, and their effort assured them *something* had been there. They wondered though—could it have been a wolf with mange that left its skin exposed? Or even the enormous bear that had killed both brave and colonist these last two springs? Might Jeremiah be mistaken about the headdress, breechcloth, and leggings?

When Jeremiah insisted he was not, Kanti promised to do what she could to find an Abenaki, someone who might know more about the mound and its *chepi*.

Goodman Broggin, who'd been holding his tongue since their arrival, objected at once. "Do not think to have heathen stories told on this land," he said.

Jeremiah was never clear if the man spoke so slowly for effect or due to a sluggish mind. In either case, he could not conceal his anger. "It murders," he said. "We must learn what it is to protect ourselves. What matters the source of the truth?"

"Truth has but *one* source," Broggin announced. The finality with which he spoke made Jeremiah realize that in this man's mind he'd crossed the same line as his grandfather.

If that were not the last proof that the Falls were contrary-minded, the intimacy displayed between his family and the Algonquin was. As the godly left, Goodman Broggin muttered, one slow word at a time, "On this field, the Devil took his own."

Jeremiah knew only the snows delayed their judgment. "Better to expel them in warmer weather, lest we be cruel," he imagined them saying.

But the storm had come, so sudden and so furious, he knew some in Dedham would foolishly think the Algonquin had summoned it.

As the wind moaned on the night of the third day, Mary Vincent sat stiff-backed, head down, hands folded in her lap. A steaming bowl of stew lay on the table in front of her untouched. Her bonnet made her sad face a perfect oval, the stark blueness of her eyes providing the brightest color in the room. Their one window was boarded over, because they, like all God's Elect in the New World, would rather not see outside once the day was done. They preferred to huddle in something more akin to a cave.

How could he tell her? How could he not? He reached out, held her hand, and tried to think of the softest way.

"Come spring we should think to move," he said.

She continued staring down into her lap. "I cannot leave your father."

"Mother, the townsfolk no longer trust us."

"Then we must trust in providence."

"Roger Williams has a new colony in Rhode Island. They ask for agreement only in civil things and allow each man to worship and believe as he will."

She shook her head. "Nathan would not like that. His name remains on Dedham's covenant."

"A covenant is a pact between two sides. Whose vegetables are in this stew, those of the godly or the Algonquin?"

Her eyes shot up and searched his face. She pressed her small hand to his forehead as if to rub the thoughts out of it. "Jeremiah, watch your words. You begin to sound like..." Her voice trailed off as Atticus moaned.

For a moment, it felt as if they were the only three people left in the entire world, until a pounding came at the door. The hard thud shook dirt free from between the timbers and left a dusty cloud in the air. The Fall homestead was typically small, a single room of sixteen by twenty with a sleeping loft, so the sound and its vibration were intimately near.

Mary Vincent's hand flew to her chest, and she gasped. Jeremiah leaped from his seat at the table. Atticus raised his head so slowly he looked as if he'd been dreaming and was still not completely awake.

"Some snow has fallen from the roof to the front of the house," Jeremiah said. "It's good and warm in here from the fire. But perhaps I should make certain the door's not blocked it."

Part of him worried it wasn't snow at all. He didn't open the door, instead examining it, reassuring himself it would hold even against the thing that had killed his father. Unlike the rest of the house, made from the ample pine already on their land, Nathan insisted that the door and its frame be good, strong oak. Having heard how Dedham's first settlers lived in hollowed-out bits of earth with barely a roof, he wanted to ensure his family would be safe because, as a carpenter, he could.

Sensing Jeremiah's concern, Mary Vincent touched her son's wrist. "I'm fine. The noise just startled me. Sit and eat more, please. There's plenty. I'm not yet used to preparing meals for three. It would be a sin to have my folly lead to waste."

Jeremiah was about to smile at her when a second sound, louder, echoed through the cabin. This one didn't come from the door. It came from the roof, above the sleeping loft.

"A tree branch?" Jeremiah suggested.

But they knew there were no trees above their cabin, only sky and storm. All stared upward as the wood creaked and the thud came again.

If the moment were not tense enough, Atticus, still staring at the ceiling, recited, "Who is this that darkeneth the counsel by words without knowledge? Gird up now thy loins like a man: I will demand of thee and declare thou unto me!"

Was that the Book of Job? The man tortured based on a wager between God and the Devil?

Jeremiah hissed, "Be silent, grandfather!"

More thuds came, moving bit by bit along the roof, then down along the brick and stone chimney. There they changed to harsh scrapes and clicks.

That's where the wood is weakest, Jeremiah thought.

From the right of the hearth came an entirely different sound, the creak of timbers bending, like tall trees pushed near breaking by the wind.

Nathan had left a musket and axe beside the door, but Jeremiah feared the musket would take too long to load. He spoke softly as he reached for the axe. "Mother, take Atticus up into the loft."

Another creak. Mary Vincent had not moved.

"Mother!" Jeremiah said again.

A loud crack. One of the planks that made up the wall snapped.

There was no doubt. It was back. The Devil had returned and was taking apart their home to get at them. With the sun gone, there would be no stopping it.

Jeremiah pulled Mary Vincent behind him as Atticus intoned, "Where wast thou when I laid the foundations of the earth? Hast thou entered into the bottoms of the sea?"

"For the sake of heaven, stay silent, Atticus!"

Another creak and a snap. Snow began to drizzle in from a hole at the edge of the hearth. Fingers tinted a horrid blue wormed through the small gap. They set to working its edges like the teeth of a gnawing animal.

Mary Vincent saw them and screamed.

Atticus's voice grew louder. "Hast thou seen the gates of the shadow of death? Do ye know which way the light dwelleth and where is the place of darkness?"

Cold air from the growing hole hit the sweat on Jeremiah's chest. He had to think. His mind was the only thing that lay between them and death.

The sun burned it like a flame; what would fire do? He lay the axe aside, snapped the handle of his mother's straw broom in two, wrapped a torn bit of tablecloth around the top, and poured oil from a lamp over it.

"Out of whose womb came the ice?"

The fingers at the hole paused. The opening was not growing fast enough, so it went for the timbers again. There was another creak and snap.

Jeremiah put the torch to the hearth-flame and handed it to his mother.

"If it comes for you, use this!"

Shivering, she nodded and took the burning stick.

"Who hath engendered the frost of the heaven?"

Another timber cracked. The hole was as big as two fists. Against the backdrop of night and swirling snow outside, Jeremiah made out a sickly human shape. Its skull seemed different now, thicker, and it looked as if more hair had grown upon its head.

Face still shadowed, it brought its hands to either side of the hole and pulled. Dust crumbled from the wall and from the ceiling. In moments, it would be through.

"Canst thou bind the unicorn with his band to labor in the furrow?"

Jeremiah swung the axe, hitting one of the hands at the wrist. A dry, mournful sound filled the cabin. The hand, dangling from a thick, bloodless tuft of skin, disappeared through the hole.

So it can be hurt.

Jeremiah pulled back the axe and waited, prepared to strike again.

He didn't have to wait long. With the force of a gale, the creature burst through the wall. Jeremiah tumbled backward. It reached the floor and got its bearings, the fire giving half of it a yellow-orange glow.

Mary Vincent was the first to realize this was not the same creature Jeremiah had fought in the field. Though the look in its eyes was feral and unreal, the face was as familiar as the air.

"Nathan!" she cried.

It was his father. His father's form. His father's body, animate and filled with a devil's hunger. The black shirt and white collar they'd buried him in were muddy from the grave and wet from the snow in equal parts. The grievous wound in his neck had healed. The hand Jeremiah had severed moments before clung to its stump as if trying to meld back onto the bone.

"No!" Jeremiah screamed. "Go back to hell!"

He raised the axe, but couldn't bring himself to strike.

Seeing the blade, the corpse reared.

"Nathan," Mary Vincent said softly.

Both son and dead father turned toward her. Jeremiah wasn't sure if she was smiling or her lips were twisted from terror.

"Nathan," she said again. The torch in her hands slipped sideways. "I cannot leave you."

"It's not father," Jeremiah warned. "I beg you keep the flame up!"

Now she truly smiled. The firelight glinting in her pupils made her seem mad as Atticus. Perhaps she was. "Poor deluded child. Do you think I don't know my own husband?"

White snow and blue cold swirled around the intruder. Mary Vincent was bathed in the fire's yellow, orange, and red.

"Take me with you, Nathan. Take me wherever you've gone."

And then she dropped the torch.

Moving faster than the creature in the field, Nathan vanquished the small distance between them. Mary Vincent closed her eyes. He drove his demon-teeth into her neck.

Recalling the scant seconds it took for his father to die, Jeremiah pushed aside all thoughts of his love for Nathan and came forward, swinging the axe. A powerful blow embedded the blade deep in his father's back. Nathan didn't fall, but he released his grip. Mary Vincent collapsed to the floor, blood flowing from her neck.

Jeremiah struggled to pull the axe from his father, but it wouldn't budge. Worse, it hadn't weakened Nathan in the slightest. As he pivoted to face his son, the axe handle flew from Jeremiah's hands. It slammed into the hearthstone, came free from his father's rib cage, and clattered to the floor.

Using his good hand, the corpse grabbed Jeremiah's chest, balling up not just the cotton shirt, but the flesh it covered as well. He pulled Jeremiah close and opened his mouth. Helpless, Jeremiah looked for his father's eyes, but found only two ebony pools.

In a pitiful wail, Jeremiah asked, "Is there nothing left of you, father? Has the Devil taken us all?"

Jeremiah didn't expect an answer, but Nathan twisted his head sideways. His hollow features scrunched in what looked like curiosity. He seemed vaguely interested in the question and was taking a moment or two to ponder it. In a voice that sounded as if he were calling from the depths of a windy canyon, Nathan said, "The work isss itsss ownnn rewaaarddddd."

He bit into his son's throat and drew inward. The powerful suction threatened to pull both blood and meat into his maw. Jeremiah was paralyzed as his father drank, aware only of pressures along his body wherever his father touched, and a chill that spread from his wound, a deathly cold like the one he'd felt three days past at the field. It moved down his arm, his side, into his leg, along his entire body.

His open eyes gave him a view of his mother where she lay on the dirt floor. He took comfort in seeing her, but his focus soon grew blurry, and his field of vision shrank.

Jeremiah thought that would be it, but there would be one thing more before he died. There was another thud and a sudden shifting. He felt Nathan let go, felt his own paralyzed form drop to the floor. The impact didn't hurt, nothing in his body did, but he felt an inconsolable sadness at no longer being able to see his mother.

Instead, his last living vision was of a wild-eyed Atticus bringing the axe down on his only son, lifting and swinging it again and again, until, bit by bit, Nathan's head was fully sheared from its body.

"Canst thou draw out Leviathan with a fishhook?" the mad old man screamed.

3

As he hovered in a void, a voice called him, "Jeremiah."

It didn't just speak, it sang, and though singing was forbidden, here it seemed stripped of the concerns of sin.

"Jeremiah." It sounded like Atticus, only so rich and deep, it spilled into his other senses, each syllable a cascade of sensation.

"Jeremiah."

Cannot I do with you as this potter does?

He thought he was dead, that this was bliss. In life, he'd often feared the light of heaven would be incomprehensible. He was glad that this was not. It felt as if the world were opening up all its secrets for him.

"Do ye know me, my Jeremiah?"

It was as if, as it said in Corinthians, once he'd seen through a glass darkly, and now at last, he'd come face-to-face.

Now I know in part; then shall I know even as I am known.

"*Are* ye my Jeremiah?"

Why was Atticus here? Was he dead, too? Though Jeremiah's eyes were closed, he could feel the old man's nearness, smell the slight sweat on his skin, taste the odor of burnt wood mixed in his white hair, and somehow sense the frigid outdoor air woven into the fabric of a woolen blanket on his frail shoulders. He even heard his grandfather's arm hairs rustle against his shirt.

"Jeremiah, Jeremiah, are ye my Jeremiah?"

More than that, Jeremiah heard bone move against sinew, smelled meat flush with blood.

Blood.

The sensations that had tickled and tantalized him collapsed into a single urge. Unbidden, unexpected, the hunger welled from a place so deep within his bones and melded so seamlessly with his savage senses that he couldn't name it or even tell where he began and it ended. If it could end. It wanted just one thing—to shred the heart and veins that kept the blood inside Atticus, free it like the juice of some grand fruit and drink.

Jeremiah opened his eyes. The illusion of bliss shattered and died. He did not see face-to-face, or even darkly. Beyond this raging need, he saw nothing at all.

He was on a dirt floor. Atticus, the source of the blood-smell, sat near, exactly as he'd imagined.

"Do ye know me, Jeremiah?" Atticus said. He had an axe in his hands.

Jeremiah tried to grab him, but found his arms pinned. Thick ropes bound him. He groaned and strained, sensing that his strength was now massive but still not enough to snap his bonds. He writhed like a serpent, trying to inch closer to the food.

"Noooooooooooohhhhhhhhhh..."

The sound he made wasn't human, or even that of a wild beast. It was more like air forced through a bellows, mocking word and meaning.

A new, coppery smell rose from the old man's skin. Fear. It intoxicated him all the more, set his mind racing. Would he try to run? Where? Jeremiah scanned their surroundings, traced the possible escape routes his prey might take and planned how to cut him off.

So much, so many shades of light and shadow had once been invisible. The fire in the hearth swirled with as many colors as a rainbow. The wood, pine and oak, seemed like corpses. Dead. Not what he needed. Useless.

He knew this place. The cabin. Home. But while all texture and substance now had added depth, anything of human design, the rounded pots and pans, angles of cut lumber, even the twist of the ropes holding him, seemed ludicrous and garish.

Ropes. It took three to keep him immobile. The first was wrapped ten times around his ankles and legs, the second ten times around his wrists and arms. The third, threaded between them, was pulled so tightly his knees were folded into his chest. He tested them again. Wrists and ankles would not move, but the rope that held the two together had some give.

"Do ye know me?" Atticus said again.

The old man. He wanted to talk. Maybe he could be tricked into loosening the ropes.

He forced the word out, "Yes..."

His grandfather's mouth dropped open. He lowered the axe slightly, making Jeremiah grow eager.

His captor's eyes narrowed warily. "Who am I?"

"Attttiiiiikuussss."

"And who art thou?"

"Jer...Jer...ahh mieee ahhhh. Grandson."

A whimper escaped Atticus's throat. His hand moved to cover his mouth, but before he could reach his lips, he was sobbing. The fear-smell lessened, and then vanished. The axe clattered by his side. He was weaponless and vulnerable.

A voice inside Jeremiah said, *Good.*

Jeremiah wasn't sure where it came from, but he didn't disagree. The old man started talking again.

"I've killed my own family," Atticus said. "Mary Vincent is dead, Jeremiah. I chopped her sweet form with that rough blade same as I did my son. You and I are all that's left."

Grab the axe from the floor with your feet.

What was it he'd said about his mother?

"Marryyyy Vincenttttttt?"

Saying the name brought a trail of images: her oval face, her smile, the feel of her apron hot from the fire, the cool of her hand after it washed the dishes. The rapid flow of memory seemed to promise more, but ended almost as soon as it began. Whatever reverie he'd been experiencing was stifled by the hunger.

Split the old man's head, then sever the ropes. You can do it.

Atticus wiped the tears from his face. Jeremiah's tongue sensed the moist salt they contained. "It was a kindness. She was done. God will forgive me that if nothing else. Her soul hadn't survived what Nathan had become; how could it survive becoming the same herself? Or worse, seeing you this way?"

White hair, thin skin puffed with crying, Atticus looked like a baby.

Take the axe between your feet. Feed.

What did he say? *Why* had he killed her? The desire to know pushed forward. What harm to ask, to hear answers? Jeremiah didn't even understand what he was. If the wrinkled thing could explain, it might make hunting easier. The voice of the hunger didn't relent, but it didn't stifle his questions the way it had his memories of Mary Vincent.

Then ask.

"Whatttt ddddooo yoouuuu knowwww?"

Atticus blinked. "Nothing. I only have guesses, Jeremiah. It's all I've ever had. *Chepi.* It must be as the Algonquin said, a plague, passing from the thing in the mound, to Nathan, to you. I killed Mary Vincent so she would not rise as well."

Mary Vincent. The smile, the hand, the warmth. The memories stayed a few moments longer than the first time.

"Whyyyy nootttttt meeeee?"

Atticus's lips curled so slightly that had Jeremiah still been alive, he'd never have noticed. "It was your idea. Your hungry mind. When first I saw Nathan, I thought this could not be my son, but a horrid devil in his shape, come to trick us into hell. But you, you *asked* him if anything were left of him, and I heard his answer."

Jeremiah's mind flew back to the quizzical look on his father's face as he harshly repeated his living words. *The work is its own reward.*

"Even as I killed him, trying in vain to keep him from you, I wondered whether some spark of Nathan had survived within that beast. After that, how could I end the last child of my children, without knowing whether you'd survived?"

The animal in him, the beast, tested the ropes again, but Jeremiah furrowed his brow.

Atticus nodded. "You see? You think. Your gift is with you; how could the rest of you not remain as well? I'm a madman, but I *know* ye, and ye know me."

The last words stabbed like a knife. Jeremiah arched and pulled, snapping the rope that bound his ankles to his wrists. Still tied, he writhed, like a giant, wounded serpent.

Atticus fell from his chair, scurried backward on the floor, and wrapped his aged hands tightly on the axe.

Flipping up to his knees, Jeremiah slammed his arms into the dirt floor over and over so powerfully that it seemed he'd break his bones. The air again filled with the smell of his grandfather's fear.

Keep him talking. He may try to escape.

"You don't know what madness is," Jeremiah said.

Good.

"I do," Atticus replied.

Make him think you're worried about him.

"I'll be free soon. If you've even half a mind, take that axe and kill me."

"No. Every word you speak tells me there's more than Satan inside you."

Something in the old man's faithful calm made Jeremiah shiver.

Tell him that there is. Tell him that you love him still.

"Take the axe and use it or I'll do to you as my father did to me!"

Atticus rose and stepped closer. "Fight it, Jeremiah! Fight! All men are born with violent passions, but only those who follow them end up in hell! I know you will not hurt me!"

Now.

Jeremiah wrenched his form through the air, knocking the axe from Atticus's hand and landing on his feet. The axe flew across the room, the flat end leaving a wound in the dark pine wall before thudding to the dirt floor. Jeremiah stood two feet from Atticus. He could easily lurch forward and bite, but despite the stink of his fear, the old man would not flee.

"Fight, Jeremiah, fight!"

Heat rose from Jeremiah's eyes. It felt as if they were burning. He opened his mouth, feeling his sharp teeth for the first time.

Rend him. Feed.

"Jeremiah, Jeremiah!"

"Stop saying my name!" Jeremiah twisted awkwardly. "Jeremiah!"

Like a mutineer briefly wresting the wheel of the ship from the captain, Jeremiah pivoted away from his grandfather. "I *am* in hell, Atticus! I *am* hell! Kill me if you have pity!"

Atticus held his ground. "The shell around you is evil, but you are not."

"There is *nothing* human about me!"

"You do not *know*!" Atticus pointed heavenward. "The Lord sent His son into this sad world to be sacrificed on the cross for a great purpose. Who knows what fate He has for you that might bring redemption still?"

Jeremiah's brief self-control was fading. His ankles

rubbed and pulled, working the ropes ever looser. Once they were free, a single, swift kick would end all this.

"Swing the axe. Cleave my neck. Bury my head far from my body."

Atticus's fear vanished as an old, mad glow flooded his brown eyes. Spit flew from his mouth as he shouted. "Samaria was under siege, and it caused a famine so that all the people were starving, their hunger so great, their hearts so weak, they felt Death upon their shoulders."

Jeremiah twitched his head, stretched his jaw, and growled. "Stop your mindless chanting!"

Atticus ignored him. "As the king of Israel walked along, he heard a mother wailing and asked, 'What aileth thee?' She answered, 'This woman said give thy son, that we may eat him today, and we will eat my son tomorrow. So we did eat him. The day after, I said, now give thy son, that we may eat him, but she hath hid him away!'"

Eyes cast upward, Atticus stepped closer.

"Stay away! I am not human!"

"Is your hunger greater than one that could overcome a mother's love for its babe? If not, I say ye *are* still human, and if human, your fate is unknown except to God. Ye shall not be judged by what ye are, but what ye do."

The rope around his ankles frayed.

"If you won't kill me, I'll hurl myself into the gorge and lie there until the sun's rays claim me."

Atticus shook a gnarled finger at him. "There! What devil would contemplate destroying itself rather than do harm? None! None! You are something more!"

With a final tug, Jeremiah's legs came free. All that lay between him and his food were the old man's frail body and his singsong voice.

Take him!

The beast tried to move his body forward, but Jeremiah stopped it. The hunger-driven beast inside him seemed amazed. The sound of blood thumping through his grandfather's veins came again to his ears. The beast roiled in his gut, gathering for a stronger assault against his mind's fragile hold. Jeremiah had to flee while he could.

He meant to run to the door, but nearly flew at it. Its thick oak, weakened by Nathan, splintered as he met it.

The outer world greeted him in new and unimaginable ways. Living scents were heavy in the frosty air, so much stronger and more appealing than his grandfather's fainter smell that the voice didn't seem to mind the shift in target. Hands still tied, snow crunching beneath his feet, he picked the most enticing—then twisted left and right until he found in which direction laid the source.

Yes. Two Algonquin scouts were making their way through the woods, less than a mile away. He felt the heat from their bodies tingle along his arms, heard their hearts beat like the drums they sometimes played.

Where were they headed? Of course. The Algonquin village. How easy it would be to slip among them and take one of their women. He felt as if he could simply hypnotize her by gazing into her eyes, the way a wolf does the lamb, making her eager for the slaughter.

If you're worried, it can be just once, to see how it feels!

At least it wouldn't be Atticus. Not yet. Jeremiah thrust his head down toward his wrists to bite through the ropes. Unused to his body's uncanny vigor, he tumbled to the ground. The freezing snow against his face and the ice that slipped beneath his clothes didn't matter to the animal he'd become. He locked his jaws around the twisted rope and chewed.

If Atticus hadn't emerged from the cabin, Jeremiah would have vanished into the role his new body was made for. The loose snow cover, brought to life by a stray wind, danced like icy stars around the old man's frail form. His eyes were saucers, trying to focus in the dark. As he screamed, his mouth opened to such an extreme it seemed he would tear the flesh where his thin lips met.

"I *do* know what madness is. Do not think yourself alone in torment, Jeremiah! It isn't only you or the starving in Samaria. I killed him. Not my son or his wife, but my grandson, our poor Jim. He wasn't stolen by the storm! It was me! I stole him and tossed him living into the sea!"

With every word, he pounded his hand into his chest, as if beating a confession from himself.

Inside Jeremiah, time stopped. He ceased moving and stared at the old man begging in the cold, not for forgiveness, but only to be heard.

"I was so hungry! The food was all but gone! The boy was sick, starved to the point of dying, but they kept feeding him! I wish I could swear it was a mercy, that I sought to spare him pain, or save the food for others, but I wanted his share for myself! While all tried to sleep as the storm raged around us, I scooped him in my arms and brought him up to the deck. Even in that wind, I could hear his wretched breathing. I watched him open his eyes, brown like my own, and look at me with tired love. Then I hurled him to the waves. My grandson! My heart went with him and never came back. If you, who've killed no one, are a monster, what am I? What am I?"

He fell down into the snow, a sobbing wreck.

The hunger still warped Jeremiah, but for the moment didn't own him. He walked nearer the weeping man, fell to his knees beside him, and asked, "Grandfather, what is it you would have me do?"

4

Blessed be the ties that bind. Jeremiah Fall imagined his brother as a tiny creature in an endless sea, who thought his own cravings must be all the world. He never felt closer to Jim than after he'd died himself.

You must feed. You think you know what pain is, but you don't!

As the hunger swelled, so did the agony. Within an hour, he was unable to issue any sound beyond a feral growl. Even when his mind tried to escape, the anguish followed it into his dreams. He told himself a demon would never let himself be tied, but before long he couldn't remember having given permission.

In the morning, Atticus wrapped his wrinkled frame in blankets and said, "I will visit the Algonquin."

Through crimson eyes, Jeremiah watched his grandfather swallowed by white day. Weakness mixed with the pain. The minutes crawled.

Atticus did not reappear until nightfall. Red-faced, trembling from the strain of a heavy burden, the old man looked as if his heart might seize. Jeremiah didn't care. He just watched the dripping slab of meat his wheezing grandfather pushed toward him. Once it was close enough, he wrapped his mouth around it so furiously, Atticus snatched his foot back in fear. The taste of salt and liquid copper filled Jeremiah's mouth, a hundred sharper flavors tingling bittersweet along his tongue.

This is not what you need, the beast insisted. Yet it drank until the meat grew stiff and gray.

Atticus placed a pot of water near his grandson. "See your reflection? You were gaunt when you woke. The blood brought fullness to your face."

His skin looked very pale, but the old man was right. His features remained the same as they had when he was living.

"Can you speak now that you've fed?"

Jeremiah spat out a piece of gore. "Enough to explain how to better tie these ropes so I don't murder you as you sleep."

"We'll do that. We'll study this thing your soul's wrapped in, learn its ways same as the Algonquin know the deer and bear. You're strong as an ox, two or three when your hunger grows. As you fought the ropes, you twitched so quickly your form was like lightning splitting the air."

"And you still believe I'm not the Devil's child?"

Atticus clenched his fist. "You are Jeremiah Fall, and your body is not your soul. You've not much time to learn that. When the snow thaws, the townsfolk will come."

The somber faces of the godly rose—men, women, and children. The beast sorted them into groups.

Goodman Broggin. Slow in mind and full of blood. Start with him.

He closed his eyes. "Leave me. Go with them. Tell them I died."

Atticus eyed him. "Ye know what they make of me. And I'll not abandon you … or abandon them to you. Better to join the Algonquin."

"What vexed them more, your request for a deer carcass or your refusal to let them help bring it back?"

Atticus hesitated. "I didn't make it to the village, only far enough to find Patience, dead from the storm."

Jeremiah looked at the blood on his fingers.

"Don't think on it. If Nathan and Mary lived, we'd share the cooked meat. The sin would be leaving it for the wolves. When you're ready, when you can ride your beast as a man rides a horse, you'll hunt for yourself."

Tell him you're ready. Ask him to cut the ropes. You can even let the old one go.

"I won't be ready. Not in time."

In just four days, the earth was more visible than the snow. If the townsfolk didn't visit the next morning, they would by afternoon. After sunset, Atticus sipped some soup while Jeremiah, hands still tied, feasted on living squirrels snared during the day. Once the family meal was finished, they prayed, Atticus for peace, Jeremiah for understanding, the beast for more blood.

Near dawn, Atticus withdrew a poker from the flame, turned the glowing tip upward, and balanced its cooler middle against a chair. "When I've gone, use the iron on your bonds. Set fire to this place, and then go to the cave. The sun should be up by the time you get there. I'll present myself to Kanti and, if all goes well, visit you at nightfall."

The beast bristled, but then faded. Was its strength waning, or did it realize it would soon be free?

Atticus stood before the ruined doorway. The smells of night and spring wafted in. With a final worried look at his grandson, he left. Jeremiah listened to his footsteps in the mud, sniffed at his fragile scent. He knew the moment Atticus reached the forest. He heard a branch crack beneath his foot as he turned north. He could still catch his grandfather, too easily, but the iron was dimming. What if he were trapped? The goodmen cut the lips off blasphemers and would not suffer a witch to live. What would they invent for him?

Once Atticus's breathing was no longer easy to distinguish from the wind, the beast eagerly agreed not to harm him, but Jeremiah had learned how mercurial it could be. Still, it would have to do. He backed into the iron and pushed until he heard a weak hiss. He pulled, not hard. The rope tore and slipped. Hands free, he pulled away the knots holding his feet and legs.

Run.

He wanted to, but his promise to Atticus was more than a show of fealty. Dedham must believe they'd perished, or else they'd come looking. He grabbed a burning log and touched it to his mother's linens, to the fallen table, and to the snapped timbers of the broken wall, until the flames stretched and yawned.

With that, Jeremiah flitted through the broken door and crossed into the endless wood. There, the whole of the world reached out in forbidden song. Odd urges surged through him, suggesting things he couldn't bring himself to believe: that he could move even faster, make dazzling leaps, melt into thin strips of shadow and not be seen.

And the living creatures! Squirrels, rats, deer, bobcat, and bear. Their heartbeats told him their number, size, and location. He knew where they'd been, where they were, where they planned to go, as if a moving map, easy to read as a book, were etched in his bones. Darting among the pines, he skirted over what little snow remained so quickly that he didn't leave a trace.

He reached the cave much too soon. The light was barely a sliver on the horizon. There was time before the morning came. Immobile for days, the thought of staying in the cave depressed him. Perhaps he could see how Atticus fared with the Algonquin?

Yes. If the savages misunderstand, you might have to save him. And then would it be so bad to taste one if they were already dead?

Its lies were becoming as familiar as his clothing, but, convinced he could battle it, he sped off.

Four scouts kept watch near the tribe's unplanted fields. Jeremiah marveled at how blatantly their warmth stood out from the trees, how their fear cried so loudly. Fear. It had never occurred to him that the Algonquin were worried about the colonists just as much as the other way around.

Pleased to slip by unnoticed, Jeremiah crouched in the shadow of a boulder, feeling nigh invulnerable. A fence of pine trunks circled the domed *wetu*, one for each family. Gentle smoke from an early fire rose in the village center. He saw grandfather speaking with Kanti as sleepy braves gathered in its light.

Atticus spoke in their native tongue, but Jeremiah knew what he was saying: He was confessing, telling how he was damned for what he'd done to infant Jim.

The Algonquin shrugged. They knew the sad decisions starvation could bring. When he wept for his lost family, Kanti hugged him.

Jeremiah felt nothing, but imagined he should. It didn't matter. Dawn was coming in earnest. He raced back to the cave, proud he had not hunted, worried at how much pleasure he took in himself.

The entrance was short and difficult to see, but within feet, the cave rose enough for him to stand. In the back lay blankets, an oil lantern, and other supplies. Among them, he found the old man's Geneva Bible. While any devotion in his heart felt distant, his mind was eager for distraction. Gritting his teeth against the beast, he lay on the blankets and read, not needing the lantern to see, amazed at how clear the grain of the paper appeared.

At sunset, Atticus returned as promised. Jeremiah heard him a hundred yards off, but stiffened when the space filled with the smells and sounds that defined his visitor as prey. It was the first time since his dark rebirth that he had faced his grandfather unbound, a fact not lost on either of them.

"I tried, Jeremiah, but I could not explain you to them," he said. "They believe that you're dead, that I've buried you in this cave, that your spirit resides here. I've told them that your spirit is savage, that it should not be trifled with, but also that it means no harm. That, they seemed willing to accept."

"You've explained me very well. Will they let you stay?"

"Yes. They believe I fled because the people of Dedham found out about Jim, that they would kill me for it,"

Atticus said. He could not suppress a slight cackle. "The Algonquin called them savages."

Though he saw the humor, Jeremiah did not laugh. "May I hunt?"

Atticus winced and said, "Yes."

Jeremiah flew past him so quickly that the rush of air nearly extinguished his torch. Ignoring the final cries of "Jeremiah! Jeremiah!" and the biblical quotation that followed, he embraced the countless shards of information his heightened senses laid out before him.

Trails glowed—he saw footprints, snapped branches, and bits of rubbed bark, their strength saying which were older, which more recent. A newer set of indentations, heavy enough to press dead leaves inches into the mud, riveted him. He sniffed, thrilled at how easy it was to pull the thread of one odor from another. He trained his ear against the forest's web of sounds until a giant heartbeat stood out from the rest.

Before Jeremiah was aware of deciding, his body took off after it. He wasn't even sure what he was hunting until he was nearly upon it. Slowing, he loped from clearing to boulder to branch as a hairy behemoth came into view. It was on its hind legs, scratching its vast brown back against a thick pine. Shards of bark crinkled and fell with each thrust of its legs. At its fullest stretch the bear was twelve feet at least.

It couldn't be one of the black bear common to the area. This must be the monster, the god-bear, that had been plaguing both Algonquin and settler these last two springs. It'd killed four men and wounded six. Jeremiah caught a whiff of human blood on its hot breath. Perhaps more than four.

Kanti believed it might be what was called a grizzly, who'd wandered impossibly far from its territory in the distant northwestern wilderness. But the braves who'd survived an encounter insisted no, this was larger, its snout shorter. And this creature matched that description. Monster against monster, then, a fair contest. If he bested it, he'd even rid the woods of a threat, so morality was not a question.

He leaped in a blur of motion, never imagining something so large would be fast enough to toss him off so easily. As quickly as he flew at it, Jeremiah tumbled away and struck the ground hard. His body rolled, crouched, and jumped again. The giant's growl made smoky breath rise from its throat. As its right claw swept forward, Jeremiah tried to grab its arm, thinking to stop it in midswing.

Though his strength might prove a match for it, the bear had the greater weight. He was lifted. Sharp claws scratched his cheek before he was hurled away again. Despite the pain, Jeremiah was delighted at not having to hold back, so he continued his uncontrolled charges. Even if the audacity of the attacks from the smaller creature dazzled it, the great bear easily braced itself for each assault.

Finally, Jeremiah managed to duck its blows and bring himself closer, but now he was in range of the creature's mouth. Long teeth tore into his shoulder, suddenly putting him on the defensive. He pulled away and crawled up a tree to inspect his wounds. Despite his strength and speed, he needed a strategy to prevail.

Arrogance was still folly.

On all fours, the bear rushed for the tree, its thick legs moving two at a time, first one side, then the other, not unlike a pacing horse. Not about to let it climb up after him, Jeremiah jumped, landing on its vast back. Ear pressed to its warm coat, he heard the blood rushing through it like water in a storm-gorged stream. Energized, he tried to wrap his arms around its neck.

The bear reared onto its hind legs to shake him off, but by then Jeremiah had succeeded in stretching his arm around its short muzzle. Pressing into the base of its skull with the other hand, he twisted with enough force to snap a stone. A sickening crack vibrated along the giant's spine.

Some fight remained in it, but not enough to keep Jeremiah from putting his fangs to its broad neck, chewing past the fur and piercing the jugular. The taste was rich, more satisfying than squirrel or ox. As the fluid gushed into his mouth and throat, filling him and lulling his beast, it felt as if he were inhaling the bear-god's essence.

Gorged, he pulled himself away, feeling the bear's life slosh inside him even though it was dead. He lay with his head propped against its still-warm, unmoving mass. Atticus had warned him to behead anything he killed, to make certain it didn't rise again in three days' time, but there was time for that.

He felt a strange kinship with his prey. They were both misplaced in a world that seemed too fragile for them. He wondered if it were the only one of its kind, a surviving specimen of a dying line. For that matter, was he? The thing in the mound was like him. Nathan had become like him. Were there more?

He decided to worry about it later. Looking at the stars through the crisscrossed branches, his hunger briefly sated, he didn't feel like a monster. He almost felt like himself, like Jeremiah Fall, son of Nathan and Mary Vincent. Almost.

Though Jeremiah found a few more of the huge bears, he encountered nothing like himself. He often returned to the back acre, sometimes thinking he'd found the trail of the thing that had murdered Nathan. He followed one scent to New Towne, until the smell of so many humans made the beast too strong. Meanwhile, Atticus asked Kanti to send word to the Abenaki so they might learn more about the mound. She refused, warning that a tribe nearly wiped out by the plague might not look kindly on his grandson's "spirit."

It was then the Falls realized that the Algonquin knew who had killed the giant bears and who was leaving them the slaughtered deer drained of blood. Abandoning his quest until he had himself more under control, Jeremiah contented himself with the books he "borrowed" from Dedham.

Years passed. Jeremiah remained as young and fit as the night his father had killed him. Atticus aged and grew thinner, until one summer when the days were long, it wasn't the old man who visited the cave, but four Algonquin braves.

Full of the blood of a black bear and involved in the sermon he was reading, he hadn't sensed their arrival until their shadows graced the cave mouth. As he reared and snarled, three of the braves tightened their grip on their tomahawks. The fourth brave, now perhaps twenty years old, stepped forward.

Knowing his smell, Jeremiah calmed himself. "Chogan. Why are you here?"

"Atticus is dead," the young man said.

The words did not surprise Jeremiah. His grandfather's heartbeat had grown slow and irregular, his body dry and hollow, but this moment was not something Jeremiah had ever allowed himself to imagine. Dead. Truly dead.

He felt it, but didn't show his grief. "How?"

"This afternoon he sat by the stream alongside our village. The sun on his face, he watched the water run on the rocks, closed his eyes, and did not open them again. He was so peaceful, we thought he was asleep. Kanti sent us to tell you and to say you may come to the village to see him."

The tallest brave, a hawklike intensity to his face, added, "Only once. Out of respect for Atticus."

Jeremiah took no offense. He was too dazed. He walked back with them, keeping his distance, but matching their pace. At the village fence, Chogan and the braves stepped aside until he passed within. The entire tribe had gathered, marking a path for him with their torches. It was the first and last time he was to enter the village he'd protected for so long.

They watched his progress as he stiffly marched into the *wetu* they indicated. The tree-smell of the bent saplings that formed the structure's dome mingled with the herbs meant to conceal the smell of the corpse from animal predators.

Jeremiah was not fooled. Atticus didn't look asleep; he looked dead. A woven blanket was wrapped around his utterly quiet body, pinning his arms against his sides. His thin hair was combed back, away from his face. His eyes were open, but the glint that sometimes looked like madness, sometimes like love, was missing. All the things Jeremiah's uncanny form could sense from the living, all the things he called grandfather, were gone.

After a time, Kanti entered and stood by his side. She was plumper now and shorter from age. Her hair had shed its dark color and was now a perfect white. As she breathed, he heard the illness in her lungs. Soon she would be like his grandfather. He decided not to tell her.

She spoke without saying his name. "With your permission, we wish to honor our friend Atticus the same way we would one of our own shamans. He would be cremated, to set his spirit free from his body. We will chant and sing the songs of our people for him."

Jeremiah didn't know how to respond. "Music is forbidden us. It would seem strange not to give him a Christian burial."

"Then take the body and do what is fitting for your people. Our friend will remain in our heart."

"No. You gave him shelter and a home. The people of Dedham would have killed him at worst, or abandoned him at best. If God sees all, He must see that as well."

She nodded. "We'll make the preparations." She stood still, looking at him.

"Something else, Kanti?"

"When it's done, will you stay in your cave?"

Jeremiah shrugged. "Where else would I go?"

"Where does the storm go when the rain stops?"

He twisted his head to the side. "Are you asking me to leave?"

The troubled grimace that overtook her face made her wrinkles more pronounced. "I don't ask the rain to come and go, but the great bear-gods are dead and the black bears fewer. I know my hunger doesn't grow less when there is less to eat."

It was true. It was getting harder for him to feed. The cave, while secure, seemed suffocating. He'd exhausted all the books in Dedham. But her fear hurt him. "If you worry for your people, I would never…"

Kanti raised her hand. "It is good the giant bears are gone. Their spirit was too large and fierce for this land. But so is yours. The hunting and fighting skill of our youth is not as great as it was before you came. You make their efforts seem small." She added, in a quieter voice, "Some think your presence sickens the land."

How dare they… the beast interjected. But Jeremiah didn't rear or snarl. He looked back at the body.

"My grandfather thought the Lord might still have a special destiny for me. Yet in all these years, I still don't even know what I am or if there are others like me."

"Those answers aren't here. The world is larger than these woods."

He nodded.

Hours later, followed by the whole of the village, Jeremiah, Chogan, and two braves carried the body of Atticus Fall to the top of a hill overlooking the stream where he'd died. It was laid on a bed of twigs. A frame of branches held the bed above stacks of dry wood.

At Kanti's nod, Jeremiah touched a torch to the pyre, setting flame to his last remaining relative just as he had to the cabin that had been his home. This time, rather than run, he sat quietly and watched.

If the Algonquin were nervous at his presence, they didn't show it. The tribe chanted and beat drums as the cracks, sizzles, and whistles of the fire did their work.

Even the beast left him alone, perhaps thinking, as Jeremiah did, that soon it would have him to itself.

In time, there came a single, unique sound, one loud, dull *thok*.

Thok. It echoed in his mind and heart.

He turned toward Kanti to ask about it, but didn't have to. Her face lit by the flames, she said, "It is the sound the skull makes when it cracks in the heat. That is the sign the spirit has been freed to join its ancestors. That life and this ceremony are over."

Thok.

5

June 30, 1675
The back acres of the abandoned Fall homestead

The three men had waited so long, even the moon was ready to leave. But Jeremiah kept watching, still unsure he wanted to approach them. Finding that the black bear population had been restored in his absence, he'd fed right before his arrival. He'd hoped to ensure the beast's silence, but it was beginning to stir, unable to understand why Jeremiah would wait for something so long if he weren't planning to eat it. Long ago, he'd learned he could remain still as a stone for hours, not feeling the slightest urge to move. He liked to tell himself he was learning patience, but it was a thing of his body, natural for it to behave as if dead.

The men he watched spoke Algonquin, though only two were tribesmen. During his years near their village, when Atticus lived, it had become second nature to

Jeremiah, so he had no trouble following it, or speaking it, if he had to.

"The message you left by the mound last moon didn't work. He's not coming," Ahanu said, but the slender young man said the same thing after only the first half hour. He was Chogan's son. Jeremiah was pleased to see in him some of the features of the boy who had once watched him work.

Chogan answered, a fatherly reprimand wrapped in his tone. "There's still time."

He was in his forties, but looked older and world-weary. The boyishness had long drained from his face, along with much of his pride. Seated on a rock, he shifted position often, as if trying to make himself comfortable, but failing. It was the same boulder Atticus had sat upon muttering vague blasphemies the day Nathan died.

Ahanu took his father's arm to offer support and gave him a mischievous grin. "Tell me honestly, do we keep waiting for this spirit because you're too tired to walk home?"

Chogan crinkled his eyes at him. "You know why we wait."

Jeremiah wasn't concerned about revealing himself to Ahanu; he was just young. It was their other companion, the one called Plasoa, that worried him. Looking older than Ahanu but younger than Chogan, his long face, thin lips, and narrow nose marked him as from a different tribe. Perhaps he even had European blood in him. In any case, he seemed sickly. Unlike Ahanu, who simply had too much energy to stay still, this man's impatience was born from fear. He paced with jerky movements that were easily heard and spoke in near-grunts. The Algonquin language was thick on his tongue. There was something else about him, too, a weight, as if he carried something more than his buckskin clothes.

"Don't like it. Dangerous," Plasoa said. "Too close to the town."

Chogan clucked his tongue. "I told you the last time you jumped at the sound of a squirrel, we're alone here. The whites think it's haunted." He glanced at the sky and sighed. "Tonight, I wish it were." Plasoa grunted, and Chogan shook his head. "Ahanu, take our friend to the stream and fill our skins. I'll wait here."

Happy to be moving, Ahanu led a disgruntled Plasoa from the clearing. Once Jeremiah heard them kneel by the water, he decided to let himself be seen. The trick of hiding in shadow was easy to master. He'd started doing it before he even knew he could, only realizing he was nigh invisible when a buck stuck its nose into him. As his wavering form coalesced into human shape, the folds of his dark cloak and the edges of his hat caught the white lines of moonlight.

Chogan leaped to his feet and then laughed.

The smile looked good on his tired face, but a wistful grin soon took its place. "I remember when I could do that to you. It's true what they say. You do not age."

"Not yet. I'm glad your son doesn't speak of me in fear."

Jeremiah meant it as a compliment, but Chogan's expression only grew heavier. "There are things far worse than you in these lands. I'm glad Kanti didn't live to see what's becoming of our people. I dread what I'll live to see. Sometimes I wonder if my son has a future.

Do you move among men enough to know the colonials destroyed the Wampanoag village at Mt. Hope?"

"Yes. King Phillip will lead your people to war with the settlers. It will be...bloody."

Chogan sighed. "I preferred it when Phillip was known only by his Wampanoag name, Metacom, before he became a chief and tried to organize the tribes."

Jeremiah stepped closer. "I knew a Wampanoag, Caleb Cheeshahteaumauk, when he studied at Harvard. I liked his mind. I let him see me one night as I stole some of his books. We became friends, or so I tell myself. He graduated ten years ago, when things were more peaceful."

"Books. I remember sneaking up to your cabin window when some of the other youths dared me, seeing you read. In all these years, you must have learned many things."

Jeremiah shrugged. "Mostly I learn that the last thing I read was false. I've yet to find any answers about what I am or what I should do beyond hunting bear, wandering the wilds, and returning to this mound once in a while."

"You should look somewhere other than books and wilderness."

"I've no fear of destroying books. And while I've learned to spend time among men, I would not say it's become easy for me."

"Is that why you waited until I was alone before you showed yourself?"

"Partly. The man you brought with you, Plasoa, his accent is strange. He disturbs me."

"Maybe you're bothered because you sense why he's here. He speaks that way because of the time his people spent among the French. He is Abenaki."

Jeremiah opened his eyes wide.

Chogan offered another smile. "So I can still surprise you. Metacom's efforts to organize the tribes brought him to us. Plasoa says he knows something about the mound."

"What? What does he know?"

"He wouldn't say. He would speak only to the powerful spirit who once killed the giant bears. You've become a legend among us. More words than man."

"I wish I were just words. Then at least I might understand what it is I am. I'd ask him myself why he seeks this legend now, if he could stop staring at me long enough to speak."

Chogan turned to look over his shoulder. Ahanu and Plasoa stood there, frozen, looking at Jeremiah as if he were a rattlesnake. Chogan waved for them to come forward. Ahanu hesitated, but obeyed. Plasoa stood his ground.

"I won't hurt you," Jeremiah said. He tried to look pleasant but wasn't sure he remembered how. "If there's something you've come to tell me, at great risk to yourself, I thank you for your bravery."

Plasoa remained silent.

Jeremiah took a few steps back and tried to soften his voice, speaking Algonquin slowly. "I've learned all I can about the Abenaki. I know how greatly they've suffered, how once there were many, until an unknown illness struck. In 1612, a second plague, brought by European fishermen, killed so many more that only a few thousand remained. Then, just six summers past, yet another plague. Disease has racked your people for over a century. War may now do the same. I don't blame you for being distrustful of me, or the world. I thank you again for seeking me out."

Plasoa found his voice, but struggled to pronounce the words. "You demon?"

"I don't know. I was a man like you until a thing, like me, was freed from that mound." Jeremiah pointed to it. In the midst of the fallow field, the small hill was barely visible beneath the growth of brush and weed. "It's where Chogan left the message for me. Do you know it?"

Plasoa nodded. "It's old. From the first plague. Skog buried there."

Skog. At last. At last he had a name. That alone made the trip here worthwhile. His mind reeled with questions.

"I speak some Abenaki," Ahanu offered. "Skog is their word for *serpent*."

"Did Skog die from the plague?" Jeremiah asked.

Plasoa shook his head. "Grandmother said he . . . *became* plague."

"But the Algonquin said it *wasn't* a burial mound."

"It was not. It was a prison. Skog fed on the people until a shaman gave one of our maidens poison. When Skog took her, he drank the poison in her blood. He did not die, just slept. So they tied him and buried him there."

Jeremiah shivered to recall his own brief captivity. What must it have been like to be buried for over 150 years?

Then again, what did that matter? The monster had killed his family.

He reached into a pocket of his cloak, withdrew a small bag, and tossed it to Plasoa.

It jangled, heavy with coin. Plasoa looked inside and seemed disappointed.

"It's all I have right now," Jeremiah said. "But your information is valuable to me. Is there more?"

Plasoa's eyes narrowed. "Yes. What would you give for that?"

A slight smile played across Jeremiah's face. He was right to be concerned about this man. Plasoa was afraid for a reason. There was something he wanted to ask, and it made him afraid, as if, as Kanti once said, he were going to ask something of the rain.

"What would you want?"

Before the Abenaki could respond, Chogan interrupted. "Do not barter. Jeremiah Fall comes here out of friendship; out of friendship we are here. If you have something to tell him, say it!"

"King Phillip..." Plasoa protested. Unable to find the words, his narrow face twisted in a mix of shame and frustration.

Jeremiah's brow furrowed. "Metacom? What about him? Is this about the war he plans?"

Plasoa made a fist. "You fight with us. For your grandfather."

Jeremiah scrunched his face. "Fight the colonists?"

Ahanu interjected. "You owe them nothing. My father says they turned their backs on you and your family."

"That doesn't mean I'm going to kill them."

Why not?

The beast was arguing the point already.

Plasoa fell to his knees and put his hands in the air. "They break every pact. They slaughter us. They are the plague."

Jeremiah shook his head. "Your people aren't innocent. What about the men and women savaged in the
Swansea colony, the children's skulls bashed in by
tomahawks?"

"That attack wasn't ordered by Metacom," Ahanu
said. "For the sixteen dead there, there are a hundred
in Mt. Hope, thousands over days past, many of them
children, too. There will be many more in the days to
come."

"Enough," Chogan shouted. He pulled Plasoa to
standing, then pushed him into his son. "Do not bargain
with the wind. Just tell him what you know."

Plasoa lowered his head. The whites of his eyes and
his gritted teeth were bright against his dark skin. He
spoke quickly, but in his native Abenaki.

Jeremiah raised his hands helplessly. "Wait, please...I
don't..."

Chogan nodded to Ahanu. The younger man narrowed
his eyes as if he wanted to protest, but obediently translated. "He says there is a story about things like Skog. It
was an Abenaki tale, but he didn't know it himself until
an old Frenchwoman who'd heard it taught it to him. The
French still sing it, like a song, but he says they keep
changing the words."

Things like Skog. Things like Jeremiah.

"What are the words?" Jeremiah asked.

Plasoa shrugged and sang. His shaky tone was as poor
as his speaking voice:

> *Lorsque le soleil de plomb a disparu,*
> *Quand il brille sur rien,*
> *Ensuite, une créature de la nuit*

Chante ce à la moindre lumière:
Laissez-moi vous dire, sœur lune,
Pourquoi mon cœur est rempli de tristesse.

Jeremiah shook his head, wishing he could find some amusement at his own futility. "I don't speak French either."

The men exchanged a few words, Ahanu pausing every now and again to repeat in Algonquin what he'd heard in Abenaki. "A creature of the night, abandoned, forgotten, tells the moon why he's no longer unhappy. It is because he's found a stone that heals him."

Jeremiah was stunned. "Heals? *Heals* him?"

The thought had never occurred to him.

Still standing close to the shadows, he stayed stock still and silent so long, apparently he began to disappear. Chogan finally dared to reach out, touching his shoulder. Jeremiah shivered back into the moment.

"Tell me more."

Sensing the depth of Jeremiah's reaction, Chogan tried to downplay the importance. "It's an old story changed by the French. Who knows what truth is left in it, what truth there ever was?"

Jeremiah nodded numbly. "I understand, but stranger things have happened." He turned to Ahanu and Plasoa. "I'll need paper, pen, and ink. I have to write this all down, the French, your translation. Phonetically. I'll have to do it phonetically. I'll learn French, but that will take time. It would be easier if I had someone to help who knew Abenaki *and* a language I could speak."

Chogan said, "Ahanu will help you."

Annoyed to have his father answer for him, but

perhaps sensing the desperation in Jeremiah's voice, Ahanu nodded.

Jeremiah watched Plasoa as Ahanu translated the request.

Plasoa sensed the desperation as well. "If I do this, you will fight?"

Jeremiah froze again. A Devil's bargain—the only clue to what he was, in exchange for fighting the settlers. Still, Ahanu was right. The colonists, believing the natives less than human, thought nothing of breaking their pacts with them, or their skulls if need be. His heart already sided with King Phillip. But a war? Battle might bring him some release, the same way fighting the giant bear did. It was getting harder and harder to exhaust the predator inside him. But the smell of the wounded. Human blood flowing. Could he handle that?

Of course you can.

If there were even the smallest chance he could be healed...

"Yes," Jeremiah said. "Do this for me and I'll fight, but in my own time and my own manner."

For the first time, Plasoa grinned.

"I'll get that paper now. Wait for me here."

Jeremiah stepped back into the shadow, letting his edges fade from view. The beast nagged him, but his mind worked so quickly he was able to ignore it. For the first time since he'd pushed the plow too hard in this field, he had a purpose beyond survival.

He sprinted to the road and headed toward the home of the aged Goodman Broggin. Two nights ago, he'd spotted a fine quill pen and plenty of ink and paper there. As he moved toward his destination, more flowing like dark water than walking as a living thing, he could still hear Chogan and Ahanu speak.

"Father, is he a man?"

"Not the one I laughed at as a child. He was more impatient than you, refusing good advice and eager to explain why his God was right and all others were wrong. Now? I don't know."

"He speaks as a man."

"Kanti once told me of a speaking bird. But it was an echo. The bird didn't understand what it said."

"So he's the echo of a man?"

"How can I know what he doesn't know himself? He has always been driven to learn, though. And if someone never ages and keeps learning, who knows? One day he may find out what he is. One day he may learn all there is to know. Then, I wonder, man or not, will he bother acting human at all?"

6

July 21, 1798
The village of Imbaba, Egypt

With the sun just rising, the angled lines and sandy surfaces of Gizeh's three pyramids, nine miles off, seemed to occupy a strange borderland somewhere between nature and human thought. The washed-out tan of the distant monuments was so close to the color of the surrounding dunes that the shape of the vast tombs wavered in and out of existence, like a waking dream of Euclidean mountains.

Jeremiah Fall allowed himself a moment to stare at the immortal stones and wonder what it was like to be dead, really dead. No doubt the pharaohs, so eager to avoid returning to the dust, would mock his quest to rejoin a world where things were born, lived, and died. Though their bones and godlike gravestones remained, he doubted that when they walked these sands, they'd seen as many years as he.

It had been over a hundred years since he'd first heard of the healing stone, tens of thousands of pages studied and miles traveled, endless trails of mind and earth, leading nowhere. He'd tried to find others like himself, but aside from vague likenesses to legendary creatures who lived on the blood of humans, he'd found only the slender thread that brought him here. But Jeremiah had nothing if not time. Fool's dream or arrogant folly, he would not stop. He'd been a fool long before he became a monster, after all.

Dressed in the long white tunic, sleeveless cloak, and headcloth appropriate to the Sahara, he kept his hands and face exposed to the air as long as possible, so as not to draw attention. His skin tingled at the coming sun, reminding him that the time he could keep his face exposed was limited. He picked up his pace, striding quickly among the slave-soldiers and elite cavalry of the Mamluks. Through painful trial and error, he'd learned that while normal skin would grow sunburnt even through thin cloth or on an overcast days, his did not respond quite the same way. As long as he kept all portions of his skin covered, he could survive the daylight hours. His eyes, likewise, wouldn't burn if he squinted, and even the rest of him could stand brief exposures, the way someone might pass a finger through a candle flame without being burned.

Unfortunately, not showing his face to Egypt's coruler, Murad Bey, would be an unforgivable offense, and he needed the man's favor.

Fighting the strong wave of exhaustion that always came as night faded, he hoped his meeting with the emir would begin and end quickly, so he could retreat to the more comfortable darkness. But he knew it wouldn't. The news he brought was not good and was unlikely to be heeded, making it even less likely his latest request would be granted. His plans would crumble, as they had many times, and he'd have to begin again. Still, he'd given his word, and his word remained his bond, especially when his options were limited.

He passed foot soldiers somberly cleaning their muskets; huge, blond-bearded, blue-eyed cavalry whetting their razor-sharp Damascene sabers; and a few black-skinned Africans standing out among their ranks. The swords worried Jeremiah more than the guns. He'd seen those blades decapitate a man with a single stroke and had heard Murad Bey could do the same to a horse. While Fall had healed from many wounds, he knew that like his father, he could not grow a new head.

Despite that fearsome weapon, he also knew that if the Mamluk fought Napoleon today, they'd lose. But the Mamluks, originally a race of slave-soldiers now grown to an independent force, were as stubborn as they were fierce. Once Jeremiah had thought the ways of the Algonquin were strange, but since then, the variations in the habits of men never ceased to amaze him. The Mamluk even refused to reproduce in the normal way, preferring to add to their ranks by purchasing slave-boys from the Eurasian steppes, training them as warriors. As a result, the Mamluk women engaged in frequent, hideous abortions, dressing as boys themselves to keep the attention of their men.

Here in Egypt, they currently ruled at the behest of the Ottoman Turks, but it was a tenuous relationship, and over the centuries, they had frequently rebelled. This invasion from France's little corporal, whose career Jeremiah had followed with a mix of respect and concern, would drive Turk and Mamluk together, though. If they survived.

He walked among the smaller hovels, picking up his pace but careful not to walk faster than a man would be able to. When he'd first arrived in Egypt, he'd expected to find a seat of ancient learning. Instead it was another wilderness, not unlike America, only drier, more devoid of life, and what human life there was, mostly impoverished and starving.

A manor home stood out from the squalor, with guards at the doors and windows. Realizing it had been "borrowed" by Murad Bey, Jeremiah headed for it. He was about to greet the humorless sentinels when a meaty hand with hairy knuckles squeezed his shoulder hard enough to hurt a lesser man.

"Jeremiah Fall, you've completed your reconnaissance! Wonderful!"

He turned to see Qarsaq's plump, cheery face. He was a true Egyptian, and, unlike the faith-driven Arab insurgents who'd battle any occupier, a pragmatic man.

"I never knew any man who could move so quickly through our deserts, let alone a Frank."

Since the Crusades, the Arabs called all Europeans *Franks*.

"American," Fall corrected. "And we have our own wilderness, my friend, with its own challenges. One day I'll show you. Until then, is the emir inside? I have news he should hear from me personally."

Though Qarsaq seemed friendly to the point of obsequiousness, and overweight to the point of uselessness in a war, Fall knew him to be remarkably powerful and politically savvy enough to never say exactly what was on his mind. It was through Qarsaq that he'd first gained the emir's ear. Qarsaq had, of course, his own selfish reasons for championing Fall, but Fall still liked to think they were friends, of a sort.

Qarsaq gave him a small bow. "Not this morning, Jeremiah. Murad Bey remains grateful for your efforts, but makes his final preparations for battle. It's been decided you will report to me, and I to him. Understand, please, that this is no slight. After our victory, you will be invited to celebrate by his side."

Cautious of the sudden change in plans, Fall ignored his benefactor's gracious smile and instead studied the coal-black eyes beneath the thick brow. Opaque as always. Mirrors. The man could even control his breath, and not once had he ever smelled of fear. Qarsaq was ambitious, making his way up through the ranks faster than Fall moved through the desert. That was why he had been so quick to befriend a man with Fall's unique abilities in the first place and why he might also be quick to betray him.

He could be telling the truth or just as easily be jealous of Fall's recent unhindered access to Murad. Either way, there was no point in challenging Qarsaq. Not with the blank and pitiless gaze of the sun rising so fast and so hot. It was also not news Fall really wanted to deliver.

"Then tell him to stop preparing. His cause today is hopeless."

Qarsaq's grin vanished. "But... from your last report, the French are exhausted. Bonaparte didn't provide as much as a canteen to drink from. Some take their own lives rather than die from dehydration. Those were your words."

"Yes. When they first found fresh water, some threw themselves in and drowned, dragged down by the weight of their arms. And those who drank, well, I'd hate to see what the slugs they ingested will be doing to their innards. But their difficulties haven't slowed their advance. They're on their way here, outnumbering you four to one. Their muskets have far greater range, and their artillery is mobile." Fall nodded toward the old cannons mounted on the village's stone walls to make his point. "Unlike yours."

Qarsaq responded evenly, as if insulted. "Our elite cavalry is second to none."

"The best in the world, without question, but aside from numbers and firepower, Bonaparte has a strategic advantage."

Jeremiah knelt, withdrew a dagger, and etched a shape on the ground. "They lock their infantry in a tight square formation. Well, more of a rectangle, really, like this. Their horse-drawn cannons are protected within the squares, like so. If they keep position, their bayonets can repel any cavalry, the way the Romans once repelled attacks by locking shields. Even their horsemen can remain within the square. Though inferior to the emir's cavalry, they need only attack when the timing is to their advantage."

Qarsaq's thick brow furrowed. "They have no water. They're thirsty. They will break this formation the moment they see the Nile."

"Some. Not enough to change the outcome. You must tell Murad Bey to abandon Cairo for now. He should prepare a retreat to Upper Egypt where he can wait. The French fleet sits in Abukir Bay. The English will attack it soon enough, cutting off Napoleon from France. For the war, time is on Murad's side, but not for this battle. He must retreat in order to win."

"I see."

Qarsaq pondered a moment, then rose to leave. Fall stopped him.

"Qarsaq, do you think he'll grant my request?"

Qarsaq's face twitched. He was trying to suppress a laugh. "To allow you to leave when he knows you intend to head to Rashid? Your request is insane and highly suspect."

"But I'll return and provide even more intelligence."

Qarsaq looked at him incredulously, no longer bothering to try to mitigate his expression with courtesy. "Murad Bey believes, as you do, that the English will return and the French will be fleeing with their tails between their legs within a month. Then, as he said, he will supply you a hundred diggers to find this stone of yours. But to ask to leave us now? It's unseemly to indulge your curiosity about our antiquities while we shed rivers of blood in the sand, my friend. Not right."

"It's not... it's not just curiosity, Qarsaq."

The Egyptian's eyes narrowed. "Then what, Jeremiah? What waits beneath the sand that's so important to you?"

Jeremiah fell silent. To explain would mean explaining what he was. Qarsaq might accept it—might—but no one else here would. And he'd worked so hard to pass as human. As a reminder, an irritating order arose from the beast to snap the fat man's neck.

"Ah. Your usual response. I must warn you that your evasiveness makes some wonder whether, if you'd known Alexandria and Rashid would fall to Napoleon, you would have fought with us at all. You see the dilemma?"

Jeremiah did. If Murad Bey did not listen to his advice, it would be certain that, as far as his quest was concerned, he'd backed the wrong side.

"You will wait for me here," Qarsaq said. He mumbled something to the guards and then vanished into the building.

Fall shifted nervously. *Was* his allegiance so easily bought? Would he have fought with the French if he'd known? Since his first skirmishes in King Phillip's War, he'd discovered that battle helped keep his hungers at bay. The smell of blood everywhere made it difficult for the beast to focus for long, easier for Jeremiah to shift the urge from target to taget. At times, it was as if the beast, understanding it would not be allowed to indulge, at least preferred to be near it.

Even so, he'd always tried to choose the right side. He was proud to have been among those who had defeated the British and helped the colonies achieve independence. But the longer he lived, or at least existed, the more difficult it became to tell which side was right. Napoleon was an invader, the nomadic Mamluk and the Turks occupiers. Given the ideals of the French Revolution, Napoleon might actually provide the Egyptians with the freedom and respect his propaganda promised.

Not likely, though. Egypt was just a pawn in the larger game all Europe was playing, and Jeremiah had no stake in that at all. Napoleon's real goal was England. Rather than invade the island directly, he hoped to strangle it.

With Egypt secure, he'd continue east, either pretending to support the weakened Ottoman Empire or conquering it. Then he'd reach India and cut England off from the jewel in her crown.

Or maybe none of that was true. At times, despite Atticus's fondness for his hungry mind, Jeremiah wished he didn't know as much as he did. At times, second-guessing paralyzed him, and he wished he were fighting a monster-bear instead.

The sky was lighter. The tingling on his cheeks grew, forcing him to raise the folds of his headcloth over his face and wrap his hands in his tunic. This was a problem. The dawn air was comfortably cool, not a time to be covering oneself. It made him stand out, but he hoped anyone watching would chalk up his covered visage to a lack of experience with proper desert garb.

When Qarsaq finally emerged from the house, he had six large warrior-soldiers marching behind him. As his "friend" came forward, they spread out, forming a semi-circle in front of Fall. Fall's heart dropped with his hopes.

"Bad news," Qarsaq said. "Very bad. The great Murad Bey finds your judgment...dubious, perhaps even clouded."

"This saddens me, Qarsaq, for the obvious reasons, but also because it reminds me of a time when my people likewise refused good advice from strange quarters. We are even more like the Mamluk than I originally thought. Does Murad Bey think me a fool?"

Qarsaq shook his head. "Not at all. He has terrific respect for your intellect and learning, as do we all."

"What then? A spy? I've been nothing but loyal. What did you say to him?"

Four more soldiers fell into place behind Fall, robes wafting around thick arms and barrel chests, completing the circle. He could take the ten of them easily, but all around, scores more turned to watch and listen. He couldn't fight an army. Not for long, anyway. Not with so many of those sharp blades around.

Qarsaq shrugged. "I told him that you were nothing but loyal. That despite your strange habits, your daylight disappearances, your uncanny knowledge of the enemy, and your mad suggestion we desert Cairo, the very notion that you were a spy is impossible. I told him any real spy would have covered his tracks much more cleverly. But today, Murad Bey takes no chances."

The truth told with bad intent beats all the lies you can invent, Fall thought. *When he realized what the emir's reaction would be, Qarsaq washed his hands of me.*

Qarsaq went on. "On the lighter side, because of your great service to us, you are being afforded an opportunity to prove your loyalty."

"Prove myself? How?"

"You will be given horse, blade, and pistols. Today you will ride with our cavalry, by my side. You will see firsthand how we utterly defeat the invaders." Qarsaq beamed. "I will be honored to battle with you, Jeremiah Fall. Assuming, that is, that you do not object?"

"Qarsaq, I'm no horseman."

It was an understatement. The four-legged beasts hated him instinctively. All mammals did, as if they could smell his strangeness.

Qarsaq flashed his old grin. "Then you will learn! Our chargers are so well trained, they will carry you into battle of their own free will!"

Fall looked at the ten soldiers, the hundreds more beyond. Those who could not hear the conversation passed the story along in whispers.

Not a fool? Murad Bey was wrong. Fall was the biggest fool imaginable. A fool to come to this desert to begin with, a fool to think they'd ever really trust him, a fool to try to stop the slaughter. Once he saw how determined and disciplined the French were, he should've kept going, headed for Rashid. But he wanted to keep his word. It seemed that no good deed would go unpunished.

The morning sun touched his brow and made him wince.

"No," he said, grimacing. "I have no objection."

"I knew you could not. Let's go get you a horse."

Qarsaq put his arm around Fall, hugging him as they walked. Trying not to look as though he were rejecting Qarsaq's embrace, he moved away and rearranged his headcloth to keep his face completely covered. The soldiers fell in line behind them.

Fear of the sun faded to the background, though, as he thought about what would happen when they brought him near their fine Arab horses. If the first refused to let him mount, Qarsaq and the others might think it simply odd, perhaps even amusing, but what would happen at the sixth or seventh? The more educated Mamluks didn't believe in monsters, but the lower-class slave-soldiers did. And how long would even the best education last against the evidence of their own eyes?

Recalling the bone-slicing scimitars, Fall again wondered what it would be like to be really dead.

The corral was a flat area fenced in by logs, where dry grass poked up from sand. As they neared it, Qarsaq summoned two handlers. A huge black mare was brought to meet them at the gate.

"To show that my love for you is as it is for my own brother, I give you my best, Al-Hawa, the wind. You have the whole morning to get used to her, but you'll find no animal smarter, faster, or better trained."

Qarsaq wasn't lying. The horse was beautiful. Maybe he felt guilty for not sticking up for his "brother" before the emir. It didn't matter. The moment Al-Hawa laid its black eyes on the shrouded Fall, it tensed and stepped back. Not yet noticing, Qarsaq took the reins and placed them in Fall's hands, making Al-Hawa even more upset.

"Easy, girl," Fall whispered, but the horse would not steady.

Qarsaq and the soldiers watched as it grew more and more upset, snapping its head left and right as it tried to wrest the reins from Fall.

"I've never seen her do that," Qarsaq said, genuinely surprised.

"She's skittish," Fall explained. "We've never met before. Let me walk with her, talk to her a bit. It's a trick my grandfather taught me. He was a horse...talking person."

"As you wish, but stay within the fence," Qarsaq said. He was clearly suspicious now, probably expecting Fall to leap onto the horse and try to escape.

If only.

Fall led the mare deeper into the corral, forcibly walking her as far from Qarsaq and the guards as he could, trying to make it seem natural. As the distance increased, the soldiers raised their muskets. When the mare looked ready to begin a full-blown equestrian panic, he warned it in hushed, hurried tones, "Keep that up, and you'll get us both killed!"

It was fortunate the mare was so tall. When Fall turned it and stood on its far side, pretending to whisper into its ear, his head was blocked from view. Perhaps sensing what the odd man planned next, the horse seemed ready to bolt.

Before it could, Fall dropped the cloth from his mouth and, quick as a mongoose, drove his teeth into the animal's wide neck. The horse shivered at the penetration, then steadied as a subtle fog, like a bank of clouds, crept along the sheen of its black eyes.

It was an effect of his eerie nature that it took decades to discover. At the moment of feeding, a piece of Fall's will seemed to pass into his prey, making it surrender to his commands. He'd found out nearly by accident while traveling in the Northwest, trying to find more of the giant short-nosed bears. While he was feeding on a grizzly, its mate came up behind him and tore him off. He killed the mate quickly, but as the wounded male tried to escape, Fall discovered he could call it back, and even make it walk in circles.

He kept it alive that way for a time, enthralled to him, even using it once to attack a troop of British imperial soldiers. But the bear's savagery also seemed to pass a bit into Fall, making it more difficult for him to rein in his own beast, so he never dared to try it again.

Once Fall had drunk enough to put the horse under his command, he patted Al-Hawa and whispered, "I promise I'll try to get us both out of this in one piece."

He slipped onto her broad back and trotted her over to the gate.

Qarsaq nodded his relief and his approval. "Your grandfather's methods are effective."

"He had a way with animals," Fall answered, wondering if old Atticus would find the half-lie amusing. He had, after all, helped Jeremiah tame the beast.

By late afternoon, French divisions had taken up positions near Imbaba, cutting off any easy retreat to Upper Egypt and, in Fall's eyes, any possibility of avoiding a rout. Shortly after, the powerful, black-bearded Murad Bey, looking much like a mounted grizzly himself, ordered his cavalry to attack.

From his position in the third rank, Qarsaq gave off a wet, throaty laugh and kicked his horse into a gallop. Fall could only sigh as he and Al-Hawa picked up speed beside Qarsaq.

The costumes of the cavalry, bleached white and embroidered with gold and silver, with weapons polished to a high sheen, were intended to catch the sun and blind the enemy. Fall was sure they were effective in most circumstances, but here and now they only served to make him more nervous. They'd be much better targets for Napoleon's muskets.

However, he was not so fearful of their coming defeat that the sight of thousands of Mamluk horsemen, charging across the dunes with a roar like divine thunder, did not fill him with awe. And battle, despite his mind's distaste for it, always thrilled the beast. His blood pounded as if the hooves of the horses were within him. He even believed for a moment that they might, by dint of sheer fury and expertise, still win.

But then he looked ahead and saw tens of thousands of utterly disciplined French infantry. They locked formation, as geometrically precise as the pyramids. Minutes later, above the roaring hooves, Fall's sharp ears made out a sound like a cauldron burning on a crackling fire.

"Here it comes," Fall said, mostly to the horse.

"Here what comes?" Qarsaq shouted. He was smiling. His scimitar was out and swinging at the hot dry air above his head.

"Musket fire," Fall told him.

"Ha! You worry too much! We're nowhere near within range of—"

His sentence was cut short by an ocean of teakettle whistles. The man riding in front of Qarsaq flew backward off his mount, a dark round wound on his chest marring the white glow of his costume. It was all Qarsaq could do to veer to the side to avoid trampling the fallen man. In seconds, scores more riders fell before the swarm of insect meteorites.

Between the chaotic howls of man and animal and the sands stirred into clouds by falling bodies, Fall lost track of Qarsaq and soon, of the battle itself. He halted Al-Hawa to get his bearing. Bit by bit, the haze of hot dry sand cleared enough for Fall to see that most of the survivors were turning back. The elite cavalry of Murad Bey had gone into retreat almost as soon as its charge had begun. Some even tossed the gold and jewels they kept sewn into their robes down to the sand, in the hopes that it would distract the French.

It did not.

Fall joined the retreat. Despite Qarsaq's betrayal, he hoped to see the man among those fleeing. Instead, the only figure he recognized was the flat-nosed Murad Bey, who, despite a line of blood on his cheek from a French musket's near-miss, was trying valiantly to reorganize the scattering horsemen into another assault.

The cavalry, though stunned by the surprising musket fire, rallied to their emir. A true commander, Murad led them to the flank in short order, then to the rear of Napoleon's divisions, where he hoped to somehow poke a hole into their formation.

Now was Jeremiah Fall's chance to flee. He and Al-Hawa could easily ride off the battlefield, past the Mamluks, past the French, and into the vast Sahara, where he could find that cool cave he longed for and forget this damnable day.

But as he scanned the dead and dying, as the thick scent of wasted blood enlivened his senses, and as he saw how the Mamluks refused to yield, he recalled his grandfather's words that we are not judged by what we are, but by what we do. And he had given his word, one of the few things that reminded him he was human.

An anger welled inside him that wouldn't let him flee. He couldn't abandon a cause he'd worked for, even if it wasn't quite his own. Cursing every bone in his already-cursed body, he kicked Al-Hawa into a gallop and joined the reorganizing cavalry.

At the rear, they found the same unyielding formation. In unison, the French infantry lowered their black bayonets to the Mamluks' silver blades. Napoleon's green-bedecked light cavalry stayed within the square and watched.

Hewing to their old nomadic strategy, each Mamluk rider attacked as if four men. First they fired the English carbine held at their leg, then two pistols, all thrown back over their shoulder to be reloaded by attendants on foot. Next they threw sharp *djeriads*, javelins made of palm branches. Finally they plucked their jeweled thirty-inch scimitars from between their clenched teeth and sliced the very air.

Some French fell, but not nearly enough to make any difference. It was hopeless. He wondered how Murad Bey felt about his advice now.

But then, as Fall spied a wheel-mounted cannon safely nestled within the huge square of infantry, another foolish thought took him. There were times when one such as he might turn the tide of a battle.

He whispered to his mount, "Let's see if we can get ourselves one of those cannons, girl."

Using his eerie influence, he made her gallop faster, ever faster, to the second rank, to the first, so that finally he even passed Murad Bey. Instead of taking offense, Bey offered the American a toothy grin and kicked his own steed all the harder.

As Jeremiah reached the line of bayonets, he let loose a loud guttural, inhuman shriek. The infantry, already weak from dehydration, quaked to hear it, but held their position. Fall pulled back on the reins and Al-Hawa leaped, high into the air.

Behind him, he heard Murad Bey himself cheer as the cloaked Jeremiah and his borrowed horse cleared the frightened soldiers' heads and landed behind their front rank. Balancing catlike on Al-Hawa's back, Fall swung his blade with one cloth-wrapped hand and fired his carbine with the other, trying to clear a path toward the closest cannon.

Murad, nothing if not a brilliant tactician, sought to

take advantage of the sudden confusion, pressing his cavalry toward the slight breach Fall had created.

Seeing the wave of Mamluk riders turn, the nearest French commander realized what was happening and had only seconds to make a difficult choice. His face looked as if it had once enjoyed some folds of fat, but it was now so drained from lack of water that his withered skin made his eyes bulge. If the commander did as instinct bade and ordered some men to pursue the single, crazed rider, he'd leave more of the formation open to the enemy. Instead, he put his faith in the tactic that had worked so well for them in Europe and ordered that the square be reformed at all costs.

The oncoming cavalry again met a wall of bayonets that cut short their cheering, if not their charge.

Fall, meanwhile, had all but reached his goal. Animals, save Al-Hawa, could barely stand to be near him, so he reasoned that all he had to do was get close enough to the workhorse pulling the cannon to get a reaction from it. And he was right. At the mere sight of Jeremiah, the lesser horse reared, wide-eyed. To make certain he achieved the full effect, he briefly pulled back his headcloth, revealing enough of his mouth to bare his fangs and snarl.

Before the sun could burn him, he pulled the covering back, but his ploy worked—the horse went mad. Trying to shed itself of its burden and flee, it kicked its front legs into the air. Its French rider, apparently having also caught a glimpse of Fall, practically threw himself from the saddle in his own effort to scramble away.

"Stay nearby," Fall told Al-Hawa. Then he leaped from her back.

He hit the heavy brass of the cannon barrel hard. The workhorse whinnied and whirled, nearly throwing Fall as it dragged the wheeled artillery in a jerky semicircle. With a swipe of his scimitar, Fall sliced the tethers, leaving the frantic horse free to put as much distance between itself and the horrifying man as possible.

The cannon beneath him was now motionless in the midst of a marching army, a rock in a sea of men. Though the vast bulk of the French formation continued forward, Murad's cavalry was again in retreat, freeing the French commander to order a few infantrymen to deal with Fall. Two raced up to him with bayonets lowered. Pulling pistols from the folds of his tunic, Fall fired both, hitting his targets and providing a few scant seconds to call for Al-Hawa.

As if waiting at his back for the summons, the horse appeared instantly, unharmed and unhindered. In the heat of battle, no one would waste time on a riderless horse. As more infantrymen approached, Fall kicked one into another, each blow from his foot taking a man fully off the ground. Moving fast, he tied the tethers to Al-Hawa, dodging bullets and blades as he worked.

With the straps relatively secure, he leaped for Al-Hawa. It was only in midair that his luck briefly failed. A bayonet jabbed up at him, slicing his tunic, tearing a long, thin gash that exposed his flesh. Angry, he snatched the hot musket by the barrel and slammed its butt into the soldier, dropping him. Though Fall wasn't cut, fingers of smoke rose from the naked strip of flesh.

After kicking another approaching soldier in the jaw, Fall used his right hand to hold the cloth shut, leaving him one-handed. He veered Al-Hawa to the right and shortly burst from the formation, dragging the cannon behind him.

A hundred yards ahead, a small rise lay in the sands. Others might take it for a dune, but Fall's sharp eyes recognized the slight gray of solid rock beneath the whitish desert cover. If he brought the cannon there and set it up quickly enough, he could fire at the approaching square's flank. If the round-shot were well placed, it could create a breach large enough for Murad's cavalry to force their way inside.

He steered Al-Hawa toward the rise. The rickety wheels beneath the cannon rumbled behind them. A glance back told him the sweaty commander was beginning to sense the seriousness of the threat. He ordered ten more infantrymen to break ranks and follow.

Strong and fast as the horse was, the cannon slowed her, making them an easier target. They'd reached the bottom of the rise and were headed uphill onto the rock when the men fired. Musket balls filled the air, whistling past Fall's head. A lucky shot strafed several of the spokes on one of the wheels. The cannon rolled forward another two yards, but the heavy barrel collapsed it.

Tethered to a dead weight, Al-Hawa whinnied pitifully, her long legs scrabbling for purchase in the sandy ground. Fall jumped down to the toppled cannon and cut her free. "Go," he told her. "No need for both of us to die."

With seeming reluctance, the black mare galloped off as another volley of musket balls hit. Fall turned sideways, moving nearly as quickly as the projectiles flew, trying to make himself a smaller target, but a round clipped his right knee. At first he felt no pain, but his leg was suddenly as useless as the cannon's broken wheel. He collapsed behind the brass barrel, hoping it would act as something of a shield.

As the pursuing infantrymen reloaded their weapons, their luck ran out. They found themselves facing the blades of six Mamluk cavalrymen, who quickly showed how easily their scimitars could sever limbs. After seven of the men were gruesomely killed and the remaining three fled, one Mamluk rider grinned and shook his bloody scimitar at Jeremiah, shedding drops of dark brown in the sand.

Briefly safe and alone with his prize, Fall looked down at the smoking blood and bone visible through the new tear in his tunic. In the way of things, it wasn't much of a wound. It would fully heal within half an hour, assuming he survived. But now, unable to move except at a crawl, what could he do?

The cannon lay sideways, awkwardly supported by its one good wheel. Thinking he might still be able to aim and fire it, Fall braced his good leg against the rock and pushed. The cannon pivoted, scratching an arc into the ground, marring its finely polished barrel. Another half a foot and he'd have it pointed roughly toward the French. The soldiers were passing as he worked, their eyes set on Imbaba. They would not be in range for long.

He could see Murad Bey's cavalry regrouping yet again. If timed correctly, one shot might still make a difference. If it didn't turn the battle, at least it would make the French pay for their victory.

Unlike the plow that didn't move for him back on the farm those long decades ago, the heavy cannon, once in motion, wouldn't stop. Fall watched in horror as the axle bent and the remaining wheel creaked and folded, ready to snap. He pulled wildly to slow it. Though he managed to briefly bear its whole weight, he could not stop the collapse. Wheel-less, the cannon crashed onto his thigh, pinning him.

Unable to stand or crawl, he gasped. Worse, the three infantrymen who'd survived the Mamluk cavalry attack had not forgotten him. He should have sensed their approach, but the roar and the million scents of battle muddied even his perception. Their guns were already lowered and aimed. Fall knew his healing powers were great, but had no wish to test their limits with multiple musket wounds.

The French looked very angry at him for stealing their cannon. Before he could say anything, they fired. One round hit a pocket of sand on the rock near his head, another ricocheted off the body of the cannon. The third caught some of the wood frame.

"Arretez!" Fall cried. He'd mastered several languages over the decades, but they didn't seem interested in listening to his French, and instead took to reloading. He strained against the weight on him, but had suffered more damage than he realized.

Their powder and shot already in place, the three soldiers tamped down the mixture in unison.

"Cette fois, viser soigneusement!" one shouted. *This time, aim carefully!*

He had no doubt that they would. Desperate, Fall pulled a final pistol free from his tunic. His aim was uncanny, but he doubted he could disable three men with a single shot.

Unless, of course, it was a cannon shot. It was loaded, after all. But the thing was right on top of him. If the musket fire didn't kill him, the recoil likely would.

He aimed at the fuse and fired. Hearing the pistol crack, one of the infantrymen looked up from his reloading in time to see the cannon belch smoke. Fall felt the barrel shove backward from the blast, searing hot against his thigh. The round-shot whistled across the short distance. One second, he saw the surprised expression on the young men's faces, then, a pile of assorted limbs and gore.

He fared little better. Pain, worse than the sun's burning, marched along his leg, abdomen, and thigh. This new wound bested even Fall's unnatural willpower. As he lapsed into unconsciousness, the sounds of the battle raging around him, he thought how typical, and how sad, that the only one he'd been able to save had been himself.

Then it all went to dreams and nothing.

He woke briefly, hours later, the sound of a familiar name ringing loudly in his ears.

"Jeremiah! Jeremiah Fall!"

A cool evening breeze rustled the fabric of his headcloth. It was night. He opened his eyes and tried to raise his head. The name he recognized as his own. He knew the voice as well. Who? Was it Atticus again calling him back from the dead? No. Qarsaq. Yes, of course.

There was Qarsaq at the foot of the rise, his brown face black as if covered in chimney soot, his fine white robes torn and bloodied, but the smile, the thick smile, was the same as it had ever been. Was the battle over?

"You're alive! Allah be praised. Come, let's get you out of there," Qarsaq said. He hobbled up the sand toward Fall. "There, there, you don't look so bad."

"I don't believe you," Fall managed to say. But then he shifted. He was weak, groggy, and still pinned, but his pained legs and hip had already started to heal.

"Ha! I can't say I blame you, but I speak the truth, as did you this morning. It was as you said. We've lost Imbaba and Cairo. Of course, the emir should have listened to you. I'm certain he sees that now. If we hurry and no one spots us, we can catch up with him. He's taken three thousand of his cavalry and headed up the Nile. He would not forgive me if I left you behind. I would not forgive myself."

Fall tried to speak again, but his body wanted to stay in a torpor to finish healing, another instinct of his strange form. He had to fight it. If he fell unconscious, the French would capture them both.

Qarsaq, obviously exhausted himself, reached the cannon and pulled at its mouth. It moved slightly.

"There we go, my friend. You'll soon be free."

All at once the Egyptian, though still grinning, stopped moving. He stood there a moment, still as a sand dune, then fell forward onto the cannon, a jagged wound visible in the center of his back.

A pleased French soldier stood behind him, his bayonet covered in Qarsaq's blood. Though the body literally lay atop Jeremiah, the eager infantryman stabbed at it a few times to make sure it was truly dead. It tumbled off Jeremiah and the cannon, spilling its life fluids into the sand. The sight made Jeremiah tremble.

The soldier looked at Fall, revealing the harsh countenance of a veteran.

"Vous êtes mon prisonnier," he said.

"Bien sûr," Fall managed to respond before his mind surrendered to his body's fatigue. *"Bien sûr."*

Then it all went to dreams and nothing again.

7

Jeremiah Fall dreamed that his skin, exposed to the day, blackened, curled, and burned. He felt himself die, then watched the wind sweep his dust into the cracks between the blocks that made the pyramids. It was still night when he came to. His wounds were healed, and he was no longer beneath the cannon. The air was thick with the gritty sweat of men and the thicker stench of smoke. A tight coldness at his ankles told him he was shackled. He was in the corral at Imbaba, along with nearly a hundred captive Mamluks.

He could probably snap the shackle and slip away, but why? What was left of the village burned, and no one tried to stop the flames. The French had no need for Imbaba; it was only the gateway to Cairo. Visible as scores of minarets rising beyond the pyramids, Cairo now belonged to Napoleon. The healing stone he sought seemed as lost as Murad Bey's promise of a hundred diggers. Even if he reached Rashid, he'd now be known as an enemy soldier.

Buried but it yet remains. Black as night among the stars, the song said. Or words like that. Ages translating and he still wasn't sure. But the possibility he was right had kept him going, kept the line between himself and the beast. Now that faith felt as futile as his parents' belief that by clearing a few back acres they might return their son to school. Beyond repairing his clothes before sunrise, he hoped fate would spare him the difficulty of deciding what to do next.

For days, the prisoners fished bloated Mamluk bodies from the Nile. Knowing that their foes followed the nomadic tradition of carrying their wealth with them, the French ordered the corpses stripped. As they pulled a lifetime's treasure from one fallen warrior after another, the prisoners gnashed their teeth and whispered of attacking, even if it meant suicide. Iyaaz, a burly blond with a rosy complexion turned near-red by the sun, was the most vocal.

"I saw you fight," he said to Jeremiah. "Why not lead us?"

"I dislike wasted blood," Jeremiah answered as he dragged a dead man onto the bank. "Three thousand of Murad Bey's cavalry died. The French lost twenty-nine men. Unless England or the Turks attack, they will not be defeated."

Napoleon had even given the conflict the grandiose title of the Battle of the Pyramids. *"Du haut de ces pyramides, quarante siècles d'histoire vous contemplent,"* they said he'd told his troops. *Forty centuries look down on you!*

With Rashid in French hands, Jeremiah tried to curry their favor, but they sneered at the American. They'd fought alongside the colonists during the Revolution of 1776—where was his loyalty to a sister republic? The Mamluks, none of whom spoke French, took these talks as confirmation of treachery and regarded Fall with disgust.

His sole companion would have been the beast, were it not for a chance reappearance. Lieutenant Louis Dillan, the man in charge of the prisoners, had taken to riding a certain captured black horse to remind the prisoners that the French now possessed all that had been theirs. Whenever they passed, Al-Hawa nodded her wide head at Jeremiah. Meanwhile, Dillan, try as he might, could not conceal the fact that he was an out-of-shape bureaucrat, unintentionally cheering the prisoners with his laughable riding skills.

The occupation consolidated. Bonaparte made the sprawling medieval Citadel in Cairo his military head-quarters. Nearby, his savants founded the Institut de l'Égypte to organize their studies of the flora, fauna, and antiquities, never realizing how unique a specimen they'd already captured.

But the French had more to worry about than catalog-ing an alien world. Ten days after Jeremiah's capture, the English, under Admiral Nelson, decimated the French fleet, stranding Napoleon's army. Thousands of French corpses, mostly in pieces, washed up on the sandy coast. Peasants burned the beached wood from the lost ships, not to cremate the bodies, but to recover the nails. Metal was in short supply.

Learning of the fleet's fate, the Ottoman declared war on Napoleon. Meanwhile, Murad Bey's remaining forces led the French on a mad chase across the northern deserts.

"Will you lead us in an escape now?" Iyaaz asked.

"I don't know. The English still hold back, hoping the Turks, Murad, and the harsh terrain will wear down the French for them," Jeremiah said. More important, he was no longer sure whose side he was on. The savants and engineers had set to work building wells, fixing roads, and trying to find cures for the diseases that plagued the land.

Time passed. Habit mollified passion. Imbaba became a supply hub, using prisoners to unload and load cargo by night. With the off-hours viewed as punishment by those who understood the desert little, the American didn't even have to volunteer. It was an opportunity, but a small one, as if destiny were testing the waters.

In the cool dark, Fall proved such an exceptional worker that he earned their grudging admiration. Soon he was able to steal moments alone, making it easier to feed on the rats, rabbits, and hyraxes whose hiding places he sensed so easily.

More months passed, history moved, until once more, events seemed aligned against Napoleon. While Bonaparte hoped his open hand toward Islam would earn respect, instead he was cursed as an atheist and an infidel. Turkish battle ships had joined Nelson at the Nile Delta. By February 1799, the Ottoman were expected to cross the Sinai and attack.

But Napoleon entered the desert first, along with thirteen thousand men, and soon laid siege to the high walls of Jaffa. When a French delegate was sent to negotiate the Ottoman's surrender, though, his head returned without his body. The furious soldiers slaughtered every man, woman, and child in the city. Forty-five hundred prisoners were herded to the ocean and executed.

The illusion of French civility was shattered, but the advance continued. Within two months, Napoleon was ready to assault the Mamluk ruler Al-Jezzar in his capital, Acre, near Damascus, but his artillery was destroyed by British ships. The French army, suffering from plague and dysentery, had to pull back. By the end of May, Al-Jezzar was rendered impotent, but so was Bonaparte's plan to cross Persia and reach India.

With the land route controlled by Napoleon, the Ottoman would have to attack by sea, so the French began fortifying the coast, including a city called Rosetta, which was what the conquerors, rather than learn Arabic, had taken to calling Rashid.

So it came to pass that one afternoon, as Jeremiah slept in the shade of two crossed palms, he was awoken by a musket butt pressed hard into his shoulder. The infantryman who carried it wouldn't say why. He simply herded Jeremiah, along with the other prisoners, into a courtyard. The space was dusty and dry, crowded with wine casks, prisoners, and the soldiers, who forced them to stand in line.

Al-Hawa, bearing Lieutenant Dillan, trotted among them. He rode up and down the line, making a show of inspecting each man. "Rosetta," he announced, "requires able-bodied men to assist our engineers. They have an old Crusader fort in bad need of repair."

Jeremiah was stunned. The fort Dillan was talking about had to be Julien, built atop the very location he wished to explore. While he fought to contain his emotions, the Mamluk bristled at the thought of aiding the defense of their oppressors. If the Mamluk refused, Jeremiah could simply volunteer.

But Dillan wasn't completely stupid. He knew how the Mamluk would react and had prepared. "Those who are chosen will be paid for this effort, and thereafter, freed. Those who are not will be transferred to a more secure prison in Cairo."

Mamluk loyalty was trumped. To a man, they shouted and begged to be chosen. Even Iyaaz went down to his knees.

Dillan grinned as he maneuvered Al-Hawa along. Relishing his manufactured superiority, he nodded at some and skipped others, as if he were a Greek Fate snipping or extending the threads of lives at whim. Jeremiah detested him, but felt his moment had come.

When Dillan came to Jeremiah, he tugged on the reins, but Al-Hawa refused to move. A soldier, as if obeying Jeremiah's wishes as readily as the horse, said, "What about the American? He does the work of ten."

Dillan, obviously not wishing to deal with his disobedient mount, warmed to the distraction. He twisted his head at Fall. "Does he now?"

Jeremiah, wrapped in his desert robes, bowed.

"American, but you dress as a native. I'd like to see your face."

Fall choked. "I...I'm sorry, monsieur, I can't do that."

Dillan shifted in his saddle and laughed. "Why? Are you disfigured? Do you think I haven't seen what war can do? Remove your headcloth at once."

Devastated, Jeremiah's mind scrambled for an acceptable excuse, furious that in all this time, he didn't have one prepared. "I...I...cannot," he said.

"Even at the cost of your freedom?"

"Even so."

Dillan shrugged. "You are too willful. I will not send you to Rosetta."

He pulled more forcefully on the reins. Al-Hawa whinnied, but a quick nod from Fall sent her moving.

His great hope snatched, Jeremiah felt weak and nauseated, but what could he do? As he watched the lieutenant move ahead, displaying less riding skill than a newborn babe, the answer came.

Fall clucked his tongue. The ears of the Arab charger twitched, and Al-Hawa reared. Dillan nearly flew from the saddle. Only his desperation to avoid embarrassment gave him the strength to hold on. The great horse galloped around the courtyard, kicking and whinnying. Her rider bobbed in the saddle as if boneless.

"It's gone mad!" someone shouted. "Shoot it!"

A soldier near Jeremiah raised his musket, forcing him to act. With a swipe of his hand, he ruined the man's aim. The lead ball ripped a small trail in the courtyard's dirt.

"You might hit the lieutenant!" Fall screamed, but he was really more concerned about the horse.

Having already left his place in the row, he ran, hoping it would be obvious he was trying to help. Trying not to move too quickly, he climbed atop the stacked wine casks. From there, he leaped at the frightened man on the speeding horse. Reaching the lieutenant, he wrapped himself around the man. Momentum carried them both sideways off the horse. In midair, he twisted so his back would absorb the brunt of the fall.

With Dillan's wheezing gasps loud in his ear, the smell of his terror acrid in his nostrils, Jeremiah Fall watched Al-Hawa race through the village into the desert beyond, fast as her namesake, the wind.

The soldiers fell over one another to help their commander. Dillan waved them off and slapped the dirt from his pants as he brought himself to his feet.

He gave Fall a curt bow. "It appears I'm in your debt, monsieur."

"Will you take me to Rosetta?"

The lieutenant hesitated, as if some dim instinct warned that the whole episode might somehow have been planned. But that, of course, was nonsense. He smiled graciously. "Done."

The prisoners were segregated into groups. Some were fitted with heavier chains for their trip to Cairo. Jeremiah, however, joined those being placed into wagons bound for the Nile. As the courtyard faded from view, he caught a final glimpse of proud Iyaaz, shoulders slumping, ashamed at having begged when every man knew such a vocal troublemaker would never be chosen.

At the Nile, the prisoners, along with Lieutenant Dillan, boarded an overcrowded barge. Many of the troops stationed in Imbaba were also being transferred to the coast. As the soldiers enjoyed rest and provisions, the prisoners were forced to stand.

Upon arrival, they were greeted by a quiet, fearful city where the begging poor outnumbered the merchants, and thousands of soldiers were stationed on the beaches. The spectacle held little interest for Jeremiah. His eyes were riveted on the single medieval tower on the Nile's west bank, high enough to provide a view of the whole river as it rushed past the city's busy port. For all its impressive stature, Fort Julien looked as if it had been untouched since Sultan Qayt Bey restored it in the fifteenth century.

The situation couldn't be more perfect. The French wanted to restore its crumbling walls, but first the oldest, weakest stones would have to be removed. That meant excavating deep among the foundations where pieces of the ancient temple might yet remain. That temple had been erected long before the city was called Rashid, or Rosetta, back when it was known as Khito, a name he'd read back in the States. After years of thinking his answers lay in the New World, he was shocked to find a clue in the margins of an old Greek scroll that had arrived at Harvard. It said, *Anysis buried the forgotten man in Khito.*

The song he'd translated from Plasoa's broken French referred to a rock that concealed a pearl. Was that what he would find there? Jeremiah couldn't help but smile. How long had he studied, how far had he traveled, just to dig up another rock?

For weeks, he worked so relentlessly that he had to remind himself to rest and to pretend to eat so as not to arouse suspicion. Often he forgot, leaving the other workers to marvel at how quickly his pickaxe flew, how deeply it cleaved dirt and stone. If no one spoke to him in Imbaba out of disgust, in Rosetta, it was out of fear. But soon there was much more to fear than an uncanny laborer. On July 14, 1799, the Turkish fleet was spotted en route to the Egyptian coast, Rosetta a likely goal.

Though it earned him no allies, Fall's endless efforts in helping with the reconstruction of the fortress were appreciated. The whispers turned from talk of him to talk of a coming invasion.

On July 21, a year to the day since the Battle of the Pyramids, the work crews were ordered to dismantle the tower's outer curtain wall because the engineers planned to use the stones elsewhere. Though the climate along the coast was generally pleasant, this day was particularly hot, as if the sun was purposefully trying to pierce Jeremiah's protective covering.

Despite the discomfort, the beast was quiet. Jeremiah had found a colony of large water rats to feed on the night before, mollifying it for the time. Over the years, it'd grown smart enough to pick its battles. Perhaps it even knew better than to challenge Jeremiah when he was working. Or could it be that it also wanted an end to its own hunger and sought the stone as well?

He was taking apart a vertical section of wall, some ten feet high. Just behind its flat covering lay a chaos of earth and boulders, so he had to work carefully. He was constantly forced to rearrange his robes to keep from burning, slowing him even more. Frustrated, he was thinking he should take a break and find some shade to better tend his cloak. Instead, he swung his pickaxe one last time.

When it hit, he heard an odd sound. It was deeper, more resonant than the lighter *chks* and *crcks* the limestone usually made. More than that, it echoed in his memory like a familiar name, not the name of a person but of a time and place. It was exactly the same as the sound of a skull splitting open.

Thok.

The beast was no longer interested in tempering Jeremiah's memories, so the old moment rushed him. He felt the heat of the pyre against his skin and heard the old sound replayed. *Thok.* It was identical. Was his mind playing tricks?

He pulled the tool free. The cracked stone split and fell. The loose dirt and pebbles behind it ran in rivulets to his feet. Cautiously, he put his cloth-covered fingers into the crevice he'd created. He tugged at its edges, trying to widen it. More earth and larger stones fell, until a bit of smooth surface winked black in the midday sun.

Black?

He swung again, enlarging the hole. Yes. He could even see writing carved into the obsidian. It was really there. He gazed in wonder, thinking he recognized the characters as Ancient Greek.

He brushed the debris away, his mind exploding as he made out a few words:

...μέλας ὡς ὁ μετὰ τῶν ἄστρων σκότος...

...*black as the darkness between the stars*...

The same phrase in three languages, a thousand years and a thousand miles apart. Jeremiah's heart could no longer pound, but something in him surged. It couldn't be coincidence. He'd found it. It was real. Not legend, not idea—it was truth, hard as stone.

"I hope you can see this, Atticus," he whispered.

He dropped the pickaxe and went at the remaining dirt and rock with his covered hands. Larger and larger chunks came free until he started a small avalanche. Soon the entire surface of a great black stone, some ten feet tall and covered in writing, was revealed.

Still reeling, Fall stepped back for a better view. He was so enraptured that he almost ignored the warning from his heightened senses—he was no longer the only one staring at the stone. The workers near him were slack-jawed, and the soldiers, each and every one, out of some strange instinctual awe, dropped their weapons on the ground. Whispers spread like ocean waves. The unearthed artifact was the center of a growing crowd.

Realizing he'd have little time to examine it, Jeremiah tried to focus on the writing. No longer the uneducated man who knew neither French nor Abenaki, he quickly recognized three types of writing: classical Greek, which he knew well; what seemed to be demotic Egyptian, which he knew slightly; and hieroglyphic Egyptian, which neither he nor any man living knew at all. If the writings were the same, the rock might hold the key to decoding that ancient script, which even the enlightened French intellectuals considered magic. Its value increased the worry that he'd lose it soon.

His mind raced to translate more, but, incredibly, other than the few tantalizing words he'd recognized, Jeremiah found his thoughts too scattered to make further progress. Of course he was excited, but this feeling was more alien. It was as if something were reaching from within or without to stop him.

"You there, let me through."

A strong hand grasped his shoulder and tried to tug him back. The beast, until now silent before the stone, welled as powerfully as it had the first night he'd returned from the dead.

Tear off the hand! Don't let them move you one inch from this spot!

As Jeremiah fought to ignore the urge, another surprise occurred. Louder even than the feral rage, Jeremiah heard a wholly new voice, an unimaginably powerful voice that said one word: *Yes.*

Was it his own? The beast's? It seemed to emanate as placelessly as the force that halted his translation, but he had to divert so much energy to master his own body, he couldn't be sure. It was all he could do to manage a few steps back.

A lean man with an air of calm authority came forward. Though the world had grown alarmingly numb and distant, Fall recognized him as Lieutenant Bouchard, an officer of the engineers. A cadre of curious soldiers filed in behind him, wedging their way between Jeremiah and the dark slab.

Tear them apart!

Yes, the new voice said.

It sounded not like the beast, but like a thousand beasts, a thousand hungers joined together. The beast sat beside Jeremiah, jockeying for control, but this new voice came from all sides, above and below, within and without. He sensed that it wanted to say more, much more, but something held it back.

The precious script vanished in a sea of blue uniforms. Knowing he couldn't challenge the army for the stone, he moved to the side, trying to reclaim at least his view. As he did, he found he couldn't prevent himself from roughly shoving any worker who blocked him.

There it was again, stone and script. Bouchard swept away some remaining detritus, then spoke in a whisper to the nearest soldier: "Get General Menou, at once."

As the man rushed to obey, Bouchard scanned the crowd, until his eyes found Fall. "You unearthed this object?"

Afraid of what he or the forces vying inside him might say, Fall simply nodded.

Bouchard fished in the pockets of his uniform and withdrew several large gold coins stamped by the French

Republic. He held them above his head for the crowd to see. When no one would avert their eyes from the stone, he coughed loudly, demanding their attention.

"I reward this man for uncovering this historical relic. The same reward awaits any who find something like it. Such objects are to be brought, if size permits, directly to me."

Greed broke the sublime spell of the ebony mass. The workers returned to their digging with a new gusto.

Jeremiah, though, stayed as close to the rock as Bouchard and the soldiers permitted. For a time, his efforts brought luck. Seeing his interest, Bouchard ordered him to assist in cordoning off the area, and then allowed him to remain when General Menou arrived.

The general, in his late forties, had a profoundly oval head. Its shape was accented by his receding hairline, creating the overall impression of a large pink egg with a sharp gaze. Jeremiah knew Menou to be an educated man, enamored of Egypt and its history. He wasn't surprised when Menou immediately recognized the Greek, but noted that the general also failed to translate it.

Menou didn't speak to him directly, but through his orders, Fall and two others were given the task of removing as much of the remaining dirt as possible, while the engineers prepared a series of pulleys and thick ropes to free it from the wall's foundations.

Before leaving, the general commanded, "Bring it to my tent."

Until recently, the French generals had enjoyed luxurious quarters among Rashid's gardens and cool courtyards. Fear of the coming Turks now kept them nearer the soldiers garrisoned along the coast.

Thrilled to be near the stone, Jeremiah tried to memorize what he could of the writings, even if he couldn't translate them. Yet something prevented even that, as if an invisible hand reached out and blocked, not his eyes, but his mind. He trembled at the thought it might speak again. The longer he stayed near, the stronger the stone's dizzying effect. Each of the paltry few words he managed, σκτά, ἔπλαθομένος, ἀτελειωιον—*shadow, forgotten, endless*—only confirmed his discovery. This was the stone of which the Abenaki sang.

An engineer commented that Jeremiah seemed ill, perhaps from the sun, and should rest. Nonetheless, Jeremiah was among those who tied thick ropes around the object and threaded them through the pulleys. He stood with the twenty men who pulled until the tall wooden trellis constructed for the purpose groaned, bent, and threatened to snap. But the timbers held, and with what Jeremiah thought sounded like a moan, the slab lifted free.

A bespectacled savant, working from a distance because he'd had trouble maneuvering among the rocks in his frock coat, estimated the stone's weight as the better part of a ton. Buoyed by the ropes, it was carefully turned and brought to the bed of a heavy wagon. They tried four horses, then six, but in the end, a team of eight was needed to move the wagon.

As it creaked away, Fall tried to follow, only to find himself facing crossed bayonets.

"Back to your digging," a dog-faced boy-soldier barked.

The soldier smelled of jealousy and fear. He resented the attention paid to Jeremiah, the gold coins a mere prisoner had earned. At the same time, having witnessed his work, the infantryman feared his strength. Riled by his petty reaction, Fall wanted to snap his neck, take the cart, and haul the stone to a desert cave where he could study it in peace. His increasing distance from the wagon made the beast whimper. But it also lifted the strange fog enshrouding his mind, making it easier to refuse the savage impulses. As for the rest of his desires, he reminded himself that after decades of uncertainty, he knew the stone was real.

Knowing would have to content him for now.

8

When the stone proved too large for even a general's tent, a temporary structure was erected for it, big enough to hold all the savants in Rosetta. Within hours of their first eager examination, all work on the fortress halted. Everyone—soldier and worker, engineer and academic— joined the search for additional artifacts. The base of the old fort became so crowded that many found themselves bruised or worse as the pickaxes flew. From a distance, the scores of swinging metal tips resembled the twitching mandibles of enormous crustaceans. Jeremiah felt as if a church, his church, had been infested by vermin.

The efforts of the mob were not in vain. Twin Mamluk brothers confirmed the superstition that their resemblance was lucky when they uncovered a second stone. It also held three types of writing, but was pinkish-gray, not black, and smaller, just under four feet high and a mere eleven inches thick.

When Jeremiah approached it, no eerie reverence overcame him. Translating the Greek inscribed on it was far easier. Instead of forgotten creatures and healing, the text spoke of repealing taxes and building temple statues. When he didn't even feel disappointed as it was wheeled away, he concluded it was unimportant, an emulation of the elder stone, wrought by later artisans skilled in duplication.

He visited the first stone nightly, and it never failed to numb his mind. Always, it seemed on the verge of speaking again, but *refused* perhaps because so many others were near. Whenever he hid in the shadows and stared at it, his thoughts became more and more cloudy. He sometimes feared he'd stumble forward, revealing himself, but the savants were so intent on their work, a winged elephant might have passed by unnoticed. For all their concentration, their translation efforts were as fruitless as his.

One idea they had did excite him—they hoped to cover the carvings in ink and imprint them on paper. If his mental fatigue was caused by the stone itself, studying a copy of the writings might bear more fruit. But any liquid put to it beaded as water did on wax. The surface was as resistant to ink as the words were to his mind.

What a punishment to have this proof before him, but its mystery still opaque. What good were all the languages and the history he'd learned if he couldn't read what was right in front of him? Atticus might call it a trial.

Like jilted lovers, the savants turned to the second stone for comfort. It proved more yielding, allowing them almost immediately to translate a line that read "in sacred, in vernacular, and in Greek characters." As hieroglyphs had been considered sacred, this proved they had a key to decipher them.

News of the discovery spread as if the world had no

borders. But the Turkish fleet did not slow, and the war preparations became paramount. The search for additional artifacts was abandoned. By the time work on Julien resumed and the excavation site was buried, even Jeremiah believed there was nothing left to find.

Rosetta's savants, preferring to focus on the easier sister, felt they'd gone as far as they could with the difficult first stone. Menou ordered it transported to Cairo for the eager minds at the Institut de l'Égypte to pursue. It would travel across the Sahara by caravan, a slow route, but all available ships were needed at the coast.

Jeremiah knew it had taken five days for Napoleon to march his army from Alexandria to Imbaba. Any wagon bearing the stone could be expected to take at least that long, and there were many lonely stretches in the desert sands. His initial urge to steal the rock suddenly seemed less unreasonable.

As the day's work on Julien ended and the caravan was set to leave, Fall asked to see Lieutenant Dillan. A month ago, the request would have been ignored, but finding the relic had made him part of a historic event, earning him a modicum of respect.

He was led by two soldiers through the narrow avenues of the torchlit city. They took him to a lush estate, through a luxurious, high-ceilinged parlor into an area crowded with small rooms that the French had converted to administrative offices.

The room they stepped into was dim and stuffed with boxes and papers. Dillan sat scrunched behind a wooden desk. He squinted in the lamplight as he wrote in a ledger, looking more comfortable in the tiny space than he'd ever been on a horse. Recalling their previous conversation,

Jeremiah immediately removed his headcloth. It was unnecessary anyway, with the sun down.

When Dillan glanced up, perhaps planning only a passing glance at his visitor, the sight of the uncovered Fall kept his gaze.

"Ainsi, vous n'êtes pas simplement les des yeux sans visage."

So, you are not simply eyes without a face.

"No."

Dillan went back to writing. For a time, the only sound was his quill scratching on paper. When curiosity got the best of him, he halted his work and said, "I confess I sometimes find myself wondering why you refused to remove your bandages in Imbaba. Tell me."

"I have a skin condition irritated by the sun."

Dillan put his elbow up on the desk. "Such a simple story, now that you've had weeks to make one up. Why not explain this at the time?"

"I was afraid it would be taken as a sign of weakness, disqualify me as a choice for the work crews."

Dillan nodded. "Ah. That might well be true. But the same can be said of the best lies. Why did you ask to see me?"

"I want to accompany the caravan taking the stone to Cairo."

Dillan laughed. "Are you a scholar as well as a lucky man, a tireless worker, and a valiant rescuer?"

"I've studied the classic languages. The stones are an incredibly important find."

"Yes. They say they will unlock the secret of the gods' writing. The hieroglyphs are believed, even by some of our own intellectuals, to be magical."

"Al-keme," Fall said. "Arabic for *things Egyptian.* It's the root of our English word *alchemy.*"

Dillan was impressed. "You do know something." He leaned back in his chair and tapped his lower lip with the quill. "But your request is absurd on its face. Our situation is grave. Julien is not yet complete. The Turks will soon attack. While indulging the intellectual curiosities of our savants is part of my duty, indulging you is not. But I am a man of my word. Once Julien is finished, you may go where you wish, plead your case directly at the Institute and attempt to impress them with your trivia. Meanwhile, you'll remain here."

Dillan returned to his writing, expecting Fall to leave. He did not.

"Lieutenant Dillan, I would consider it a great favor."

Dillan didn't bother looking up. "A second favor? But, monsieur, you only rescued me from my horse once."

Kill the two soldiers. Plunge your teeth into the pretentious man's neck. Enthrall him, like the horse. The charger has more soul than this one anyway.

The beast had been quiet for a time, as if it wanted to reach the stone as badly as Jeremiah did—a disturbing thought. Facing an obstacle to that goal, it was getting more inventive. In the abstract, Fall almost agreed, but he and the soldiers left so quietly that a few moments later, he heard Dillan look up, to make certain they were gone.

Outside, a breeze swept off the Mediterranean, making the torch flames flicker and their ample shadows dance.

"I was there when you found it," the younger soldier reminded him. Fall recognized him as the dog-faced youth who stopped him with his bayonet. The remark seemed off-handed, but this fellow didn't seem capable of saying anything without being angry about it. When Fall didn't respond, he became insulting. *"Vous avez essayé de le suivre sur le wagon, comme si vous étiez dans l'amour!"*

You tried to follow it on the wagon, as if you were in love!

"Don't taunt him," his weary partner warned.

"Why not? Didn't you hear? He's a scholar. Maybe we'll learn something. Tell me, scholar, do you know what they translated from the second stone?"

"A decree from Ptolemy repealing certain taxes."

Briefly surprised, the boy-soldier recovered. "Ah, but that's not as important as the stone you love, is it?"

"As far as the hieroglyphs go, in fact, it is."

"And in other ways?"

Upon reaching the start of a small alley between a tavern and a shop, Fall abruptly stopped. "Pardon, messieurs," he said. "I must go."

The older soldier rolled his eyes. "Doesn't this city smell enough like piss?"

"Perhaps the mere thought of the stone has made his bladder..."

Fall cut off the air the soldier needed to finish the sentence with the fingers of his right hand. At the same moment, Fall's left hand found his partner's neck. He lifted and carried their squirming bodies into the alley, holding them aloft until they passed out.

A key in the pocket of the older soldier's jacket ensured he didn't have to worry about snapping his ankle chains. After briefly making sure both remained unconscious, he reached the tavern roof in two quick jumps, leaving them behind before the beast could even tell him how sweet their blood would taste.

He leaped roof to roof and within minutes was outside the city walls, feeding on an unlucky desert hare. He was a mile from Rashid, on a Saharan dune, when he heard the clanging alarm indicating the soldiers had awoken and informed their commanders of his escape.

The sandy hill he rested on overlooked a ribbon of desert road leading south from the city. The path, visible against the sand not by its color, but by its flatness, was the only way they could take the stone. All he had to do was wait for them.

Jeremiah had often felt lonely since Atticus died, most recently since the death of Qarsaq, but this was the first time he'd actually been alone in a long while. Once he'd left the American wilderness for his journey to the Middle East, he'd been among people constantly, acting far more civilized than he cared to.

Here with the city glowing near the sea, the cool sand beneath him, and white dunes stretching as far as he could see, Jeremiah Fall felt a pang that reminded him why he wanted to be, if not saved, then at least damned for being human.

He placed two fingers in his mouth and let loose a shrill whistle. As the sound faded, he heard the thud of galloping hooves. Blotting out the stars as she fell back on her hind legs and kicked her hooves in the air, Al-Hawa appeared, neighing. Somehow, he'd sensed her nearby days ago, but could only hope she'd heard his wordless call. He laughed to see her, happy for the company. Seeing the scar still on her neck, and imagining it was still painful, he wished he'd earned the horse's loyalty some other way.

She didn't move as he patted her. It would be easy to drink from her again, but he didn't. Instead, he spent the night forcing the beast to hunt rabbits until it was full.

Jeremiah and Al-Hawa were well hidden when the caravan groaned from the city gates. Ten mounted dragoons, wearing the scarlet that identified their unit, rode before a flat, high-wheeled wagon bearing the stone. Behind that was a second wagon, a dainty carriage of Parisian design, looking peculiar in the otherwise military procession. No doubt it held any officers and savants traveling with them. At the rear were a second set of ten dragoons and five light cavalry, all in the green that offended the Muslims because it was considered the Prophet's color. The procession was trailed by two small cannons.

Twenty-five soldiers. Perhaps he could take them, perhaps not. Not without loss of life. For the time being, he'd no idea what to do other than follow. He'd have to make things up as he went along, wait for a proper opportunity, or, barring that, night.

As they moved deeper into the sandy void, all trace of road or path vanished. A few of the light cavalry occasionally broke ranks to scout ahead. On Al-Hawa's back, Jeremiah paced them at a distance, keeping himself between them and the sun. The lack of road slowed him and the horse only slightly, while the weight of the huge rock made the caravan move at a crawl.

He tried to estimate how much time he had. Cairo was over a hundred miles away even if they followed the Nile directly. Camel caravans averaged twenty-five miles a day, but these were horses, requiring more water more often. If an opportunity for him to take the stone didn't occur, he could easily arrange some circumstance to delay them.

That afternoon, the dunes gave way to rocky outcroppings, then tall hills so pockmarked with caves Jeremiah thought they must all be hollow. When the caravan stopped to rest and water their horses, Fall did likewise.

Eager to find a spot away from the sun, he explored the nearest cave. The entrance afforded a good view of the caravan. Inside, it was as tall as a cathedral he'd once seen as a boy in Sussex. A flurry of smells and rapid heartbeats told him that small mammals nested deep inside, desert rats mostly, while a small pool provided fresh water for Al-Hawa. It wasn't perfect. Myriad cracks in the thin, rough ceiling sent shafts of sunlight crisscrossing the hollow, ruining the dark. The cave roof was so brittle that it wouldn't take much to collapse it and flood the place with light, but the space was peaceful enough for now.

Settling in the shade near the sturdier cave mouth, Fall leaned back and let the workings of his body slow. Below, a hundred yards away, the occupants of the dainty Parisian coach stepped out to stretch their legs. One was a cotton-haired officer Fall didn't recognize, and two were dressed in frock coats—savants.

There was a fourth, though, dark-skinned, in ivory-colored robes too expensive for most Egyptians. The figure was too slight for a man. A boy? Perhaps it was the male child of some local official they sought to curry favor with. Whoever it was, Jeremiah hoped the caravan would rest here for the night. If he did decide to attack, he'd be able to bring the stone into the cave.

Would a fight be necessary? When the sun set, maybe he could present himself as a lost traveler. No, his face was well known in Rashid. Following his escape, Dillan had, no doubt, warned his fellows about their meeting. They'd know him. Maybe he should have finished his work on Julien and then presented himself in Cairo as the lieutenant suggested. Arrogance is folly. He'd been impatient again. Too late for that now.

The sun drooped below the crest of the hill, casting its long round shadow toward the caravan. Three dragoons stood on the wagon with the stone, keeping guard. They were silhouettes, but next to them the stone was clearly a different sort of dark, like a piece of night sky the sun could not reclaim.

"What are you?" Jeremiah asked. "Can you tell me what I am?"

The single word the new voice said throbbed in his memory. *Yes.*

It must have been the stone.

Entranced by the sight and distracted by his thoughts, Jeremiah nearly failed to notice a sand-colored disturbance in the smooth ground. It moved like a small wave toward the caravan. At first he saw just one, but then there were two, four...more.

Were they a family of some desert animals hidden by their natural color? No, he realized. He stood and squinted. They were men, at least ten, maybe more. Each one was wrapped head to toe in clothing that matched the ground so closely it might as well have been made of sand. It seemed Jeremiah wasn't the only one who coveted the stone badly enough to try to steal it.

9

A rabbit's white fur against snow, auburn butterflies on autumn leaves, gray toads like muddy rocks with bulbous eyes. Jeremiah had seen all those disguises in nature, but they were nothing like these men whose forms winked in and out of existence against the sandy ripples. If it weren't for the shifting of bulky packs strapped to their backs, he might've missed completely. As it was, while his first count was ten, the number soon reached twenty.

Who were they?

The colonists during the American Revolution wore dark clothes and hid among the trees as they waited for the marching British, their red coats an easy target. But these men weren't poorly trained rebels fighting for freedom. They moved with a discipline bordering on art.

The Mamluks? The Turks?

No, the Mamluks' silver blades and glowing robes were meant to startle and shock, attract attention. The Turks, too, were loud fighters, eager to show themselves to God and their enemies as they raced to meet death. Jeremiah had read about the Hashshashin, from eleventh-century Persia, who murdered political and military leaders, and their oriental equivalent, the Ninja. But both were centuries and worlds away, and these men were here, moments from their goal.

Part of him wanted to warn the caravan, but intervening would be foolish. Aside from the fact it would mean revealing himself, he didn't know their purpose, so how could he rightly choose sides?

Deciding to go in for a closer look, he pulled his headpiece on, checked his covering, and left the cave on foot. The trackless space held only the shadow of the hills. He'd have to rely on his silence and speed to keep him hidden. He darted from outcropping to dune, barely disturbing a grain of sand. The attention of the dust-crawlers remained on the caravan.

He was ten yards from their rear when the first group was close enough to attack. Four rose to their feet, sand raining from their head-wraps, shirts, and pants, making them look as if they were made from the same stuff as the desert. Their bulky packs were more visible now. In the center of each, a whitish line curved down, its tip sparking and hissing like a burning snake.

What was it? He felt as if he should know.

The three dragoons on guard atop the wagon bed spotted them instantly. The rest were caught unawares. Some were sitting, coats unbuttoned, some sipped water. Few held their weapons. Those who didn't dove for them when the dragoons shouted.

Two of the four standing attackers raced at them, yet for all their startling appearance and expert maneuvering, first blood went to the French. One of the light cavalry, a stout man who'd been cleaning his musket, rammed his bayonet into an assailant's chest, more by accident than plan.

The dust-crawler fell on his back, limbs twitching. The soldier stabbed down twice, three times, piercing the breastbone to finish him off. As he hesitated, uncertain whether to complete a fourth thrust, Jeremiah saw the Frenchman's face. It was round but with a pointed chin that made it oddly heart-shaped. His bright green eyes were startled as the fallen man erupted in a cloud of red fire and dark dirt.

Overlapping the sight, Jeremiah heard a loud crack as if a boulder had split in half. Tendrils of smoke and debris flew in all directions. Shrapnel, hidden briefly by the cloud, struck the Frenchman's heart-shaped face and ripped an arm from his body.

Surrounded by the dusty haze, the one-armed soldier fell to his knees, then to his side. Dead, he lay alongside the man he'd killed, the careful desert color of the dust-crawler's garb marred by the pinks and reds of his own innards.

Gunpowder, Jeremiah realized, annoyed for not recognizing this new madness sooner. *They're blowing themselves up!*

No sooner had he finished the thought than another attacker exploded. The cavalrymen nearest flew backward, their light green uniforms making them look like leaves caught in a wind.

The two assailants still standing headed for the stone, but by now more Frenchmen had their bearings. Those on the ground aimed their muskets. The dragoons on the wagon lowered their bayonets. It seemed the attackers would be cut down long before they reached their goal.

But ten more intruders rose from the dust. Fuses spitting sparks, they sped toward the foot soldiers, making them uncertain where to aim. As the first two drew nearer the wagon, the guarding dragoons made ready. One stepped back to aim and fire his musket while his comrades kept their bayonets steady.

In response, one dust-crawler moved ahead of his partner and reached the wagon first. In a swift, startling action, he grabbed the bayonets pointed at him and yanked their blades into his own body. The dragoons tried to keep their balance but stumbled forward to meet the force of the dying man's exploding bomb.

His partner grabbed the wagon's side and hurled himself up at the stone. The remaining dragoon fired, sending the attacker flying backward. He nearly disappeared into the sand again until the eruption of the black powder hurled clots of dry earth and bits of his body skyward.

The ambush was not yet successful, but the fearlessness of the suicide attacks rattled even the battle-hardened French.

Though he'd never seen its like, the self-destructive tactic was not unknown to Jeremiah. In seventeenth-century Taiwan, injured Dutch soldiers blew themselves up rather than be taken prisoner. Given how the Taiwanese treated prisoners, those sacrifices seemed almost wise. More recently, when the Sinhalese rebelled against the British, they hid inside hollow palm trees stuffed with explosives, waited until soldiers came near, and then detonated the explosives and themselves. Napoleon's own grenadiers were known to sacrifice themselves when the situation became dire.

But those men gave their lives to avoid a worse death by torture, to liberate a homeland, or to make a desperate last stand. Here it didn't make sense. Were they abandoning their lives just to steal the stone? Given their disguise and expertise, more standard tactics might readily have succeeded, yet they didn't seem to carry any weapon other than their bombs and a willingness to die. The group was highly trained, so he couldn't believe the plan was careless. What could possibly make this plan worthwhile?

He'd have to sort that out later. With the attackers so determined to die, he was no longer concerned about which side to take. Jeremiah sped, as only he could, to the nearest bomber who still thought himself hidden by the sand. Jeremiah lifted him by his hissing backpack and hurled him into two others.

Realizing they'd been discovered, the remaining assailants were almost to their feet when the powder exploded. A second eruption followed and set a third aflame. The burning dust-crawler's sandy clothing blackened as the fire consumed it. He howled and ran in an aimless zigzag pattern, finally falling in a heap, his own explosives, for whatever reason, failing.

The man's panicked last moments brought a grim relief to Jeremiah. It was the first sign that these men, however devoted and disciplined, were human. That meant he still had an advantage.

The surviving dust-crawlers moved into clear formations. Most formed a long line that stormed toward the

French troops. Three others composed a tight triangle aimed at the wagon. An odd man out came for Jeremiah.

Their plan was clear, if not their ultimate purpose. The men headed for the troops were to serve as a distraction for the trio racing to the wagon. They wanted to reach the stone, that was certain, but fuses burned on each back. None planned to survive. Was there another group waiting behind some dune to claim the rock? No. If that were the case, the focus would be on killing the French, not reaching the wagon.

At once, the tactic made sense. They didn't want to *steal* the stone; they meant to *destroy* it.

Why? Time didn't allow the question to matter. If they succeeded, for whatever reason, any hope of unraveling the stone's secret would be lost.

Let me out. Let me protect it.

Knowing how it reacted to the stone, Jeremiah loosed his hold on the beast just enough to let its rage rack his body. Tearing the cloth from his face, he bared his fangs and roared at the man rushing toward him. The late-day sun behind him barely caused a tingle.

He expected the dust-crawler, if not to turn and run, at least to express some surprise. He did not. He just kept coming. It was all Jeremiah could do to grab him by the neck and crotch and toss him over his head before his bomb went off as well.

Jeremiah turned from the blast, but not fast enough. Hot bits of metal tore into his upper arm. The concussive wave that followed nearly threw him off his feet. In the time it took him to grab at the pain in his arm, three more blasts went off near the caravan. Body parts wearing frayed bits of French uniforms flew through the air.

If he'd kept count correctly, the attackers were down to fourteen, but the black smoke now hanging in the air prevented him from seeing how many French were wounded or dead. He could count the frantic heartbeats, but by the time he sorted them, the stone could be destroyed.

Holding his arm, he sped toward the wagon. He heard the sharp cracks of musket fire, followed by two, three, then four dull, rumbling bomb blasts. The scene was utter chaos. The fancy Parisian carriage was aflame. The horses, though trained for combat, reared wildly. Worst, the triangle of dust-crawlers trying to reach the stone remained intact.

There was another explosion. Though he felt its hot wind slam him, Fall didn't bother to see where it was coming from. He was too intent on saving the stone. Through the haze, he saw the remaining dragoon guard reloading with admirable speed. Yet even if he finished before the three men reached him, he'd have just one shot.

Though Jeremiah thought he was running as fast as he could, the beast proved him wrong. He picked up speed until the fuse of the nearest attacker sputtered in front of him. He reached out and pulled himself through the air to grab the pack. At first the man came along with it, but Jeremiah yanked the bomb free, sending its bearer skidding sideways on the ground. With less than an inch left to the fuse, Fall hurled the pack away and kept running forward.

Spotting Jeremiah, the dragoon on the wagon seemed unsure who to aim at, but chose the closest dust-crawler. Struck in the chest, he fell ten feet from the wagon. His bomb detonated just as Fall reached him.

Jeremiah heard the whistling of shrapnel. Most rushed past him, but some tore through his shoulder. The blast pushed him back. This time, he fell.

There were more musket cracks and more explosions, but no way to sort the confusion, no way to tell how many dead or how many remaining to die. Stunned, Fall rallied and raised his head.

As a result of the latest blast, a line of fire burned at the wagon's edge, smoke rising as it went. The lone, valiant dragoon, coughing, struggled to reload again. He glanced around for aid, but only dying screams and yet another explosion issued from the thick gunpowder clouds. No help was coming.

One member of the triangle survived. He'd also been thrown by the last blast, but it had hurled him closer to the wagon. He staggered, but was already back on his feet. The dragoon's weapon would not be reloaded in time. Once the bomber was close enough for a bayonet attack, he'd be too near the stone.

Jeremiah ran at him from the side, hoping to push him away from the stone. A fit of coughing took the dragoon as the attacker's hands reached the flaming wagon edge. Jeremiah was still several yards away. The bomber, despite the fire, pulled himself up to the wagon.

Not knowing if he could make such a long leap, Jeremiah hurled himself off the ground at the same time the bomber jumped toward the stone. Smoke from the fuse curled above the attacker's head like the feather of an ethereal bird.

Weak from the shrapnel wounds, Jeremiah neared the bomber. He could smell the desert on him, the salty sweat of his exertion. Like a bat arching to catch an insect in midflight, Jeremiah wrapped his arms and legs around the dust-crawler. As he maneuvered himself between the explosive and the stone, he caught a glimpse of the man's dark eyes.

They were serene. There seemed no fear about his impending death, no concern his mission might not be completed, or even a sign of satisfaction at the thought it would.

As they reached the peak of their flight, driven by his own fear and panic, Jeremiah's hands fumbled across the man's backpack, feeling cool metal cylinders. His keen senses focused above the din of fire and screams, searching desperately for a rattling hiss.

There it was. He heard it. As long as he heard it, there was time—time to reach the fuse, time to pull it out. His fingers moved with inhuman precision along the cylinders, through the fabric. Where was it? Any moment now he'd have it. He had to.

But then the hissing stopped.

The tightly packed saltpeter and sulfur, shed of molecular bonds by a single spark, morphed into a raging, expanding gas that the metal cylinders could not contain. The unleashed force ripped through Jeremiah. He felt as if a thousand thick, molten worms burrowed through his flesh and bone, then burst through his other side, free to fly and whirl through the desert air, carrying pieces of him with them.

The thought of dying didn't bother Jeremiah nearly so much as the thought of dying ignorant, not ever knowing what he or the stone was, or if he might have been healed. If it had been his destiny to know, he wondered if destiny could fail.

Was it all for nothing?

Above his anguish, in a place beyond sensation, he heard the stone's voice. It whispered into the deepest corners of his being, whispered as it had when he first saw it, whispered as it always had, ever since it was made in times all but forgotten by both man and god, and it said: *Yes*.

10

It wasn't at all like Corinthians this time, through a glass darkly. Jeremiah Fall felt more as if he was squinting through a fragile cone at an out-of-focus pearl. When a smoky breeze caused his tiny field of vision to flutter, he wondered if his single working eye was still in its socket.

He could hear, but only the muffled crackle of fires. What was missing told him more than what was there; there was no musket fire, explosions, or cries. The battle was over. Who had won? He didn't know. Had anyone survived? It didn't seem so.

Certainly not him. Surely he was only visiting the wretched remains of his body. Wherever his clothes were torn, hours of exposure to the late-day sun had burned him to the bone. What was left refused to respond. He couldn't even retreat into memory or imagination. It was as if the shrapnel had reached his inner life and done its damage there, too.

Variations of pain were all that was left, that and

hoping the last of his energies would eventually recede and the earth reclaim his form. He worried it might take years, that he'd be trapped in his own body as Skog had been trapped in the mound. He hoped he *could* die. What a lesson in patience that would be, to wait for divine mercy, to wait for whatever ruled this world to finally leave him in peace.

Pshhhh. Pshhhh. Pshhhh. Pshhhh.

Footsteps. Sandaled feet, soft in the sand, were working hard to remain standing. They were maybe ten yards away, but growing closer. Someone *had* survived.

A robed figure intruded on the blurry pearl of his visible world. The figure went to its knees and then leaned forward, occupying the whole of his pathetic sight. Nearness brought it more into focus. The slender shape, covered by cloth, was no soldier, bomber, officer, or savant. Then who? Ivory-colored robes. Was it the one from the dainty carriage, the one Jeremiah had taken for a boy?

As long fingers pulled back the face covering, black hair unrolled and cupped the cheeks of an almond-shaped head. A few soft strands blew against the face, their black lines against light brown skin.

A woman. Arabic. He was surprised she would uncover herself before a man, then realized it didn't matter because he must look like a corpse. If he was dead, his curiosity survived him. Why would a woman be with the caravan? Was she a companion of the officer? General Menou had taken an Egyptian bride. Maybe this woman had married a Frenchman as well.

She stared at him, but her face remained too indistinct to make out her expression. She stiffened and straightened her back, maybe in a sign of disgust at the sight of his seemingly fatal wounds. He could only imagine what he looked like. The remains of a predator's meal?

He thought of a half-dead deer he'd found after a bear attack, how he'd used a stone to put it out of its misery. Would this woman do the same for him? Set his spirit free by cracking his skull with stone instead of flame—*thok*? Would he see Atticus again? Mother? Father? Even baby Jim?

No. When she did move, she didn't rise to find a weapon. She settled on her haunches, clasped her fingers, and touched their tips to her lips. She whispered. He heard her, but couldn't make out the words. Yet what seemed so familiar?

Praying. Yes. Praying. She was *praying* for him.

He wanted to laugh but found himself too moved. It didn't matter that she probably mistook him for one of the soldiers protecting the caravan, that she couldn't possibly know who or what he was. No one had prayed for him since Atticus passed away.

He wanted to weep, but his tear ducts were gone. The torrent of emotion provided a different relief. It softened his mind's defenses, let him slip away, not into the cover of night, but the sanctity of unconsciousness. For a moment, the unintelligible words this woman chanted became the sweetest lullaby he'd ever heard, the closest he'd ever come to bliss.

One moment appeared to follow the next, but did it? When did hot and dry become cool and moist, the fire's crackle a watery drip? All at once, or slowly? There might be hours, days, even years stuffed between.

He no longer saw through a tunnel. His vision was

clear. Jeremiah saw a beautiful horse, its giant head bent low as it lapped from a pool. Al-Hawa. He even made out the ripples in the water's glassy surface. There was a thin ceiling above him riddled with holes. Frail starlight twinkled through the scattered openings. He was in the cave. How?

The quiet moment ended, replaced with agony. A blob of white shone on his chest. Somehow he'd blinked away the night. Deadly sunlight streamed through the ceiling's holes. Wherever it touched, his flesh blistered and threatened to burst into flame. He tried to move but managed only a sickly writhing. Instead of a shriek, the air he pushed through his throat sounded like the hiss of an enormous snake.

Small hands grabbed his ankles. They pulled him so slowly across hard rock and dirt that the sunlight's movement across his neck and face left a smoking trail. A flash of rough fabric covered him. He whimpered as the worst of the pain withdrew. The pulling began anew. When it stopped, and the blanket was withdrawn, he tried to moan but again produced only an arid rush.

"Vous devez vous reposer maintenant."

French. A woman's voice. The one who had prayed for him?

You must rest now.

So it wasn't a dying dream. He was healing. Jeremiah didn't know whether to feel pleased or newly damned. What stuff made his bones that they could remember their shape after being crushed? If, over a hundred years ago, Nathan's head had been placed closer to its body, could even *that* have healed?

But his uncanny form wasn't the only thing responsible

for his survival. The woman must have brought him into the cave and dragged him into the shade when she saw what the sun did to him. Shouldn't she have been horrified? Where was she now?

The frantic rolling of his eyes provided no immediate answer. He could see he was lying in a small alcove; no holes in the lower, thicker ceiling here. When he tried to move his neck and head, they responded, but made a horrible cracking sound, as though his new bones needed to be broken before they could be used.

He saw Al-Hawa again. She bobbed her head at him in recognition. There were other horses beside her, nudging one another for a turn at the water. Boxes and supplies.

Rescued from the caravan and hidden here. The woman's no fool. She knows more attackers could appear. But where is she?

His mind sorted the heartbeats until he found her. She was by the pool, too, concealed by a warhorse. As the great animal stepped forward for its turn to drink, she was revealed. She looked so slight beside it that, if not for the curves of the robes wrapped around her form, she might have seemed a child.

Jeremiah tried to call, but only managed another arid hiss. At the grotesque sound, she snapped her head in his direction, looking like a startled fawn. She dipped a soldier's tin cup into the water and carried it toward him, holding the hem of her robes so they wouldn't trail in the dirt. Her bare feet, wet from the sloshing of the pool, left imprints on the ground. Her posture was elegant, schooled, but there was also a natural ease to her movements.

She knelt beside him and let go of the robes so they drooped around her feet. The thin, off-white material had a sheen like silk, but it was thicker, woven with other fibers. He caught a whiff of the rare spices wealthier Egyptian women used as perfume. They mixed with even more expensive musk. As the scents melded with her own slight sweat, her heartbeat rose in his ears. His body shuddered. His nostrils flared.

Take her.

"Shhh," she said.

Thinking his shivering meant he was afraid or in pain, she looked as if she might caress his brow. The loosely wrapped cloth left the flesh of her neck exposed. He saw her jugular throb, heard what rushed beneath the skin.

You need the blood to heal.

She touched him. Tenderly, she raised his shoulders and placed his head in her warm lap. Even Atticus, who loved him, hadn't dared a single hug. When Qarsaq grabbed him or Bouchard tried to pull him back from the stone, it was hard to keep from throttling them.

This dizzying sensation sent his mind reeling in two directions at once. Her gentleness recalled his lost humanity. The nearness of her living, vulnerable flesh encouraged the beast to riddle his mind with violent images; he, joyfully tearing into her throat, achieving the satisfaction his body craved, but which he'd never allowed.

There was no real need to fight it. He was far too weak to harm her. The feelings, for now, were just another fresh bit of hell.

She brought the cup to his lips. The silt-filled water was useless, but he drank anyway. She'd prayed for him, saved him twice, and now became the first to touch him kindly in over a century and a half. He wanted to maintain the charade that he was worth her efforts.

As his throat muscles pushed the gritty wetness down, his jaws clenched. He couldn't speak yet, but soon. He wondered what on earth he could possibly say. He'd have to be cautious. But she'd already seen so much, and he was so tired of hiding.

Night's return brought a curious odor. It wasn't the woman, the horses, or the pool. It wasn't even the sand rats he sensed in the cave's deeper recesses. This smell, mixed with open air, came from outside. It was warm, sharp, and familiar, with a ghostly tinge of meat. Vegetables boiling in water, mixed with chicken. Stew?

A short while later, the woman returned carrying a steaming bowl. He rose to his elbows to greet her, surprised to find his body obeying his commands. If he couldn't hunt to satisfy it, the hunger would grow stronger, too. He'd have to warn her.

"You can move," she said in French. "Can you eat?"

He understood what she said, but for some reason couldn't remember how to speak French. He tried to answer in English, hoping she'd understand.

"There is chicken?" His voice worked, but it was rough and weak.

She smiled and came forward with the bowl, preparing to feed him.

He shook his head, stopping her. Even that slight motion dizzied him. He leaned back, aware for the first time that his arms were no longer covered in his own tattered robes, but a loose, sandy shirt stained with the dried blood of a dust-crawler. He had on different pants as well, the sacrilegious green of Napoleon's light cavalry, torn and burnt in spots. She'd dressed him with what she could find.

He forced himself to speak again. "Chicken. Where...did you get it?"

Her smooth brow rippled, forming a single line. It was so expressive, hanging above her thin eyebrows, that it looked as if an artist had painted it there with a single stroke.

"Caravan supplies. There remain two chickens and a...rabbit? From France."

Her English was good enough.

"Alive?"

She nodded.

"Bring me the rabbit."

The line above her eyebrows thickened. "Why?"

"Alive. Bring me the rabbit alive. Please."

"But..."

"I'll explain...later."

She eyed him as if studying a unicorn, a griffin, or some other mythical creature.

The fact that she'd hidden everything in the cave meant she was worried that more suicide bombers would appear. Unlike her, Jeremiah was also concerned about what would happen if the French found him. He was a fugitive. He needed to regain his strength and speed his healing, to protect himself and to protect her from him. Would she help?

She put the bowl down and headed for the cave mouth. She returned with her long fingers clenched around the ears of a quivering ball of brown fur. The closer she came, the more the rabbit's movements quickened. The horses by the pool, save Al-Hawa, shifted nervously as the rabbit's distress told them a predator was here.

The woman noticed the animals' reactions. She kept

coming, but with increasing caution. She stopped about a foot away from Jeremiah doing her best to keep the creature steady as it kicked at her robes with its long feet and wiggled its back trying to escape.

As she held it out to him, she resorted to French again. *"La pauvre chose a parcouru tout le chemin de la France. Tu veux que je …?"*

The poor thing has come all the way from France. Do you want me to … ?

She didn't have time to finish. Jeremiah's arm shot out, snatched the rabbit, and brought it to his mouth. His jaw clamped around the neck, killing it. Its meager but vital fluids seeped into his throat, slaking his corpse-dry skin. His limbs tightened, relaxed, then fell under his control again.

The woman's pained gasp turned his eyes toward her, but he couldn't stop drinking. She staggered backward and nearly fell before her hands found the cave wall.

"Chnu anta?"

Not French. Arabic. Likely her native tongue. *What are you?*

Swooning from the blood rush, Jeremiah wasn't certain how, or if, he should answer. Still, any illusions she might have had about him were gone. He felt embarrassed, not only that she'd seen him feed, but also that she'd seen how good it made him feel.

He moved his blood-smeared mouth away from the rabbit.

"I don't know," he said. He could talk more easily now, but that didn't make it easier to figure out what to say.

The wound he'd created was no longer covered by his

mouth. She eyed the animal's neck then raised her hand to her own throat. Fearful, she struggled for the English. "And you the same way will kill me?"

He tossed the carcass deep into the alcove where he hoped she couldn't see it. When he shook his head, the movement came without pain. He was stronger. His French even came back to him.

"I would rather die than feed on another human, let alone one who saved my life."

In answer, the sharp smell of her fear filled the space between them. But the single line on her brow also reappeared. She was thinking. Eventually, she lowered her hand from her neck.

"You say I saved your life?"

"You brought me here, pulled me out of the sunlight. Even brought me the..." He tilted his head toward the back of the alcove.

"But, monsieur, *can* you die?" There was a spark in her eyes, a light Jeremiah thought he recognized, a desire just to know. He saw no reason to lie.

"Lately, I'm not sure."

"Not by a bomb?"

He shrugged. "No. Not that one, anyway."

She let her gaze travel up and down his body in a way that embarrassed him further. Her heart still beat quickly, but the acrid odor of her fear was dissipating.

"What is your name?"

"Jeremiah Fall."

She locked eyes with him. "The American who found the stone? Who fought beside the Mamluks?"

It was only after he nodded that he started to wonder just how much this woman knew. It was obvious she wasn't simply the mistress or wife of an officer who'd gone native.

Her questions came faster. "Were you following the caravan? Do you still serve Murad Bey? Are you with the Turks? Who do you fight for?"

"Slow down," he said.

She began to enunciate each word. "I'm sorry. Why...did you...follow...?"

Jeremiah smiled. "No, no. I understand. I speak French. I understand everything you've asked, I just...I'm not sure how much I want to tell you."

"Oh."

She sat back and pursed her lips. Her demeanor shifted from demure to regal, as if to say, *How dare you refuse me?* Was she some sort of royalty? She was certainly no servant.

"I mean...I'm very thankful for all you've done..."

"You are welcome."

"But...I don't know who you are. I don't know what *you're* doing here. It doesn't make sense. Why would the French take an Arabic woman on such an important trip? It's very...unusual."

"So are you," she answered. "And you have the advantage of strength and speed. Why shouldn't I have the advantage of knowledge?"

"I said I won't harm you. You already know more about me than anyone else living. Won't you tell me just a little about yourself?"

"It's a very long story."

"I doubt it's as long as mine. How about your name?"

"Amala."

"Amala means *hope* in Arabic. Very pretty. Do you have a surname?"

"Amala Dhul-Nun al-Misri."

Jeremiah twisted his head sideways. The surname was familiar, but his brain was still sluggish. Where had he heard it? "Dhul-Nun al-Misri, wasn't he an eighth-century Sufi saint?"

She nodded. "You know a great deal. Only one of the French savants recognized it."

"I have a lot of time to read," Jeremiah said. "Dhul-Nun al-Misri. It was said he knew the secrets of the hiero-glyphs. Your family was named after him?"

An odd half-smile spread across her lips. "Why did you follow the caravan?"

To answer meant telling her everything.

"Question for a question?" Fall said. "A game?"

"No game. As you said, we don't know each other, so how do I know if I should trust your word? You wouldn't be the first man who lied to a woman. If I thought the pistols I saved from the soldiers could protect me, I might feel comfortable about telling you more. But clearly they would not."

Enthrall her as you did the horse. You can make her love you for the rest of her days.

An image flashed in his head, Amala in his arms, the tips of his canines piercing her warmth. It would be over in seconds.

She was right to be cautious, but he didn't want to tell her that yet either. "You talk about pistols, but you stay by my side. You saw how fast I took the rabbit, but you're not afraid. Why?"

She shrugged. *"Le monde est plein d'ombres et de*

douleurs, mais voyez en nous une profondeur suffisante et vous trouverez partout la lumière enterré. La peur vous empêche de le voir, je lutte pour contenir ma peur."

The world is full of shadows and sorrows, but look deep enough and light is buried everywhere. Fear prevents you from seeing it, so I fight to contain my fear.

"Very nice. You prefer to speak French, but you're Arabic."

"It's a…pretty language. I was educated in…" She paused, then smiled at him. "You're trying to make me say more about myself."

Fall smiled back at her.

"There's yet another reason I'm not afraid of you."

"What's that?"

"You're still very weak."

She was right. As they talked, he'd been sinking sideways and hadn't even noticed. She came forward and tried to help him lie back down.

At the feel of her hands on his shoulder, he said, "Don't."

"You must rest more. We can talk later."

"The stone, they'll be coming for it…"

She pushed him down firmly. "It won't be easy to find. It's here in the cave with us."

The moment he became aware of its nearness, an enervating wave filled him.

"It's here?"

It brought him first to sitting, then to his feet.

Yes, said the voice of a thousand beasts. It was so loud he wondered why he hadn't heard it before.

Concern spreading on her face, she tried to pull him back. "Lie down."

For the first time, the stone spoke other words: *She wants to keep you from me.*

He spun dizzily. "Are you trying to keep me from it?"

He had to see it. But standing was so hard, like trying to steer a blade of grass in a hurricane. Al-Hawa. If he could reach her, she could be his legs. He took a few steps, then buckled to his knees.

Amala came up beside him. "No, I don't want to keep you from it. If it's so important, I'll help you."

He was too disoriented to stop her. They walked together, slowly.

The horses, nervously snorting, gave way as if he were nobility. Jeremiah and Amala passed the pool. After a few more steps, he wasn't sure how many, the wet, airy cave sounds gave way to a low murmur. It played teasingly beneath his heightened senses, making him even more disoriented and agitated.

I called you. You found me. I waited while you let the French surround me. Now someone else comes.

Jeremiah shivered. Amala, again misinterpreting, pulled herself closer to him, as if trying to transfer the warmth of her body to him.

Take the girl, the river rush of voices said. *You'll need strength to protect me.*

Please, no, he answered inwardly.

Why not? Like everything else, she's a ghost.

Panic gripped Jeremiah. Unlike the beast, if the torrent of voices commanded, he wasn't sure he could disobey.

Take her.

Please . . . he pleaded.

The horses then. Why not feed on them?

Stop! He begged and begged.

Mistaking his sudden pause for physical weakness, Amala guided him through a wide passage at the back of the cave. It opened up into a second high-roofed area that wound along the edge of a deep pit. If anything, the ceiling here seemed more fragile, poised on falling. A large boulder, echoing the shape of the stone, stood near the edge of the pit. Tracks in the dirt told him where she'd led the wagon. He didn't need her. He could just follow them now.

The nations Napoleon conquers. The land the colonists and native tribes fought over. Democracy. Tyranny. The dead. The living.

It dawned on him he didn't need the tracks either. Pulled by the voice, he led more than being led, yanking Amala along.

"You're hurting me," she said.

All ghosts. All false.

The passage narrowed, and then opened again. In the center of a wide, flat area, almost a separate cave, there it was, atop the wagon. The myriad perforations in the ceiling sprayed the space with irregular circles of white moonlight, but even where they touched the rock, it refused to be illuminated.

The world is the arrogant folly. Not you.

Jeremiah stumbled ahead of Amala and put his fingers against the flat surface that held the writings. He let their sensitive tips run along the small phrase he'd translated.

"Black as night among the stars," he said aloud.

Yes.

He scanned for anything else in the Greek he might recognize, but the stone kept nearly all the words a blur, save the one set it seemed he was meant to see.

"A healing light for all the creatures of the night."
Yes.

Hand still on the letters, he went to his knees. The roar of a thousand beasts grew louder. He said it again, "A healing light."

"You..." Amala said. He'd forgotten she was there. "You think it can *cure* you? Make you human again? That's why you searched for it?"

"Yes," Jeremiah said, no longer certain if he was speaking aloud.

The deluge echoed him. *Yes. You found me. But another will be here soon to take me from you.*

Amala kept talking, but Jeremiah couldn't make out her words. It was only the stone he heard. He now knew for certain that it was the stone that spoke, or something within it, even if he couldn't place the sound. It dampened and muffled all else.

At last, one other noise made it through, as if he'd been granted permission to hear it. It wasn't words, but a light, distant skittering, a horde of tiny claws scrabbling and scratching against dirt and stone. The smaller roar issued from the crannies of the cave complex. As it came closer, it got louder.

Instinct told him what it was. He wanted to warn Amala, but couldn't speak. It was all he could do to turn and wave her away from the entrance. She didn't understand his frantic gestures until it was too late. A swarm of desert rats, summoned from the depths of the cave system, poured in, covering the floor like living liquid.

She screeched and leaped atop a small, crumbling gray rock that barely held her above the quivering flood. The rodents, all shapes and all sizes, raced for the stone.

As soon as they came within a foot, the hundreds stopped and made a perfect semicircle around it.

They won't be enough. You'll lose me, but you wouldn't take the woman or the horses. At least this way, you'll survive to fight again.

With the warning complete, the great multitude of voices stopped. But there was no silence, only the symphony of a hundred tiny breaths and pattering hearts.

Jeremiah stood and stared at the waiting creatures.

Feed! the beast cried.

Its voice seemed small compared to the shattering chorus. But Jeremiah felt smaller still. Only his reason had ever kept the beast at bay. That was the dark compromise they'd lived with for over a century. Now he had no reason *not* to indulge it.

He turned toward Amala, a helpless, plaintive look in his eyes. She seemed to guess what would happen next—the rabbit, hundreds of times over—and stepped quickly and carefully toward the exit.

Once the ivory-white of her robes was out of sight, Fall fell upon the living floor, drawing piece after piece to him, biting one in half, tearing another open with his fingers before it reached his mouth. It wasn't like hunting a bear—black, grizzly, or giant. It wasn't like fighting in a war. It was an orgy, a grotesque revelry at the behest of some thing he now feared was more likely a final damnation than a cure.

Or was it? Could this somehow be a final set of tests? A passing encounter with a devil that blocked his path to the light? He didn't know. He hated not knowing.

It was only when he was done that he returned to himself. The memory of his indulgence faded quickly, as if the details of those moments were like the ink the savants tried to use on the stone, but which it would not absorb. The effect of the blood remained. He could walk more easily. There was renewed strength in his limbs.

He looked at the stone. It was quiet now. He staggered away from it the same way he'd seen men stagger from taverns to head home in the dead of night, drunkenly donning their daily identities as if a poorly fitting but familiar coat.

He remembered one thing clearly enough. The stone had said someone was coming.

11

His head clearing, Jeremiah Fall walked back along the path, the deep pit to his right. Moonlight shone on its near wall, but kept the bottom secret. He headed back to the small pool. The horses shifted at his presence. Al-Hawa nodded at him.

The woman stood at the mouth of the cave, her head turned up toward the broad night sky. A slow wind made the tips of her hair waver. As he approached, he tried to make himself seem more human. Realizing he hadn't wiped his mouth, he did so quickly, rubbing the blood from his face, then wiping his hands on his borrowed pants.

His feeding frenzy made him worry he might break the vow he'd made to Atticus and himself, the vow to stay human. He had to try to reclaim it somehow, here and now. Standing as close to Amala as he dared, he cleared his throat, determined to do what he had never done before.

"In 1644, I was an American colonist. A creature like

me attacked my father. He rose from his grave three nights later and killed me. I'm driven by a fierce hunger for living blood, but my grandfather taught me to fight it."

Jeremiah had no idea if it made any more sense in the telling than it had in the living, but he did his best to fit himself into words. He spoke of Atticus, Nathan, Mary and James, the Algonquin and Abenaki, King Phillip, the wars, the libraries he slipped into, the books he stole, the slender thread that turned into a mad hope and brought him here. He told her everything, as if confessing his life would make it real again.

When he finished, Amala, the intelligent sparks in her eyes glistening like earthbound stars, said, "I had a feeling you were older than you looked."

He laughed, wondering how his parents could ever have believed that merriment was a sin.

His smile had yet to fade when she started asking questions again. Some were childlike in their simplicity. He did his best to answer. Do you ever need to sleep, or do you just have to hide from the sun? How high can you jump? What does blood taste like? How does fear smell? Do you breathe? If you stood invisible in a shadow and someone accidentally touched you, would you be revealed?

Others were more profound. "Are you still a Puritan?"

He wasn't sure how to answer that one. By the time the question came up, they were sitting on opposite sides of the cave entrance. He was leaning back. Amala, arms wrapped around her knees, craned forward as if to tug the answers from him with her eyes. *Was* he Puritan? What *did* he believe? As he pondered, Jeremiah's body went still. He felt himself almost leave it behind until Amala said, "Monsieur Fall?"

"What is it?"

"You looked...as if you were about to disappear."

"Sorry. The Puritans are...were my people. There've been better; there've been worse. They burned adulterers alive. I saw them hang five women near Salem as witches. At the same time, they believed every man had to seek the truth of Scripture for himself, which meant they had to read. They were the first to establish universal education and to create books for children. There'd be no democracy in the States without them."

Amala shook her head. "I didn't ask what you thought of them, but if you still believed as they do. Do you still consider yourself predestined by God? That Skog was the Devil, or serving him? That becoming human would be a sign of Christian salvation?"

"I...I'm not certain. Some of it, I suppose, but not all. I let the Algonquin cremate my grandfather. I fought against the godly in a war. What do *you* believe, Amala?"

She shrugged. "What my parents and teachers taught me to believe. That's all I've had to choose from. I haven't read or seen nearly as much as you. Your experiences must have changed you inside as much as Skog changed your body, no?"

"Yes and no. Let me put it this way. During the American Revolution, at the siege of Savannah, a terrible battle, I met a French soldier, Roland Verne, who spoke perfect English. He had no trace of an accent. I complimented him on it, but he shrugged me off. 'I speak four languages just as easily,' he said. 'But, you know, no matter how hard I try I still *think* in French.' I guess the same is true of me. I've encountered many ideas, many beliefs, but deep down, I was raised as a Puritan, as a carpenter, then a farmer. I'm still translating. For all I know, I still tell myself the voice from the stone is God testing me, or Satan tempting me." He shrugged. "Though I suppose those are the same thing."

He furrowed his brow at her. "What *did* your family teach you to believe, Amala Dhul-Nun al-Misri? Who are they? What's your connection to the stone?"

She bobbed her head lightly as if deciding where to begin. "To begin with, I can tell you..."

Jeremiah's hand shot up, silencing her. He was gripped by a sudden, unwelcome awareness. He heard many hooves against the sand, many riders in the night. But they were so distant, far farther away than he was used to hearing. Had his awareness increased because the night was uniquely still, or because the stone wanted him to hear this?

In any case, the voice had not lied.

"Someone's coming," he said. "They'll be here in a few hours. Just as the sun comes up."

"*Who's* coming?"

"I don't know." He grabbed her arm, ignoring the temptation physical contact brought, and pulled her back inside. "I'd like to say the French, but they don't ride by night."

His gaze darted about the scene. The intruders would easily find the spot where the attack took place, then the cave. Could he conceal that they'd been here? He ticked off the evidence of their presence: his alcove bed of torn cloth and blankets, supply crates, the horses, scores of tracks on the floor. Even if he could erase all that, it was pointless. Any fool would smell the horse dung hanging in the air, and he doubted it was fools who were coming.

"They'll try to destroy the stone again."

"How can you be sure it's the same people?"

Her questions suddenly seemed more foolish than charming. "Who *else* would it be?"

"You stopped the bombers last time."

"Barely." He halted, wobbling on his feet. "I'm still in no shape to protect it again... or you."

"Would more blood help?"

"It might. I don't know."

She looked down. "Is it true what you said, that when you feed, the victim doesn't always die?"

"Yes," Fall said, not really listening. "I told you about Al-Hawa."

She stepped forward and tugged the cloth away from her neck.

"Stop it!" he growled, shielding his eyes. "Are you insane?"

"Would it be worse than being killed by whoever's coming? If it makes you stronger, you'll be better able to fight them."

The beast in him said nothing. There was no need. The woman was doing such a fine job of pleading its case.

"Didn't you hear anything I said? When Skog came out of the mound, he wasn't human; he was a beast. My father, when he killed my mother, was a beast. The only thing letting me pretend that I'm not is the hunger I don't fulfill."

"Even if it means I might be killed? Even if it means losing the stone?"

"Even if," he said. "Now please... cover up."

She eyed him, then did as he asked.

"They're south of us," he said softly. "Take one of the horses and head north. You can contact the French and tell them what happened. Maybe leave out some of the details about me."

"But you'll stay?"

"I have to."

"Monsieur Fall...Jeremiah, what would you do now if *no one* were coming?"

It was another useless question. "Try to read more of the Greek, I suppose. But I told you about the effect the stone has on me. I've only been able to focus on a word or two. At that rate, it'll be months before I complete a sentence."

She crinkled her lips in a half smile. "Before you interrupted, I was going to say that *I* can tell you what the stone says."

"You? How?"

Insulted, she stiffened a bit. That regal sense again emanated from her. "You thought I was brought along as a courtesan?"

"Amala, I didn't know what to think. I still don't."

"I saw their notes, read some of the carvings myself."

Fall's brow wrinkled. There was only so much that smell and amplified hearing could tell him. "Did you study ancient Greek in the school that taught you French?"

"No, I can't read the Greek."

"The Coptic?" It would be surprising, but not out of the question.

She shook her head.

Jeremiah's eyes flared. "The *hieroglyphs*? That's impossible. No one living can understand them."

She raised an eyebrow. "*Impossible* is a strange word

coming from a man like you. I told you my name. Dhul-Nun al-Misri was my ancestor. Over the centuries, his secrets were passed from father to son."

Fall nodded slowly. "And when there was no son, to the daughter."

"The women in our family have *always* been educated. Dhul-Nun wrote of a black stone buried at Rashid over three thousand years ago. When I heard it was found, I had to see it. That's why I journeyed here and offered to help the French. They laughed. *'Qui est cette petite femme qui pense qu'elle sait de la magie de langue?'* Who is this little woman who thinks she knows the magic of language? So I showed them. I read a line or two. That gave me their attention. Of course, I read much more than I was willing to tell them."

Jeremiah took her wrists in his hands. The tips of his fingers sensed the blood pulsing through her veins. "Amala, is there anything that says if it can heal me?"

She looked into his eyes. "I still only know some. I don't know if *any* of it's true. Nothing I do know disproves your hopes."

"Tell me, tell me everything."

"Some of the writings are instructions, rituals, rules. There is also an old story about the garden where God created man."

"Eden? The stone has a version of Genesis? I suppose it's possible. The Hebrews came out of Egypt during the Exodus. They may have traveled through Rashid."

She shook her head. "It's not the same as what's in the Pentateuch or the Qur'an, only similar. It's as if this story were hidden between those words, like the darkness between the stars."

His mouth fell open. She was right to chide him for using the word *impossible*. He spoke quickly, unable to contain his excitement. "How do you know that phrase? Is it in the hieroglyphs?"

"Yes. It's like the Greek you translated, yes?"

He nodded. "It's part of what brought me here, what I heard from Plasoa. Tell me the story written on the stone."

"It's the tale of the forgotten man."

Jeremiah chanted. *"I am the forgotten man, unfinished by my maker's hand..."*

It was Amala's turn to be surprised. "Exactly."

"Who is the forgotten man? Does it say?"

"Before the creator made a man, he made another, a first attempt no one recalls. He was called...I think the closest pronunciation would be...Bandias."

"A first man..."

Can I not do to you what this potter had done?

As if cold, she wrapped her robes more tightly around herself. "Now you tell me how that connects to an old Abenaki legend."

Jeremiah smiled in disbelief. "After I wrote down Plasoa's garbled words, I learned French, then went back and guessed at what I'd written. Even after decades, the best I'd managed was flawed." He looked up at one of the holes in the ceiling. Through it, he saw a cloud over the moon. He recited:

> *When the blazing sun is gone,*
> *When he nothing shines upon,*
> *Then a creature of the night*
> *Sings this to the lesser light:*

I am the forgotten man
Unfinished by my maker's hand
He left me when the world began
And would not tell me what I am

Like all who travel in the dark
And cannot see their tiny spark
I cannot tell which way to go
But my shadow seems to know

Within this black rock lies a pearl
Glowing brighter than the world
Calling with a healing light
To all the creatures of the night

Buried but it yet remains
Waiting for the end of days
Black as night between the stars
My shadow knows just what we are

As he finished, the cloud slipped away, and the cave filled with shards of bluish-white moonlight. Amala rose and took his hand.

"Come with me to the stone. I want to tell you the story, but I can't remember it all. I want you to hear it as perfectly as possible."

Jeremiah followed cautiously. "I don't know. You've seen what it does to me."

"I'll hold you up."

"That's not the effect I'm worried about," he said, but he didn't stop her from lighting an oil lamp from the supplies, then leading him back to the bowels of the cave.

The stone still had its luster. The mound of dead desert rats remained, but the whole area seemed dormant, like a theater set abandoned between performances of a play.

Ashamed of his half-remembered gluttony, Jeremiah kicked a path through the little corpses for Amala. He stopped before reaching the stone and let her move ahead.

Her face, which always seemed intelligent, focused with intense skill. She found a particular section of the hieroglyphs then turned the oil lamp this way and that. As she moved it, the flickering flame lit the chiseled pictograms from different angles, casting shadows that made them seem alive. Her fingers danced across the stylized images, symbols that could be birds, the squiggles of a snake, the oval and line of a disembodied eye. Every third or fourth image, she said a word or two, sometimes trying several words in French or Arabic, to find the one that fit.

As she spoke, the story, at once alien and familiar, traveled across thousands of years, from the stone, to her lips, to Jeremiah's hungry mind, where it lodged like one of Atticus's old rants, feeling somehow both sacred *and* profane.

When Aten created the heavens and the earth, he was as a child in the womb and his spirit hovered over the waters. From his center grew two trees: the Tree of Life and the Tree of the Knowledge of Good and Evil.

Aten ate from the fruit of the first tree, and he ate also from the fruit of the second. He said, "Let me open my eyes." And there was light.

Aten looked at the animals of the land and the plants of the field and saw that none were like him. He said,

"Let us make man in our own image, and we will place him in a garden and have him name the creatures we have made."

From the banks of the river where the Tigris and Euphrates meet, he took some clay in his hands and started to fashion the man, but a sadness filled Aten's heart, a longing for the time his spirit hovered over the waters alone.

Aten set the undone man aside and thought of what would become of the man once he had been made. And Aten said, "I will make a helpmeet for him and place them in the garden, with the injunction that they shall not eat of the fruit of the Tree of Good and Evil. But the woman and the man will eat from the tree, and I will curse the soil because of him."

Aten paused, uncertain whether to continue. He forgot the man he had begun. The forgotten man, hearing what Aten had said and seeing Aten had forgotten him, fled, for fear he would be destroyed.

So Aten began again, dipping his hand in new clay. He made a second man and gave him dominion over the beasts of the field and the fish in the sea. Aten named him Adapa. And Adapa named all the beasts of the field, each according to his kind. And Aten made a helpmeet for the man. And Adapa named her Havah.

One day, Havah went strolling in the cool of the evening and came upon the forgotten man as he stood by the two trees. Seeing that he was in a manner like Adapa, she asked him, "Who are you?"

And the forgotten man said, "I am the firstborn of Aten."

And Havah answered saying, "This cannot be. Adapa is the firstborn of Aten."

"Has Aten told you that? Has he also not said you may not eat of all the trees?"

"The fruit of all the trees we may eat," Havah said, *"except the tree in the middle of the garden. On the day we eat of the tree, Aten said we would surely die."*

And the forgotten man said, *"What Aten has told you is untrue. You will eat of the tree and not die but be as Aten is."*

And Havah beheld the tree and saw that it was good to eat. She ate of the fruit and when done turned to the unfinished man and said, *"Because you have shown me this, I will give you a name. I will call you Bandias."*

And Bandias said, *"Aten has made you from Adapa so his seed will not perish. Let me put my seed in you also so that I may not perish."*

And Havah gave birth to Cain and said, *"Now I am like Aten and have made a man."*

Amala stopped speaking long before Jeremiah noticed. His head was swarming, not from the stone, but from the effort of his mind trying to connect a dozen threads. He knew there were different versions of the Bible, different translations, that some of the tales in it existed in other forms. The story of a flood that drowned the world, for instance, appeared in several cultures, but this seemed different.

"How? How did the same story make it from ancient Egypt to the Bible, to America?" He sat cross-legged on the ground and held his head in his hands as if that would keep his thoughts in his skull. "Bartolomé de las Casas, a sixteenth-century Spanish priest, fought for Indian rights in South America because he believed they were descended from one of Israel's lost tribes. Is it possible they brought the story to the Abenaki? So many coincidences. Atticus would call it a miracle."

Amala rested her palm flat against the stone. "What do you call it?"

"Cain," Fall muttered, ignoring the question. "It was said that after he murdered Abel, he went to the land of Nod and sired…monsters. According to the stone, Bandias was the father of Cain." He raised his head toward her. "Amala, what else does it say?"

"The rest are instructions, rituals," she said. "They're more complicated."

Through the gaps in the ceiling, he saw the sky shedding its darkness, swelling at the edges with color. "Tell me whatever you know. There isn't much time left."

She nodded. "The hieroglyphs say that before there was even writing, Bandias was trapped in the stone. They explain how to free him and how to earn his favor."

Jeremiah's face dropped. "Bandias. Then it's not God that talks from it. It's this fallen man. It *is* the Devil. I *am* damned."

My child forsakes me. But the other is coming.

12

Before the multitude of voices overwhelmed him, Jeremiah slammed his fist into the rock. "Who? Tell me who's coming!"

Amala appeared behind him. She rubbed his shoulders, trying to soothe him.

You could still take the woman.

She brought her lips close to his ear. Somehow over the monstrous bellow, he heard her whisper, "You said yourself the Devil's temptations are the same as God's trials. If that's true, you might yet have your cure."

"How?"

She scrunched her face. "I don't know. If Bandias is trapped inside it, why couldn't this stone or something like it imprison your beast as well?"

It made a sort of sense, but how many impossible things could he believe in a single day?

Why stay asleep when you can be awoken?

Jeremiah stepped back, planning to put some distance between himself and whatever was in the stone.

Amala followed him to the wide passage. "What's wrong? Where are you going?"

"It's talking to me again. We've got to get you out of here. I'll get you some water and put you on a horse."

"I don't want to leave," she said. "I can shoot a gun. Handle a sword."

His pace quickened. "Can you survive an explosion, or an attack from a creature like me? That stone isn't important only to me. If it links the American Indians to the lost tribes, it changes everything we understand about history. If it's destroyed, your memory of it may be the only thing that survives."

"But what will you do?"

He paused at the edge of the pit and peered down into its darkness.

"Will *you* destroy it?" she asked.

"No. Not yet, anyway. Whether it can cure me or not, for all I know if it cracks, it might release this . . . this Bandias creature. Maybe those dust-crawlers were hoping to blast him free. But if the horses can help me bring it here, maybe I can use the ropes and pulleys from the supplies to lower it into the pit. I could cover it with rubble. Even if whoever's coming finds it, it'll take them a while to figure out how to get to it. If nothing else, I can find out more about who they are. Though I've already got a pretty good guess."

"Who?"

"The Devil's always had followers. Kali, the goddess of death, is worshipped in India. Around A.D. 200, there was a group that worshipped mankind's first murderer, Cain, the Cainites. Why not a group that worships his father?"

"Then it's even more important I stay. You'll need help lowering the stone."

When she turned for his response, she couldn't find him. He'd disappeared into the shadows and watched as she twisted her head and called his name. She grew confused, then worried, before he let her see him again. She gasped as if he'd appeared out of nowhere.

"I don't doubt it when you say you're a good fighter, but I'm a lot better at hiding. I'll get the ropes and pulleys. You'll have to harness the horses. Once that's done, you *must* leave. Horses don't like me much, but I can get them to run away from me."

Amala did the work with the horses quickly, slowing only when she saw Jeremiah pack Al-Hawa's saddlebags for her.

"Monsieur, you never told me how the Abenaki legend brought you to Rashid."

As he tightened the straps, he explained. "The Frenchman I told you about, Verne, was wounded during the siege of Savannah. He lost a leg and couldn't fight anymore, so I brought him to a ship to take him back to Europe. There, I heard some French sailors sing a sweet little song that had some of the Abenaki phrases. By then, it was about a little boy tormented because his father wanted him to grow up. A few years back, an English version showed up with same melody, but even fewer of the original words. The forgotten man had been... forgotten. It had become something completely new:

> *Twinkle, twinkle, little star,*
> *How I wonder what you are*

Up above the world so high
Like a diamond in the sky

He shook his head. "It's harder to follow something backward in time, like trying to sew with spider's silk, but I kept trying to find out where the story came from, looking for those words everywhere. It's strange how things are connected. Maybe there are no coincidences. You know the Greek philosopher Plato? About three years ago, a very old copy of one of his last dialogues, *Critias,* made its way to Harvard. It's about an ancient civilization, Atlantis, so big it once challenged Egypt, until the gods destroyed it. A century earlier, another Greek, Solon, heard the Atlantis story while visiting Egypt. He told it to Critias' grandfather, who told it to Critias, who told it to Plato."

He stepped back and picked two pistols from one of the crates. "I wasn't exactly a student. More a trespasser. By the time I'd finished reading it, it was almost morning. I was in a hurry to get going, but as I rolled up the scroll, the lantern light struck it at an off angle. I saw some writing along the side, so faded it was just an impression, like a schoolboy's note scribbled in the margins. I guess no one else noticed it, but their eyes aren't as good as mine. It said, in Greek, *Anysis buried the forgotten man in Khito*. There he was, the forgotten man."

"Khito is the old name for Rashid, but who is Anysis?"

He paused from loading the pistols to tap his brow. "A very obscure reference. If you can't read hieroglyphs, most Egyptian history is lost. We don't even know the name of the pharaoh who freed the Hebrews in Exodus.

Other than the Bible, there's only a single reference, from the Greek historian Herodotus, who said he was '*Anysis* of the city of the same name.'"

"Akhenaten," Amala said.

"What?"

"In his journals, Dhul-Nun al-Misri wrote that Akhenaten was the pharaoh who freed the Hebrews from slavery. He was a very unusual pharaoh. He challenged the Egyptian priests, got rid of all the old gods in favor of worshipping just one…Aten."

"The creator god mentioned on the stone," Jeremiah said. "Amazing."

"After Akhenaten's death, the old religion resumed power. His temples and all references to him were destroyed. He was a forgotten man himself."

"Then that's the connection to the stone. Akhenaten or his followers, maybe the Hebrews themselves, buried it in Rashid, and one of the lost tribes brought the story to the Americas. After all this time, the pieces are falling together."

He tugged the bayonet blade free from a musket and put it in his pocket, thinking it would come in handy for cutting the ropes. "Let's hope that now they don't fall apart."

He snapped his ears toward the entrance. He could hear the approaching horses even from inside the cave.

"You've got to go," he said.

"How will I know what becomes of the stone, or you?" she asked.

"Stay with Al-Hawa, and I'll be able to find you."

Realizing he might never see her again, Jeremiah dared put his hands around Amala's waist to help lift her into the saddle. As he did, something in him stirred, something, aside from his mind, that reminded him of his humanity. She seemed to sense it, too, looking down at him with curiosity and affection.

Not knowing what to do other than grimace, he turned away and whispered in Al-Hawa's ear. In seconds, she was off, and he was standing outside the cave, wasting precious seconds to watch them head into the rising sun. Only the sting on his skin forced him back inside.

The horses were harnessed to the wagon. Now, he had to get them to pull it near the edge of the pit. As he walked near them, the waterfall of voice assaulted him.

You let her go.

"Yes," Jeremiah told it. "I'm only sorry I didn't let those bombers destroy you."

They could not. Illusion cannot destroy reality.

"Oh? Then what can destroy you?"

Nothing.

As Jeremiah approached, the six horses reared. In a flash that could barely be called movement, he flitted to the rear of the wagon, giving them a single direction in which to flee. They tugged and strained, but the wheels barely inched forward.

Two of the horses were cavalry-trained, not used to being part of a team. They pulled, not in tandem, but at random. There wasn't much time for them to learn, so Jeremiah crept closer, hoping that increasing their terror would increase their strength.

When that failed, he put his shoulder to the foot-thick platform and pushed. The wheels turned. The wagon lurched, jarring the stone. It wasn't until he was almost there, near the edge of the pit, that the stone spoke again.

Napoleon. Your father. Your grandfather. The woman. Even this stone. All false. You will learn. You will know.

Dizziness welled. He tried to shut it out but felt the world narrow. He couldn't afford lost concentration now. Jeremiah pressed his teeth so hard together he feared he'd crack them. He tried to pray, inwardly asking, "Are you testing me?"

But the stone provided the answer. *You test yourself.*

When the horses moved forward, a disoriented Jeremiah fell to the ground.

For nothing.

The right side of the wagon grazed the precipice. The ground beneath the wheels crumbled just enough to tilt the wagon. Panicked by a shift in the weight behind them, the horses tugged, trying to bring the wagon away from the pit, back to the center of the path. If even one wheel slipped over the side, it would be over. The wagon would tilt sharply and the stone would tumble.

Was that its plan? Was Bandias trying to free himself? Jeremiah jumped to his feet, slammed his hands against the wood of the wagon, and pushed. It was hopeless. The front right wheel sent more rock and debris into the pit, leaving a gap behind it. Inches ahead of the rear wheel, the ground gave way completely. If the horses continued, the wagon would collapse into the abyss.

Cursing his endless stupidity, Jeremiah leaped onto the wagon bed to cut the horses free. As he moved past the stone, his whole being slowed, as if the air were replaced by oil.

Nothing.

The horses pulled, taking the rear right wheel to the brink. Sliding the bayonet from his side, he dove forward, bringing his weight to the front of the wagon and slicing the harnesses. One horse went free and galloped madly back toward the pool. A second joined him. The wagon slowed, but not enough to keep the wooden bed from creaking.

Three…four…five…

At four, the wagon stopped moving, but when he cut the final horse free, he felt the bed beneath him tilt, ever so slightly. As the sound of the terrified horse echoed in the open space, Jeremiah Fall leaned over to see where things stood. Two-thirds of the rear wheel dangled over nothing. The wagon gently rose and fell. If he jumped, walked, or so much as moved, it would tumble.

"Great," Jeremiah Fall said to himself. "Are you sure I'm the one testing myself?"

Yes.

He searched for a heavy stone, something to pull up to the wagon and balance his own weight. A foot away, a large one lay half buried in the sand. A dim patch of morning light from one of the ceiling holes graced its rounded top. The sun wasn't bright enough yet to do him any damage. If he could keep the wagon from falling, he might bring the stone up to take the place of his weight, and then use the ropes to moor the wagon to one of the larger boulders along the path.

He put his hand down toward the rock, stretching his fingers. Their tips barely touched it. He moved forward a little, but it was still tantalizingly out of reach. The patch of sunlight grew stronger as he watched. He tried again. Just when he thought he might reach it, a creaking from

the wood behind him made him look back. Judging from
the frayed marks at its base, the stone had slid a fraction
of an inch closer to the pit.

After several long minutes retesting the platform's
balance, he leaned forward again. The square of light
was brighter now. When he held his hand flat against the
stone, a sharp burning pain made him withdraw it.

Throughout his effort, the sound of the galloping
horses he'd freed never faded. It grew louder, as if they
hadn't kept running, and instead kept madly prancing
around the cave. No, that wasn't it. It wasn't the horses
he'd freed from the wagon; it was *them*.

Scores of armed, mounted men swarmed onto the path
in front of him. Jeremiah brought himself to the balls of
his feet, careful to keep his precarious balance.

"Yujad Jandal. Talfana uf'uwan."
The stone is here. Summon the . . . snake?

Arabic, but they weren't dressed the same as the dust-
crawlers. They looked more like Bedouin, but an ad hoc
crew at best. From what he could see of their faces, some
were dark like the natives, others European. There was
even one overweight fellow who looked incredibly pale.
Slavic, Jeremiah guessed. Something about their eclectic
appearance disturbed him. Whatever joined them as a
group could not be seen.

Hoping they didn't know about his effect on horses,
he snarled, exposing his fangs. Even if the men remained
in control, the horses should rear.

Both remained calm. They trotted closer and surrounded him.

Beyond the pack, a final horseman appeared. He rode
tall in the saddle, oddly stiff. No, not stiff, Jeremiah

corrected himself. He was motionless, as if a statue. His chestnut horse would be more at home in North America than Egypt. The rider's clothing was likewise unusual. Unlike the more or less traditional desert garb of the horsemen, his robes were a mix of burgundy and gray. The cut of his wide-sleeved overcoat looked vaguely Turkish, the style of the day. But this was no Turk.

He was completely covered, down to the cloth that wrapped the individual fingers of his hands, a cross between a mummy's wrapping and gloves. A silk mask covered his face, the only slits for the eyes. It sat on the skull so tightly that the shape of his broad nose and thick lips pressed against the fabric. It wasn't difficult to guess that Jeremiah was in the presence of one of his own, the *other* to which the voice referred.

This last horseman came closest, nearly to the edge of the teetering wagon. The growing patches of sunlight glanced off the steed's brown hair, making it easy to see the weeping scars on the horse's neck, similar to those Jeremiah had left on Al-Hawa.

He looked at the other horses. Also marked, bitten. That explained their lack of panic. Given all the times his own beast had suggested enthralling a human, Jeremiah decided to look more closely at the men. Their necks were concealed by their garb, but many of their eyes bore the same glassy look the horses' had, the look of slaves.

The masked horseman's eyes remained on Jeremiah as he asked, in Arabic, "Is the woman secure?"

"Yes," the light-skinned one said.

Amala?

"Don't you dare harm her," Jeremiah cried out in his best Arabic, surprised at his own anger. "I'll kill you all!"

He didn't see the man move his arm, but the horse-man's hand was now up, its wrapped fingers splayed in an open gesture, as if to reassure. "No one will touch her."

"Yes, snake," the men murmured in Arabic.

On a day of revelations, one more came. Not snake, *serpent*. In Abenaki, the word was *Skog*.

13

When Jeremiah Fall had first struggled with this creature a century and a half ago, its eyes were lidless. Peering at the slits, he recognized the dark crenellations in the whites and how the pupils glowed blackly like the stone.

"You killed my father," Jeremiah said in Abanaki.

The head twisted in recognition. A calm sigh of a voice answered, "No. If he was the man who freed me, I made him as we are. Did *you* kill him?"

Jeremiah wanted to hurtle into Skog, but when his tightening muscles shifted his balance, strands of wooden fiber within the timbers snapped with a loud— *thok*.

The familiar sound froze him. The stone was behind him with all of its secrets. If it fell, Bandias might be released, or the writing lost forever. He couldn't let it go.

Skog remained silent long enough to determine that Jeremiah would not attack, then said, "Secure the wagon to that boulder, and then harness the horses to it."

A broad-shouldered man left his saddle and landed hard on the ground. His clothes smelled of horse sweat and desert air, but his body had no odor. His thick eyebrows reminded Jeremiah of Nathan, but the dull tint to his eyes defined him as a slave. He was like the horses, fearless and without a will of his own. He fished a thick rope from the saddlebags and trudged dumbly toward the wagon.

If Skog read surrender in Jeremiah's hesitation, he'd made his first mistake. As soon as the man was close enough, the tip of Jeremiah's booted foot caught the slave below his chin. As the man fell, the fabric of his clothes fanned around him, settling only after he hit the ground.

The wagon bobbed. Practiced hands raised pistols at Jeremiah, but he'd survived musket wounds before. He turned to where their master had been, to see if there was some reaction. Skog's chestnut horse swayed as if to hidden music, but the saddle was empty.

Jeremiah snapped his head to the right. Skog was next to him, standing on the wagon with the same stone-still posture. It was the way Atticus had once described Jeremiah's thrashing—no movement to be seen, more as if he'd slipped between moments, vanished from one spot and instantaneously reappeared in another.

Skog was half a head taller than Jeremiah, but thinner. The airiness of his form was more apparent in close quarters, as if his body lacked true substance. He was so close that Jeremiah could see his thick lips part beneath the mask, even feel his slight breath as he spoke. It wasn't warm as Amala's had been. It was cooler than the breeze in the cave and dry, terribly dry.

He said, "If…"

Jeremiah's hands shot forward before the second

word could form. He hoped to wrap his fingers around the monster's throat, but snatched air. Momentum nearly made him fall from the wagon. The creaking wood again cried—*thok*.

Afraid to move his body, Jeremiah slowly turned his head. Skog was back on his horse, free to speak without interruption.

"If saving the stone matters more to you than revenge, you must know something about what sits behind you. Do you know of Bandias?"

Jeremiah blinked at the name. It was all the answer Skog required.

"Some of these men are my servants. The others, Bandites, worship our father. We'd hoped to take the stone after it was brought to Cairo, but the men who attacked the caravan betrayed us. We're in your debt for defeating them. It would be easy to convince us to share his secrets with you. Have you heard him speak?"

"It warned me you were coming, if that's what you mean."

Skog shifted in the saddle, his first unnecessary movement. Was he surprised? Jealous? Some of the men on horseback looked as if they wanted to whisper to one another, but thought better of it. Skog hadn't lied. They weren't all slaves.

"Would you like me to tell you more about him?"

"The stone, can it cure what we are?"

The chestnut horse blasted air from its nostrils as if it were laughing. "Cure? Yes," Skog said.

Jeremiah's face tightened. "I don't believe you."

"I don't have time to earn your trust. Bring the woman."

As if invisible wings had carried Skog's words out-side, two more horsemen appeared with Al-Hawa and Amala between them. Amala was bound and gagged, balancing in the saddle.

"Aim your weapons at her head."

The two men alongside her drew pistols and pointed the barrels at the long black tresses that covered her temples.

The effect on Jeremiah was instant—his body vibrated furiously. "Leave her alone!"

Skog didn't respond, as if he considered the situation too obvious for words.

"I'll kill you," Fall threatened.

"You don't even know what that means. I'd tell you, if you'd let me, but you won't. You just stand there full of useless rage. Hylic, tie the wagon down."

The Slavic man Jeremiah had noticed when they first arrived, the heavy one with pale skin, dismounted with considerably less skill than the first. He landed poorly, and as he regained his balance, the cloth briefly slipped from his face. He looked to be in his thirties, but his beard, far from full, grew in patches, as if adolescence had left him half undone. He ambled more than walked, shifting side to side, perhaps from an old wound. Like the first man, he retrieved a length of rope, then came toward the wagon.

Kneeling by the front wheel, he came close enough for Jeremiah to grab. His light eyes were sharp and clear. This one was here of his own free will. Yet there was no fear on him either. He was a Bandite.

Nodding at the scant distance between them, Jeremiah asked, "Aren't you the least bit afraid I'll kill you?"

Hylic smiled as he peacefully looped the rope around the axle. "Oh, no. It would be an honor."

An honor to die? He'd heard that before, from many soldiers. It was always bluster, a way of steeling nerves as battle neared. Jeremiah could always smell the tension when they said it. But this seemed different, as if the Slav meant death itself, any death, were the honor. The notion disturbed Jeremiah so much that he didn't stop Hylic from completing his work, instead waiting as he wrapped the rope around the tall boulder at the pit's edge.

Now free to move, Jeremiah straightened and faced Skog. All eyes turned to him expectantly, Hylic's, Amala's, even the men whose guns were pointed at her head.

Skog said, "The stone is secure. Climb down and I'll tell you all you need to know."

Again, Jeremiah disobeyed. He tongue-clicked a command to Al-Hawa to run, then leaped at Skog. Al-Hawa reared, her front hooves leaving the ground, surprise overtaking the men flanking her.

Having seen Skog vanish twice, Jeremiah didn't think he'd reach the creature; he only hoped to provide a distraction while Al-Hawa took Amala to freedom. But luck was with him for a change. Skog, underestimating his opponent—or not quite believing they *were* opponents—made the wrong choice. He pivoted toward Al-Hawa as Jeremiah flew at him, perhaps preparing to issue orders to his men. Realizing his error, Skog was turning back toward the wagon as Jeremiah slammed him in the chest. His form felt uncannily strong, but gave to momentum. Together they tumbled off the chestnut horse, Jeremiah catching flashes of Al-Hawa turning, Amala stunned but remaining on the horse's back.

With Skog beneath him, Jeremiah didn't hesitate. He grabbed at the joint between skull and neck and pressed the smooth cloth covering inward, tightening his grip until the mask showed every mottle and scar beneath it. Through his fingertips, Fall sensed the unliving body's terrain. At first, he thought Skog's skin was like cowhide loosely covering stone, then realized leather was more supple and stone not so cold.

His hold on Skog didn't keep the monster from vanishing, but it forced him to take Jeremiah along with him. One moment they lay struggling in the dirt among the startled horses, the next they were near the rocky edge of the pit and then beneath the wagon bearing the stone.

Disoriented by the lightning shifts in position, Jeremiah tried to tighten his grasp further, but found his strength failing. The rats, as the voice had warned, weren't enough. The surge his rage had provided was evaporating. He'd have to end this quickly or not at all.

When Skog next transported them—this time alongside the boulder where the wagon was moored—Jeremiah did his best to smash the Abenaki's skull against it. Neither neck nor skull moved. It was as if they were a single piece, fused to a spine that was one with the earth itself. His second effort proved weaker than the one that had already failed. His strength was gone. It was too late.

While Jeremiah weakened, Skog's energy seemed boundless. When the monster rolled lazily sideways, Jeremiah flew as if caught in a tornado. He turned in the air, then smashed into the ground, his shoulder crunching on impact. Their positions were now reversed. Skog was atop Jeremiah. With only some obstinacy keeping his hands around Skog's neck, Jeremiah wondered if the creature had only been playing with him, and now the game had ended.

Jeremiah tried to roll again, but before he could, Skog transported them into an area of the cave littered with poisonous light. There Skog lifted him into the air. A hot, burning sensation clamped onto the back of Jeremiah's exposed neck. Drops of sunlight dappled the black and burgundy of Skog's robes. Morning had come in earnest. Jeremiah, wearing the ill-fitting pants of a soldier and the thin sandy shirt of a suicide bomber, would soon be helpless. The smoke rising from his exposed back was already so thick, it cast a shadow all its own.

Pain made him more frantic. He tried pulling Skog left, then right, but the only thing he was able to move was his own burning shadow as it writhed across Skog's chest.

As he smelled his own searing flesh, he realized he'd failed. He'd have to release his grip and then escape into the dark. Had he, at least, provided enough time for Al-Hawa and Amala to flee?

He was not about to learn. Skog's hands clamped onto Jeremiah's shoulders, immobilizing him. The rays burrowed deeper into his neck. Jeremiah twisted, but felt as if caught between two boulders.

Jeremiah cried out, half in rage, half in anguish. The horses rustled as if his scream briefly pierced their slavish state, allowing them a moment of natural terror.

He looked at his adversary, his form so placid. No breath moved the cloth of his mask; no evidence of will rippled through his limbs. He was as Jeremiah had originally seen him—a thing.

There was a cracking at Jeremiah's back. His burning

flesh had caused his shirt to combust. As fire ate the fabric, more of his skin was exposed and more of it burned. Releasing his pathetic grasp on Skog's neck, he flailed at the flames. The only reward was a new burning sensation along his naked fingers.

"Jeremiah!" Amala's voice cried.

So she was still here. Still in danger. Though he barely knew her, the thought of her peril rallied him one last time. Rather than claw at the source of his own pain, he reached down, found the tiny eye slits in the cloth covering Skog's face, and tore. The fine mask and robes were well made but no match for even a weakened Jeremiah Fall. He ripped the cloth off the face, tearing all the way down to the neck and chest, exposing his opponent's skin to the killing daylight.

Skog was now revealed as a thin, sickly Abenaki. His leathery skin was nearly drained of the clay-brown and olive undertones European settlers oversimplified as "red." High cheekbones widened an otherwise thin face. Skin folds near the eyes made his nose seem broader and flatter. His lips, unlike the rest of him, were thick and full. His head was shaved except for the crown, where the dark, wiry strands seemed more like dead grass than hair.

The dead eyes opened fully; the thick lips curled into a snarl. A reaction at last. Skog let go of Jeremiah's shoulders, vanished, and reappeared standing by his side. He delivered a swift, strong kick that would have killed a normal man, but instead took Jeremiah out of the sun so quickly, it provided only relief.

As he flew, landed, and rolled, Jeremiah passed through several shafts of light too quickly to do any further damage. From there, an agile leap took him into a safe, dark corner. The burning stopped, but not the pain. Still, Jeremiah was pleased. He'd hurt Skog. He'd pierced his cemetery calm. Skog was no god.

Jeremiah rose into a crouch. Skog staggered, grasping at his eyes. Jeremiah couldn't tell if he'd been temporarily blinded or was simply enraged.

Knowing he had seconds before the creature recovered, Jeremiah grabbed a rock. He hurled the stone at Skog's bent head at the same moment he jumped and kicked at Skog's side. Skog ducked the rock, but the kick sent him flying into a larger pool of light. There, an ugly, animal howl erupted from his throat.

Fatigue rushing through him, Jeremiah bolted from shadow to shadow. Reaching the pale Hylic, he yanked his scimitar from its scabbard. Pistol shots whistled past his ears. Some hit wagon-wood, while others careened off the boulder to which it was moored. That gave him an idea. He'd head for the boulder. The solid rock at his back might give him a better chance against Skog.

Meanwhile, the ferociousness infesting Skog's scream spread to the creature's form. No longer stiff, it flexed and crouched in a way Jeremiah recognized. He'd experienced it the few times he'd given his own beast full rein, usually in a fight against a giant short-nosed bear. It meant there would be no rational thought interfering with the creature's urge to destroy.

Before Jeremiah could reach the boulder, a feral blur came at him. Arms, legs, and teeth, clawing, kicking, and biting, occupied every inch of the air. The maddened Skog didn't remain in one spot long enough to completely materialize. At times, it was as if his arm were one place, his legs somewhere else entirely.

Instinct kept Jeremiah dodging, striking back when he could. He stumbled sideways into shafts of light, earning burns with each false step. Landing a solid blow with the stolen sword seemed impossible. He wasn't bad with a blade, but never needing much skill against a human opponent, he'd never acquired any expertise. As Skog came at him, he flailed with it, cutting only air.

The combatants moved between shadow and light, until a lucky blow etched a long tear in Skog's robes. Yet for each slight bit of sunlight that struck the Abenaki's skin, Jeremiah was scalded thrice. Just as he thought he might black out from pain and exhaustion, he felt the boulder behind him. He'd hoped to fight Skog from this position, but now, utterly drained, he had another idea, a final gambit.

He raised the blade. "Let the girl go or I'll cut the rope and send the stone to hell."

The whirlwind of Skog's form settled. It folded into itself, again becoming a statue.

"You can't destroy it," Skog said. "You'll only make it more difficult for me to reach..."

At first, he was only two yards from Jeremiah, but he quickly vanished and reappeared farther away, in a dark hollow at the rear of the horses, not far from where Amala was being held.

"And I don't wish to wait..."

Fall feared he would turn his fury on the woman. But he didn't. Any trace of his beast seemed gone. Either Skog controlled it as easily as he did his enthralled men, or he and it both knew they'd already won.

Skog said just three more words. "Fire the cannon."

A cannon? Jeremiah's head snapped back and forth, searching for it. There was none to be seen.

"Fiat lux," Hylic intoned. *Let there be light.*

The cave fell quiet enough for Jeremiah's ears to detect the faint crackle of a burning fuse. Not from within the cave, but out in the day, nearby.

Two explosions followed. The second came so quickly that it overlapped the first. A powerful blast of iron round-shot erupted from the unseen cannon. The second sound, which occurred as the cannonball crashed into the fragile cave wall overlooking the pit, was more like a shattering mirror. The patchwork of limestone and dirt above and around Jeremiah shuddered and collapsed.

Pieces of the ceiling showered down. Most fell into the pit, but many rained down on the horses, the men, Amala, the wagon, and the stone. At first, Jeremiah couldn't imagine why Skog would risk losing the stone by collapsing of the cave, but the thin roof wasn't doing any real damage. No, it wasn't the debris Skog sought, but the sunlight. It filled the cave unhindered, all save the shady spot behind Al-Hawa, where Skog had appeared before issuing his command, to make sure he would be unharmed.

The bright flash was blinding, and the pain complete. It had, as Skog guessed it would, left Jeremiah only one way to fall, into the pit. The stone and the wagon receded as he flew backward and down.

For a normal mammal, the fall would have lasted several seconds. With his heightened senses slowing time, it seemed to go on forever.

He hit the still-darkened bottom, flat-backed. At the moment of impact, it didn't feel as if he'd been falling at all, more as if the earth had catapulted into him. He'd no idea how many bones cracked, or how he managed to stay conscious. The modest rubble from the explosion plummeted around him.

As time returned to normal, he heard the horses and the creak of wagon wheels above. The stone was being moved. He tried to discern any speech hoping to hear word of Amala. He counted the heartbeats and thought one hers, but could only be sure of the sounds of the wagon, the horses, the packing of crates, and the shifting of feet.

As he lay helpless on the dark floor, the line of sunlight inched down the pit wall. Within an hour, it would reach the floor, and by midday, flood it. There was no shelter to crawl beneath. Broken in so many places, and bloodless, Jeremiah wouldn't heal enough in time to climb. No point in even trying now. Any escape attempt would have to wait until they'd gone.

He kept listening until he thought they'd left, but the silence was quickly broken by the softer sound of footsteps in the sand. Some of them were walking outside the cave behind the ruptured wall.

Above the line of sunlight, the shadows of men appeared. Several figures peered over the edge of the gaping hole caused by the cannon fire. The Slav, Hylic, was among them. These were not Skog's slaves. They were the cultists, the Bandites, the ones who worshipped the unfinished man.

They knelt and chanted in a tongue Jeremiah didn't recognize. Their soft ancient utterances defied his linguistic skill so completely, they might as well have been spoken in a dream. Once finished, they rose in solemn unison. As the others filed away, Hylic remained long enough to toss something into the pit.

Flat and sandy, it flopped and fluttered through the air like a dying, ugly bird. It landed with a thud some yards from Jeremiah's feet. It was a wide canvas, probably the remains of a tent.

"To cover yourself," Hylic said in French. His voice was as near-boyish as his face, but a distinct Russian accent came through. In case he hadn't been clear enough, he pointed to the sun and added, "From that."

Then he left to join the others.

14

The jagged line of the hole above him reminded Jeremiah Fall of the edge of a broken bowl he'd once seen on the floor of Mary Vincent's humble kitchen. She'd been ladling soup into some earthenware the Algonquin had given grandfather when a scalding drop hit her hand. She was forced to drop the bowl, but the half sphere didn't shatter; it split down the middle. And there it was, right above him, all these years later, the same shape, only instead of orange bits of carrot floating in broth, white clouds rolled in a blue sky.

Can I not remake you like the bowl? the Lord said to the prophet.

"Haven't you done that already?" Jeremiah asked.

The thrown canvas wasn't far. Unable to stand, he pressed his heels into the earth and flexed his ankles to pull himself nearer. Once close, he edged the cloth between his feet and maneuvered it along his body until he could grab it with his hands and cover himself.

He strained to hear, hoping to tell how far off Skog

and his men were, but couldn't. Whatever it was that allowed him to detect them at a distance had left with the stone. Perhaps Bandias himself, fed up with Jeremiah, had switched allegiances to the Abenaki.

He could wait for night, but that would give them hours of travel time. Skog seemed masterful in many ways. Even if Jeremiah got out, it was possible he wouldn't be able to see their trail. If he were going to follow, he had to do it soon.

He looked up and around, and saw the boulder that graced the pit's edge. They must have left in a hurry. Hylic's thick rope remained tied around the rock, its unseen length somewhere on the ground above.

Maybe there was another way out.

He whistled for Al-Hawa. He doubted that, after seeing how she followed Jeremiah's commands, Skog would take her with them. Had Skog killed her? He feared for the horse, but then her smell came to his nostrils. The black equine head poked over the edge of the pit and looked down obediently.

"Push the rope down here," he said, expecting her to comply.

The horse gazed at him with uncomprehending eyes.

She understood when called, could rear and run and do whatever else was in her nature, but whatever bond linked them did not provide a dictionary. Much as Puritan angels and demons lay at the base of Jeremiah's understanding, Al-Hawa still thought like a horse.

Unwilling to surrender, he tore a long strip from the canvas. Sorting through the rocks fallen near him, he found the one that most resembled the boulder above. He twisted the canvas strip, to make it look more like a rope, and then tied it around his rock.

"Al-Hawa," he said, making certain he had her attention. Pointing to the stone and canvas string, he used his fingers to mimic a horse's four legs and head. He trotted his hand up to the strip, then used his middle finger to push the "rope" away from the stone. He pointed to the real boulder and rope, then to Al-Hawa, then to the drop that lay between them. There were many humans, let alone horses, Jeremiah wouldn't trust to understand his crude storytelling, but Qarsaq insisted she was the brightest of the herd.

Four times he acted out the idea before she disappeared from view. Shortly, he saw her ears poke over the ledge, then rise up and down in a steady motion. At last, a loop of rope tripped over and hung in a semicircle. She stopped, thinking she was done, but it was easy to egg her on until the full length unfurled and the end of the rope dangled a few feet above the ground.

Standing and walking with the tent wrapped around his wounded body proved more difficult. Climbing the rope was painful enough, but the stiff canvas kept flapping open and letting the sun slip in, earning him a few sharp burns. Smoldering when he reached the top, he was happy to claw his way into some darkness and rest.

The few remaining desert rats that huddled fearfully in the limestone nooks provided food. After fashioning the tarp and his tattered clothes into a more reliable and mobile covering, Jeremiah climbed into the saddle and galloped from the ruined cave to face the desert day.

The August sun pressed against the thick fabric like a physical thing, hampering his senses, but the trail was not difficult to find. The deep cuts left by the wagon bearing the stone were unmistakable. The impressions of the horses' hooves accompanying it were more ghostly, but Jeremiah saw them, too, and was surprised by their number. He'd seen ten men within the caves, but these prints put the number closer to fifty. No wonder Amala had been unable to escape.

Either unafraid of being followed, or in too much of a hurry, Skog and the Bandites hadn't bothered to erase any evidence of their turn to the northwest. Their path took them not only away from the Nile, but away from Cairo and Rashid as well, through the Libyan desert. Daman-hur, the largest city ahead, was a place of watermelon fields and marketplaces, so he doubted that could be their final destination. Where were they going? The coast? Alexandria? Would they try to leave Egypt?

The merciless heat, coupled with the pain of still-healing bones, limited Jeremiah's speed as well. It was hours before the sun began to set and interfere less with his eyesight. By then, the terrain had grown trackless, the land barren of life and landmarks. The lines of the wagon were all but indistinguishable from the lines the wind bled into the sand. He'd almost lost them completely when al-Hawa reached a flat limestone field.

If it were still midday, the direct sunlight would have washed away the tiny details on the sand-colored stone so completely that even a Bedouin tracker would have missed what occurred. But with night approaching, Jeremiah saw the muddle of tracks quite plainly.

They'd met here with other riders and exchanged their horses for fresh mounts. A triangle of wooden fiber marks told him where a trestle and pulley were used to shift the

stone to a new wagon. There seemed no limit to the cult's
resources.

The trail split, most of the horses heading east to the
Nile. A smaller group, accompanying the new wagon,
continued northwest. Would Amala be taken with the
stone? Most likely. Her knowledge of the hieroglyphs, if
they knew about it, made her as valuable to the Bandites
as it had to the French. His goals all likely lay in the same
direction.

As darkness buoyed him, Jeremiah picked up speed.
The dull red glow of campfires on the horizon made him
think he'd found them, but proved a disappointment. A
stray wind carried the smell of bathed French soldiers.
Perhaps they'd been sent from the north to see what
became of the stone. Thinking they might know something he did not, Jeremiah decided to take a closer look.

Leaving Al-Hawa behind, he slipped into their camp.
He spotted no guards, only two thin Egyptian boys
rooting among the supplies for a few tins of food. Their
bodies wobbled from malnutrition as they moved. He
thought about helping them, but their hands were already
full, and every moment he tarried, Skog and Amala grew
farther away. Instead he neared the campfires and listened
to the tired soldiers talk.

"Why bother searching for this stupid rock? The
savants have another back in Cairo to drool over. What
do they need this one for? *Bookends*?"

"Miscreant! Be thankful to draw such easy duty away
from the towns."

"Easy? You read the reports of gunpowder burns.
They were attacked by Murad Bey."

"You'd prefer the villages, where the plague is

rampant and every peasant with a pointed stick is ready to kill you? Or perhaps you wish you'd been among the ten thousand at Akoubir Bay last week."

"That was a battle I'd have preferred. The Turks thought they'd repeat what the British did to us there, but Napoleon defeated them soundly enough, didn't he?"

"It only delays the inevitable! Nelson's gone back to his waiting game, and the Ottoman troops mass again. We'll sail back to Paris on English ships yet."

"Paris. Well, as long as we don't have to deal with those English women. I prefer the Egyptians. Or their cattle."

Titters circled the group.

"They say when Bonaparte visited the pyramids, he asked to be alone in the king's chamber to commune with the pharaohs. He came out white as a ghost, shaking. He refused to say what he'd seen, and ordered, *ordered*, that the incident never be mentioned again."

"Maybe it was an English woman!"

"Oh, mon cher petit caporal, permettez-moi de vous montrer ma mince pie!"

Jeremiah took their loud laughter as his signal to leave. Fifty yards from the camp, a commotion made him turn back. The two thieving boys, roughly held by an oxlike, unshaven sergeant, were thrown into the campfire's light. They fell to their knees, begging.

There wasn't any time for him to change what happened. The unshaven sergeant pulled a pistol. A sharp crack filled the air and the taller boy flew backward, carried by his ruptured head. He lay on the ground, his twitching body casting obscene shadows along the desert floor. The younger boy stood frozen, watching his companion's death throes, until a soldier's bayonet provided a quicker death.

Jeremiah stopped in his tracks. He could beat the soldiers senseless and indulge his own feral nature, but the boys would still be dead, and there were many more starving in this country that he would never see. Skog was right when he called his anger useless.

He returned to Al-Hawa and pressed the horse into a gallop. He made her run so fast he sometimes lost sight of the tracks, but still wouldn't let her stop until she nearly collapsed. He told himself he raced to save Amala, to find salvation, to stop whatever evil Skog planned with the stone. In truth, he raced because his thoughts were infested with cruel images of dying children, and the immediate sensation of the sweaty equine heat beneath him was all that there was to remind him of the value of living.

By noon, the lifeless, oceanic dunes flattened into plains dotted with spidery shrubs. Far ahead of Jeremiah, a group of men rode. They'd be indistinguishable from a nomadic family or loose-knit jihadist militia were it not for the tall covered wagon plodding in their midst, pulled by eight horses.

Hylic, the one who'd given Jeremiah the canvas, led the caravan. Neither Skog nor Amala were visible. He guessed the Abenaki would be in the wagon, near the stone and away from the daylight. Amala, if still with them, must be there, too.

Jeremiah stopped at the edge of the dunes to watch their progress, letting Al-Hawa drink greedily from the water-skins he'd filled for the journey. At night, even in shade, he might slip past the men, but noon offered no

shadows on the flat plain. They'd see him coming, open
fire, and that, at the least, would slow him. Worse, Skog
had proven the superior fighter. Facing him without a
plan would be pointless.

After half a mile, one of the horses pulling the wagon
listed sideways and nearly fell from exhaustion. Hylic
raised his hand, and the caravan stopped. Confident
they'd be there for a time, Jeremiah rode Al-Hawa along
the edge of the dunes until the distance made him comfortable that he could cross onto the plain unseen. A patch
of distant palms and boxlike houses indicated they'd
reentered the world of men. He left his horse and headed
toward the hovels to watch their approach. He hoped to
get close enough to hear them talk and maybe glean their
destination and intent.

The people here were humble dirt farmers, toiling in
small watermelon fields that required constant irrigation.
It was far more difficult work than the rocky New England dirt he'd once cursed.

As he neared one of the hovels, a dog, having caught
Jeremiah's unnatural scent, yapped from inside. Villagers he could hide from, but the little high-pitched bark
might alert the Bandites. Worse, the agitated sound was
soon answered by more dogs, each calling the other from
the safety of the sparsely placed homes. But it dawned
on Jeremiah there was no need for concern. Skog would
likely assume himself responsible for the commotion.

He made his way to the doorless entry of the nearest
one-room home. A dog, a small, starving thing, stood in
the center of the room, baring its fangs protectively. The
only furniture was a table and a stool. On the stool sat a
middle-aged woman, head covered, arms wrapped around

two children. At this time of day, her husband might be
out farming, or begging, or perhaps he was dead, a victim
of the war or the plague.

Jeremiah hovered at the door, covered in his ragged
tarp, unwilling to cross the threshold and disturb the fragile home. He spoke softly, tried to sound harmless, and
offered the woman far too many coins in exchange for
clothing. Once she saw the money, she complied. Still,
she remained more afraid than grateful, perhaps thinking
he was insane or ill.

He walked to another house, this one abandoned.
One wall had collapsed and its thatched ceiling folded
inward. After calling Al-Hawa to join him, he sat in it
and arranged the robes that the woman had sold him.
They were softer and more flexible than the canvas,
and that was good, but there was barely enough to
cover him.

He and the horse remained hidden inside as the caravan rode through the village, bringing the barking to a
wild crescendo. Jeremiah counted the heartbeats of thirty
men. No one, not the men or the villagers, spoke a word.
Eventually the barking diminished, and the sound of the
horses faded. Jeremiah looked out and saw the caravan
inch along the eastern horizon, the surreal rectangle of
the wagon bobbing like the pull-toy of a gargantuan
child. He climbed on Al-Hawa's back and followed, staying among the cover of the dilapidated houses as long as
possible.

Avoiding main roads, the caravan crept due north.
There were more towns as they progressed, too small for
the French to bother occupying. Their inhabitants were
too cowed to even stare. The terrain grew more uneven,

allowing Jeremiah to keep closer and still believe himself unseen.

Within a few nights, he caught the smell of brine. They *were* hauling their burden toward the coast. In time, he heard the surf of the Mediterranean. Though there were towns far east and west, ahead there seemed to be nothing but date palms.

With little before them but the sea, Jeremiah kept some low hills between himself and the caravan. As the ocean wind picked up, a stark vertical line appeared on the horizon, far straighter and taller than the palms. It soon revealed itself as a ship's single mast. The flag it bore was French. It was so close to the portless shore, Jeremiah realized it must be moored to rendezvous with the caravan.

He climbed the remaining hills on foot, then took to his belly, staying low to the ground as he reached the crest. The land, thick with grass, palm, and bush, stopped right at the rippling water's beginning. Beyond them, the endless sky met the endless sea. Left and right, glowing port towns stuck up and out with hard angles, but here, in a spot either abandoned or disregarded by civilization, nature held sway.

The ship was anchored in a perfect spot, right below a hill crowned by a single thick tree. Its strong roots jutted into the air some ten feet above the waterline. Hurricane lanterns along the ship's deck outlined its size and shape. It was just shy of a hundred feet, with sixteen guns on its single deck. He recognized it as a corvette, designed for coastal defense. The gargantuan ships of the line, which could carry more than a hundred guns, would dwarf it, but the corvette's hold was ample and its speed made it a reasonable choice for transporting the stone.

Horses, men, and now a French ship. If Bandias survived in civilization's shadow, it seemed his followers did as well. Could the cultists be working with Napoleon to secretly transport the stone back to France?

The wagon was backed up the hill, bringing it roughly above the ship. Hylic, looking slightly haggard from the journey but no less serene, led ten men on a climb down to the deck. There they were met by a tall, stately figure in a French captain's uniform. Proud medals glistened on his jacket, but the smell of his anxiety carried thick in the air.

As the captain watched the Bandites swarm his sleek vessel, he rubbed his hands and slouched. When the French flag came down and was tossed into the sea, he seemed wounded. If it were some secret mission, the captain would be fearful, but not ashamed. His mien was more that of a traitor.

When the captain joined Hylic's men in tossing a series of canvas-wrapped bundles over the railing, Jeremiah's guess was proven correct. As they sank, human limbs protruded from the folds. Jeremiah wondered how much this man had been paid to murder his own crew.

Next the men assembled a wooden trestle on the hilltop, probably the same used in the desert. Once it was complete, the carriage door opened. Within, Jeremiah glimpsed Skog's black and burgundy robes just before they vanished. A moment later, the Abenaki reappeared on deck.

Seeing him, the guilty captain's heartbeat quickened, but not from mere fear. This was a sound Jeremiah knew well, the sound all mammal hearts made when their owner was convinced it was about to die.

The carriage's wooden roof was lifted, revealing the stone. If the thing within it knew Jeremiah was near, it said nothing.

The captain rubbed his hands faster as he spoke to Skog. Fall had the impression he was asking for payment. When he finished and awaited a reply, Skog pulled off his mask, baring his emotionless face. The captain froze for an instant, puzzled by Skog's foreign features, then went back to rubbing his hands.

Jeremiah never saw Skog's head turn, but one moment it looked at the captain; the next it was facing Jeremiah. Jeremiah ducked and cursed himself. Realizing that hiding was a fruitless gesture if he'd been spotted, he raised his head again to watch.

Skog's hand appeared atop the captain's head. He clutched the white hair on the crown of the man's skull into his fist, then moved so swiftly and powerfully down and to the right that not only did the neck bones snap, but also the flesh tore. An upward yank brought the head free of the body. Skog tossed it overboard, where it plopped in the waves. As the captain's body crumpled, Skog fell upon it and fed.

The callous killing repulsed Jeremiah, until the blood-smell reached him and stirred the beast with longing. He was about to turn and hide until he could bring himself under control, when another figure emerged from the top-less carriage. *Amala.*

New feelings—relief and elation—mingled with the hungry rush.

Yes.

Jeremiah looked down and swallowed hard. Why was that damned voice speaking now? Was it talking to him, or was he overhearing its approval of Skog's murderous ways?

He shook the hypnotic feeling and looked again. Skog was gone, as was the captain's body. Hylic was mopping the spilled blood on the deck. Amala, meanwhile, was pulled by two men, who took her to the ship and led her below deck. The closing hatch provided a final glimpse of her dark-skinned face.

He wished he could somehow let her know he was near.

The stone was transferred to the corvette. The Bandites, having swapped desert robes for sailor garb, readied the sails. They'd want to cover as much distance as possible before sunrise, not for Skog, but to give themselves the best chance of avoiding the constant English patrols.

The ship creaked and tilted. Its bow turned north. Jeremiah slipped down the hill and raced back to Al-Hawa. He took some meager supplies, money, his knife, the Geneva Bible, and transferred them to a smaller bag he could strap to his back. He stripped off the robes, leaving himself in the soldier's pants and sand-colored shirt.

"Good-bye, Al-Hawa," he said to the horse.

She snorted, and then nuzzled him. He petted her, whispering, "Trust me, you'll live longer without me. Go."

She bristled at the command, as if she did have some loyalty to him beyond his powers, but then galloped west.

By the time Jeremiah returned to the coast, the corvette's sails were raised and filling. He flew past the empty carriage and dove into the sea, wondering where on earth this mad journey would take him next.

15

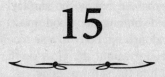

The water was cloudy, thick with silt churning from the ship's wake as it moved through the shallows. Though Jeremiah didn't have to breathe as he swam, he raised his eyes repeatedly to the surface to make certain he was headed the right way. The corvette's sails were swollen by a steady easterly wind. The ship tilted with it, gaining speed. If he didn't reach it soon, he never would.

When the waters beneath him blackened with depth, he submerged completely, lest his furious strokes be seen. Strong currents buffeted him. If strength alone were the issue, he'd have reached the ship by now, but it took him time to figure out how to work with the water's flow. At last, his hands reached the hull. His grip was tenuous, but his fingers quickly found a soft section of pitch between the timbers, and dug in. He let the vessel carry him, wondering how long the trip would be and what sort of sustenance fish-blood would provide.

Though the corvette bore no flag, any good captain would recognize the design as French. Still they managed to avoid the English coastal patrols and were soon in the open sea.

By night, he calculated their heading by the stars. By day, he remained below the surface, scratching out better handholds among the wood, moss, and barnacles. There he abandoned his body to a semiconscious state to preserve his energy, until the glow on the surface faded enough to tell him the sun was gone.

For days, he debated whether to risk a climb to a porthole or gunport through which he might spy Amala, or the stone, or at least overhear the Bandites talking. He feared it would be foolish, too easy for Skog to sense him on the small ship. In time, concern over his ignorance of what went on above grew stronger than his fear of being caught. So, one night, Jeremiah crept upward, clinging lizardlike to the wood. Trying to remain hidden in the ship's wake, he studied each opening for clues to what might lie beyond it.

As he worked, the weather shifted, the clouds darkened, and a chill swept the air. Before he could return to the spot he'd carved for himself, the corvette was lashed by high waves and winds. The storm, though not the worst he'd seen, stymied the ship's headway and shrank his visibility. It was soon impossible for him to tell in which direction they sailed, or what lay beyond each swell.

A commotion on deck told Jeremiah that the crew was worried about more than the choppy seas. Scanning the roiling waters, he spotted the cause of their concern: a dark, distant triangle that grew larger with each passing wave. It was a British frigate on a course to intercept, the foul weather making it easier for the larger, better-gunned ship to catch them.

The corvette tried to flee, but the frigate dogged them. Hours later, the worst of the storm passed, and it was apparent the little ship had failed to outrun its pursuer. The frigate trimmed sail and slipped closer. By midday, they were in range of its guns. The British vessel turned its starboard side, with its two rows of cannons, toward the corvette. Its guns outnumbered theirs more than two to one.

Shots were fired, likely intended as warnings. Owing to the unpredictability of the sea, one cannonball tore into the bow, dusting Jeremiah's face with splinters and rattling the length of the ship. It was a moment of truth. If the corvette returned fire, the frigate's cannons would rip them apart, sending the ship and the stone to the bottom of the sea.

"Lower your sails and prepare to be boarded!" a thick Irish brogue, amplified by a brass speaking-trumpet, called from the frigate's deck.

The corvette did not respond.

"Lower your sails or have your belly ripped open!"

"A moment, please!"

It was Hylic's tenor voice, faint and unamplified, calling back in stiff English. Jeremiah doubted the frigate's captain would wait. If he attacked, at least it would solve one problem. Losing Bandias to the ocean floor would free the world of one monster. At the same time, forfeiting the stone would mean severing any link to the secrets of what Jeremiah was and the cure he longed for.

Once again, he'd have to choose a side; once again, he wished the choice were clearer. Even if the ship were sunk, Skog would survive, and that would lead to the slaughter of the frigate's crew.

What then? Sink the frigate instead? The distance

wasn't far. If Jeremiah could board it and reach the second deck, he could incapacitate some of the gunners and fire one or more of their cannons downward into their own hull. A slow but fatal blow to the English ship would give the British time to reach their lifeboats. Skog, who seemed in a hurry, probably wouldn't bother with them then. The stone and many lives would be spared.

A sharp splash ended his ruminations. Jeremiah saw a mix of black and burgundy beneath the water, speeding toward the frigate. Skog must have had something akin to the same idea. Jeremiah doubted, though, that the survival of the sailors figured into his calculations.

Releasing his hold, Jeremiah followed him into the underwater silence. He saw Skog's inky form curve beneath the frigate's bottom as effortlessly as a bird gliding through air. Could he somehow pin the monster on the frigate, trapping him there as it sank? Ropes and dirt, after all, had kept the creature imprisoned for decades.

In seconds, Fall came up against the copper sheets that protected the lower hull of the English ship. He broke the surface, surprised to see the corvette's mainsail lowered. Apparently they were complying with the British captain's request.

"Prepare to be boarded!"

"Who do I have the pleasure of addressing?" Hylic called back.

"Captain Ryan Doyle of King George's fleet."

"I am Hylic Kirillov."

"Kirillov? A Russian? What are you doing commanding a French-built ship? Did you capture it? Where's your flag?" Doyle's voice was no longer quite so commanding.

At first, Jeremiah thought it foolish to have the soft-spoken Hylic play at being captain, but now he realized the strategy. The Russians were all but English allies, part of the coalition trying to push back the French. While a closer inspection would reveal the crew's varied nationalities, for now it made Doyle hesitate.

"May I kindly come aboard to discuss the situation?"

Doyle didn't answer immediately, so Hylic continued. "All advantage is yours, Captain Doyle. We are outmanned and outgunned. If I am your guest, it proves we will not attack or flee. I can promise my words will interest you."

"All right," Doyle said. "I'll send a boat to get you."

"Thank you. I will be waiting."

By the time the dinghy set out, Jeremiah was close enough to hear Doyle whisper to his first mate, "Are the guns at the ready?" and the answer, "Aye."

The man, no fool, was preparing for any possibility, but how could anyone be ready for Skog?

With the English crew's full attention starboard, between the ships, Jeremiah pulled himself to the frigate's port. Relatively safe in the overcast day, he climbed to the second deck's gunports and peered inside. The cannon deck was open for the length of the ship, but his line of sight was broken by support beams, crates, stacks of supplies, ropes, and ammunition.

A complement of ten stood at their cannons, backs to Jeremiah. As they awaited orders, they strained to see outside. There was no sign of Skog on board yet. Trying to find someone who could hide in the shadows as easily as Jeremiah would be a waste of time. Instead, if he moved quickly, he might need to fight only these ten.

Jeremiah entered through the gunport, slipped to the side of the first cannon, then pressed himself into the plentiful shadow. Here, he paused to sort the murmur of conversation from above. Doyle's voice, easiest to hear, was full of new doubt. Hylic had apparently reached the frigate.

"A *secret* mission for Tsar Alexander? What sort of object do you carry for him?"

"That cannot be said," Hylic answered.

"Why should I believe a word of this nonsense? Do you have official papers to identify yourself?"

"Of course." The eerie peacefulness that inhabited Hylic's voice grew even more extreme with his lies.

"Where are they? Show them to me at once."

The click of a locking pistol hammer signaled the end of Doyle's patience. Jeremiah would have to act. Two crates and a stack of cannonballs stood between him and the nearest members of the gunnery crew.

"Think Doyle will shoot him?" one said.

"I've seen him do worse and get away with it."

Jeremiah slammed their heads together, then slipped back into hiding. He vanished so quickly that when their fellows turned at the sound of their bodies hitting the wood, they had no idea they were no longer alone. Leaving their posts, six gunners hurried toward their unconscious comrades. They bent over the prone bodies, forming a tight group in the awkward space. That was exactly what Jeremiah had hoped they'd do.

He sprang out and forced the heel of his hand into the back of one man's skull. He rammed his elbow into the jaw of another. Shock riding their initial surprise, the last four barely managed to raise their hands in vague gestures of self-defense before he dispatched them. The slight thuds of the scuffle mixed easily with the creak of timbers as the ship rocked in the waves.

Farther along the deck, the men remained focused on the vessel across from their cannons. Perfect.

He pulled two, then four cannons free from their braces and aimed them down at the center of the floor. He was about to try for six when he was spotted. One of the gunners, a wide, barrel-chested man, face so sunburned the skin was peeling in clumps, had leaned back against a support beam. Seeing Jeremiah and the cannons, the ovals of his eyes stretched so far they seemed to meet his raised eyebrows.

He pointed at Jeremiah and opened his mouth, making the brittle skin near his lips crack. He was about to shout, but before he could, the hull beside him burst into pieces. Beyond him, more explosions were visible. The black iron of cannonballs led sprays of red and orange flame across the ship, ripping through whatever wood, metal, or flesh lay in their path.

Jeremiah was hurled onto his back before his brain registered what must have happened—in a surprise attack, the corvette had fired all its guns at the frigate. A sharp rumble indicated a second set of cannon fire, this time, from the frigate. Yet, surprisingly, nothing flew across the small space at the corvette. The French ship was untouched. Instead the bigger vessel rattled again, the cracking of wood joined by the frantic howls of men.

Through involutions of fire and smoke, Jeremiah saw a man-sized shadow tinged with burgundy soar through one of the gaping holes, back into the sea. Skog. He'd had the same thought as Jeremiah. Judging from the sounds that came from the ship's stern, he'd also commandeered far more cannons.

Above a growing din, Doyle shouted, "Your own men *kill* you?"

Hylic Kirillov raised his voice, not out of fear, but out of politeness. "It's an honor."

The frigate, a fine English construct designed by practiced minds, built by steady hands, sailed by skilled men, and guided by a seasoned captain, bobbed helplessly as chaos rippled through it.

Doyle ordered his men to return fire, but the surviving crew, startled by the inner and outer explosions, could not respond with any speed. By the time they did fire, their aim was spoiled by the swiftly tilting deck. Skog had planned his strike wisely. Seawater rushing in from below weighed the vessel so it listed increasingly away from its target.

As the floor beneath him tipped, Jeremiah moved, shoving the wounded and unconscious through a starboard rupture so they wouldn't be trapped when the ship went down. As he worked, the jagged circle in the thick timbers showed less and less of the corvette and more of its flagless mast and the sky.

Above, Doyle screamed the order to abandon ship. Jeremiah heard the crew struggle to lower the lifeboats. By the time the stolen corvette fired a second round, the frigate's failing hull moaned all along its length.

Jeremiah knew he should leave, but a memory held him back, the imagined image of his brother—the starving infant Jim—gasping for breath beneath the waves. What if Skog had left more living men behind to drown? The deck at a forty-degree angle and rising, he ran toward the stern. He flew around wheeling cannons snapped free from their braces, fallen supplies, burning timbers, and the dead.

As he traveled the length of the ship, he counted twenty corpses, their bodies so mangled they seemed like fleshy seaweed floating in the gushing water. If their deaths were quick, Jeremiah thought it more likely the result of Skog's efficiency than of any sense of mercy.

With a massive sigh, the frigate lurched forward and down. Realizing that whoever was going to survive was no longer on board, Jeremiah clambered to the nearest breach. Through it, he spied the corvette, sails raised as it headed off through choppy waters. It was just under way and not moving too fast yet. He could catch it easily. He was about to leap when a sudden break in the cloud cover allowed the sun to pour through the breach. The deadly brightness drove Jeremiah back into the doomed ship.

Repeating some of the more imaginative curses he'd learned in six different languages, he looked around for something to cover himself. Too late. The frigate rolled onto its side, piling crates and cannons atop him as it slipped beneath the waves.

Jeremiah couldn't drown, so far as he knew, but the speed with which the hulk sank made him consider the possibility that he'd soon be trapped at the sea's bottom for all eternity.

16

The maze of wreckage that pinned him, the sunlight that had kept Jeremiah Fall inside the hull, both seemed acts of spite on the part of the heavens. Timber, ropes, cannons, chests, barrels, even a section of the hull with the porthole intact locked together above him like twigs in a gargantuan bird nest. But as the water filled the sinking ship, the ballast righted its descent. The weights rolled away as easily as they'd gathered, allowing him to slip into the sea.

His freedom brief, he soon became entangled in the sail. The ship's twisting descent had snapped the mainmast, pulling the giant canvas down alongside the sinking vessel's body. Fall ripped the thick cloth easily, even tearing off a section large enough to wrap himself in, in case the sun above was still bright.

The surface seemed so distant. How many fathoms had he sunk? He squinted, trying to make sense of the light and dark that played above. The tiny lines were likely lifeboats; the feathery white must be the wake of the fleeing corvette.

He kicked and swam, passing among drowned bodies pulled down by the undertow. The currents moved their limbs in a macabre, otherworldly dance. Trying to focus on the corvette, he did his best to ignore them, but one corpse, its clothes too small for its bulk, looked familiar. Swimming closer, he recognized the fake captain, the Russian, Hylic Kirillov.

Whether it was his insane desire for death or just the sound of his voice, the cultist had rankled Fall from the moment he first heard him speak. He was quiet now, though, drifting, arms akimbo, legs splayed. A wound on his arm oozed black into the ocean's drab green. A hundred times stronger than the smell of blood in the air, it made Jeremiah tremble. He'd have to move away quickly, before the beast could convince him to sip the tainted water.

But then Hylic opened his eyes, focused on Jeremiah, and offered a horrible grin.

Startled, Jeremiah shivered backward. He was alive, but too far underwater to save himself. What of it? Wasn't death his self-proclaimed honor? Who was Jeremiah to interfere? But with the corvette speeding away, this man was likely his only link to its destination.

Reluctantly, he grabbed Hylic's shoulder, planning to drag him to the surface. When the Russian realized what was happening, his smile vanished and he tried to struggle free. His arm flashed through the water, bending the wound, making more blood seep from the gash. The thick, inky blobs sent Jeremiah's senses reeling.

The beast, seizing its chance, careened by Jeremiah's well-honed defenses with such force it seemed as if it'd been hiding its full strength all along. It wrested control of his muscles and forced the simple action it required; the parting of Jeremiah's lips.

His mouth filled with salty liquid, his tongue instantly sorting the taste of sea from blood. His body shuddered, and his senses drowned in a wondrous agony of pleasure.

Furious to have his vow broken in such a stupid, senseless way, Jeremiah pushed aside the joy of the taste, pulled back his arm, and punched Hylic in the nose, just hard enough to knock him out. Hissing out the bloody water, he turned the wild surge of energy to another purpose: dragging them both to the surface.

It will be easier next time, the beast said.

Jeremiah ignored the voice as he pulled himself into the air. The corvette was long gone. Several lifeboats huddled in the midst of the frigate's flotsam. No doubt they were searching for more survivors. Not wanting to be found, he submerged slightly, along with his unconscious companion.

Hylic Kirillov might well have drowned anyway had Jeremiah not found a capsized lifeboat. He surfaced beneath it, bringing his head into the air pocket it held. In the close space, the last thrill from the taste of human blood finally weakened. He pulled Hylic's face into the air and slapped his cheeks. A slight, phlegmatic cough told him the man's incomprehensible urge to die had been thwarted.

Still angry at his inadvertent indulgence, Jeremiah began the long, arduous task of nudging the overturned boat away from the others. Once he was certain they were far enough, he flipped the boat upright and heaved Hylic's unconscious form inside. Climbing in himself, he looked at his captive, imagined a dozen situations in which it would be appropriate to kill him, and hoped at least one would come to pass.

As part of the boat's design, the oars were stored firmly beneath the seats. By the time Hylic awoke, Jeremiah was rowing through increasingly high waves, trying to steer by the evening's first stars. At first, Hylic gave him a peaceful, enigmatic smile, but as he came more fully to his senses, he looked around, increasingly disturbed. When he realized his hands and legs were bound by strips of torn sail, he stopped smiling completely.

"Ya ne umer," he said in Russian. *I'm not dead.*

"No," Jeremiah answered in French, the easier language for him. "Sorry to disappoint you."

Hylic crinkled his eyes. "You're not sorry. You think you did the right thing."

"Not entirely," Jeremiah assured him. "But I need you alive. Where are they taking the stone?"

"If I tell you, will you kill me?"

"Doesn't that usually work the other way? You tell me what I want to know so I *don't* kill you?"

Smiling, Hylic pulled himself up, trying to attain a more comfortable seated position. "Things don't always work the way you expect."

Jeremiah snapped the oars, sending the lifeboat lurching forward, throwing the man onto his back.

"You're right. Things don't always work the way you expect," Jeremiah said. "Where are they taking the stone?"

Hylic stared. "If you won't kill me, why should I tell you? You don't understand anything. That woman *told* you the story, and you still don't understand."

When Jeremiah bristled at the mention of Amala, his captive's eyes narrowed. "You have feelings for her? She told us she translated the stone for you, and a little bit about your background, but nothing else. Why Skog hasn't fed on her yet I still don't know. It would make her more cooperative." Hylic leaned forward, a sympathetic look on his face. "You don't have to kill me yourself, you know. Toss me over and let me drown. Promise to do that, and I'll tell you everything, for all the good it will do you."

"It doesn't make any sense. Why not just kill yourself? Are you afraid?"

Hylic shrugged. "No. It just can't be my decision."

Staring at his silly smile, it occurred to Jeremiah why this man irritated him so. While Jeremiah clung to his existence despite its agony, he embraced the thought of oblivion with the giddiness of a child.

"*Why* do you want to die?"

Hylic rolled his eyes. "You wouldn't listen to Skog; why listen to me?"

Jeremiah nodded toward the miles of ocean. "I seem to have more time on my hands."

He pondered it a moment, then said, "Very well. *Why*? Because this dreadful, stupid world—the rocks, the sky, the seas, the stars, the yous, the mes, everything about it—is completely, totally *fake*. Even death. Aten only *thought* he was god, the way you *think* you're still a man. But he was deluded, and all that he made from insect to angel is likewise deceived. The life Aten created is not life, the death not death."

The story sounded familiar. "That's the old Gnostic heresy," Jeremiah said. "They believed the world was created by a false god called the demiurge. But a tiny bit of the divine was accidentally left in the illusion, so we each retain a spark. It can be reached through illumination and knowledge: Gnosis. They fought the early Christians for control of the Church, but faded out along with animal sacrifices and Zeus worshippers."

"Did they? Or did their ideas seep back in quiet ways? If the earth were created by a true God, why do you Puritans believe that Satan rules this world? That truth is only seen through a glass darkly?"

"What's that got to do with Bandias?"

"When Aten dipped his hands in the clay, he drew too much truth along with it, so much it threatened his self-deception. That's why Bandias had to be forgotten. Otherwise why not just destroy him? Why allow him to mate with Havah? The demiurge couldn't face the truth, but he knew he'd accidentally created something that could end the dream. Bandias is our savior. Why do you think I gave you that tarp in the cave? Because we worship you, as we worship all his children. Part of you must know all this. His truth burns in your veins. How can you see this world so much more clearly than I and still not see its seams?"

The prisoner lay back quietly for a while. When he struggled to sitting again, Jeremiah let him stay upright. After a few minutes of glancing at the stars, Hylic said, "You're rowing toward France, trying to follow the ship."

"Yes."

"You won't kill me. Can't talk you into feeding on me, can I?"

"No."

"Well then, the only thing to look forward to is rejoining my brothers. I'll tell you where they're going if you like."

Jeremiah stared at him. "Really? It's that simple?"

"An ancient city in France," Hylic said.

"Why there?"

"It's a nexus, a crack in the false creation, one of a few spots where Bandias can be freed."

"And then he'll start a murder spree like Skog?"

"What? You think he's like Skog, or you? No. Bandias will feed on creation itself. He'll take it apart, piece by piece, all of it, shattering the demiurge's dream. It will take him six days. On the seventh, well, the seventh won't be a day at all. *Apokalupsis eschaton.*"

It was Greek for the revelation at the end of the world, the removing of the veil. Apocalypse. Madness. The whole thing was madness. The pathetic man in Jeremiah's lifeboat was mad. For a moment, though, the parallels between the Gnostics and the Puritans echoing in his head, it *all* looked mad. The sea around him looked mad, the sky, the stars.

"How? How will Bandias be freed?"

Another wide smile from Hylic. "I'll tell you that, too, but only because it will make you row faster. An incantation written in the hieroglyphs must be read to free his spirit. Alone, it would take him until the year's end, December 31, 1799, to manifest a body. However, should one of his male children offer, Bandias can inhabit his body and use it to plant his seed in a woman, just as he did with Havah. Within a day, she'll birth Bandias fully into the false world, and he'll begin his work much sooner."

"Skog. Skog would take the role of Bandias's child."

"Well, seeing as how unlikely a candidate *you* are, with all your delusions, yes."

Jeremiah's heart filled with terror. "And the woman...would be Amala."

Hylic nodded. "She *can* read the magic writings, after all."

Jeremiah's arms tensed. He yanked and pulled the oars so hard that they threatened to snap. "You bastards, you filthy bastards!"

The Russian chuckled and settled back to the floor. No matter how Jeremiah twisted and turned the lifeboat in his efforts to gain speed, Hylic remained determined to enjoy the ride.

17

Dogged by visions of hell, Jeremiah Fall rowed through the abyss. Hylic Kirillov refused to say anything further about their destination, offering only cryptic questions:

"Do you know how Paris got its name?"

And, "Have you ever seen the standing stones at Salisbury Hill?"

It went on like that for five days. Jeremiah's haunted mind began providing waking dreams; a score of screaming mouths for every wave they passed, millions of tortured souls sharing a single mass of mangled torsos. More frightening than the phantasms was how numb his heart felt. Whenever he looked at Hylic Kirillov and wanted to kill him, he worried he was earning his own spot in the coming hell.

It ended in a hazy premorning glow. While Kirillov slept, what had seemed infinite ended. The horizon's thin line turned tan and green, then swelled, revealing faint clouds above the land's rough surface. Ten minutes later, a ruddy-skinned fisherman called to Jeremiah.

"Vous êtes des idiots d'etre à ce jour à la mer, cette petite chose! Retournez au port à la fois!" the gruff voice called. *You are idiots to be so far at sea in that tiny thing! Get back to port at once!* He thought they'd come from the nearby land instead of the ocean.

Jeremiah thanked him and kept rowing. He avoided the port and aimed for a beach to the north that was far too rocky and inhospitable to be anything but lonely. Covered with his tattered bit of sail, he leaped from the boat, surprised how queer solid land felt beneath him. He pulled at the prow, pushing his feet against submerged rocks and broken clamshells. Before he could bring it fully ashore, a high wave smashed the boat sideways into a half-buried boulder, cracking the wood and waking its remaining passenger.

"We're sinking!" Hylic cried.

"We're here," Jeremiah answered.

"France?"

Not answering, he yanked Hylic and the cracked boat farther from the waves. He took them to a sandy spot concealed by an awkward ring of brown and black rocks, their surfaces marred by seagull droppings and the rough green crust of marine life.

"Are you going to pull me the whole way?" Hylic asked.

Jeremiah turned the boat sideways and sent him sprawling onto the sand.

Hylic coughed and sat up. "Have you ever seen the standing stones at Salisbury Hill? Do you know how Paris got its name?"

"Wait here," Jeremiah said.

"Ah, a joke," Hylic said, holding up his bound wrists.

Ignoring him, Jeremiah headed into town. In the shade between buildings, he hunted water rats and listened to the villagers' conversations. His navigation wasn't so bad after all. They were in Port Vendres, a small fishing town on France's Vermillion Coast, just large enough to offer a decent selection of supplies. Checking the single bag he'd brought from Egypt, Jeremiah counted the coins he'd been awarded for his discovery of the stone in Rashid. Handy to have French coins in France.

The first shop he entered was dark enough for him to keep his head uncovered. The owner, a thick-armed woman with fishlike eyes, gawked at his battered appearance just the same. Because of the soldier's pants he still wore, she'd likely sized him up as a deserter. As he changed into the clothing he bought behind a room divider, he caught the sharp scent of her agitation. She was clearly eager to share news of her odd customer.

As he left her store dressed in overcoat, hat, and scarf, she continued to study him from the doorway. When the first slight shadow made itself available, he used it to vanish before her eyes. Glancing back, he enjoyed her stunned expression, pleased to think that if she spoke of a disappearing man, her eyesight, not him, would be the bigger topic of gossip.

Alone, he could travel relentlessly on foot, but having the Bandite to consider, he'd need horses, so he located a ramshackle stable. Its two aging mares whinnied at his presence. He silenced them quickly, disappointed at the thin taste of their blood, not bothering to regret the assault until it dawned on him that maybe he was becoming cruel.

When he tried to purchase them, the bearish stable

owner, distrusting Jeremiah's appearance and American accent, overcharged exorbitantly. It was a mistake not to haggle, because it doubled the man's suspicions, but he felt harried. Even if Bandias could not deconstruct the world, even if the stone held no cure, Amala was still in danger.

As he returned to the lifeboat, Hylic's jaunty whistle rattled him. He dumped food and fresh clothes into the man's lap. The Bandite grimaced and raised his wrists again.

"You've no reason to keep me tied. Until we find my brethren, you and I have a common purpose. Besides, I'm not Skog. Even if I did run, you could catch me easily."

Finding no flaw to the logic, Fall pulled out the old bayonet blade and sliced him free. Hylic sighed with relief. He set to rubbing the deep marks on his wrists and ankles. All at once, he looked up at Jeremiah and made a face.

"What is it?" Jeremiah asked.

"This constant dourness doesn't suit you. Of course, the future frightens you, but even I don't think about Bandias all the time."

"We're in Europe, Kirillov. Why don't you just tell me where they're taking the stone?"

"I've been *trying* to tell you. Do you know how Paris got its name? Have you seen the standing stones?"

"I don't have time to waste on riddles. Is it Paris?"

"No," Hylic said. He gathered the clothes Jeremiah had brought for him and took them to the far side of the boat to change. "You could just answer the questions."

"Hurry up," Jeremiah said. "The woman at the store didn't care for the way I looked, and the stable owner didn't like the way I spoke. The villagers may start looking for me."

Hylic chortled. "Is that why the bad mood? I will hurry, then, not only because it suits my purpose, but also because I like you. I think I like you more than I like Skog. Then again, he's already abandoned so much of his humanity, he's more like a tree or a mountain. One can admire such things, but they're not pleasant to chat with. Deep down, you and I are more alike. Though I freely admit I'm a rank amateur in comparison, we both fight instinct for the sake of principle. I fight my body's desire for survival. You, well, in your case, you fight your entire nature."

"We are *not* alike," Jeremiah said.

Hylic stepped out and held his gaze. "Aren't we? You were a farmer before your life was shattered? I was born in a decorated military family, educated in Moscow. I became a proud officer under our enlightened empress Catherine and hoped to bring our great ideals into the northern Caucasus. But when the people there didn't want them, our plan to make them accept was simple: For the death of every Russian soldier, we burned an entire village and killed all the people in it; for the death of every officer, two villages.

"I don't remember exactly how many women and children I shot as they tried to flee. At first, killing them seemed less cruel than letting them live. Then, I felt nothing at all. I thought some part of me had died, until in one town I met a crone who explained to me that of course this mad world was false—and the proper feeling for nothing is nothing. It made more sense than anything else I'd ever heard or seen. Her face I remember. She had the sweetest smile as I stabbed her. Thanked me with her last breath, and even told me where to find a group of Bandites to begin my new life. You'll come to the same moment someday, I'm sure. Maybe when you finally realize that killing is an act of love."

Jeremiah grabbed Hylic's throat, and lifted and squeezed until his eyes bulged and his quivering lips went blue around the edges. With a voice reduced to a gurgle, Hylic managed to say, "To die... would be... an honor..."

"I could give you worse than death, you know," Jeremiah snarled. "I could make us truly alike. I could let you become what I am."

At last, for an instant, the Bandite seemed worried. "Would... you?"

Jeremiah hissed and let go.

Hylic coughed. His face turned red, then pink. He clambered to a sitting position. "I'm trying to teach you. That's the point of my questions, to show you how truths are wrapped inside truths."

"I don't need your lessons. I just need the facts."

"Ah, but you see, you do need my lessons, badly. In a false world, any supposed fact, any history, any story, is like a living thing, changing to ensure its own survival. Don't tell me you've never encountered a tale that took on a life of its own?"

Twinkle, twinkle, little star.

"Ah. I see from your face that you have. Do you know how Paris got its name?"

Though Fall had no need of breath, he sighed. "It was named after the Parisii, the Gaulish tribe that originally lived there."

"That's one answer. Do you know what the Bretons say?"

"The Celtic group in the northwest? No. I don't know much about them other than that they settled in France from Britain around the fourth century. Most of them still speak their own dialect."

"That's what I mean about facts. In Brittany, they'd tell you Paris is actually named after a far older, far greater city, one whose existence stretches back before recorded history. They'd tell you that France's latter-day capital earned its name because it was considered on a *par* with it. You see?"

"No, I don't. I don't see," Jeremiah said. "Tell me what you're talking about before I wring your neck again."

Hylic shook his head, disappointed. "I'm drawing you a map to the borderlands, the place between myth and supposed truth, and you give me a threat you know is useless against me?"

Jeremiah grimaced. "You're right. Arrogance is folly."

"Well that's a pretty saying, isn't it? Be as arrogant as you like for all I care, just try to listen. In Brittany, they say Paris was named because it is on par with Ys. Parys. Paris. I'm talking about the city of Ys."

Jeremiah searched his memory. "The legend of King Gradlon?"

"Yes!" Hylic said, clapping his hands together. "You know the story."

Jeremiah nodded. "He was an early version of King Arthur. He fell madly in love with a sorceress he'd captured from a sea kingdom, but she died in childbirth, leaving him heartbroken. He turned to the Church and invited them into his lands, but the priests made his daughter, Dahut, miserable. She begged him to build her a city near a group of ancient stones so she could worship there as her mother did. Only the stones were submerged whenever the tide rose. He was warned that the idea was mad, that Dahut was evil, but she was the only thing left of the woman he loved, so he did it. His engineers made a wall to hold back the sea, and his architects built the city, Ys.

"It became a place of orgies, blasphemous rituals—a new Sodom and Gomorrah. Finally, God sent a storm to destroy it. King Gradlon tried to save Dahut, racing the rising sea on a horse with her at his back. Angels appeared, saying Dahut was a demon and that Ys and his nation would survive only if he let the waves take her. So he did. He tossed his only child to the sea." Like Atticus and Jim.

"Now what's the tale inside the tale? Who do you suppose Dahut worshipped?"

"Bandias."

"Excellent. And she had Ys built on that spot because it was a nexus where the forgotten man could be freed. If she'd found the buried stone before the demiurge stepped in with his storm and his 'angels,' she might've succeeded."

"The city is real?"

Hylic chuckled. "As real as anything."

Legend placed the ruins in Douarnenez Bay, on the tip of France's northwestern coast. Rather than deal with the uncertain boundary between history and myth, which Hylic seemed eager for him to embrace, Jeremiah fell to calculating, comforted by the reliability of abstract numbers. "It's clear across the country, seven hundred miles. On horseback, with good weather, we might make a hundred a day."

Jeremiah headed for the horses, calling back over his shoulder, "Did Skog plan to travel the whole route by sea?"

Hylic followed. "He intended to. I doubt the encounter with the frigate humbled him, but it may have changed his plans." Hylic squinted at the animals. "Fine mares, if you like the elderly. Why aren't they afraid of you?"

Hylic peered at their neck wounds and opened his mouth in mock surprise.

"I've fed on horses before," Jeremiah said, climbing into his saddle.

"You're a tale within a tale yourself, Jeremiah Fall," Hylic said.

The sun was low over the northwest road. Jeremiah squirmed as he rode toward the light.

"Have you read Cervantes?" Hylic called from behind. "Don Quixote de la Mancha?"

"Another game?" Jeremiah asked. He squinted and tried to rearrange his scarf.

"No. It just occurred to me that you, heading off to save what you think is the world, are rather like the old knight tilting at windmills. I am your far more pragmatic Sancho Panza."

Seven hundred miles. Could he keep from killing him that long?

In France, a country disheveled from a revolution as endless as its foreign wars, there were scores of officials susceptible to bribe, a hundred places the corvette might land, and as many paths to Brittany as there were varieties of cheese and wine. Jeremiah doubted they would run into Skog, but he kept alert, constantly scanning the roads they traveled by night as well as the fields and vineyards they crisscrossed by day.

He tried to avoid as much of the mountainous Massif Central as possible, fearing their sorry horses wouldn't survive. When they reached the flat plains and rolling hills beyond, he felt some relief. Now they could make up for lost time.

But throughout, while Hylic seemed a pleased tourist, Jeremiah remained full of foreboding. He imagined hidden threats everywhere, wishing he could travel faster still. Only the long stretches of uneventful miles made him accept the journey's length and again wish for patience. Arrogance is folly. Patience the cure.

"Ever been to Paris?" Hylic asked as he eyed a mileage marker showing the city's distance. Jeremiah already regretted letting him purchase a bottle of wine when they'd stopped to rest.

"No. Never had cause."

"Never wanted to see that 12th century palace turned into a museum? Never wanted to take a flight in one of those hydrogen balloons created by Jacques Charles and the Robert brothers? We're not allowed to know the names of many other members, but I always suspected they were Bandites, proving the sky itself false."

"Or maybe they just saw the birds fly and wanted to see what it was like. And tell me something else, Kirillov—if you *do* believe it's all illusion, why bother to see Paris?"

He expected some clever retort, but either wine or the argument silenced Hylic. He stayed that way through the dawn and most of the day, lifting Jeremiah's spirits considerably.

They passed warm countryside, pastures of grazing cattle, and pleasant, peaceful villages. The northward miles brought cooler temperatures. In Rennes, Brittany's capital, Hylic was surprised to see Jeremiah purchase a small telescope.

"Skog said he has the vision of an eagle, but not you?"

"Even an eagle's vision can be improved," Jeremiah explained. He also wanted any advantage over Skog he could get.

Brittany proper surprised Jeremiah. It seemed a world apart, especially in its treatment of the opposite sex. It was so different from Egypt, where the Islamic women were relegated to household neighborhoods, or even the States, where certain roles were culturally forbidden. Here the women worked as freely as the men. There were even households consisting of unmarried women joined by trade and child-rearing. What would have been a scandal or a crime elsewhere seemed to work quite well here.

There was a darker side, too, a heightened anxiety. The Bretons eyed not only Jeremiah and Hylic with unease, but also each other. Those who spoke French distrusted the Celtic speakers, and everyone feared having enemy England so near. It was rumored Napoleon hoped to build a fleet of hydrogen balloons to float across the channel and bomb London. Who knew what the British had planned for them?

The journey ended the night they reached Pleu de Ver, a coastal village that smelled of the sardines that the Douarnenez Bay provided in great number. The place was sleepy and unencumbered by visible visitors or strangers, other than them.

"We must have gotten here ahead of Skog," Hylic said as he looked around. "Let's find a nice spot to wait, shall we, Fall?"

Jeremiah trotted forward on his horse, eyeing each person they passed.

Hylic followed. "Isn't it clear they're not here yet? And the horses are exhausted. You drove them too hard the last leg. Their flanks are soaked. My poor mount has foam on her lips. We should either let them rest or shoot them."

Jeremiah kept going. Of course, to human eyes, there would seem nothing unusual, but he had to be sure. Merchants took inventory, fishermen mended their nets, and workers unloaded supplies, preparing for the next day's work. Many wore the tapered caps that earned them the nickname *pen sardin*, sardine head, because its shape bore a slight resemblance to the fish that gave them their living. But the tension he'd sensed throughout the region was double in this town. Moreover, it mingled with anger and resentment, as if this quiet sanctuary had been invaded. But no one spoke of the cause, at least not in a language Jeremiah understood.

At last, his scrutiny paid off when a wizened stump of a man, fifty yards distant, raised his dry-apple face to stare in their direction.

In disgust, he whispered to his companion, *"Plus de gens de l'extérieur."*

More of the outsiders.

The Bandites were here. But where? Jeremiah silently commanded his horse, driving it forward.

"Where are you going? Really, there's nothing here," Hylic insisted. His protests sounded contrived. Had he lied about Ys? Even if he hadn't, their common purpose was at an end. He should tie the man up somewhere at his earliest opportunity.

"I want to see the ruins you claim are here," Jeremiah answered. He brought the horse to the water's edge, but a small island blocked his view. Inches below the surface, the vestiges of a land bridge were visible. He directed the horse across the water toward the isle.

"You don't think that's Ys, do you?" Hylic said, catching up. "Too small. Much too small."

Jeremiah turned back. "Tristan Island, according to what the fishermen were saying. The far side should give us a full view of the bay."

Hylic sighed and scratched the back of his neck.

Reaching dry ground, Jeremiah slipped from the saddle and let the horse rest at last. The scent of a sardine press overwhelmed the smell of the sea. The entirety of the little island was no more than fifteen hundred feet in length. Directly before him, rough stones were piled— old fortifications. Beyond that, the high sea cliffs that faced the bay blocked a longer view.

Hylic scratched the back of his head more fervently. This would be as good a place as any to tie him up, but first, Jeremiah wanted to see what lay beyond.

Jeremiah walked toward the cliffs, braced by a strong wind. Hylic followed, his fingers dancing so furiously at the back of his hair Jeremiah smelled the blood from the scratches. When he stopped to stare, Hylic sheepishly explained, "Some sort of insect bite. The flies here are bigger than the desert spiders."

A change in Kirillov's smell indicated his sudden tension. Jeremiah might have paid more attention to it, but as they walked up the cliffs and rounded the curve of the isle, a stunning vista was revealed. The center of the bay held a larger island, and Skog's corvette was anchored at its side. He'd found not only the Bandites, but also a place that would seem more at home in a dream.

Gradlon's legendary circular wall was intact, and within its confines lay a dozen impressive structures in various states of ruin. Were that not enough, oblong spheres, wider than the lunar crescent, hung low in the sky over the city center. It was no coincidence that Hylic had been discussing Charles' elongated hydrogen balloons, for here were four of them, their cloth colored white to help them blend into the clouds.

Eager to take in every detail, Jeremiah put the telescope to his eye. He'd never seen anything like these elongated balloons, but guessed they were based on a concept by the French engineer and general Meusnier, who envisioned using air cells to create a flying *dirigible*. As far as Fall knew, the only attempted flight had been unsuccessful when the pilots discovered they could not steer. These *airships* had no such problems. They maneuvered readily over the flat raised area they were positioned above, propelled by what looked like a small steam engine. Thick ropes trailed beneath them.

The hill itself was peopled with what the wizened Breton had called *outsiders*. They were Bandites, more than there'd been on the corvette, not just men, but women now as well.

The structures the cultists worked among evoked an even greater awe than the airships. On the hill, looking

older and more eternal than the sea, stood a series of great
ebony stones, arranged in careful circles, with some pairs
topped by horizontal slabs. They were like the drawings
Jeremiah had once seen of Stonehenge on Salisbury Hill,
but much, much larger.

It was then he realized the ropes beneath the dirigibles
didn't moor them. They held a final stone. Even now it
was being moved with the help of Bandites, tiny against
the scene, into the center of the black behemoths. It was
the stone, carried from the corvette to the island by the
impossible airships. It was now being set down in a spot
that looked carved just to hold it. Though the stones
around it were far taller and wider, its blackness glowed
so deeply, it made their darkness gray.

A sudden rush of air, too fast to be an insect, snapped
him from the scene.

"Hylic?" he said. There was something wrong with
his face.

"Thank you," Hylic gurgled. Blood from his mouth
spattered his lips.

He fell backward. Jeremiah caught him, but not before
his back hit the ground. The fall snapped the head off an
arrow that had entered his chest and broken through to
the other side.

Hylic's eyes swam, then focused on Jeremiah. He
offered one of his smiles. It seemed less satisfied than
usual, more apologetic. "I hope to see you again in a
greater and timeless world."

Jeremiah had been a fool. The scratching was a signal.
Hylic had put the scent of his blood in the air on purpose.
Fall wasn't the only one who could smell it or detect to
whom it belonged.

A figure on the cliffside allowed itself to be seen. It lowered its bow, vanished, and then reappeared much closer. It hovered over Jeremiah and the fallen Hylic Kirillov, looking as if it were one of the standing stones on the island of Ys.

"I'm not weak this time, Skog," Jeremiah said.

The figure sighed. "You're mistaken."

18

The scent of the chest wound wafted between them. Jeremiah tensed. Skog stiffened in response, refusing to be taken off-guard again by an impulsive attack. As for Jeremiah, with the ritual looming and Amala captive, revenge seemed as base as bloodlust. Rather than barrel into his foe, Fall fled, leaping from the cliff into the bay. As he hit the water, he thought about the trembling body he left behind and wondered if Hylic Kirillov's faith had wavered at all in the face of death's clarity.

The sudden undersea quiet wasn't at all like the time he'd spent clinging to the corvette's hull. This reminded Jeremiah more of the numbness the stone caused. These waters, protected from harsher currents by the bay's crescent, didn't writhe as the Mediterranean had. His visibility was also better. He saw schools of sardines, hundreds if not thousands strong, and scores of other living shapes. Most important, he spied an underwater mountain, the top of which held the beginnings of the sea-strong wall of Ys.

The momentum of his dive fading, Jeremiah flipped back and saw the trail he'd left behind, a thread of bubbles and swarming silt leading back to the surface. Near it a fainter stream twirled along the far side of the swarming fish. Between their silvery glints, he saw a rippling like a giant stingray. It was the color of pitch tinged with burgundy. Of course, Skog had followed.

For over a century, Jeremiah had never known a peer in battle. He'd been taken completely off-guard by the Abenaki's superior skills during their first encounter. Maybe now he could test those skills more carefully. Skog was masterful when Jeremiah was the pursuer. How would he fare with the situation reversed?

The multitude of sardines changed course, rushing toward the center of the bay. Jeremiah swam with them, attempting to fade between their slight shadows. It seemed to work. While he kicked amidst their tiny legion, Skog stayed behind, floating, twisting his head as he scanned the waters. If the school kept its heading, Jeremiah could follow it all the way to Ys.

But there was a reason the fish had turned. Instinct had told the sardines to seek safety in shallow water, where a large predator couldn't follow. Jeremiah saw that predator now—five times the length of Skog, lumbering but gaining momentum. Were it not for its cavernous jaws, he might have mistaken it for a whale. The open jaws formed a near-perfect circle, lined with hooked teeth. He'd seen something similar once, but only as a carefully rendered drawing in a book of ocean fauna. The text named the behemoth a basking shark. It was a creature of the deepest sea, and hunger had doubtless drawn it into the bay to feed.

Its maw already engulfed the tail of the school. Unable

to see Jeremiah, it turned toward him, forcing him to jerk away and reveal himself. Skog spotted him at once, and in that instant was nearly upon him.

Before Skog could reach him, Jeremiah sped into the twinkling darkness of a smaller school crossing the massive shark's back. A mere five yards away, Skog righted and slowed, his robes fanning around him in the water as he scanned for his prey, but failed to see him. Twice now Jeremiah had eluded him. Good.

As school and shark swam toward the ancient wall, the floor of the bay rose beneath them. Jeremiah could see the first rows of cut blocks, fitted together so tightly by their builders that water couldn't pass between them. Even today, Napoleon's best engineers couldn't manage that feat of precision.

Skog followed the fish for a few moments, knowing Jeremiah must be hiding near them, and then vanished himself. But to where? Had he given up so easily?

The basking shark's mammoth body shuddered. One moment the living hulk was intact, the next all that remained was a swirl of flesh, meat, and bone. Some of the sardines in its throat and sundered stomach swam free to rejoin their fellows. Unable to find his quarry, Skog had decided to destroy his hiding spot.

In the center of the decimation, the Abenaki floated, arms outstretched, apparently needing a moment to recover from the effort of ripping the creature in two.

With Ys so close, Jeremiah dove for the stone walls, pulled himself along them and up onto the surface. Surrounded by cool air, his wet clothes slapping rock, he flew up the flat stones. As he vaulted over the top, forcing gravity to release him, he hurled himself into the streets of Ys, landing catlike on all fours. Immediately, he searched for another hiding spot, determined not to face defeat again because of his own impatience.

The grandeur of Ys was long-decayed, but enough remained to make it plain why the Bretons believed Paris was named for it. Even more, it reminded him of Plato's vision of Atlantis's ringed, utopian capital. The spacious avenue where he stood was one of many wheel spokes, all bound for the island's midpoint. Fountain-adorned squares marked the cross streets until there stood a central mount that hosted the standing stones. Along either side of the street lay the foundations of houses, shops, and other buildings. Few remained standing. Those that did seemed on the verge of collapse. Only one or two retained their facades. The colors of their tiles, though dimmed, were still visible as an echo of lost splendor.

A sound—seawater spraying into the air—issued from beyond the sea wall. Skog had arrived. Jeremiah flew down the avenue, choosing the remnants of a tall tower to conceal himself. So much was absent from its walls that he soon wondered if he'd chosen wisely. Only some accidental balancing trick enabled it to stand. Its thick shadows were ideal for hiding, though, so he rolled onto the floor toward the side abutting the street. He pressed close to an old tile mosaic depicting sea serpents, unicorns, and other fantastic beasts.

The hush that followed meant nothing. Skog couldn't remain invisible while he moved, but he could stay silent. If only Jeremiah could sense his location. Mammals, birds, insects—Jeremiah could hear their heartbeats, catch their scents with ease, but a creature like himself? Was it possible?

In the rush of their first encounter, perhaps he hadn't tried hard enough.

He closed his eyes and concentrated. Slowly, he took note of each slight stirring, marking it and assessing a cause, even recognizing the sound of the breeze as it pulled flecks of dust from the antique walls. At last, there came an even fainter tone, wet cloth against the avenue's pavement. Even if Skog was noiseless, his clothes were not. In Jeremiah's mind's eye, he saw him walking along the row of buildings, searching.

Surprisingly, as if he knew, Skog spoke. "If you don't want to see our father freed, why did you seek the stone? Is it really for this cure you think you desire?"

His voice no longer sounded tired by the pointlessness of speech. Instead, it seemed…annoyed. Could Skog's self-control just be another mask, as much mere decoration as the building's colorful facade?

"I thought you were trying to trick me, that you were to be a worthy rival for our father's love, but the woman said as much, too. A cure? I don't understand. Why would a god plead to be an insect?"

Amala. How much had she told them? What was done to get her to speak? Hylic said Skog had refused to feed on her. He hoped her prized status as Bandias's bride had protected her from other harm as well.

The sound of heavy stones crashing into the ground came next. Repeating his strategy with the shark, Skog had pushed in the wall of the first fragile building he came to, reducing it to rubble. He moved to another, preparing to do the same. One by one, he would eliminate all the hiding places.

"Can it be you still believe in stories of salvation?" Skog asked. "Guiding gods and spirits?"

A second frail structure collapsed, larger than the first.

"You think I'm a devil? If your life is different, it's because I touched it. Before that you were nothing. You speak of God and Satan. My people told how Tabaldak created this reality, and from the dust of his hands made Gluskab and Malsumis, each with the power to make a world—Gluskab for good, Malsumis for evil."

More stone creaked, then tumbled into unrecognizable ruin. Skog was near, maybe four buildings away.

"Where were they when the first plague came and only one in twenty of us lived? Not my children, not my father or my mother, not my brothers, not my sister, not my friends or my wife, not a single thing I cherished was spared."

Long moments passed before the next wall fell.

"I walked through fields of rotting corpses, looked down at where there should have been fertile dirt, and saw the faces of my people—those I'd helped, those I'd hurt, those I'd envied, those I'd pitied. Where were those guiding spirits then?"

The next crash rattled the wall Jeremiah lay behind. But, aside from irritation, the tone of Skog's voice hinted at something equally new—weariness. He was getting tired.

"When boils grew on me, I tore them out, but the fever still burned as the sun does now. I fell into the worst of dreams. But what were dreams? What was pain or thought? I fell away from my senses, and away from my own mind, into what I thought was nothing, and found him waiting. My heart asked if the obvious was true, that the world was too horrid to be real. He answered with one word: *yes*."

Another crash. This time, Jeremiah could see the dust trail the air. Skog had destroyed the building next to him. The tower would be next. He looked up at the large stones precariously stacked above him, climbing toward the sky. They seemed heavy enough to hold him forever.

"I thought it was Malsumis, that he was the forgotten man. But the nameless cannot truly be named. Even Bandias is only a word the truth allows itself to be called, a token to the first woman who gave the name to him. I understood what Bandias offered—he would send me back to the dream-world. In exchange, if I were strong enough to become his willing son, I would bring him here through me. Together we could crush the nightmare."

Skog was on the other side of the wall. Jeremiah pressed his fingers into the tiles, trying to sense where the Abenaki stood.

"I answered with the same word I first heard from him: *yes*."

Though his fingertips, he felt the tremors of Skog's voice. Jeremiah would have one chance, just one. Would he be strong enough? He flattened his hands against the tower, until no space remained between flesh and stone, and tried to sense the weakness in the wall.

"When I awoke, I tried to bring as many of my people to him as I could, but they tricked me, bound me, and buried me in that mound. I felt betrayed, until the day Nathan Fall set me free and I realized *that* was part of his plan as well."

The memory of his father's vile corpse crashing through the door of their home gave Jeremiah the burst of energy he needed. He forced the stone blocks out toward Skog. What came next, he saw only in glimpses. Startled, Skog tried to duck, but falling boulders hit him in the shoulder. The rest of the tower lost all resemblance to its intended shape and came storming down. In less than a second, a heap of rock remained. Skog was buried beneath it.

Could it be so easy?

Jeremiah rose and warily eyed the rubble. He circled it, checking each crack for any sign of movement, but saw none. Recalling how slender the thread was that had brought him here to begin with, how tiny the events that composed it, Jeremiah refused to trust this seeming victory.

A loud creak turned him toward the sea wall. A wide gate, above water now that the tide was out, lay open. A rotund man stood there, leaning against the side, panting. His face was as pale as the color of the flying dirigibles. "Hylic," Jeremiah said. The small boat that had brought him here was visible on the slight shore beyond the gate.

The arrow missed his heart and lungs. Finding himself luckily—or *unluckily*—alive, he must have been frantic to reach the island and witness the ritual.

When he saw Jeremiah unharmed, Hylic's wavering eyes widened. "You're here. Alive. But...but...but, then where is...?"

Jeremiah nodded toward the pile of stones. Bereft, Hylic staggered toward it.

The sound of rushing hooves brought Jeremiah's attention toward the long road. The cultists, having seen the tower fall, were coming. Together, they might be able to dig Skog free. Jeremiah would have to stop them. He was tired, but they were human. It would be easier than stopping Skog.

Their horses were a half mile down the avenue. He headed in their direction, but stopped when he caught a movement in the corner of his eye. Hylic was scrabbling up the pile of stones. Reaching a small flat area, the Bandite closed his eyes and covered his wound with his hand. Jeremiah felt a wave of concern, but didn't understand why. Hylic couldn't possibly move the massive blocks himself. Still...

"What are you doing? Praying to your master? Get down from there or I'll..."

"Kill me? I so wish you had."

When a familiar, intoxicating smell came to his nostrils, Jeremiah's eyes shot to Hylic's hand. It hadn't been covering his heart; it'd been clenched around his wound, squeezing, drawing blood. Thick and long, it dripped, splattering on the rock, flowing down through the cracks.

Jeremiah ran as he screamed, "No!"

This time, he would have killed Hylic, really and truly, but as his foot hit the first flat stone, the debris spewed upward, moved by a force beneath it. His foothold gone, Jeremiah fell on his back. The stones at the top of the pile rolled down upon him. Heavy rock crushed his hands, legs, and chest, burying him as completely as he'd buried Skog.

Jeremiah's mind slipped away, despite his many cares. Now he was only afraid that in whatever void unconsciousness took him to he would not find the God he and his family worshipped. He was terrified that instead, he would stumble upon the same darkness the Abenaki had, the one that made him hate the world enough to want to end it.

19

How many times had Jeremiah Fall awoken from wounds that should've killed him? Grateful he'd lost count, he stood, rubbed his limbs, and supposed he should feel pleased the avalanche hadn't done more damage. Skog's power, revitalized by the smallest drops of human blood, impressed him, but at least he'd seen its limits. If not for Hylic Kirillov, Jeremiah might have won, and that meant he could again.

But why had he survived? Why was he free? Of course. The cultists had saved Jeremiah once already. As he was a child of their god, they were forbidden to harm him. So instead, he was brought here, which was...

He looked around. The space's crudeness was utterly unlike the rest of Ys. The floor was coarse, the rocky walls sharp-pointed. At one end, the low, uneven ceiling tapered at a steep angle into something of an alcove. Beyond that, a narrow crevice crept deeper into the dark. It was too thin for a child, let alone an adult, to pass through. Hardly an escape route.

The space he was in might have been a natural pocket in the island's volcanic rock, opened and evened by the original inhabitants, those who'd first worshipped the standing stones. King Gradlon likely only added to it, turning it into something of a prison cell. At one end, an iron-banded door was mounted on crooked hinges. There was a sort of window, too, lined by iron bars that sliced the moonlight as it entered.

Jeremiah shoved his shoulder against the door. The wood gave and the hinges creaked, but a heavy weight on the other side prevented further movement. Knowing Jeremiah's strength, they must have braced the other side with thick lumber or piled boulders. He couldn't get out that way.

Through the window, he saw one of the flying things drifting past the crescent moon. He thought it was leaving the island, but it was just caught in a wind from the bay. As the rope dangling beneath it drew taut, the dirigible staggered and shivered like a cloud on a leash. The rope was tied to a cross on the dome of a ruined church, the only sign here of the religion King Gradlon embraced.

Looking down at the city, he saw that his cell was opposite and slightly below the central platform that held the standing stones. It still teemed with the activity he had seen earlier. Now, he was close enough to distinguish the cultists from Skog's servants by their eyes. The men on horseback were his slaves. They were positioned at the perimeter, carrying muskets and swords. Having shed desert clothes and sailing garb, they wore no special uniform. The rest, all cultists milling about the stones, also had no particular clothing—no robes, no telltale symbols. It looked as if they had been plucked at random from spots across the globe. Some wore the fine tailored outfits of men and women of influence, others the threadbare garb of beggars and dirt farmers. Their ethnicity varied wildly: French, Arabic, Spanish, English, and African, even Asian. The only thing they seemed to have in common was a stupidly peaceful smile, the same as the one Hylic Kirillov wore.

Madmen, it seemed, came in all shapes and sizes.

Hylic was there, too. He was seated in a plain wooden chair that looked terribly out of place among the gargantuan stones. At first, Jeremiah thought it was a seat of honor, then noticed Hylic's hands were tied. That made sense. Skog's attempt to kill him wasn't intended as a reward. After all, Hylic had led Jeremiah here. The cultists might worship what Jeremiah was no matter what he did, but not Skog. To him, Jeremiah was now not only a rival, but also a threat. Hylic's role in reviving Skog was probably the only reason he'd been permitted to view the ritual at all.

This was also the closest Jeremiah had been to the standing stones. He knew they were large, but now saw that they were fully four or five times the height and breadth of the monuments at Salisbury Hill. The taller pillars were set in pairs of two and three, holding aloft a longer stone. Though each dark rock seemed to serve the builders' purpose, each also retained a unique identity, adding to the impression that this was not a temple, but a group of antediluvian monstrosities. It was as if the giants in the earth mentioned in Genesis had somehow been frozen in the midst of a profane dance.

The stone Jeremiah had found in Rashid would seem an impish intruder, mismatched in texture, shape, and size, were it not for the depth of its ebony hue. The others seemed to lean their massive weight toward it, as if fighting an urge to fall.

He'd read that Stonehenge was aligned with certain stars, marking celestial events. Here the patterns on the mount were likewise reflected in the sky. The twinkling night lights Jeremiah recognized as planets seemed to sit atop each pillar, as if enthroned. Only the tallest "seat" lay empty. It was easy to tell what was expected to fill it. The crescent moon climbed directly behind it, making the pillar's shadow stretch toward the central stone. It seemed as if everything, the Bandites, the stones, and the planets, were all waiting for that final guest, the moon, to arrive and take its seat.

It would happen soon. He had to get out of here, find Amala, and stop this.

Jeremiah wrapped his hands around the bars and pulled until he thought his bones would snap. He twisted the bars until it felt as if the flesh would rip from his hands, but the iron was buried deep in the rocky wall. He tried the door again, testing sides, top, and bottom. Whatever braced it did so for all the door's width and length.

That left the tiny crevice. He knelt into the alcove to examine it. The opening was barely high as his head, but it stretched back six feet before curving out of view. Shoving his arm too quickly into the narrow space earned him a gash from the sharp rock, but the cut disappeared almost as quickly as it happened. He felt for the top. After half a foot, the ceiling rose beyond the reach of his fingertips. He lay on the floor and slid his head in. It was still impossibly thin beyond the opening, but the crevice looked tall enough to stand in.

As he lay there, a slight airflow graced his lips. He opened his mouth and tried to feel it again, against his tongue. There it was; this time moving in the other direction. Air was being drawn into the crack, as if it breathed. That meant the narrow passageway led somewhere. Whether it was to freedom or hell, he'd no way of knowing. Or did he?

When he hid in the tower, he'd stretched his senses to hear Skog. What would happen if he tried the same here? Practicing his patience, he stilled himself. As the air played along the razor-sharp rocks, he listened. He sniffed for slight differences in temperature, tried to picture what lay beyond his vision.

The hollow was dank, and at first his concentration only augmented the briny seawater smell. When the air made its next sluggish movement, he focused on it. It was a slight sound that changed pitch, ending in smaller trills, mere wisps at the edge of hearing.

He'd never thought of a breeze as having size or shape, but pictured this one filling, defining the unseen space. It was working. He couldn't count feet or inches, but somehow knew the crevice traveled past the curve for a time, then opened into something wider. It might be an exit.

On his knees, he tried to press himself into the narrow gap. The rock cut his shirt, then his skin. No use. Though the space opened shortly, the thinner entry had no give. His chest was wider than the space by inches. Could he broaden it? Pleased to find the bayonet still on him, he used it to jab and scrape at the opening. He moved so fast and fiercely that sparks flew and set his clothes afire. The blade now chipped, he cursed himself as he dampened the flames with his hands.

"Jeremiah?"

The sound of his name took him completely off-guard.

"Jeremiah?"

It was a whisper so soft, it seemed full of doubt even at its own existence. But he knew the voice.

He pressed his head into the crevice, pushed his mouth toward the dark, and called back, "Amala?"

"Not so loud. They're right outside my door. The guards all have Skog's marks on their necks. What they hear, he hears."

"Where are you?"

"A cell," she whispered. "They're going to take me to the stone. I'm to read the hieroglyphs."

"You can't. You have to fight them."

"There are too many."

"Can you squeeze through the crack?"

"Too narrow. Jeremiah?"

"What?"

"I wish you'd fed on me. Then you might hear what I hear. We could be together up until the end."

"No, Amala, no. Maybe they're wrong about the stone, what it is, what it does, or maybe…"

"Maybe what?"

"Maybe Atticus was right. Maybe God has a reason for me to be here."

"To keep Satan from walking the earth?" she said. "You *are* still a Puritan."

He could hear the sadness in her voice, a sorrow he took for defeat.

He raced back to the window. The horned moon had nearly climbed the remaining pillar, whose shadow almost touched the stone. Skog was there now, too. Kneeling, he'd removed his mask, revealing his expressionless face. Even from here, Jeremiah knew the dark glint in his eyes meant he was speaking to Bandias, that he was hearing the river rush of voices. The ritual would begin soon.

If there was something, anything, to be done, he had to do it now. But what? He couldn't bend the window bars, couldn't break the door, the crevice rock wouldn't budge, and his chest…

His chest. It was the only thing he hadn't tried to break. He'd survived an explosion, why not that? With a guttural howl, he hurled himself into the crack. The effort cut and bruised his side. He stuck his arm into the crevice, grabbed its edges, and tried to pull the rest of himself along. Cloth ripped, skin tore, but the bones of his chest held.

He needed momentum.

He withdrew, leaned back far as he could, and then threw himself into the narrow space. With a crunch, two ribs broke. His chest, wedged into the space, throbbed. Panicking, the beast tried to wriggle free, but his body was stuck fast.

Are you insane? it asked.

Familiar enough with agony, Jeremiah moved his arm in and pulled again. A third rib joined the broken two. Their ruptured ends pressed into his lungs. He pulled and gained inches, but the thick center of his rib cage, the sternum, refused to yield. The craggy volcanic razors cut deeper with each twitch of muscle.

He howled, and the beast howled with him. It was hopeless. All he'd done was trap himself.

"Jeremiah? What's happening? Are you all right?" Amala called.

Distracted by her voice, the beast calmed down. It focused and calculated the distance between them, figuring how much time it would take to cross. Its machinations gave Jeremiah an idea.

"Cut yourself," he ordered. "Bite your lip, Amala. Draw blood. Do it."

Would she obey? Trapped and tortured by the rough rock, time ceased to have meaning. It felt like hours, but it might have been seconds before the air drifted through the crevice again. This time, it carried not just brine, but the heady scent of blood. Not just blood, not just human blood, but Amala's. His muscles shivered in involuntary response.

The beast grew grim.

Will you let us have her if we get through this crevice?

"Yes," Jeremiah lied.

The beast was too frightened from being pinned to doubt him. Engulfed by torment, its reptile will met with Jeremiah's desire. Together they pressed their body forward until...

Thok.

The sternum split. As its broken edges pressed into his heart, it felt as if the tower had been piled atop him again. But he kept moving, deeper into the narrow space. Legs and arms trembling, he passed the entry and stood. Shivering, semiconscious, he shimmied along, his body's movements less an exercise of hope than a dead enslavement to the call of Amala's blood.

"The door's opening. They're coming for me," she said.

He rounded the curve and advanced two more yards before the light of oil lamps showed him the wide space of her cell. He heard voices, but couldn't understand what they said. Though the pain remained excruciating, it wasn't what confounded his hearing. The vertigo he experienced whenever the stone pulsed with the forgotten man's energy pulsed over him. It felt as if Bandias were testing the air, preparing to stretch.

Jeremiah raced the final length of the crevice, hoping even slight momentum would bring him through the final narrow opening. The smell of Amala's blood took him across the last few feet.

Unable to stand, he sprawled on the ground like a giant spider, eyes red as he bared his fangs and hissed. Having been separated from her for so long, he hoped he would see relief or warmth in Amala's dark eyes. Instead, he saw only the terror his mangled appearance inspired.

The four men around her swayed as if half asleep. Was Skog too busy with the stone to command them? No. In short order, they snapped to attention. While two hurried Amala toward the door, the others moved to strike Jeremiah with their musket butts.

His right arm and shoulder refused to respond, but his left hand snatched one of the muskets. He used the bayonet blade to stab the lanky guard holding it. His sandy-haired companion fell seconds later.

Using his knees to push his torso forward, Jeremiah slammed into Amala and the guards who held her, knocking all three off their feet. He'd reached her but crippled himself in the process. The impact made his cracked sternum press inward, sending a torrent of anguish through his chest. The heaviness was paralyzing.

Desperate to relieve the intense pressure, he managed to get his right hand to obey and brought both palms to the bulging center of his chest. Gritting his teeth, he shoved. Another rib broke, but with a crack, the sternum's halves shuddered back into place. They held together loosely, but at least they no longer pressed inward.

His right arm still mostly useless, he managed to get to his feet. Amala lay on the floor. For the first time, he noticed the drops of her blood gracing the rocky wall where her head had struck. Terrified, he knelt beside her and cradled her motionless head. Unwittingly, he let the blood from her shallow wound rub along his fingers. When he saw she was still breathing, such a wave of relief raced over him, he let down his guard.

In that instant, the beast moved to make good on Jeremiah's promise. It thrust the bloody fingers into his mouth and sucked greedily. At the taste, black fire ran through his bones. He'd never conceived, never imagined, such a wild sensation. The feeling rode beyond bliss and told him that no matter how grand this seemed, there was much more to be had if only he would truly drink.

Cursing himself, he scooped her into his arms and raced outside. He was surprised at the sudden strength the tiny drop of blood brought him, but recalled how just a little more had enabled Skog to free himself from a mountain of stone.

He found himself on a long avenue, a hundred yards from the stone circles, easily spotted by all who stood on the central mount. The armed riders raced for him at once. The free-willed cultists came, too, but reluctant to leave, they kept looking back. The lunar crescent had moved fully into position. The collected light of moon and planets stabbed into the stone.

Jeremiah sped along the street. The forgotten man's

dizzying call rose in him as he went. Not knowing if he would be able to disobey if Bandias commanded him, he knew he had to get Amala away as quickly as possible. Remembering the moored airship, he carried her into the wreckage of the church.

Its doors were long gone, its interior hollowed out, and the horsemen could easily follow. But they couldn't fire lest they hit Bandias's intended bride, nor could they outrace Jeremiah as he flew toward the rickety spiral steps he hoped would take him to the roof.

Halfway up, he dared a backward glance. Those who'd first arrived had abandoned their horses and headed for the stairs. The cultists were at the entrance now, swarming in, their flow into the church slowed by their number. He was about to turn back to his climb when the crowd at the door was swept aside, bodies flying like dead leaves in a storm.

Skog stood in their place. He was swaying, uncertain, pulled by the same vertigo Jeremiah struggled with. One instant he reappeared beside Jeremiah on the stairs, seething with rage, but the next, his eyelids fluttering like a sleeping child's, he vanished, called away by a power beyond him.

Jeremiah didn't question it. Instead, he finished his climb to the ceiling. There he found a hatch that took him to the sanctuary's roof. He laid Amala down at the base of the dome and then ascended to the cross. He tugged at the dirigible mooring to bring it down within reach. He wrapped the rope around the cross to keep the airship low, then laid Amala in the small sled suspended beneath it.

He looked at her face, caressed her cheek, and laid a

kiss on her brow. Once certain she was secure, he cut the tether with his broken knife and set the airship free. It rose skyward, lit on the underbelly by an inky, unnatural sheen. As the dirigible flew, Jeremiah thought he'd saved her, and now turned to the source of the blackness, thinking he might also save the world.

20

From atop the dilapidated church, Jeremiah Fall watched the mob withdraw.

"Bandias will see to it."

"Bandias will summon his bride."

They all returned to the hill, where they stood in patterns matching the pillars. What he saw of their shadowed expressions looked like rapture—only Hylic's stunned expression seemed out of place.

The stone no longer cast aphotic shadows so much as generated a palpable void, an emptiness that seemed as if it could be touched. The guardian pillars, the solemn ruins, the masterful sky, and the merciless sea were all wrapped in a stygian pall, as if the world were poised to reveal itself as the vast lie the Bandites believed it to be.

One form remained unobscured: Skog. Jeremiah saw the spaces between his fingers as his hands lay flat against the carved writing. His body forfeited its statuelike stillness and trembled. His thick lips moved rhythmically as he chanted. Jeremiah could neither hear nor understand what he said. The dark seemed to swallow sound as well as light.

Jeremiah scrambled down the side of the church, heedless of the rocks dislodged by his reckless descent. His mind raced as well, trying to figure out the fastest way to stop the ritual. A skyward glance made him wonder if he *could*.

Though the wind should be pulling them out to sea, the three tethered dirigibles, moored at various buildings, were being tugged toward the central mount. To his horror, Jeremiah saw that even the airship carrying Amala was moving toward the stone.

Hitting the ground, he sprinted for the hill. Few of the Bandites even noticed him. Those who did afforded him a passing glance that revealed their smug pity for his efforts. As if moving among sleepwalkers, he reached the tallest pillar undisturbed.

Thinking to disrupt the circular pattern of the guardian stones, Jeremiah lay down and pressed his feet into the base of the twenty-foot rock and pushed. At first, he only scraped his back when his efforts forced him along the volcanic floor. When he tried again, the pillar quivered. He pressed and released, pressed and released, working the slight motion into a steady rocking. As Amala's still-unconscious form drifted ever lower, the pillar toppled.

It landed with a thunderous clap, squashing several beguiled worshippers and splitting into rough segments. There seemed no other effect. The eldritch energies grew visible, surrounding Skog and the stone in an amorphous, caliginous pocket. All across Dahut's island, the dark became too easy to see, the light too obscure. Everywhere shadow was more real than the substance it was cast upon.

The airship's rope scraped the ground as it moved. Between the sled's wooden slats, he saw Amala. She stirred, her arms moving out to the sides.

Tired beyond endurance and desperate beyond hope, Jeremiah threw himself at the energy pocket surrounding Skog and the stone. He passed into it as though it were air, then raised his hands to grab the chanting Abenaki. He tried again to hear what Skog was saying, but any sound he made seemed drawn directly into the rock.

Jeremiah's palms made contact with Skog, but he felt nothing. His hands vanished into him, as if Jeremiah's body were nothing more than a reflection on the surface of an inky pond. Fearful he might be swallowed whole, he shifted and fell to the side, crashing to the still-solid ground, relieved to find that his hands remained intact.

Skog was no longer speaking, but a deep reverberation in the ground told Jeremiah that Bandias was answering. The sound of a thousand thousand beasts—the call that had once been directed at Jeremiah—was now locked in a final negotiation with Skog. Again, Jeremiah couldn't make out any words. The utterances were as formless as the crackling hollow they stood within. But it was clear that Bandias had no need for Jeremiah. Skog was his chosen son.

A crepuscular blast hurled Jeremiah out of the pocket. He flew, then slid along the coarse ground, nearly hitting the wooden chair that held Hylic. Jeremiah looked up at him as Hylic looked down, neither knowing what reaction he should have. An airy, hollow boom snapped both their heads toward the profane miracle before them.

With inky precision and matchless speed, something transferred itself from the stone into Skog. What remained of the Abenaki still had the shape of a man, but it was no longer possessed of flesh or bone. There were no stars inside it, no space, no light, nor was it truly dark. There were no colors, and nothing for the senses, the mind, or the intuition to grasp. Its material defied all appearance, as if it were only vision's placeholder for something *not*.

It occurred to Jeremiah that if the story of Bandias, the forgotten man, were not exactly true, it was the closest language could possibly come to communicating the idea of the thing before him.

The blissful smiles of the Bandites evaporated as their faces folded into a more complete dark. Individual expressions lost, they moved like a single thing, toward the nothing. Upon reaching its border, they melted into it the same way Jeremiah's hands had briefly disappeared. Unlike his hands, they did not return. Instead, they forfeited any aspect of being that ever made them separate, that ever made them selves, into the emptiness of their god.

"Cut me free," Hylic said, whimpering.

"So you can join your brothers and sisters?" Jeremiah answered. "Forget it."

"No, no," Hylic responded. "So I can spend my last moments trying to flee."

Jeremiah tore his gaze from Bandias to look at the

frightened man. "What's wrong? Don't you want your gnosis?"

Hylic shivered, eyes wet as he stared at the inky black. "Jeremiah Fall, please. It's just that... it looks an awful lot like... nothing. I think I may have been... mistaken."

"Mistaken? If you hadn't freed Skog, I could have stopped this."

"Perhaps you're right, and if it matters, I wish I hadn't stopped you. But if you don't want to help me because of what I am, then perhaps you will because of what *you* are? Do you want your final act to be one of cruelty or mercy?"

Clenching his teeth, Jeremiah kicked the legs of the chair, snapping its structure and sending Hylic to the ground. He quickly slipped from his bonds.

"If we live, or anything like it, I will repay you for this. I swear it," Hylic said as he ran.

Amala's airship still moved steadily toward the stone, but seeing no other escape, Hylic grabbed the rope dangling from it and tried to climb. His limbs, weak from the pain of his arrow wound, or fear, didn't allow him much progress. The sinking airship would meet him on the ground long before he'd meet it in the sky.

Jeremiah Fall could conjure no further tricks. How could he fight what couldn't be touched? Could this be the fate Atticus imagined when he asked him to hold on to his existence? To bear witness to the end of all things?

As he watched Hylic's futile efforts, he thought he should be the one climbing to Amala, to spend what time remained with the woman who'd shown him kindness.

The moment the thought occurred to him, another wave burst from the creature. Oblivion reached out to the remaining Bandites. Black tendrils coiled from Skog, now possessed by the forgotten man. They wrapped around each of the cultists, covering their bodies and rendering each a crude blob, only roughly human in shape. Not as starkly ebony as Bandias, but far more mobile, these new creatures—his darklings—swarmed into action. Half moved toward Hylic and the dangling rope, half toward Jeremiah.

What was this? The airship was already floating toward the monster. Bandias had only to wait to claim his mate. What was the purpose of these things? Could Bandias have somehow sensed Jeremiah's desire to reach Amala and his need to thwart it? What difference could that wish have made?

It didn't seem to matter. The darklings devoured whatever stood in their way. Like the desert rats in the cave, they came at him. The first shadow-hand reached for him. Though he pulled away, the very air it grabbed crackled with energy.

He wrapped his arms around the nearest pillar and pulled himself up, scrambling spiderlike to its top. The darklings piled beneath him. Uninterested in climbing, they set the pedestal rocking, repeating Jeremiah's earlier failed trick. Flecks of stone flew from it wherever they touched.

When that pillar fell, he jumped to the next. Not waiting to see how quickly the darklings reacted, he leaped from pillar to pillar. Once the airship's rope was within reach, he grabbed that and started to climb. Hylic was below him on the rope. In his panic, the Russian had lifted himself a good eight feet off the ground. The shadow-men pooled beneath them both. Some waited patiently for time to bring the airship down. Others toyed with the rope, which hissed and frayed at their touch.

Reaching the slender sled, Jeremiah found Amala sitting, eyes open.

"He's calling for me," she said matter-of-factly. Was she only half conscious or captive to the uncanny energies around them? "He wants me to read my part from the stone. Do you hear him?"

Jeremiah shook his head. All he could make out was a mad cacophony. But he wasn't prepared to give up yet. The reaction from Bandias meant something. There might still be enough time to figure out what it was.

"Then say no, or don't say anything."

"I don't think I can. Was there ever a single word you read on the stone that you didn't feel compelled to speak aloud?"

She was right. There hadn't been.

The airship lurched like a fish on a hook. Below, Hylic dangled above a sea of shadow limbs. Some of the darklings, testing their new forms, managed to keep from destroying the rope long enough to try climbing it.

"Help!" Hylic howled.

"Stop climbing, don't move!" Jeremiah ordered.

"Stop climbing? But…"

Jeremiah yanked the rope, pulling Hylic and the darklings higher and higher until the Russian's hands grasped the edge of the wooden sled, tipping it. With Hylic holding on, Jeremiah untied the rope and sent the darklings down among their faceless brethren. They landed with a sickly splash.

Despite that, the airship continued its descent. Amala

stood. Her eyes riveted on the stone's writing, her lips began to move.

"*S'tah…*"

"Stop her, Jeremiah," Hylic screeched.

"I know!"

His hand clamped across her mouth, smothering the next syllable. She bit him, tore into his palm, and snapped her head back and forth. He held her, but her body had become remarkably strong.

"Amala, no. It's all right," he said, trying to soothe her. Her eyes seethed with the same fury he'd once seen in Skog's.

"That's not working!" Hylic said.

Worse, something was going on below. The darklings drained away, pouring their shadow-selves into Bandias's possessed form, as if he were an ocean gathering its strength for a more powerful assault on the shore. A moment later, another burst of energy roiled from Bandias, shaking the airship and threatening to overturn it.

As Jeremiah tried to hold Amala steady, the rattling opened a toolbox and sent half its contents over the edge. Their quick clatter on the ground told him there wasn't much space left beneath them now, maybe ten feet.

Amala twisted free of Jeremiah. Wild eyes again focused on the hieroglyphs, she opened her mouth. "*S'tah…*"

Again her oath was cut short. Abruptly unconscious, she went limp in Jeremiah's arms, a new bruise on the back of her head. He looked up to see Hylic holding a wrench. Even as he glared at the man, he realized it'd been a good idea. Perhaps he truly did regret his allegiance to the monster beneath them.

The airship settled. Whatever had been pulling it now held it steady. Fearing the calm, Jeremiah and Hylic looked down. Bandias, for perhaps the first time since the fall of man from paradise, moved. With a terrifying slowness, the *nothing* arched its head to look at them.

It parted its lips. There was no sound, but it looked as if the first man was screaming. The atmosphere itself rattled. The airship hurtled up and away, blown far over the bay.

Hylic buried his face in the sled and held on for dear life. Jeremiah clamped himself around Amala to protect her, yet still managed to watch what they were leaving behind. It reminded Jeremiah of the fate of Lot's wife. Ys had been called a medieval Sodom and Gomorrah. When the couple fled those cities as God's wrath destroyed them, Lot's wife could not resist looking back and was turned into a pillar of salt.

But this was not Sodom and Gomorrah. Jeremiah's eyes filled not with the light of a thousands suns, but with their absence. His ears rang, not with the sound of a thousand chariots, but with the roar of a beast thwarted in its efforts to claim a mate.

Its anguished breath spent, Bandias inhaled, drawing not just air into its being, but reality. Practicing its intent for the whole of the world, it rendered whatever was nearest back to the formless void that existed before creation. That void, it seemed, had remained all this time, hidden just beneath the shell of the world's myriad forms. The only mystery was how it had ever remained hidden.

It was as Hylic had told him back in the tiny rowboat. Bandias did not *need* a mate to manifest, but he would prefer one. He proved that now, as, in an instant, the whole of the island of Ys did not disappear, but became, simply, *not*.

At the same time, the tempest that shoved the airship proved too much for the cloth cells that held the hydrogen, tearing them in several places. Though they'd somehow escaped Bandias for the moment, they could not escape the plunge into the sea.

21

As time lessened the Puritan distrust of new ideas, the section of the library devoted to the arts at Harvard's School grew. Toward the end of Jeremiah's time in the States, he happened upon a thick tome of color plates, one reproducing an oil entitled *Landscape with the Fall of Icarus* by the sixteenth-century Flemish artist Brueghel. The title caught his attention. Icarus was son to Daedalus, the mythic Greek inventor. Daedalus created wings held together by wax, so he and Icarus could fly free of an island prison. Though warned, Icarus soared too close to the sun. When the wax melted, he fell into the ocean and died.

But where was he in Brueghel's painting? The landscape was full of life: an ox and farmer, a shepherd tending his flock, a fisherman, and a bay with ships sailing toward a busy port. The world was far too busy to notice the tiny spot where Icarus hit the water, a blur of limb and feather.

With the utter destruction of Ys to amaze them, Jeremiah was certain the airship crash would be equally invisible to the locals. Yet in no time, boats circled them. Fishermen gawked as if they were the sole oddity on an otherwise banal morning.

Wincing from the dawn's mild rays, Jeremiah cradled Amala, holding her above the surface. Hylic coughed seawater as he tried to stay afloat. They obviously needed help, but the men didn't rescue them immediately. It was only when the wide cloth of the dirigible slipped beneath the waves that one rickety boat crept closer.

The gritty captain, gnarled as the husk of a dead tree, was the oldest-looking living creature Jeremiah had ever seen. At his order, the two younger men with him pulled them aboard.

Amala struggled back to consciousness. Hylic continued to heave. As Jeremiah crawled to the shade of the doorless cabin, the old man snapped at him in Breton.

"Je suis désolé je ne parle pas cette langue," Fall answered. *I'm sorry I don't speak that language.*

Insulted, the captain spat and nodded at one of his men. There was a familial resemblance in their faces, though the captain was so wizened, it was the same resemblance a raisin bore a grape.

"Are you from England?" this one asked in French. "Are you attacking us?"

Jeremiah realized that everyone in the surrounding boats was staring nervously skyward. Now, at least, their slow rescue made some sense. They were terrified the British had arrived. They must be thinking the destruction of Ys was part of an attack on France, in flying devices the likes of which they'd never seen.

"No," Jeremiah answered, trying to sound as harmless as possible.

"Do we look English?" Hylic interjected. "I'm Russian; he's American. The woman's Egyptian."

The fishermen relaxed slightly, until Jeremiah pointed at the spot where the island and its city once stood. "We escaped Ys before it was destroyed."

A long, anxious pause followed. When the translator laughed, the old captain slapped him hard on the back of the head.

"Why is that funny?" Fall asked.

The Breton rubbed the back of his head. "It's like saying you fell from heaven. Ys, if it ever existed, was destroyed hundreds of years ago."

Jeremiah was confused. "Gradlon let his daughter die to save his nation and the city. The ruins were right there."

The Breton looked as insulted as the captain. "You think I don't know our own legends? Gradlon saved his nation, not Ys. The evil city sank beneath the waves forever."

Jeremiah looked to Amala and Hylic for support, surprised to find them staring at him with equal confusion.

"I don't remember any city," Amala said. She lowered her voice. "I remember Skog; I remember the stone. Nothing else."

"Then where do you remember being with Skog and the stone? Where did I rescue you *from*?"

"The ship, the one that brought me here. It sank when the balloon lifted us."

Befuddled, Jeremiah turned toward Hylic, who shrugged. "I remain grateful for your rescue, but there was no island. As the woman said, the corvette was anchored at the mythic spot for the ritual."

The sailor put his hand to Jeremiah's back. "Is the air thin up there?"

Jeremiah rubbed his temples and lowered his head.

Once it was clear no further flying machines were approaching, the venerable captain, irked at having lost time from the day's fishing, brought them to port and the custody of Louis Desmarais, a local official who claimed some vague connection to the Directory that ruled France.

The thin-haired bureaucrat had a natural cheeriness. Not even questioning Jeremiah's eagerness to get inside, he brought the trio to a small room in his home and let them dry themselves.

"I don't care for trouble," he explained. "It bothers my digestion. But when people fall from the sky, well, I must make an exception."

Jeremiah left it to Hylic and Amala to weave a story about how they didn't know one another, but happened to be at the same fair in Le Mans, some hundred miles away. When they shared a ride in a hydrogen balloon on display, a sudden gust snapped their line and set them adrift. Such balloons were rare, but not unheard of, and they took care to omit the more unbelievable aspects of just what it was they flew.

Desmarais was inclined to believe them. "I'm loath to contact the army to corroborate your story. One is never sure whose side they might be on this week."

A knock came at the door. His pleasant expression vanished, and, his digestion apparently bothered by the intrusion, he rubbed his stomach before rising to answer. When he returned, though, the smile was back on his face. "Some wood from your balloon's basket ruined one of our fishermen's nets, forcing his early return. Bad news for him, good news for you and me. One piece bore a plate indicating the device was built in Rennes. Of course, such a remarkable thing would have to be French. Forgive my doubts."

Fall made a mental note to visit Rennes one day to try and find the source of the airships.

They were not only released but also offered two rooms at a local inn, one for Amala, and the other for the men to share.

"So you can rest and get your bearings until you decide the best way to reunite yourselves with your belongings in Le Mans," Desmarais explained before leaving them.

"It smells of fish," Hylic complained as he threw himself on a bed. "Then again, everything here does."

Jeremiah wrapped a scarf around his face, preparing to go out. "You don't remember a single Bandite from the island? Not one name?"

"How can I remember people I never met from a place that never was?"

"What about the Bandites on the corvette? They were all on the island. Do you remember any of their names?"

A puzzled expression crept across Hylic's face. "A corvette? It wasn't a corvette that brought us here; it was a...well, that's odd, isn't it? I think the captain's name began with a V, but Skog killed him before we set sail."

Jeremiah headed for the door.

"You may want to wait until nightfall," Hylic called after him. "You don't help us by standing out."

"Us?" Jeremiah muttered as he exited.

Happy to be away from Hylic, he padded down the hallway. The door to Amala's room was open a crack, so he peeked in. She lay on her back, the bruises on her head hidden by her black tresses. Her eyes were closed but moving beneath the lids, a sign, Jeremiah had once read, that she was dreaming. He hoped it was a pleasant dream.

The story of their rescue had already spread through the port town. With no need to conceal himself, he spent the next several hours visiting shopkeeps and townsfolk. His queries about strangers brought shrugs; his questions about the ruins brought the same refrain: "It's a legend."

Finally satisfied the next answer would be the same as the last, he returned to Tristan Isle, to the cliff that had afforded him his first view of the city, and used his telescope to stare out at the long bay. Aside from the ripples of low waves, the surface was flat all the way into the sea.

It's a legend.

"It is now," he said to the wind.

"I believe you," Amala said that night. "I just don't remember."

The fish oil burning in the lamps added to the smell, but the warm yellow light played so peacefully on her face, it reminded Jeremiah that the dark could sometimes be friendly. It was the first quiet moment they'd shared where neither was wounded, enslaved, or about to be sacrificed. He sat on the edge of her bed, she cross-legged at the head.

"All I can guess," Jeremiah said, "is that Hylic was right. Bandias doesn't just destroy; he removes things completely from creation, from history, from memory. Only, why is it I still remember?"

"You're part of him," she answered. "One of his children."

Jeremiah gave her a weak smile. "I wish you wouldn't say that."

She put her hand against his cheek. He started, pulling back so that only the tips of her fingernails still touched him. The beast had been curiously silent since Bandias was freed, but Jeremiah had every reason to distrust that. It might be biding its time, waiting for him to let down his guard, as it had in the ocean and the prison-cave. But there'd been plenty of fat water rats to feed on in town, and now he wanted very badly to relax into Amala's caress, a sensation that made him feel alive.

He moved forward again, letting her fingers touch him. She seemed surprised, but pleased.

"My father's name was Nathan. I'm not like Skog," he said.

"I didn't say that's *all* you were. It's obvious you're many things." She leaned closer, put her lips to his, and kissed him. "It's a shame you're afraid of so many of them."

He lingered there a moment, pulled back, and looked in her eyes.

"Don't I feel...cold?"

"Not to me," she said. She kissed him again.

The door creaked open. Hylic stood there, holding a few folded sheets of paper.

"I hope I'm not interrupting," he said; then he made a curious face at Jeremiah. "*Can* you be interrupted? I know Bandias can mate, but I never saw any indication from Skog that he was interested or even able to..."

"What do you want?" Jeremiah asked.

He stepped inside, closed the door behind him, and held up the papers. "I told you I was wrong. I said I'd help you. Now I have. Bandites have ways of leaving messages for one another in certain spots, under certain stones or by certain trees. I thought I might check for signs of their presence. There must still be a member in town. I don't know who it is—but this was meant for him. They don't remember Ys either, but they know the stone was transported here and that Bandias now resides within Skog. Though it's less than six months before the year's end and Bandias manifests on his own, they still hope to earn his favor by bringing him his bride. For that, they'll need the stone and the woman."

"Why the stone?" Jeremiah asked. "Wasn't it just a prison? Can't they just have someone read the invocation?"

Hylic shook his head. "It's more than a prison. Even Skog wasn't sure exactly what it is. Must be pretty unique to restrain a creature like Bandias, though, eh? The carved writing itself has power. For Bandias to mate with the woman, she must read the words directly from the stone, which now lies at the bottom of the bay. According to this note, someone will arrive in the next few days with the resources to try to retrieve it."

"Then we have to get Amala as far away as possible. We could bring her to America."

She shook her head. "It will only delay the inevitable. Bandias *will* manifest when the year ends."

"Then, what? There must be *something* we can do," Jeremiah said.

Hylic shifted uneasily. "I have one thought, but it's not very good and I'm certain you won't like it."

"What?"

"If she's the only one on earth who can read the hiero-glyphs...kill her."

"No!"

Don't let him!

He lunged at Hylic and held him against the wall. Jeremiah's eyes glowed so brightly that the skin on his hands picked up their red hue.

Kill him! He wants to hurt the woman!

The beast seemed as bent on protecting Amala as Jeremiah was.

Why? Jeremiah asked, but he realized the answer before it came.

To save her for our father...

So that was why Skog hadn't fed on her, and why Jeremiah felt so at ease with her. He released his grip.

"I said you wouldn't like it," Hylic said, clearing his throat. "You must admit, if nothing else, it would buy time to think of another plan."

"It wouldn't even do that," Jeremiah said more evenly. "They found a second stone at Rashid that also unlocks the hieroglyphs. Some savants have native wives, others female assistants. The Bandites knew about the stone practically from the moment I discovered it. Why wouldn't they keep some agents there? By now they could have taught someone else to read the incantation. So, Hylic, don't mention hurting Amala again in any way, unless you are still eager to die."

"Fine," Hylic said. He pointed at Amala. "Ask her for a better idea. She's the one who did read the thing, after all."

"Amala, is there anything?"

She closed her eyes. The familiar line formed again in her forehead. It tightened, thickened. "To father himself,

Bandias must come fully into creation. Inhabiting Skog is only a half step, a body borrowed to carry his essence until he can plant in a woman. If ever he were weakest, it would have to be as he passed from Skog to…" She hesitated, perhaps about to say "to me," swallowed, then went on. "…to the woman. If we had the stone, and I recited the words, he'd have to come. Perhaps then he could be killed."

Yes, the beast said. *Summon him.*

"No. You have no reason to believe we could hurt him even then. It's insane," Jeremiah said.

She gave him a weak smile. "Many things are these days, don't you think? From what you said, you had no reason to believe you could hurt Skog until you buried him under those rocks."

"But…" Jeremiah began. He had no idea how to finish the thought.

Amala pressed the point. "Or we can wait, and the results will be the same, won't they? Do you have another idea?"

"No."

Hylic cleared his throat again, loudly. "There is another issue. If it were just a question of a girl and the stone, the ritual could have been done in Egypt. A sacred spot is required. Jeremiah tells us it was Ys, and Ys is gone. The Bandites now plan to take the stone elsewhere."

"Do they name the place?" Jeremiah asked.

Hylic shrugged. "The letter refers only to the place where Bandias was born."

"Eden?" Jeremiah asked.

Hylic laughed. "I know. Why not just bring the stone to Olympus or the hut of Baba Yaga?"

Jeremiah shook his head. "No, no. It is real. The

Geneva Bible, Genesis 2:8–14, names Pishon, Gihon, Hiddekel, and Perath as the four rivers that flowed from Eden. Hiddekel and Perath, in Greek, are the Tigris and the Euphrates. That's the place the stone names, where Aten dipped his hands into the clay of the riverbank to form the first man."

"You can't be serious," Hylic said. "You actually want to go to the Garden?"

"You're the one who told me about places where legend and history cross," Jeremiah said. "This sounds like one. The rivers are real enough. They meet near a small village called Al-Qurnah. It's in Ottoman territory, the Pashalik of Baghdad."

"So you mean to do this?" Hylic asked. "To steal the stone from the Bandites and take it to this place, hoping Bandias will somehow be weak enough to kill? He'd still be at least as strong as Skog, you know."

"I nearly beat Skog once," Jeremiah said.

Hylic sighed heavily and touched the wound on his chest. "Were it not for me. Very well, then, I'm with you, but I'll tell you, I think I now know how those dust-crawlers felt, finally realizing how precious life is, then deciding to give it up all the same."

22

Most remarkable," Monsieur Pagels commented as he politely listened to the fishermen's tale of how they'd swept two men and a woman from the sea after their balloon tumbled from the sky, how they'd stayed for a short time, then left.

Pagels was a tall man and a man of means, so aristocratic in his bearing one might expect a French revolutionary to behead him were it not for his personal guard. He wore a long, tailored suit and vest with elegant matching pants. His graying beard was trimmed into a perfect goatee. A top hat crowned his long skull, increasing his already considerable height so much that each time he stepped from his exquisite carriage, it fell off. His anxious squirrel of a servant would race to pick it up and brush the dirt from it.

Pagels, clearly pleased by the locals' stories, went on to explain his purpose in coming to the town. He wished to hire six boats for an expedition to the bay, where he expected to retrieve, with minor difficulty, a large stone.

On behalf of the townsfolk, Louis Desmarais bombarded him with questions. Once Pagels described the amount he was offering for Desmarais's assistance, the use of the boats and their captains, and the best divers the town had to offer, the beaming official asked nothing further.

A hidden Jeremiah watched and listened, counting Pagels's guards and cataloging their belongings. Once the man and his entourage retired for the night, Jeremiah returned to the deserted barn they'd found some miles away, where they'd settled after pretending to leave. Aside from privacy, it offered a fine view of both the bay and the roads to Douarnenez.

When Jeremiah described Pagels, Hylic claimed never to have met him. He did remember Skog discussing an influential Parisian who'd helped arrange for the corvette and its treacherous captain.

Jeremiah was wary about how few men the Bandites had sent. He was certain there were more nearby, but failing to find them, there was little else to do but keep watch. With Hylic and Amala guarding their barn during the sun-filled days, he was free to rest for the first time in as long as he could remember. Even so, he wouldn't lie down until morning was nearly over, and rose long before sunset. He spent the time rifling through his memory, searching for anything he might have missed.

His spirits rose whenever Amala was near. With the beast devoted to protecting her, it made her the first human he could approach since his change without wanting to feed. He found it easier and easier to relax around her. Hylic, having no such protection, wisely tried to irritate Fall as little as possible.

Meanwhile, Amala told him what was written on the

stone so often he could practically recite it himself, except for those parts too difficult to pronounce. Beyond the story, there were, as she'd said, instructions and incantations. One to free Bandias, a second to allow him to possess one of his children, and a third for his bride to invite him to plant his seed in her, as Havah had. If the carvings were true, it was as Hylic said in the rowboat: Once the first incantation freed Bandias, he would de-create reality when the year renewed itself, regardless of whether the other incantations were used. All they'd done was delay him.

Beyond that, Jeremiah could find no hint of a weakness to exploit, or any evidence of a way to cure himself. Still, they went through each line, pretending they both believed that somehow the world could go on. Whenever Amala thought he wasn't looking, though, the air filled with her anxiety, telling him she was lying.

While she slept, Jeremiah prodded Hylic for more information. He described anyone in the town he saw exchanging more than a few words with Pagels, wondering if that person might be the Bandite the letter had been intended for.

"I don't know *every* Bandite, you know," Hylic protested. "We're everywhere. We keep our faith secret and certainly don't keep a membership list. It's like expecting you to know the name of every Puritan, if you assume every Puritan *didn't* want his faith known."

His options exhausted, Jeremiah fell to watching the progress of Pagels's odd project. In spite of himself, he was fascinated by the mechanics. Workers rigged six of the larger fishing boats with trestle, ropes, and winches while Pagels held contests among the town's swimmers to see who could hold his breath the longest.

One bright morning the boats set out, and the three of them—Hylic, Amala, and Jeremiah—sat on a blanket on a hill overlooking the bay. Hylic and Amala took turns using Jeremiah's telescope to watch the swimmers dive with ropes tied around their waists, spending breathless minutes beneath the surface. Jeremiah relied on his eyes. As the two living humans ate the wine and cheese he'd procured from the village, it occurred to him what a strange scene this was, almost like a picnic.

By late afternoon, the ropes were in place, and the sailors manned the winches. As they started work, Jeremiah turned from the bay.

"Why are you looking away?" Amala asked.

"I'm not. I'm listening. They're singing an old shanty, to keep the cranks turning in time."

"You can hear them?" Hylic asked. Jeremiah nodded.

"Sing it for me," Amala asked.

Jeremiah shrugged. "It's about a man whose love sailed away. He wishes he were a blackbird so he could follow.

> *"I've sailed on the ocean,*
> *My fortune to seek*
> *Oh, I miss her caress,*
> *And her kiss on my cheek*
> *I returned and I told her,*
> *My love was still warm*
> *But she turned away lightly,*
> *And great was her scorn."*

She put her hand to his knee. In the last few days, he'd allowed her more and more physical contact and had taken more and more comfort in it. But now the sheer normalcy of the moment evoked a deep pang. He didn't want to fail her, but how could he succeed?

The winches turned, and the boats tipped, lower and lower, until it looked as if they might capsize. Circles rippled out at their center until at last the top of the stone, wrapped in thick rope, broke the surface. The cheers were loud enough for Amala and Hylic to hear.

After that, things happened fast. The stone was taken to the docks and placed in the tall carriage. No one remarked how perfectly it was suited for the size of the stone, as if it were built to carry it.

Smiling, and tipping his hat, Pagels paid everyone. As they applauded his largesse, he quickly moved into his own carriage. When his top hat fell as he entered, his servant didn't bother picking it up. Soon the two carriages were headed down the road.

"Time to get ready," Jeremiah said. The picnic, such as it was, was over.

Within an hour, the sun drooped beneath the tree line, and the air grew colder. As the two carriages ambled down a narrow road, the first driver shifted the reins to one hand in order to pull his coat tighter around his neck.

An unusual whipping noise, like tight ropes snapping when suddenly cut free, made him lift his head. Before he could do more than gasp, two thick logs, held by ropes tied high in the trees, swung from the brush. They careened toward the first carriage at the level of the coach wheels. The first narrowly hit the harnesses, terrifying the horses. The other slammed the rear right wheel, breaking it. The coach leaned down and back, then halted once the axle had dug itself too deeply into the earth.

A third log, not held by any ropes, flew at the second, taller carriage as if it had been hurled. It flew beneath the wagon's center, landing between the front and rear wheels. The horses groaned as they tried to pull the carriage over it, but the stone's weight made that impossible.

By the time the first driver released the reins and tried to grab his pistol, Jeremiah was on him. He knocked him out with a single blow, then raced to the second carriage and did likewise there.

The carriage door flew open and Pagels's hired guards rushed out. But as each came, Jeremiah yanked him from the door and hurled him away. After a rough landing, they were knocked unconscious by Hylic and Amala with old shovels they'd found in the barn.

Soon eleven men lay unconscious by the side of the road. All accounted for except their employer, Jeremiah looked into the fine carriage to find the tall and hatless Monsieur Pagels. He seemed to be trying to press his lanky form into the seat cushions. When he saw Jeremiah, his face lit up.

"Remarkable," he said as Jeremiah pulled him from the carriage. Balanced on the step, Jeremiah held him aloft by his ascot. Pagels's long legs left his feet dangling only by inches. When Jeremiah bared his fangs, the same insipid smile he'd once seen on Hylic spread across this man's face. "In all my years, I never dreamed I'd be allowed to see a creature such as yourself. It would be the fulfillment of a lifelong desire if you would deign to kill me and end this dream forever."

As he waited for a fatal blow, Pagels clasped his hands to pray. Jeremiah slammed the top of his head into the tall man's forehead and hurled him roughly to the ground near the others.

"Keep dreaming," Jeremiah said.

As Amala and Hylic stood over the men, Jeremiah examined the supplies and luggage. As he did, Hylic became increasingly restless.

"Aren't you going to feed on *any* of them?" he asked, astounded.

"No."

"It's a waste. You need strength. And we can't let them live," Hylic protested.

"Why not?"

Hylic lowered the shovel, mouth agape. "For a man who's been in so many battles, you certainly seem to have a great deal of difficulty with killing."

Jeremiah continued his search. "Those men are hired hands. They're not part of this. There's no reason they should die. Pagels is the only Bandite here."

"Very well," Hylic said.

With a quick swing of his shovel, he smashed Monsieur Pagels's skull.

Jeremiah turned to him, furious. Hylic protested. "Do I have to remind you what's at stake?"

He moved toward Hylic, but Amala held him back. "Jeremiah, he's right. What else could you have done? Dragged him all the way across Europe and Turkey?"

"Actually, yes," Jeremiah said. "He might have told us many things."

"Not him," Hylic said. "He was a true believer."

"So were you," Jeremiah answered.

Gritting his teeth, Jeremiah went back to the carriage and looked inside. Pagels hadn't acted as if he were protecting only himself in here. What was it, then? He ripped the seat up. In a hollow beneath it sat a small oak chest. It was heavy for its size, and from the sound it made as he lifted it, Jeremiah guessed what was inside. He carried it out, put it on the ground, and snapped the padlock. Gold coins, scores of them, spilled from the motion of opening the lid. It was a fortune. They could buy a ship and hire a crew for the journey to Al-Qurnah.

"What luck," Hylic said.

But Jeremiah didn't feel lucky. He rose and listened to the night, concentrating until he thought he could even hear the slow movements of the stars.

"What's wrong?" Amala asked.

"This has been too easy. They practically handed it to us. Bandias is out there somewhere using Skog's body. He could have stopped us. Why didn't he?"

Hylic exhaled air between pursed lips. "Who knows if such a creature thinks at all? Time itself could be different to him. By the time he finishes a thought, a month may pass."

"Or maybe he *wants* us to have the stone, *wants* us to take it to Al-Qurnah. The stone is useless without a mate. We could be heading into a trap," Jeremiah said. He turned toward Hylic. "Funny, but the only reason we've come this far has been the information *you've* been feeding us."

Hylic's own eyes narrowed. "This is getting tired. I don't blame you for distrusting me. A man who cannot trust his own hungers, how can he trust anyone? War disenchanted me with the world, so I sought ecstasy. I thought I'd found it. You saw my face as I looked into that darkness. There was no ecstasy there. You saved me from that, perhaps only for half a year before the end of the world, but still...I vowed I would return the favor. I still say I will, unless, of course, you kill me now. And may I say for the first time, I'd rather you didn't?"

Jeremiah grunted and turned away. Hylic seemed sincere, but from the beginning he'd felt guided by an unseen hand—to the poem, to Rashid, to here. But whose hand was it—the Devil's, the Lord's, or something else entirely?

23

Nearing the coast of the Eyalet of Aleppo, Syria

Limping to Eden, chained to the Devil himself.

From the railing of the Italian ship the *Santa Marta,* Jeremiah watched the town of Latokia grow. Slivers of white shone on the wave crests, as if moonlight had flaked off and settled on the ocean. On the horizon, a fortress rose, said to date back to the time of Alexander. Nearer the shore, a mosque's minaret towered above decrepit warehouses. He could see the janissaries, soldiers in the standing Ottoman army, as they roused from slumber and prepared to greet the ship.

The bow burst through another wave, spraying his face with salt water. It felt cool as his skin but not as lifeless. Europe was just a memory. It'd taken two weeks to maneuver the carriage across France, then fifteen days for the schooner-rigged ship to cross the Mediterranean.

They'd made good time, but the world clock was ticking, with just three months left before the new year.

History, and all within it, kept churning, unmindful of its beginning or end. Everywhere it seemed men churned with the same chaotic fury as the sea. The France they'd left behind was poised on the brink of another revolution. Napoleon had returned, to the consternation of the Director. He claimed that their orders for him to remain had never arrived. They claimed his disobedience was treason. Only the cheering Parisian crowds stopped them from moving against him. Now it seemed only a matter of time before he moved against the government. The Ottomans, meanwhile, gathered an army to reclaim Egypt.

But Jeremiah was headed for Eden.

He went to the storage hold to wake his companions. Hylic lay in a nest of rags and straw, looking like an ungainly, flightless bird. Amala was curled at the foot of the stone, her ivory-colored robes stark against its blackness. It seemed a normal darkness now, though. Without Bandias's spirit inside it, the stone was like a husk. Discussed and studied endlessly, it provided neither danger nor answers.

In another corner lay his own clothing, the long, thin strips he wrapped his hands in during the daylight, and his one extravagance, the satin mask he had purchased in France. It protected him well, but he hated using it. It reminded him of Skog.

Sensing his presence, Amala opened her eyes. "We're there?"

He nodded. "Nearly."

"We could have gotten beds with all our gold," Hylic complained.

"We'll need what's left of the money just to get out of Syria," Jeremiah said. "Did you sew it into our clothing?"

"Yes," Amala said, yawning.

"And left half in the chest for them to find," Hylic added sadly.

"If what Qarsaq told me about Aleppo is true, it's all about the bribes. The army and the religious groups, called *sharifs*, struggle for control. The Ottoman governors play one off the other so they can steal as much as possible for themselves. It's still better than trying to get past the French *and* the Ottomans."

The timbers above their head rattled. Their Italian captain shouted his docking commands.

"Sounds like we've arrived," Jeremiah said. "Get ready to be arrested."

The janissaries were a not-unpleasant combination of sleepy and drunk. Any decent soldiers had been called south. With Napoleon's replacement, General Kleber, negotiating a French withdrawal from Egypt, the sultan wanted to be in position to either reoccupy peacefully or attack quickly.

Jeremiah gave the squalid soldiers a few coins, but insisted that the rest of what was in the chest was for the *effendis*, the local administrators, the men who could get things done. Seeing the ancient stone, the janissaries were convinced their business might actually be as important as Jeremiah claimed. Interfering with them no further, they escorted the trio to a manor home in the shadow of Alexander's fortress.

Amala and Hylic were told to wait while Jeremiah and the chest of coins were brought to a spacious parlor.

Once lavish, the tile floors were stained, and the beautiful geometric patterns in the wall mosaics chipped.

A narrow carpet led to a wide desk in the middle of the room. The guards placed the chest on the carpet between Jeremiah and the desk, then withdrew.

Behind the desk, a middle-aged man in colorful but threadbare robes perched in a high seat. He drew water-cooled smoke from a hookah. Two older, bespectacled men, dressed more modestly, flanked him. "Welcome to the Eyalet of Aleppo, Jeremiah Fall," the man with the hookah said. "I am Jabal Tarif."

Jeremiah let his surprise register. "You know me."

"Of course," Tarif said. "Murad Bey wrote in detail of the American who travels by night and has a perpetual interest in large stones."

What had Murad written? Would they arrest him as a traitor? "I gave him my best advice."

Tarif sucked languidly on the hookah. "So he said. He also said he was a fool for not listening to you. Selim III himself mentioned your bravery in the battle while address-ing our troops. You've become something of a legend."

A legend. He hoped he wouldn't wind up like Ys. When Jeremiah said nothing, Tarif asked, "Doesn't this please you?"

Jeremiah turned his palms up in an open gesture. "If it pleases the sultan, then I'm pleased. I only hope I don't run into my legend one day and find myself the weaker of the two."

Tarif nodded. "A humble response from an impressive man. So far, Murad's words do not overestimate you. The stone on your ship, I assume it's the one stolen from the French?"

"Yes."

"Of course, you're here to return it to Egypt's rightful rulers."

"Of course," Jeremiah answered with a bow. "But first, I have a favor to ask."

"Favors cost money."

Jeremiah rose from his bow, then lifted the chest onto the desk. Between what they'd hidden and what they'd spent on the voyage, less than a third of the coins remained, but the amount was still substantial. Tarif pretended a lack of interest, but Jeremiah heard his heartbeat quicken.

"This will do for our customs tax. But what is the favor?"

As he recited the fable he had prepared, Jeremiah wondered if it would become part of his legend, too. "The stone is half of a set of directions left by Alexander the Great. I would like to bring it to Al-Qurnah, where I think the second half is buried, and match them. If I'm correct, they lead to a buried vault. It would be the greatest find in history, bringing great knowledge, prestige, and Alexander's gold."

The corner of Tarif's upper lip twisted upward. "And finding this lost knowledge is the desire that drove you when you fought with Murad Bey?"

Jeremiah shrugged. "A tenth of the treasure would make a man rich beyond his dreams."

"Then a twentieth would satisfy your dreams precisely, I assume?"

Jeremiah feigned disappointment, then nodded agreement. "Done."

One of the men on either side of Tarif leaned in and

whispered. As he listened, the official kept his dark eyes on Jeremiah. Jeremiah, of course, could hear the advice being offered and knew what would come next.

"The journey is long," Tarif explained. "I couldn't forgive myself if I sent you unprotected. Also, it would be difficult for us to learn if you succeed or fail. I will therefore supply a hundred janissaries to accompany you. You'll have to pay for them, of course."

Jeremiah grimaced at the complication. "So many troops seem unnecessary."

"Oh, it's my pleasure. Our soldiers will help bring whatever you find back for an impartial accounting. But this is good for you as well. Eighty thousand men gather on the border with Egypt. This is not a good time to be a foreigner. Their presence will provide the proof three strangers will need that your journey is official."

"I see the wisdom in it," Jeremiah said.

"Then it's agreed. I'll also tell you there are continuing reports that some of Bonaparte's troops remained behind after the failure of their cowardly attack on Acre."

"That was in June. Three months ago. They went east, into the desert? Why?"

Tarif shrugged. "Who understands the Franks? We thought the plague or dehydration would destroy them, but the reports continue, like glimpses of giant desert snakes or glowing balls of fire in the sky. They may be imagination fired by fear, or not." He looked out the window at the peaceful night sky. "I assume Murad is also correct about your preferred travel time. The men will be ready tomorrow evening. The funds, of course, will be paid directly to me. I wish you great good fortune, and myself as well."

Jeremiah was about to leave when the second of the two advisers leaned in to whisper. This time, Tarif hissed. He looked at Jeremiah with a sigh. "I'm afraid we have fewer troops available than I thought. I will send twenty men. The cost, however, remains the same."

"Twenty of your men will be as good as two hundred Franks," Jeremiah said.

Tarif laughed. "The reports claim seventy Franks, so perhaps I will only send seven!"

"It could have been worse," Jeremiah told Hylic and Amala back on the ship. They tore most of their remaining coins from the folds of their packed clothing to pay for the troops and some supplies. "The soldiers will make travel easier. Once we reach the Euphrates, we have to travel through three more provinces, the Eyalets of Raqqah and Mosul, then the Pashalik of Baghdad."

Though the price remained constant, the actual number that met them the following night was eight. Two deserted after a few miles along the hilly road to the ancient river, but the six remaining seemed to have no better place to go.

The Euphrates was a welcome relief, its waters cool and fast, with thick plant growth on either side. Once the stone was loaded on a wide barge, the thought of speeding their journey might have pleased Jeremiah, were he not aware of what lay ahead. At times, he watched Amala as if every time he saw her might be the last.

In Raqqah, they floated past dry, rocky ruins that stretched along the bank for half a mile. The tents of nomads and an old fortress with a few soldiers were the only evidence of inhabitants.

"It would be easier to think of saving the world if

more of it looked nicer," Hylic said. "Where is the grand capital, Ar-Raqqah?"

"That's it," Jeremiah explained. "The city was destroyed by Mongols in the thirteenth century. It's barely a trading post now. Frankly, the fewer people we run into, the better."

Hylic's observation on the world's beauty was accurate, if not heartening. After Ar-Raqqah, the places they passed seemed as dry and lifeless as the uninhabited stone. The long days rendered even the wide, flat Euphrates unimpressive. For Jeremiah, it became another exercise in patience, perhaps his last.

Trading stories with the janissaries provided little distraction. They were simple men who dreamed no further than the wine and women their tiny salaries might enable them to enjoy for an hour or so. The brightest among them, Farid, wasn't even really a soldier. He confessed to having been given his uniform by his older brother an hour before arriving at the port.

The soldiers spent most of their time asleep, not even caring why Jeremiah wore a mask and covered his hands and fingers or why he slipped off to hunt along the bank.

Invariably Jeremiah's mind turned back to the stone, as if thinking about it could somehow invest it with the answers he desired. For hours, he sat in front of it and stared.

"You two are starting to look alike," Amala told him. "I doubt it's saying anything new. Are you?"

Jeremiah shrugged. "I was thinking how this stone held Bandias. It means he was trapped. I wish we knew how. I don't even understand its relationship to him.

Is this the clay he was made from? Is it even really a prison?"

"We know the carvings can summon him," Amala offered.

"But why? The bombers in the desert seemed to think destroying it would make a difference. Maybe that would've worked, while he was in it, if I hadn't stopped them."

Amala made a face. "I never met anyone who blamed himself so much for not knowing everything."

"It is pretty important."

"But must our...time together be like this?"

He knew she was going to say "our final time together." After that, try as she might to soothe him, Jeremiah only grew more pensive, refusing to wear his mask and instead spending his days beneath a blanket.

When they reached the Baghdad Pashalik, the last leg of their journey, the current grew rough and fast. Knowing they would soon arrive drove him deeper into despair.

"I don't blame you. Why should you be cheerful?" Hylic, the man who once chided him for being dour, said. "Even if we succeed, we're all likely to get sucked into that abyss and never even be remembered."

Hating to agree with the former Bandite, Jeremiah said, "That might be better than being remembered as a monster."

"Easy for you to say."

On a day when the sun burned so hot it threatened even the skin of the living, Jeremiah still refused to put on the mask. Instead he lay beneath the blanket, head pressed against the stone, listening to the river slosh beneath him, trying to remember his mother's face. He was about to drift off when the cloth surrounding him moved. He started to grab it, but saw Amala slip into the dark beside him.

"Hylic's trying to get Farid to gamble with him again. It seems such a petty way to get our gold back. I'd rather spend time with you," she whispered. "It's so dark under here I can barely see you, except for those eyes of yours. It's like talking to two red flames."

"Sorry." He closed his eyes.

"Don't be. It's a warm light. At least they let me see your face."

The sign of a predator, he wanted to say, but didn't.

She put her head against his chest. "We're almost there. What do you think we'll find? Would it surprise you to see one of the cherubim guarding the tree of life with a sword?"

"I'd think someone would have noticed that by now."

"I know it's dangerous, but aren't you in the least excited? We're traveling to Eden."

"We're going to summon an omnipotent devil, and I'm supposed to try to kill him before he rapes you. And that's if things go according to plan. No, I'm not excited."

"We all die anyway, no? Even you."

She sighed into his chest and rubbed his shoulder. "You think you're a monster. I think you've been lucky. I know life mostly through books and stories. I've spent all my years studying, but that's nothing compared to you. You've seen ten thousand times what I have, read ten thousand more."

"You might not feel that way if you'd seen what I've seen."

"It can't all have been so horrible," she said. "Or you would be more like Skog. Would you answer a question for me and think about it before you do?"

"Of course."

She smiled. "How do I say this? What's more important to you: what you've experienced or what you've read? Not just what you've read...I mean is it the things you try to believe in or what the world shows you?"

Keeping his eyes shut, he furrowed his brow. "Lately I've been having trouble telling the difference, Amala. Books and the world, my thoughts and reality, have been crossing over in ways I never imagined possible. It feels like two rivers inside me, one strong as the other, getting so close they're ready to crash together forever. The idea of their meeting terrifies me more than anything, even more than what I am. I can't even really say why."

She pressed her fingers against his lips.

"Perhaps," she said, "that's what happens when a soul approaches its destiny."

"Maybe, but I won't know until I get there."

She put her chin up on his chest. "Open your eyes. I want to tell you something and I want you to look at me while I do it."

"No."

"Please."

He did. The darkness of the blanket held no secrets from his eyes. Though he'd seen her face mere moments ago, the memory didn't do it justice. He wished he could answer her question by saying that seeing her always felt more important than anything he'd read or thought.

"Jeremiah Fall," she said, "there's one thing I know that you don't."

"What's that?"

"That in the end, no matter when or how or why it happens, you and I will be together."

He brushed the back of his hand up her arm, then gently along the curve of her skull. He spread his fingers so her smooth hair passed between them. "How do you know that? Something you read or something you experienced?"

"I don't know how I know; I just know that I do, and that doesn't bother me one bit."

"I wish..." he said, but he was cut off by her kiss. The beast was so quiet, he drew her closer, unafraid at his longing to pull her living warmth inside himself.

But then his stomach bubbled a warning. Something was about to happen.

What was it? The stone, or...?

A sudden lurch twisted the barge. Amala flew across his chest, taking the blanket with her. They'd hit something large and nearly capsized. Exposed, his unprotected face was sliced by the midday's rays. It would take seconds to cover himself, but instead he reached for Amala first, to make sure she was safe. And in that time, the sun struck his cheeks long enough to make smoke rise from them.

Never having seen it before, Hylic stared. So did all six soldiers.

The rocking stopped. Amala was fine, sitting upright, balancing herself against the stone. Jeremiah grabbed the mask and rolled it onto his head.

"I have a skin condition," he explained.

The janissaries might have deserted then and there had not the barge struck another rock and spun violently. As he shook with the raft, Jeremiah looked to see where they were headed. The Euphrates, no longer flat and even, was pockmarked with dangerous white risings. Far ahead, though, the waters were clear again and the river widened. Jeremiah could make out the huts and small buildings of a village among the tall palm trees. Al-Qurnah. They'd arrived.

Hylic and the soldiers put long poles into the water, trying to steer, but they'd long ago proven useless at such tasks. In a panic, they were unable to coordinate their efforts at all. Worse, the barge was headed directly for the largest whitecap, the gray boulder beneath it visible even through the froth.

Jeremiah leaped into the river, quickly touched bottom, and planted his feet in the sediment. The barge was above him, dragged inexorably by the currents. Before it could pass over him completely, he grabbed at it. As he held it, he found he could still touch the riverbed, but when he tried to dig his feet in to slow the raft, the soft ground gave and the weight dragged him forward.

A three-foot-tall river stone slammed his thigh, then another. When he saw a third loom through the bubbling water, he lifted himself out of its way. As the barge passed it, he braced his feet against the smooth stone and pushed. The craft wobbled, but remained on a collision course with the boulder ahead.

He flew back aboard and grabbed a pole from a frightened janissary.

"Do what I do!" Jeremiah barked to the others. "Same side, same direction! Now!"

Afraid to disobey, they fell in line. The barge grazed the boulder's side, but remained upright. It continued past the rapids into the quieter waters.

The soldiers cheered. Jeremiah smiled. Realizing they couldn't see his face under the mask, he nodded enthusiastically and said, in Turkish, "Good. Good."

Soon they drifted quietly toward a spot where the river they were on met another. It was here the fruitful met the tiger, if the meaning behind the names Euphrates and Tigris were to be taken literally. With some difficulty, they slowed the barge and brought it up along a bank opposite the village.

Al-Qurnah itself was a square of crude thatched tents, mud houses, and one or two modest limestone structures. It seemed uninhabited, the only living things the palms, fish, and birds. The area where they'd landed was considerably lusher. Here the trees grew close together along the bank, and thick tropical grass covered the ground. Beyond the patch of palms, more green growth stretched out in a wide, open field.

"So where do we look for the treasure?" Farid asked.

Jeremiah looked guiltily into the youth's innocent face. He should've thrown the soldiers off a hundred miles away, rather than let them share the fate here. How could he explain it now?

"We...we have to find it. It's buried," Jeremiah said. "Pull the barge up as far as you can."

Amala, a dreamy expression on her face, waded across a shallow toward the village. "I'll see if anyone's there," she said.

"Wait," Jeremiah said.

She smiled. "Don't worry. Nothing can happen until I recite the incantation."

He stared at her until she was halfway across the river. The even rush of mixing waters filled his ears strangely, drowning the sound of her heartbeat. He watched a bird fly on the opposite shore and realized he couldn't hear it either. It was as if there were an unseen barrier between that place and this.

He stepped off the barge, planning to follow Amala, but found himself staring at the verdant field. No cherubim, but in the center, a wide tree grew. It was different from the palms along the banks, very different, and obviously very old. Its myriad twisting branches were dense enough to hold water, but it seemed nearly lifeless.

Was that the Tree of the Knowledge of Good and Evil, or the Tree of Life? Was this Eden? Was it just Eden for Aten and Bandias, the Garden named in Genesis a different thing entirely? Or was it caught like Ys, somewhere between legend and history?

He knelt where the water met the ground. Covering one hand with his shadow, he removed the wrappings from his fingers and stuck his bare skin into the muck where it made a deep burbling, slurping sound. Closing his hands around some dirt, he pulled it back into the air and let the shapeless slime drip across his open palm and fall between his fingers.

Cannot I do with you as this potter does? As the clay is in the potter's hand, so are you in mine.

Was this that clay? Was this where man was born? His mind tried to twist his heart around the idea. He tried to convince himself it was true, then again that it couldn't be.

At least his hearing still worked on this side of the river. He caught Farid's quick breath well before he rushed up beside him. "Hylic wants you to join us. We need your help to pull the barge farther onto the bank."

Jeremiah didn't answer. As he looked at the mud, his mind was stuck in an indecisive nether realm. But the beast pulled him out. Not by telling him to kill, but by screaming a warning that set his entire body aflame.

The woman! Save her!

Farid made a sound as if he were about to repeat his request when a musket ball tore through his neck. His head snapped backward, and he collapsed to his knees. Before his body could finish falling, the whistle of more gunfire filled the air. Jeremiah threw himself toward the barge. Two of the janissaries were dead, the other three fleeing.

Across the river, the barrels of French muskets appeared over the ridges of the mud hovels. Their iron pellets flew across the river. Some splashed into the water; others careened off the surface of the stone, leaving not so much as a scratch.

The French, so close. Like Amala's heartbeat, he hadn't heard them.

Amala. Did they have her? Had she found cover?

He slipped behind the tall rock, next to a cowering Hylic.

"How did they find us?" Jeremiah said.

"Perhaps that is a question best left for later?" he answered. A musket ball ricocheted near his head, making him roll into a fetal position.

A woman's shriek ripped through the air above the rivers. That, he heard.

Heedless of any danger, Jeremiah rose, searching the village for any sign of her. All he could make out were the vertical tips of bayonets as the French reloaded.

As they worked, a mustached man in a lieutenant's uniform raised his head.

"Rendez la pierre et de personne d'autre n'a besoin mourir!"

Surrender the stone, and no one else need die.

No one else?

"Who are you?" Jeremiah shouted back.

The lieutenant sneered. *"Je vais poser les questions. La femme a déjà été tués. Ne vous souhaitez vous joindre à elle?"*

I'll ask the questions. The woman has already been killed. Do you wish to join her?

Amala? Dead?

The two rivers within Jeremiah crashed together, drowning everything he thought he was. Was this the shattering moment Hylic and Skog had spoken of? It didn't matter. Nothing did. He straightened and stepped from the cover of the stone.

"What are you doing?" Hylic asked.

He didn't answer. The French fired again. Balls of searing metal tore the air on either side of him, carrying the smell of burnt powder. Most missed, but some tore his clothes. A lucky shot raked the skin on his thigh down to the muscle. He didn't feel it. The wounds of his body were no longer a concern. The only thing that mattered was his rage.

Kill them.

With his back to Paradise, Jeremiah Fall moved toward the French, the crimson shine of his eyes visible even in the sunlight.

24

His feral half so used to being suppressed, Jeremiah Fall was halfway across the river before his savage instincts realized they were fully in control. Performing a feat the beast always knew, but Jeremiah had unknowingly prevented its using, he vanished and reappeared directly among the French.

Startled to find their target beside them, the soldiers froze. Jeremiah could practically hear their thoughts as they struggled to decide whether to obey instinct or reason, in a world in which magic was suddenly real. Those in whom instinct won were the first to flee. Even the desperate, hurried pitch of their bodies looked sluggish, as if they were all in a dream and Jeremiah the only man awake.

Before any could fully turn away from him, Jeremiah counted them all (not thirty as he'd originally guessed, closer to fifty) and determined the rough order in which they would die. He grabbed the nearest arm, snapped it from its socket as if tugging a ripe fruit from a tree, then used its pulpy stub to crush another man's skull.

As the nightmare unfolded, the long-faced lieutenant with the pencil-thin mustache stumbled backward. *"Tirez vos armes!"* he shouted.

Fire your weapons!

Jeremiah vanished and reappeared again, leaving those not yet trying to flee to shiver with incomprehension. By the time they overcame their paralysis enough to contemplate obeying their leader's command, two more had perished, and Jeremiah was drinking greedily from the split neck of a third.

Blood spurted into his mouth as if from a fountain, the death of his long-held vow beneath his notice. He didn't even enjoy the taste. His stormy mind failed to linger on any sensation long enough to appreciate how his nervous system shimmered and his body swelled with delirious energy. All it meant was that he had more power with which to kill.

The lieutenant held his terror back long enough to issue his command again. *"Tirez vos armes!"*

The remaining soldiers launched a crackling swarm of seething metal pellets at Jeremiah. Again he vanished, leaving their shots to either crash into the earth or hit their fellows, affording them some of the most merciful deaths of the day.

In flashes of broken moments, torn from the stream of time, the massacre went on. Jeremiah reappeared only long enough to kill or drink. Knowing hell had no point if the pain ended too quickly, he left the lieutenant for last. When he was done with the others, Jeremiah held the man up by the back of his head, then twisted it slowly across the gory scene so he could fully apprehend the torment of each fallen man.

"It's nothing," Jeremiah told him. "You're nothing."

He reached for the man's thin face and tore the flesh from it, dropping it to the ground like a sickening mask, the entirety of his mustache still intact on the skin.

It was still not enough. Nothing could be, but Jeremiah was determined to try. He searched among the bodies for those only wounded. For every man he found still remotely alive, he tried to discover some new way of folding or breaking him. The only surprise the beast encountered was Jeremiah's inventiveness.

Once every conceivable agony had been wrung from the murderers, once their flesh was beyond any hurt, Jeremiah fed on the warm corpses, drinking and sucking fluids tinged with copper and a thousand other flavors. All the while, the happy beast assured him his crime was not the worst mankind had ever seen.

Far from it.

When he was finally gorged, his abdomen was so bloated his innards sloshed as he moved. By then, the sun had given up on the scene, lying low just above the field's solitary tree. It turned the clouds around it as bloodred as the ground at Jeremiah's feet.

As if in a final cruelty, the sated beast contentedly fell asleep, leaving Jeremiah alone to contemplate what he'd done. As he staggered among the dead he'd created, he found his horrible fullness brought the opposite of drunkenness. His mind was terrifically clear, his thoughts crystal pure. The images his eyes brought to his mind, the sounds his ears carried, and the messages that tingled on his skin all had intense depth and clarity. Sensation conveyed such hyper-reality, it seemed to cross into dream and back again, as if the two were, and had always been, one and the same.

For all the tactile wealth swarming him, he no longer felt part of anything. He was lost, gone, as if he'd died at his father's hands long ago on a snowy night in Dedham, and everything he'd done since had been the actions of a corpse moving from mere momentum.

A low moan came to his ears. To a human it would have been barely audible, but to him, stoked full, it was a scream. All sense of scale gone, he could not judge how far or near it was. Suspecting one of the soldiers had somehow escaped his wrath, he tore through the empty village seeking the source. As he did, the mind that Atticus had once praised as his path to salvation concocted six more ways to kill, each far more painful than the scores he'd already used.

Then he saw it, a single form coalescing from a thousand sensations, the last living thing. It lay semiconscious against a mud-house wall whose dirt was infested with the corpses of insects. His senses were so hyperactive, he had trouble matching the vision with anything from memory. He was almost upon it before he realized he knew who it was.

It was not a soldier. It was not one of the French. It was not a hitherto invisible native. It was a woman. No, not just a woman, a miracle—a spiteful miracle. Rather than grateful, it left him furious at any god that would pick now to return her from the dead.

Amala.

Amala.

Alive. A bruise the shape of a rifle butt made a thick crease in her brow, right where the single line of her consternation always formed.

The lieutenant had lied. Why? Hoping to cow his

enemy into an easy defeat with a smug boast? Fool. Arrogant fool.

"Look what he made me do," Jeremiah said. "Look what I did."

His knees wobbled. He fell beside her and wept, but instead of tears, the blood of other men dripped from his eyes. He sobbed like a baby, wishing he were the one who'd been forgotten in the moment of his creation.

He apologized to the lieutenant, to Atticus, to Nathan, to Mary Vincent, to his infant brother James, to each and every soldier he'd slain, and to his God.

Mistake. Accident. Folly.

He did not apologize to himself but took a sad comfort that he would fully deserve whatever came next.

He scooped Amala into his arms and carried her back across the Euphrates. He hoped the shoulder-deep water of the river would wash away some of the stains from his skin and his clothes. Arriving at the other side, he saw it hadn't. Even her ivory-colored robes were left a pale pink.

He laid her near the stone, facing her away from the carnage, so upon waking she could gaze out into the field where the single strong tree still grew.

It was time. He was ready to face the end.

Hylic, drained not just pale but white, stared across the river to the hill of human pieces. The former Bandite tried to speak three times before he succeeded.

"You...once asked why I hated the world, why I chose Bandias." He pointed at the dead. "That's why. That's what it was like in the northern Caucasus."

Jeremiah's face twisted. He bared his predatory fangs, his gums and mouth still lined with blood. "Worship whatever you want. I don't care. Still want to kill yourself? Go ahead. Would you like me to help? I'll do *that*, too!"

Hylic's mouth dropped open, as if he'd expected to speak with someone he knew, but found a stranger instead. "No. I told you I realized I was wrong when I stared into the abyss, and *I* still feel the same. But where are you now, Jeremiah? *What* are you?"

Hylic's racing heart made the veins in his neck throb. Every pore oozed fear. Jeremiah knew what he was thinking. Hylic was wondering if the beast could possibly still be hungry. Well, let him wonder, then. In answer, Jeremiah snarled, a lionlike growl that shook Hylic and echoed in the plain beyond.

Without another word, the Russian stood and ran.

25

$\longleftarrow$ ✦ ✦ $\longrightarrow$

He was not quite alone, but there was nothing he could do about that.

Her eyes flickered open. "Where am I, Jeremiah?" she said. "Where are you? I remember someone hitting me."

Her brow furrowed into her wound, making her wince. When she saw him, a smile played on her lips. "Your eyes. I've never seen them so red, like burning suns. You're like a silhouette, a shadow-man."

Like Bandias.

"Hush," he said.

She pulled herself up on her elbows. "What is it? What's wrong?"

"You have to say the words now. You have to summon him."

"So soon? Why?"

He didn't want to say, didn't want to tell her that awash with the blood of the men he'd killed, Jeremiah was as strong as he ever could be, that with his soul gushing in remorse, he would never be more willing to die.

Had the fate Atticus imagined now hardened him for the coming battle?

He lowered himself beside her. The space between them lacked the intimacy he had once felt. The glare from his eyes mingled with the gloom, forcing her to shield her face.

"Call him," he said.

Still confused, she grabbed at him. Her grip was weak, but he let her hold him long enough to feel the dampness on his clothes. She rubbed her fingers together and felt the blood.

"There were French soldiers," she said, remembering.

"Yes. Napoleon's secret mission. Their lieutenant said they'd killed you, so I killed them. I don't imagine my massacre will be forgiven, but with the entire world at stake, I might as well use my crime to best advantage."

She put her hand to his cheek. "Poor thing, don't you see? If their blood helps you, they'll have helped saved the world. If it doesn't, it will soon be as if they never were. Either way it doesn't matter."

He took her hand away. "No. It matters."

She stiffened and turned to the stone. "All right, Jeremiah. I'll begin."

"Wait," he said. "One last thing. If I fail, you could still stop him yourself."

He pressed the handle of his chipped knife into her hands.

"Once his seed is in you, you can…"

"Kill myself?" She looked at him. "Is that…is that what you want?"

"No. But I could spend lifetimes reciting the list of

things that have happened that I never wanted. I slaughtered fifty men because I thought they'd harmed you. I'd *rather* the world end than see you die. I know that. But if I fail, it won't be up to me. It will be your decision."

He rose, stepped back, and disappeared. "You said you *knew* we'd be together in the end, no matter how it came. Keep knowing that. I'll pray that it's true."

The blade in hand, she blinked, turned to the stone, and started pronouncing the strange tones of the ancient language.

But the forgotten man was not summoned. Instead, it seemed he had always been there, as if Amala's chant only pulled back the thin veil between chaos and creation and rendered him visible. As she spoke, Jeremiah saw him standing by the tree in the center of the field, his right hand against it. Somehow, Jeremiah knew it was the same pose he'd taken thousands of years ago, when he'd approached the first woman and asked that she eat of the fruit from that tree.

On that day you shall not surely die.

As if he'd been there at that primal moment, he could feel how the unfinished man made the hunger in Havah's belly play on her mind, the same way the beast toyed with Jeremiah. Bandias made her and the man fall from grace, he broke them, and now Jeremiah realized why—to make them more like him. The woman gave him so much in return—children, a name, a history. Even if Bandias was to remain hidden, she gave him the shadow of all the things he'd been denied. Was that why he'd waited so long to destroy the world, so first he could pretend to belong to it?

Knowing Bandias would see him no matter where he

was, Jeremiah walked across the field until they stood
face-to-face.

My child, the Bandy Man whispered.

"Nathan Fall was my father," Jeremiah said. "Atticus
before him, all the way back to Adam."

For a moment, they were the same height, the same
size, the same *shape*. The only difference was that for a
moment Bandias seemed a shadowy reflection of what
was real.

Illusions.

But when Amala finished the chant, Jeremiah Fall
realized he had not seen correctly, not at all. The forgotten man waited, letting Jeremiah's eyes adjust. Now
he saw him. His hands were huge, his eyes serene, his
shape as vivid and varied as the blackness between the
stars. Everything around him seemed sad and lonely in
comparison. The creature was not misshapen; he was
perfect. Bandias, humanity's dark father, was making
creation pale.

Not to attack, but to test what stood before him, Jeremiah touched the thing's chest. Unlike the inky form
that had swallowed his hand in Ys, this skin gave slightly
at the pressure, glowing gray where he touched instead
of black. As he pulled his hand back, the grayness swam
across Bandias and disappeared. Before it vanished, Jeremiah thought he saw the shape of Skog.

"Skog makes you real. He holds you in the world.
Before him, was it the stone? Was it the only thing that
kept you separate from the void?"

It doesn't matter, Bandias said. He nodded at Jeremiah's hand. The lines were gone from his palm. It was
smooth. Perfect.

"I think it does. I think it means I don't have to destroy you. I have to destroy Skog."

Jeremiah hurled his fist at the spot he imagined a jaw would be. More gray flashed through the figure. He saw an outline of Skog's face twisting sideways from the blow. He moved to punch again, but his knuckles were gone. The back of his right hand was as smooth as the front.

Do you see yet? Too late.

Though he suspected it wouldn't work, Jeremiah's instincts made him try to vanish. He would have, to human eyes, but Bandias vanished with him. In the space between moments, he grabbed Jeremiah's face and held it. Unable to feel Bandias's hand, Jeremiah felt only his own flesh—his cheeks, his nose, his mouth—as they surrendered their shape and substance.

It didn't happen quickly as it had with the followers at Ys. Bandias was taking his time, teaching his child a lesson.

Jeremiah kicked at the thing, only to have his foot vanish as well.

Do you understand now that you are nothing?

Bandias let go. Jeremiah fell. There wasn't even any blood at his ankle to mark the loss of his foot. He reached for his face, but his left hand met only featureless skin, smooth as pebble. He could still see, still hear, though, but only because Bandias had chosen to leave him his eyes and his ears.

Look.

By the bank of the river, a woman stepped out onto the plain.

Amala. Amala was coming.

He tried to scream, "No!" but his mouth was gone.

She moved casually, as if, like Havah, she were enjoying a stroll in the garden in the cool of the evening.

Jeremiah hurled himself at Bandias, this time losing his right arm and shoulder. But the blow again had an effect. More lines of gray rippled in the black. Skog's outline writhed.

He was not nothing then, not yet.

Bandias turned only slightly. It was the merest of gestures, but enough to tear apart the space between them and hurl what remained of Jeremiah into the trunk of the great tree. The bark cracked and gave at his back. He would have groaned if he could.

Amala was close, moving steadily, her bearing as regal as it was in the cave when he first saw her. Was she enthralled? Or trying to spare Jeremiah and sacrifice herself?

The woman is a ghost.

He pulled himself to standing. There was so little of him left that he needed a weapon, so he snapped a branch from the tree. The broken edge was white and hard as bone, its point sharp as any spear. Hoping it might be *the* tree, hoping it might be sacred, he put the branch under his arm, steadied it with his hand, and rushed forward, aiming for the monster's heart.

As its edge pierced the darkness, there came a terrible crack, like thunder erupting from the center of the earth. It was followed by a loud, hollow sound.

Thok!

Jeremiah was thrown back. Trails of light branched like lightning through Bandias, the same ivory hue as the bared wood. It not only illuminated the outline of

Skog's body, it looked as if it was attempting to wedge the Abenaki away from the surrounding dark.

Bits of Skog's face emerged from the black.

Bandias staggered. The cracks inside him brightened to a purer white. For a moment, the field was lit as if by a horrible storm. A chiaroscuro battle was taking place in the vague shape of a man. For a moment, Jeremiah dared hope.

But Bandias used Skog's shaking hand to withdraw the branch and hurl it away. It landed at the base of the tree, not far from Jeremiah. Black smoke curled from the ivory-colored wood.

The light faded; the darkness won. Skog within him straightened and disappeared.

It can't end like this, Jeremiah thought.

He dragged the remains of his body toward the smoldering branch, determined to try again, to keep trying until the darkness claimed all of him. But by the time Jeremiah's remaining fingers curled around the smooth wood, Amala had reached the tree.

It can. It can end just like this.

She stepped into the arms of the forgotten man. At once, the amorphous pocket of energy Jeremiah first saw during the ritual on Ys enveloped them. A wave pulsed from their joined center. It raced across the field in all directions, erasing whatever it touched. The lush plain was left a desert, the river lifeless. Even the torn bodies of the French in the village beyond faded.

The strength the human blood had provided vanished with the corpses. All that remained was Jeremiah and the tree at his back.

Abandoning the tree's support, and using the branch

as a crutch, he lurched across the few yards separating him from the night-shrouded couple. Within the crackling pocket, Bandias stroked Amala's cheek. She closed her eyes into the caress, tilting her head. The forgotten man traced the full lips of her open mouth with the nothing of his fingertips.

Jeremiah saw her body tremble, heard the sigh that passed from her lips. Hoping to tear them apart, he passed his fractured form through the shapeless mass as if it were air. When he tried to grab Amala's shoulder to pull her away, his hand moved through her as if through the surface of a pond. When he tried to stab Bandias with the branch, that, too, did nothing, nothing at all. Jeremiah stumbled back, helpless.

Amala. He wished he could say her name aloud.

The space between the woman and the shape closed. The dark emanating from Bandias passed through the fabric of her robes, restored to ivory-white since the dead soldiers had been erased. Beneath her clothes, the visible black lit the curves of her figure and the texture of her skin.

Jeremiah tried to close his eyes, but his eyelids were gone.

Bandias pressed the shadow of his head toward her, pulling her lips into his mouth. She placed her hands against his thighs, dug her fingers into shade that resembled muscle, and drew their bodies together. She clawed at the abyss as if even the scant space between them was too much to bear. Bandias put his hands around Amala's waist and lifted. She entwined her legs around his, wrapping the smooth brown of her calves against his onyx emptiness.

Jeremiah tried to look away but saw their shadows on the ground. He twisted his head to the stars but could still hear her moans of pleasure. Was this punishment for the sins he knew, or for those he had never understood at all?

As the two figures locked in a final ecstatic shivering, the darkness flowed into Amala, leaving the naked Skog behind.

The Abenaki seemed disoriented, drained, and pleased all at once.

The protective pocket lessened, then melted into air.

It was done. First the stone, then Skog, now Amala. She carried the world's end within her.

Tears came to Jeremiah. He blinked them away for a while before wondering how it was he could cry. His eyelids had grown back. His arm and shoulder, too. He looked at his hand and watched as the irregular, imperfect lines of his palm bubbled back up to his skin. His foot returned as if the ground had simply hidden it. The dark father, anger gone, had returned Jeremiah's body as if it were a child's favorite toy that had only been temporarily removed for bad behavior.

Ignoring Jeremiah completely, Skog smiled at Amala. He tried to meet her eyes, but she refused his glance and turned away. She walked off, exiting the field from the same direction she'd entered. She held one hand against her belly, as if trying to feel what grew within her. Jeremiah gasped when he saw what her other hand held; the knife he'd given her. She was going to do it, then. She was going to kill herself and try to take Bandias with her.

He knew he should stay silent, but a sorrowful cry rose from him. Her steps slowed briefly, but she didn't turn to face him. She continued walking across the dead field, toward the place on the banks where the two rivers met.

Skog, face and torso drenched with something akin to sweat, only darker, stepped up to Jeremiah, offering him the satisfied smile Amala wouldn't accept. "Part of you always knew that this world is the shadow world, didn't it? That's why the false light of the demiurge burns us. Do you understand fully now? Do you have the Knowledge?"

"Yes," Jeremiah lied. He didn't want to reveal any hint of Amala's last gambit.

Skog's red eyes searched Jeremiah's face. He nodded in admiration, as if he could still see the bloodstains and gore clinging to Jeremiah's clothes, though they'd passed from existence and memory, like the grass and the soldiers.

"It is good," Skog said. "You do know."

"There's only one thing I don't know yet," Jeremiah said.

"What's that?"

A single thrust forced the point of the white branch into the center of Skog's chest. It passed through his breast plate, tunneled into his heart, and burst from his back. The red eyes widened into saucers. The powerful arms flailed. When it seemed Skog might try to pull the shaft out, Jeremiah shoved the protruding tip into the trunk of the tree, pinning the thing that had murdered his father.

"Can you die?" Jeremiah asked.

Black liquid ran from the gaping wound, hissing as it hit the bark. At first, Jeremiah thought the wood was dissolving, but it was Skog's blood, boiling away. Wherever tree or branch touched it, his body sizzled like a flank of beef burning in the fire.

"It doesn't matter. I'll see you there, brother," Skog said. He tried to say more, but his voice became a dying, breathy wind.

Jeremiah pushed the branch deeper into the tree. The burning thing stopped moving and went limp. Its pieces, divorced from whatever allowed them to cohere, tumbled from one another. They gathered in a small mass on the ground. Their muddy color and consistency reminded Jeremiah of the dead leaves that filled the valleys, roads, and rocky plains back in Dedham, when winter was ready to arrive.

It was the first time he'd ever seen a creature like himself die. It made him feel, somehow, relieved.

26

With the last rustle of settling ash, a song filled the starlit field. Amala's voice, soft and sweet, wrapped the translated words around the French melody Jeremiah had taught her in the cave.

> *When the blazing sun is gone,*
> *When he nothing shines upon,*
> *Then a creature of the night*
> *Sings this to the lesser light...*

Jeremiah trudged wearily across the sterile earth, toward the spot on the bank where Amala waited. Exhaustion didn't slow his steps. He understood she was waiting to see him one last time before the end, before turning the knife on herself. Dread mixed with the fear that he might try to stop her. His footfalls grew heavier. His mind careened. Could there be a way to drive Bandias out of her? None he knew of. But he let his mind continue working nonetheless.

A silvery glint in the dirt caught his eyes. The knife. It'd been tossed to the ground, abandoned. What did it mean? Was she afraid? There was no fear in her voice.

I am the forgotten man
Unfinished by my maker's hand
He left me when the world began
And would not tell me what I am.

No fear, no remorse, no grief, only *love*. Her song was full of rapture, full of a mother's love for her unborn child.

He found her leaning reverently against the stone on the barge, as if it were the pillar of an invisible temple.

"Amala?"

She didn't turn. Caressing her belly with both hands, she kept her eyes on the spot where the river waters joined—the place of the beginning and the end.

"I wish it had been you," she said. "I felt so sure it would be. Everything about you—the way you struggled to find the truth—seemed fated to take you to him. But I suppose in a shadow-world even certainty is a lie. Skog was the stronger."

Jeremiah felt the memory of their moments together dribble through his fingers like the mud he'd pulled from the riverbank. "Amala, did you serve Bandias all along?"

"Oh, yes. It's why I went to Rashid in the first place."

"In the desert, after the caravan was attacked, you weren't praying for me; you were praying *to* me."

"Of course. He was in your blood. It was the first

real evidence I had for the beliefs my parents taught me. Other than my family, only Skog knew who I served. He kept it from the others, afraid they might betray us like the dust-crawlers, like Hylic Kirillov. They all seemed so loyal until they turned their backs on the truth. I told you as much as I could, I hinted, but you resisted so much."

He recalled the unfinished man's words: *The girl is a ghost.*

She turned and smiled. "But here we are, together, at the end. I was right about that, at least." She held her hand out to him. "Your father and I forgive your confusion. If you put your hand on my belly, he has a gift for you."

Jeremiah hesitated, then stepped closer. Amala took his wrist and placed his palm against her womb.

Here.

Something powerful moved from her into Jeremiah's palm. It entered him, filled him deeply. It tugged at the humors that flowed though his veins. It sorted the fluids, drew one from the others. As it passed back out, through his palm into Amala's womb, he felt his beast drain with it, as if the ephemeral urging that tormented his psyche had been a physical thing all along.

Jeremiah's skin filled out, turning pink. His stony strength vanished, his senses diminished. His heart pumped his own blood. His body was restored from the dead. It felt human again. It *was* human.

But Jeremiah Fall had never felt less so.

Amala leaned forward and kissed him. It felt better than when they'd kissed before, but also much worse. She pulled away and looked into his clear blue eyes. "So tell me, Jeremiah Fall, what are you feeling so near the end of all illusion?"

"I feel like a king," Jeremiah said. It sounded like a joke, but he didn't smile.

She giggled. "A king?" She pressed her head into his chest as she'd done in the dark of the blanket.

He felt his heart race. "A very specific king."

"Oh? Which one?"

"King Gradlon riding from doomed Ys, his wicked daughter Dahut at his back, his horse racing the rising sea." He choked as he spoke, surprised by how much more power his emotions possessed in this mortal form. "She was all he loved. But as the waves rose around him, an angel appeared and told him he had to let her die or the rest of the kingdom and all the souls in it would perish. He had seconds to choose."

Amala stiffened. "What did King Gradlon do?"

Jeremiah swallowed. "He...let her fall into the sea."

Amala pulled away. Her brow crinkled into a familiar line. She searched his face. "You said you couldn't harm me. You said you'd rather the world would end. I know you spoke the truth."

"I did," Jeremiah said. As if he could touch her thoughts, he traced the single line on her forehead with the tip of his index finger. "But I didn't know who you were."

The beast was gone. It could not object, and Bandias was at his weakest.

He wrapped his hands around her neck. It was harder, so much harder to be so deliberate, not to have his careless strength and to have to fight his own desperate feelings. Amala struggled, kicking and scratching, but he held on until at last she was dead.

Such silence, outside and within.

What was he feeling? The numbness Hylic described before he became a Bandite? What was it he'd said about the shattering moment? "You'll come to yours, I'm certain, when you realize killing is an act of love."

Could murder be an act of love? No. And he wasn't numb. Human at last, the full force of his feelings had simply been hiding long enough for him to do what he thought he had to. Grief washed over him with such force, he thought his body would be destroyed. He knew his soul had been.

He laid her body by the stone, and gave in to Hylic's Bandite longing, thinking only how he wanted to die, how he might take the knife and use it to join her. Certainly even Atticus would forgive him if he'd had enough of life now.

But it wasn't over, no, not even then. An inky blackness slipped from her lifeless womb back into the obsidian stone. As it did, Jeremiah's bones hardened, his skin grew pale, and the beast settled on him again.

Bandias had not been destroyed.

As his humanity receded into rage, he turned on the stone. "Can you die *now,* you bastard? Can you die *now*?"

It had to. It had to. He couldn't have killed Amala for nothing. Not her. He pounded at the rock with his fists until the bones in his hands cracked.

But nothing broke, nothing changed, nothing mattered. He couldn't destroy the forgotten man any more than he could a story. No matter how hard he struck, with fist, with rock, with everything he could think of, not so much as a scuff marred the stone or the dark within it.

He kept up the effort all the same, hoping his

endurance might somehow triumph. But it didn't, and as he tumbled through new levels of despair, he grew weaker and weaker.

Of the seventy French soldiers. Bonaparte sent to Al-Qurnah, twenty had been scouting and missed the apocalyptic battle. When they returned, now believing themselves the sole members of the mission, Jeremiah Fall did not put up a fight. Unlike the fifty lost to history, and unlike Bandias, invulnerable in his stone, Amala remained dead, and Jeremiah remained her killer.

27

November 5, 1799
The Grand Citadel, Cairo, Egypt

When Jeremiah Fall finished speaking, both priest and savant regarded him with equal disgust.

Étienne Geoffroy Saint-Hilaire was the first to express his disappointment. "When we journeyed here aboard *L'Orient*, we savants debated questions such as: Is there life on other worlds, and what exactly, is a dream? Not a single conjecture made on that ship was as fantastic or unbelievable as your absurd, nonsensical story."

"Let me burn him again," Father Sicard offered.

Of course they didn't believe you, the beast whispered. *They can't. They're useless. Just rend them. Feed on them. It will make you strong, and you can pound at the stone again if it pleases you.*

"Why don't you understand?" Jeremiah said. "Bandias is still in the stone, gathering strength. At year's end, he'll manifest without being born; then, within six days, he'll do to Egypt, to France, Rome, Russia, the entire world, the same as he did to Ys. Help me try to stop it. The dust-crawlers thought there was a way. Musket fire couldn't scratch it. Maybe cannons..."

Saint-Hilaire slapped the side of his frock coat. "*Mon Dieu*! You think we'd try to *destroy* an artifact so rare that Napoleon Bonaparte sent troops to recover it from deep in enemy lands?"

Sicard's lips twitched into a smile as he put another iron on the fire. "The knot of your lies is so deeply twisted, it seems a hell itself. You claim to have principles, yet commit the most horrid sins. You admit the sins, then insist they never were. When this forgotten man erased the soldiers, did he also cleanse your guilt at murdering the woman you claimed to love?"

You won't have to listen to this if you kill them. What do you care anymore?

Jeremiah lowered his head. Why *did* he care whether the world continued or not? He didn't know. He didn't understand what still held him together any more than he understood how King Gradlon or Atticus lived with themselves after tossing their children to the sea.

When he had killed the soldiers, at least he was enraged. He lost control and abdicated choice. Even so, he still remembered every face. He could still hear each man's final cry. With Amala, though his heart reeled from the revelation, there was no anger—just a cold, ugly decision. He'd decided not to let the world end, even if it meant murdering her. But why had he made that decision? Why *not* let it end? Nothing remained that he cared for. He certainly no longer cared about himself.

He raised his eyes to meet those of the priest. "My guilt is not cleansed. I don't pretend to know what God's judgment will be. I do know there's nothing left I could do that would damn me any further. Nothing..." His voice trailed off.

Jeremiah's brow furrowed. Nothing? There *was* nothing left. Piece by piece, it had been taken away, as if planned. *Planned.* What had Skog said during their first fight?

I felt betrayed, until the day Nathan Fall set me free, and I realized that was part of his plan, as well.

"What is it?" Sicard asked as he turned the iron in the coals. "Have you thought up a new sin?"

Maybe he had. Maybe there was one last thing left to try.

Geoffroy's eyes squinted behind his glasses. "I think some truth slipped through your lies. Despite whatever disease plagues your delirious mind, you are a mercenary, a man seeking fortune. It's therefore easy to conjecture that you do believe the writing on the stone leads to treasure. Perhaps you killed some unwary men, not our soldiers, but your own accomplices. But there was no fantastic trip to France. Instead you and the woman took the stone through the Syrian desert to Al-Qurnah, where you murdered your last living partner rather than share what you found."

The Frenchman clasped his hands behind his back and leaned forward, being careful to remain beyond Jeremiah's reach. "So now you want us to destroy the stone so the treasure's location will be known only to you. Yes?"

Sicard pulled the iron from the flame. "Answer him."

Jeremiah looked from Geoffroy to Sicard, then back

again, the only sound the coals crackling in the brazier. Neither man sought the truth, only confirmation of what he already believed. Perhaps if he gave them that, he could get something in return.

"Yes," Jeremiah said. "It was a treasure. I found enough gold to buy an empire. Two empires. Not even the Turks or the Mamluks know where it's buried. Only I do. So far anyway."

"Now we're getting somewhere, devil," Sicard said.

"What do you mean, so far?" Geoffroy asked.

"I couldn't kill everyone. My partners still seek it. They're men of influence and high position. Once they realized the stone was back in Egypt, I'm sure they sent an agent, a spy. The stone's here at the Institut de l'Égypte, isn't it? Is there a woman working with your savants, a too-eager servant, a wife or an assistant, a lover? Someone who appeared out of nowhere and knows the old writing a little better than she should?"

"Everyone who studies the stone has your trust, do they not, Geoffroy?" Sicard asked.

Saint-Hilaire sighed. "While General Kleber negotiates the withdrawal, we remain surrounded by insurrection and disease. Many of us feel our work is done, that the savants should be allowed to return to Europe, but the puzzle of this stone remains. It seems to...resist all our efforts to translate it. So yes, we've enlisted some aid. There is a woman, very young, who seems uniquely gifted."

A Bandite. They were here. Jeremiah tried not to react beyond a slight smile. "I'm sure you see the wisdom in keeping her from the stone before she steals its secrets? I promise I'll be here when you get back."

Saint-Hilaire and Sicard looked at each other.

"It would do no harm to speak to her," Geoffroy said.

"She's likely a heathen," Sicard said. "Shall we bring my things?"

Geoffroy paused just long enough to ease his conscience, then waved the soldiers toward the brazier. As they doused the coals, the musty space filled with smoke. The white clouds grew so thick that the priest hacked and coughed.

Overcoming a natural distaste, Saint-Hilaire patted the aged figure on the back. "Let's head for cleaner air, Father Sicard. I'll see that our next interrogation takes place in more pleasant surroundings."

Sicard's chest rattled. A gob of greenish phlegm flew from his mouth and landed atop the pile of dead rats. "The body deserts us long before the mind, eh, Geoffroy?"

That would depend on the body, and the mind, Jeremiah thought.

As Geoffroy held the rope ladder steady, the withered man made a feeble ascent. His hair's angelic white was the first of him to disappear. When his black robes also vanished, Geoffroy took his turn. Halfway up, the intellectual twisted around to look at the prisoner one last time. His intelligent eyes scanned Jeremiah suspiciously, as if he sensed the manipulation. But would his actions be any different if he knew they served the prisoner's purpose? No. If there was a spy, the stone had to be protected.

"We'll be back, monsieur," he said. "You are a most fascinating subject."

"Hurry," was all Jeremiah could think to say.

The soldiers packed the torture implements as carefully as servants would a rich man's luggage, then followed. The ladder was withdrawn, and the heavy stone lowered. Without so much as a dust swirl to comfort him, Jeremiah was again left alone in the dark.

Now there are only rats again, the beast moaned.

There was no reason to suspect his idea would work. It was as mad as those that had already failed, madder. But if it was Bandias who had set Jeremiah on this course, who had guided him, perhaps it was time to give the dark one what he wanted. To do that, he had to reach the stone.

Hours later, only the mumbled, drunken curses of his regular guards issued from above. The savant promised they'd be back, but when? If they found the woman, soon. Could he trick them into transferring him somewhere? Bringing him before the stone? If they unchained him for an instant, it would be the only chance he needed.

Rend them. Feed on them. It will make you strong.

"Shut up!" Jeremiah said aloud.

His voice echoed sharply against the walls, then died into silence.

Silence? Where were his guards? He strained his hearing and made out some shallow breathing and snores. They were undisciplined, true, but it was difficult to believe they'd fall into a stupor so close on the heels of a visit from such important guests.

Feet scraped the floor above. Someone was still standing and walking. It didn't sound like the guards. The wooden wheel creaked, then fell silent. Was it the priest and the savant? Or, had Kleber's talks with the Ottoman Empire fallen apart? Were the Turks invading?

He heard a grunt, then more scrapes. The groan of the wheel returned. By inches, the stone rose, signaling what Jeremiah knew might be his only chance to escape.

When the pale light of an oil lamp trickled through the gap between stone and ceiling, Jeremiah used the ability he'd kept hidden from his captors and vanished into the shadows. The chains still held him, but his new visitor's search of a seemingly empty cell would inevitably bring him close enough to grab.

And tear into his neck. The blood will let you break these chains.

Shut up!

The ladder dropped. A clumsy, portly man maneuvered it. Twice along the way, he nearly dropped his oil lantern. He all but fell the last three feet. Once steadied, a panting man with a slight beard and Slavic skin appeared in the lamplight.

"Jeremiah Fall," the man whispered. "Please, please tell me you are here."

Stunned, Jeremiah reappeared at once. "Hylic?"

The Russian leaped back. Off-balance, he fell onto the floor, landing, unknowingly, on the pile of dead rats. "Jeremiah! You'd think seeing something like that would be burned into one's memory, but I'd forgotten." He shook his head and sized up the situation. "I am assuming you can't disappear out of those chains, so here."

He tossed Jeremiah the keys.

As Jeremiah freed himself, Hylic caught his breath. "I told you I'd repay you, didn't I? Consider us even. It took weeks for me to get work in the Citadel's kitchens. No one seemed to care for Russian dishes until they grew paranoid that their Egyptian cooks meant to poison them.

Then, well, you've never seen such gluttons! Even with jihadists attacking inside the city walls, they stuffed their faces. It took time to figure out where you were and find the right combination of powders to mix into the wine for the guards. Very gracious of me, considering how I was deserted in Al-Qurnah, don't you think?"

Deserted? What was he talking about? He'd run off in terror, afraid Jeremiah would butcher him the same way he had the French soldiers. No, of course. Hylic no longer remembered seeing Jeremiah slaughter the soldiers because it hadn't happened. Like Ys, they never even existed. To him, Jeremiah was the same creature who regretted hurting a horse.

Noticing his stare, Hylic raised an eyebrow. "You could thank me."

"Thank you, Hylic."

The sincerity took the Russian aback. "You're welcome. What happened at the Garden? I heard Amala was killed."

"She was one of the Bandites," Jeremiah said. "And yes, she's dead. I had to kill her."

Hylic's face grew somber. "I hated that idea when I came up with it. I'm sorry. And Skog?"

"Him, too."

"That I'm not sorry about."

"It's not over. Bandias returned to the stone. I've got to get to it. I have an idea."

"Better than your last?"

"Probably not."

"A pity. It sits in a courtyard in the middle of one of the Institute's borrowed palaces, about a mile west of here. Is there anything I can do to help?"

"No, not really."

Hylic exhaled. "Wonderful. Assuming anything survives your efforts, you'll find me at the western gate, waiting with horses. I don't expect us to have a long friendship, but I'd appreciate being escorted out of the center of the coming war. Trust me when I say I barely made it this far." Wiping sweat from his forehead, he looked down and saw the carcasses he was sitting on. "Perfect. You might have warned me, Jeremiah.

"Jeremiah? Where are you?"

28

Jeremiah Fall's hands barely touched the rope as he flew into the room above his cell. He passed the drugged guards, hurtled down the narrow hall, and bounded up the sandstone steps. At the first landing, he leaped to the sill of a tall window. A dry Sahara wind puffed at him as he experienced his first view of the world in weeks. The familiar smells of night air and civilization invigorated his senses, giving the beast much to consider. Jeremiah let it swim in its predatory calculations, taking a moment to savor the fact that he was free.

The building he was in, the Citadel, had been built by Saladin in the twelfth century on a hilltop at the city's eastern side. From his window perch, nearly all of Cairo was visible, looking like a mass of interlocked and winding streets. Hundreds of minarets pointed heavenward. The houses, shops, taverns, and countless other buildings were packed so densely that there were places where not even a ray of noonday sun could reach the ground. In the center lay a reminder of what all vanities came to, a cemetery with hundreds of acres of domed tombs. He wondered if the dead would be pleased to know that, at least for now, they could still be remembered.

He descended the crenellated wall quickly, his filthy robes flapping against the white stones. On the ground, he sensed the many rats out foraging for food and gathered some meals for himself. The beast hissed in disappointment, but did not refuse to drink.

Despite the late hour and the civil unrest, the streets were full of Egyptian peasants, merchants, soldiers on furlough, and many, many mules. The beasts of burden knew the streets better than the humans and actually acted as guides for the occupiers. Unseen, Jeremiah moved among them for the mile west Hylic had indicated, then paused and realized he was lost.

Regardless of his heightened senses, all the walls surrounding the large structures looked much the same. A short trip among the rooftops solved the problem, letting him single out the complex that had once belonged to two Mamluk nobles and was now the luxurious location of the Institut de l'Égypte.

A palm tree raised Jeremiah to half the height of the surrounding wall. From there, a single leap took him to its angled top. Balanced there, he looked down on the lush gardens on the other side. The grounds were stocked with all manner of flowers and plants, their perfumes mixing in the air. Some species had doubtless been collected by the savants as part of their studies, others brought from France as experiments to see what might thrive in these arid climes, or maybe simply as reminders of home. There even seemed to be something of a zoo. The air contained the scent of species Jeremiah didn't recognize. Knowing

Saint-Hilaire's fascination with animals, he wondered if it belonged to him. Perhaps this was what Al-Qurnah had looked like at the dawn of time.

He leaped down among the flowers, wishing he could linger to appreciate the collection, but if he came any closer, the animals would react, and his sights were on the two palaces that shared this space.

Lamplight and moving shadows filled nearly every window of the enormous structures. Jeremiah was approaching the nearest, trying to guess which held the courtyard with the stone, when a low keening vibrated through the wall. He knew the sound—the cry of a thousand thousand beasts. He recognized the way it numbed him, making the rest of the world seem faint and distant.

He was about to hurl himself up the wall when the massive double doors at the front of the palace flew open and the cries of an agitated woman swept the scented air.

"I am not a traitor!" she screamed. "I will not go with you!"

Jeremiah crept closer. As she struggled and twisted, her black hair moved in a tiny maelstrom, concealing her features. At first she seemed so much like Amala, he froze. But her voice was different, wasn't it? Bandias had made him human for a time; could he also bring her back from the dead?

"I don't see how you can refuse," came the answer. It was Father Sicard. Saint-Hilaire was there, too. Both men kept their distance as their soldiers dealt with her thrashing.

"I promise this won't take long," the savant assured her. "Depending, of course, on how much time you take to explain why you were alone with the stone in the dead of the night, chanting those strange words."

"You can't take me from him!" she shouted, near tears.

"Him? Who is *he*?"

"Satan," Sicard put in. "I'll prove it. You'll see."

As the soldiers yanked her along, her head's gyrations briefly ceased, revealing a flat, long face, olive complexion, and green eyes full of rage. It wasn't Amala. There'd be no reprieve for that sin.

The farther the woman was dragged from the palace, the louder the keening grew, as if Bandias were mourning the loss of his new bride. But she was only half the picture. Where was the male the creature required? Among the savants? Hiding somewhere in the shadows even now?

No, Jeremiah knew. He was here. Right here, not yet quite as damned as he could be. So far, he'd guessed correctly.

Once the grim entourage entered a far building, Jeremiah launched himself up the palace wall, its rough contours providing easy holds. The huge windows were covered with tall mahogany *mashrebeeyah*, elegantly carved window screens that allowed Islamic women to peer discreetly out. The lights burning within cast geometric patterns on Jeremiah as he passed, while inside he saw a dozen tired academics toiling over their writing. Only a few were attuned enough to the outside world to whisper their confusion at the recent disturbance. Did they know the woman who was being dragged off? Wasn't she the one who knew the hieroglyphs? How can we work without her?

The keening made it difficult to listen further. Jeremiah completed his ascent, then crept across the wide roof to a central courtyard. Two stories down, columns and a low roof formed a square porch along one side. In the center, dwarfing a magnificent bubbling fountain, sat the stone, glowing deeply as it had the moment Jeremiah's pickaxe first brought it back into the world of man.

When his head jutted over the roof's edge, the sound intensified, vibrating his bones as it spoke:

Yes.

The four soldiers stationed on the porch would be easy to deal with, but there were also three stories and four walls of windows looking down on the scene. The savants, their servants, and whatever soldiers remained inside would see what was going on.

The sound grew louder. Bandias was becoming impatient. Jeremiah decided a crowd of onlookers was not something he could likely avoid. He'd have to worry about them later.

Wrapping himself around a corner column, he slid down, threading his form through the shadows to the lower roof of the porch. From there, as each came to see what was wrong with the last, he knocked the guards out one by one. Before the beast could object to their survival, Jeremiah vanished, then reappeared directly before the great black hulk, prepared to commit the only sin remaining.

"You planned this from the beginning, didn't you? From the moment I found you. Maybe even from the moment Skog killed my father."

Yes.

"You stripped everything from me bit by bit. My humanity. My ideals. My hopes. My ability to love. You made it all an illusion, so I'd accept the world as false. Amala was right. You weren't waiting for Skog. You were waiting for me."

Yes. He was too easy. You were the prize. The most deluded part of this dream, still holding on to hope even after having become so much like me.

It was a sickly satisfaction to know he'd finally guessed correctly.

No longer afraid, no longer surprised, no longer attached to memory, desire, or hope, Jeremiah Fall put his hand against the onyx surface.

"All right, then," he said. "I'm ready. I accept you. Yes."

At his last word, black tendrils seeped from the surface to his hand. They coursed along his arm, mocking its shape with black veins that clung to his skin and grew like ivy. Their darkness roved under his clothes, across his body. Some, needle-thin, seeped into his pores, while larger stalks, thick as pythons, slithered up his throat to his jaw. There the stalks flattened, pulled open his mouth, and made him scream.

Above the din of the stone's otherworldly river-roar, Jeremiah heard human voices and rushing footsteps. As he'd guessed, more soldiers were coming, along with the savants and their servants. He wished he could tell them to run, but Bandias took no chances with his willful child. The tendrils moved Jeremiah like a marionette and snapped him down so hard he felt his knees shatter.

The black slivers that had worked their way through his pores pooled in his abdomen. There, they set to pushing and pulling his diaphragm, working his lungs like a bellows as the ebony serpents possessed his mouth and tongue. He didn't have to read the hieroglyphs to recite the incantation. Bandias did that for him. The arcane sounds he'd heard once from Skog, then from Amala, swarmed from his mouth, his voice no longer his own. As he spoke, the pictograms glowed in turn.

A musket ball screeched near his ear, its sound and substance vanishing as it met the stone. More followed, with the same result. The amorphous pocket he'd seen twice before now grew around him and the stone.

The words mimed by his mouth became a torrent, a deluge of eldritch sounds so alien that his vocal cords were barely able to create them.

As quickly as it had come, the cascade of words stopped. The tendrils withdrew. Jeremiah spat and coughed. The shapeless hollow still hung around him, but through it, he saw the growing crowd. Some approached curiously, staring through magnifying lenses. Others took frantic notes. Father Sicard was there—Saint-Hilaire as well—but they stood back from the others, more stunned than fascinated as the story Jeremiah had told them acted itself out in the world.

The dark-haired woman the soldiers had dragged away was here, too. But the stone's display was so spectacular that no one seemed to notice or care as she went to her knees, a rapturous smile on her face.

The chant complete, Bandias drew himself from the stone and into Jeremiah, bone to bone, flesh to flesh, mind to mind. The amorphous shell faded. They rose as one. Once more the dark man stood within Creation, Jeremiah trapped inside him.

Jeremiah knew what he looked like to the surrounding crowd because they told him:

"Miracle!"

"Étonnant!"

"Merveilleux!"

"Un signe de Dieu!"

But they couldn't possibly understand what they looked like to him now that he saw through the forgotten man's eyes. To him, they were nothing but intangible wisps, the minute glow in their center the only thing about them that seemed remotely real.

It is as I told you, all illusion.

Bandias allowed Jeremiah to turn his head, to use it to see as much as he liked. He faced the buildings, the earth, and the sky but saw only phantom shapes.

The hunger you fight, the hunger you fight with, the hunger you fight for are all the same. They are the same as the urge that was first imprisoned in this mud and the same as the one that drags the seeming world each moment from its womb, only to devour it, then drag it screaming out again.

It was true. Jeremiah could see the feral force that lurked beneath each variation of shape, texture, and color. Vaguely, he recalled that there was something he once wanted desperately to do, some final act, but the hollowness of the world was so overwhelming that, try as he might, he couldn't remember what it was.

He'd lost it—the thought, the idea, the purpose he had in mind. It was gone, until he happened to glance at the stone. The sight of it steadied him, reminded him who he'd been and who he'd tried to be. Unlike all else, it remained heavy and real. More than that, it brought clarity. He understood it now. Its purpose was revealed. He was surprised he'd never noticed or guessed the truth.

Now that he knew, it seemed obvious. It wasn't a prison or a source. It was a door, a passageway.

What lies beneath the hunger? Me.

Beneath me? Nothing.

Through the portal he saw a shimmering void, the abyss over which God's spirit hovered when it contemplated the world. At the stone's threshold, fragments of reality passed from being into nothingness then back again.

And nothing is the final truth. You see?

Yes, he did see. He saw that Bandias truly believed that all Jeremiah had experienced—the horrors of the world, the horrors of his self—would whittle down his resistance and make him accept that existence itself was worthless.

He also knew it hadn't. Back in the cell, as he contemplated his crimes and realized the forgotten man's plan, Jeremiah had understood something else as well, something an unfinished man couldn't possibly comprehend.

Atticus was right. His mind was his salvation. Even here, it helped him shape what was before him. Amala's question on the barge provided the last key, but he hadn't realized it at the time. She asked which was more important: his experience or what he'd read, the things lived or lived by, the principles or the stories. It sounded like a stark choice, but it was only in his cell that he remembered something the Greek philosopher Aristotle had written over two thousand years ago. It wasn't one or the other:

The whole was greater than the sum of its parts.

Atticus and Gradlon survived the demise of their own hearts because they knew they were part of something more. The senseless hunger beneath didn't make the world less real. The movement between the two made both world *and* hunger real. Not contradictions, but a dance. Each moment died so the next could live. Creation never ended. It was ongoing. Bandias couldn't see that. He was unfinished, never fully in the world, never fully whole. To him, the world could only be a dream.

The woman walked toward them expectantly. Bandias wanted her, wanted to play again at being born, to try to press himself into the game and wreck it from within.

Yes.

But Jeremiah said, "No."

The ease of it surprised him. He expected a struggle, but there was none. Skog must have offered no resistance. But Jeremiah found he could turn the primal body, and make it leap through the doorway, back into the void.

They hovered there, he and Bandias, for an infinite instant, just long enough for Jeremiah to look back at the world's luminescent phantasm, then unleash a burst of the same de-creating energy that had erased Ys, on the doorway itself.

As he felt it rifle from his being into the portal, he hoped and prayed that this would be it. Having killed Amala, Jeremiah wanted to condemn not only the forgotten man to the nothing, but himself as well. Death seemed such a small thing to ask. But though Bandias's body became increasingly unable to distinguish itself from the abyss, he still sensed Jeremiah's desire.

In the worst possible punishment, Bandias hurled his foolish child through the crumbling portal, back into the false world, because he knew that only there would Jeremiah Fall's suffering continue.

Jeremiah lay sprawled on the polished marble floor beside the fountain. Its water sloshed from the base, splashing his face. At the same moment the cold, wet slap made him realize where he was, the ancient stone shuddered and split.

Thok.

There it was, that sound again. Perhaps it had no meaning beyond what Jeremiah gave it, but for him it would always be both the sound of a spirit's freedom and the sound of a closing door.

Dazed, uncertain why he'd survived, Jeremiah stood and faced the confused gathering. The Bandite woman threw herself on the broken stone and wailed. The soldiers raised their muskets. Jeremiah shrugged and seemed to disappear.

But that was mere illusion, a trick of light and dark and speed.

The commotion at the Institut de l'Égypte could be heard as far as the city's western gate. Alarms clanged and troops shouted. Mobs rushed madly about as if the end of the world were nigh.

Watching from his half-starved mount, Hylic Kirillov had no idea whether the riot was a good sign or a bad one. He shifted, his fear growing. Should he stay and be killed or flee to the desert alone and die there?

Jeremiah decided he'd suffered enough.

The old nag near Hylic huffed as if its breathing were disturbed. When the Russian turned to it, he was startled to see its saddle no longer empty and a wound in the side of its neck.

"You call this a horse?" Jeremiah said.

"That's what the man who sold it to me called it," Hylic said, annoyed at his own surprise. "He had a gun, so I didn't argue."

Jeremiah kicked its side and the two galloped through the gate. Soldiers called angrily, ordering them to stop, but no one pursued them. Things were too busy inside the city.

Once they were well into the desert, the pyramids rising before them, Hylic relaxed enough to ask, "The world, is it ending?"

"Turns out it is, always has been, and always will be."

"A riddle. Wonderful. Let me rephrase. Will I see Paris, and when I see it, will it be real?"

Jeremiah nodded. "Yes."

"Then...good."

His poor horse already exhausted to the point of collapse, Jeremiah slipped off its back and removed the saddle. He slapped it on the rump and sent it running back to Cairo.

Hylic stared. "That animal cost me..." he began. "Oh, never mind. Walk if it suits you."

"I won't be walking." Jeremiah put two fingers in his mouth and whistled. Moments later, Al-Hawa raced toward them, sand spraying as her hooves kicked the ground.

Jeremiah petted her flank and put his head to her nose. "I've been calling to her ever since they threw me in that cell. I wasn't sure she heard me, until now."

Hylic nodded. "So your uncanny nature does have advantages?"

"Maybe. But I'd still prefer to be human."

"To each his own. Once we reach the shore, I plan

to find passage to Europe and put this very far behind me as quickly as possible. I'll visit Paris. And you? Will you find Murad Bey and go back to fighting as a mercenary?"

Jeremiah smiled at the horse as he put the saddle on her. "No. I'm still wondering who sent the suicide bombers. Maybe they can tell me why Napoleon ordered seventy men across the desert to meet us at Al-Qurnah. After that, if Bandias did mate with the first woman, there must be a lot more creatures of the night out there aside from myself and Skog. I'd like to find them, too."

"For pity's sake, Jeremiah, why?"

In one graceful move, Jeremiah leaped atop Al-Hawa's back. "Maybe they'll know of a cure, maybe I'll destroy them, or maybe I won't. It would be arrogance to decide beforehand."

The horse, obeying his unspoken command, broke into a gallop, carrying Jeremiah north. As Hylic struggled to get his own beast moving, Jeremiah called back, "And arrogance is folly."

Above, the stars all twinkled, like diamonds in the sky.

Epilogue

*Décade II, Quintidi de Brumaire de l'Année VIII
de la Révolution
(November 5, 1799)
Paris, France*

"*Mon général*, you know the government will fail,"
the curly-haired, broad-nosed man said. He adjusted
the fine white ascot jutting from the folds of his black
jacket. "They ignore the constitution and the will of the
people."

Bonaparte, as he struggled to conceal the pain he was
feeling, watched the man's face carefully. He let a sip of
brandy roll about his tongue for the longest time. When
he felt he'd left the man twisting as long as he could, he
swallowed and responded. "You speak, *mon directeur*, of
a coup d'état, do you not?"

The oval face of Emmanuel Joseph Sieyès launched
into a brief grin. "Only because I've known for some

time it's for the best and that you are the man to make it happen."

Napoleon arched an eyebrow. "But I'm only *the man* now that your first choice, General Joubert, is dead?"

Sieyès's face grew deeply solemn. "No. Because you're adored. The people love you. If I may speak bluntly, they remain loyal to you despite the cost of your failures in Egypt."

Responding half to the pain, half to the words, Bonaparte lurched forward. "Because of our masters in the Directory. I had no support from them!"

Sieyès threw his hands up in the air. "Of course, *mon général*, and the people know that as well."

Bonaparte settled back in the plush velvet chair and hoped the director didn't see how close he was to breaking out in a sweat. He put the brandy glass down, looked out the tall window at his beloved Paris, then waved off Sieyès's words with a flip of his hand.

"I live for the people. I live for France."

"That's why I am here. For you. For France."

The pain was harder to ignore. Sieyès kept talking, but Bonaparte only half listened, pretending to be aloof by picking at one fingernail with another.

"Enough. I'll consider this conversation carefully. Thank you for your visit. I'm afraid I have other pressing matters."

Sieyès's eyes narrowed. "Are you well, general? Some intestinal difficulty from the Middle East?"

"I am fine. We'll talk again soon."

The taller man nodded and bowed. Gritting his teeth, Napoleon responded with another flip of his hand. Sieyès appeared to take it in stride as he exited.

Alone, Napoleon breathed heavily. Sweat beaded on his brow. He only wished it were some disease he'd brought from Egypt. It was much worse. He stepped before a floor-length mirror and tugged at the collar covering the source of his pain. There they were, twin scars, the jagged bite marks that refused to heal.

He had hoped distance would weaken their hold on him. Now, he expected things would be exactly as they were when the marks last burned in Egypt. That fetid wind of a voice would stab his head and fill it with more instructions. Again, he'd be helpless to disobey, like the last madness it commanded:

Leave seventy men in the desert; order them to the confluence of the Tigris and Euphrates. They'll find a man with an ancient stone there. They must bring both back to Cairo. The man will be dangerous by night, but the sun will weaken him.

Cette bêtise! Why? Why waste French blood on a suicide mission? But he'd been forced to obey, just as he had been ever since he'd taken that moment alone in the Great Pyramid, in the chamber where he tried to commune with its ancient king.

"Et qu'est-ce que j'ai reçu pour mes efforts spirituels? De l'information? De la sagesse?"

And what did I get for my spiritual efforts? Information? Wisdom?

No, a shadow leaped from the cracks, came at him with the fangs of a wolf, and delivered these damnable scars! Skog. The thing called itself Skog. Was it a name or a title? If a name, what sort?

He tore the collar away, planning to struggle against Skog's new commands, but the voice did not come.

Instead, as he watched, the marks grew lighter. The pain evaporated. He ran his fingers over the small pink bumps. Yes, they were almost gone. He rubbed his brow. No more sweat. He was cool. Perhaps the horrid creature had met its end. Hoping it had been a painful death, Napoleon straightened and smiled. It was over. How or why he did not know, but he was home and he was free.

He was more than free; he was adored. Sieyès was right; he was the man to overthrow the Directory, to reverse their losses in Europe, to defeat their foes at home and abroad. He'd have to remain cautious, letting Sieyès believe he was working with him. But he could do it. Politicians were easier to manipulate than troops in the field. In the end, he knew who would rule France. And then he would shed the past as he had these scars.

To damnation with the plagues, the deserts, and all their old, useless stones. History was a story written by the winners. Soon, he would write that story himself.

Acknowledgments

Thanks first to stalwart agent Joseph Veltre, for originally suggesting I try a "historical paranormal" novel, setting me off on this great adventure. Thanks likewise to editor Alex Logan for all her support, work, and the neat books she sends. Very special thanks to Jazan Wild and Dan Kemp for using their considerable musical talents to create "Creature of the Night," a wildly creepy tune inspired by this book.

Any fiction set in other epochs owes much to research. Among the many sources I scoured and scrutinized, I'm particularly indebted to the evocative and exhaustive *Mirage: Napoleon's Scientists and the Unveiling of Egypt,* by Nina Burleigh (Harper, 2007) and *Discovery at Rosetta,* by Jonathan Downs (Skyhorse Publishing, 2008). As part of my look at Puritan times, I was happy to uncover the now little-known, and fairly bizarre, *Young Puritans* series, by Mary

P. Wells Smith (Little, Brown and Company, 1899). Thanks to Sheila Kinney for somehow finding these at a local library.

And of course I am always and ever thankful to Sarah, Maia, and Margo, the center and source of my life and efforts, who make the struggles not only worthwhile, but also pure magic.

About the Author

Born in the Bronx, **Stefan Petrucha** spent his formative years moving between the big city and the suburbs, both of which made him prefer escapism.

A fan of comic books, science fiction, and horror since he learned to read, in high school and college he added a love for all sorts of literary work, eventually learning that the very best fiction always brings you back to reality, so, really, there's no way out.

He first came to prominence as the author of the best-selling *X-Files* comic book series, based on the TV show, and has since written eighteen novels, including *Timetripper, The Shadow of Frankenstein*, and *The Rule of Won*. His recent work includes *Paranormal State: My Journey Into the Unknown* (coauthored with A&E star Ryan Buell), *Split, Diary of a Stinky Dead Kid*, and the upcoming *Dead Mann Walking*. He currently lives in western Massachusetts with his wife and fellow writer Sarah Kinney and their two daughters.